UNDEFEATED

Undefeated series: Book 1

STUART REARDON

JANE HARVEY-BERRICK

Stuart Reardon Publishing

CONTENTS

DEDICATION

To Emma
Without you there would be no happy ever after.
Stu x

THIS SPORTING LIFE

There are no stars in this game. Just men like me.
David Storey, 'This Sporting Life'

PROLOGUE

It's a beautiful game.

It's a hard game.

And even on a good day your body is battered and bruised. It's a brutal game with blood, mud and dirt.

See this scar on my cheek? Rugby.

See this scar running through my eyebrow? Rugby.

I have a lot of scars.

I have 13 scars on each arm from keyhole surgery, knee surgery, scars on my forehead and the back of my head, scars on my knuckles. I've had both eyelids stitched, surgery on both shoulders, suffered a broken nose twice, and spiral fractures in my hands. I've broken my fingers so many times, I don't even count those. I've had cartilage cleaned out of my left knee, two medial ligament grade-two tears on each knee, three lots of surgery for Achilles tendon injuries, and once I put my bottom teeth through my top lip. Getting stitches in your mouth isn't much fun. They tug when you eat or speak.

There's nothing nice about rugby. Maybe that's why I bloody love it.

Chicks dig scars? Yeah, I've heard that, too.

In my experience, they're not so keen on being around while you're healing. Being the loser who's benched, not so sexy. Being the guy who's career is going down the toilet ... I'm looking a lot less appealing now.

Trusting a woman when you're at your lowest—dumbest, stupidest mistake ever.

Beat me, break me, butcher my heart.

I'm coming for you. And this time...

I'm going to win.

1

CHAPTER ONE

"Bloody hell! Is this what I think it is?"

Kenny peered at the small velvet box nestled inside Nick's kitbag.

"I have no idea what you think half the time," Nick said calmly. "Your mind is in a different galaxy, far, far away."

"Fuck off! Seriously? You're going to ask Molly to marry you?"

Nick had been seeing Molly for nearly three years. She'd been angling for a ring and he thought why not? All the guys he'd gone to school with were married by now, kids on the way, why not him? He was twenty-six, reasonably well paid, owned his own home, and the next obvious step was to settle down.

"Yeah, I think it's time."

Kenny gave him a strange look.

"Is she pregnant?"

Nick laughed out loud.

"No, you mad sort! What you asking me that for?"

Kenny slapped him around the head and yelled, "Then what are you doing it for, you idiot?"

It was no secret that Ken and Molly didn't like each other, although Nick's life would have been a lot simpler if they did.

"You're being a dickhead," Nick said. "But I want you to be my Best Man."

Kenny gave an evil grin. His front four teeth had been knocked out in a game two months ago and Kenny was waiting for the end of the season so he could get implants. He looked like an overgrown vampire.

"Oh yeah! Best Man's speech! I'm down with that."

Nick had a feeling he'd live to regret this decision.

"When are you going to ask her?"

"At the after-party tonight."

"Your funeral, pal."

What a knob, thought Nick, shaking his head.

"Why are we friends?"

Kenny frowned.

"Dunno. Low standards?"

All through his prep and match warmup, Nick had a strange feeling in his gut, a knot of anxiety.

He pulled out his lucky boots, placing them next to his gum-shield on the bench ready to use. He wasn't as superstitious as some players, but he liked his lucky boots. Although they were beginning to wear out and that made him nervous.

He also had a favourite pair of Speedos to wear underneath his rugby uniform, but that wasn't anyone else's business.

"Last game with your mates," said Kenny, his voice wistful. "Now you're leaving us behind, you'll be too big-time for us lot in the second division. All change for you—you'll forget all about us."

Nick laughed and thumped his friend on the back.

"Like I could ever forget you, Ken."

Kenny didn't smile and something flashed behind his eyes, but then the captain called to signal them out onto the pitch and they didn't speak again.

The sky was slate-coloured, boiling with dark storm clouds, and even on a late Spring afternoon, the fans huddled together, their applause dampened, with rows of seats standing forlorn and empty. Not many had followed the team to this last away-game of the season.

Nick glanced at the sparsely filled seats, disappointment souring his attempts to be positive. No matter what, he was still determined to play his best. But if the team had been in with a chance of promotion to the Premiership—the rugby super league—the stands would be full. Not today; not with a slow slide toward the lower half of the table after a mediocre season. Not even for the last game of the year.

As the ref blew his whistle to start the match, rain began to fall with heavy drops that rapidly turned the pitch into a mud bath, Nick and the other players slipping and sliding, clothes clinging wetly, slapping against his skin.

Nick hated games like this. He was a Fullback whose speed and acceleration, agility and power won his nickname, 'The Rocket'; his speed could also win matches. But on days like this, mud weighed him down, clinging in heavy clumps to his boots so that every time the referee paused the play, he was hooking out clods from between the studs with his fingers, hoping to improve traction on the field.

The captain signalled the Backs to keep the action close—fewer mistakes on short passes—and Nick shook his head in frustration, water dripping across his mud-streaked face. He swiped at his eyes with his shirt, exposing his hard, flat stomach and part of his muscled chest as he felt the cool rain against his hot skin.

The game was even slower now as the ball became slippery and muck clung to Nick. The wind raged, sending stinging rain into his eyes, and the unseasonal cold bit deep into his bones. At the other side of the pitch, Kenny was leering at his opposite number and probably saying things that would get him sent off if the ref caught him.

Every player was battling the elements, and Nick had lost his advantage of speed. He couldn't rely on his ability to run the ball downfield; the best hope was that they could keep their opponents pinned to the try line.

The game was rough and bruising, and Dennis, playing on the left wing, put his bottom teeth through his top lip after a brutal tackle, colouring his shirt with splatters of rusty red as blood dripped down his chin. He grimaced ghoulishly, poking his tongue through the wound.

Nick winced. *Been there, done that and got the scar to prove it.*

Dennis walked off swearing, his voice a whistling lisp because he'd bitten his tongue, too. They'd stitch him up at halftime so he'd be back to play the second half.

The game restarted. Nick swore when Kenny got flattened at the bottom of the ruck, disappearing under a mountain of heaving, kicking, swearing man-flesh, and the paramedics started to unpack the stretcher. But then the Hooker freed the ball and the game rumbled on. Kenny sat up, shaking his head like a wounded bull and staggered back into position.

Nick was relieved that he wasn't hurt, and the fans sent up a muted cheer.

Finally, the ball was passed sloppily in Nick's direction, and he plucked it from the air, gripping the slippery leather and racing up the field, his eyes squinting as he tried to see through the pelting rain. Sensing the line was close, he flung himself forward, feeling the bone-shaking jolt through his entire body as he crashed onto the pitch, sliding forward and carving a muddy groove.

This! This was what he did, what he lived for. Nothing could compare.

Adrenaline shot through him as the referee blew his whistle.

Nick picked himself up, grinning at his teammates when they high-fived him, celebrating as the points were marked up on the scoreboard. Then the kicker stepped forward, wiping mud from his eyes, as he attempted the conversion. He focussed on the ball, glanced up to the sticks, then struck the ball perfectly. The team held their breath as the ball hit the stick a glancing blow, then sailed through the goal posts. Cheers erupted as another two points had the fans leaping to their feet.

Nick clapped, relief filling his chest. Every point mattered in a close game.

He breathed out heavily. His body, shorts and legs were coated in filth, his face smeared, and he spat out mud, nearly losing his mouth guard. He rolled his neck from side to side, ignoring the aches and bruises of his abused body.

Rugby was a hard game, a brutal game, even when you weren't getting tackled, kicked, punched or head-butted. He loved it.

It was the only try of the match so far, and now they had seven more much-needed points.

But at halftime they were trailing by nineteen points and the team was losing focus. Coach let them take a drink and eat something sugary for an energy boost, then listened to them bitch for a minute before giving them a bollocking, spittle flying from his purple face.

"You're playing like you're half asleep out there! There're too many dropped balls, too many missed tackles. You're not a bunch of bleedin' amateurs! You're supposed to be professionals! Come on! You can do this! Keep kicking the ball back—they'll struggle to score if they're forced to play on their end of the field. And get your completion rate up—you can win this!"

They had to believe they could still win. No one was giving up. Being on the losing side week in, week out was mental torture. You played until your dying breath.

But the team was sluggish and morose, tired by the long season and drained by the foul weather, their bodies aching, muddied and bruised.

Nick gritted his teeth in frustration. The job of the Fullback was to attack, but Coach wanted the play to be short and safe and sensible. This was rugby—it was meant to be hard and tough and dirty.

He kept his mouth shut. Arguing with Coach never ended well.

They jogged back onto the swampy pitch and Nick couldn't help noticing that most fans had already given up and gone home, leaving just a handful of people at either end of the rain-sodden terraces. He shouldn't blame them—it was horrible weather and a scrappy, slow-moving match. But he did blame them. The team was playing their hearts out, and where were the supporters? Already in the pub, slagging them off.

A hot jet of anger pulsed through him. But as he moved into position, he forced himself to think positive, his mind slithering back to the tactics they'd discussed. His brain felt as muddy and weary as the rest of him.

Frustrated with himself, he took that slow-burning core of anger, using it to push himself to move faster, dragging his feet out of the mud and nearly losing a boot as he slogged across the field, thick thighs pumping, blood pounding in his ears.

Then one of the opposing team fumbled the ball and threw it forwards.

"Knock-on!" Nick yelled, raising one hand.

But the referee hadn't seen the ball being dropped forwards, half-blinded by the lashing downpour.

Nick's teammates detonated with a volcanic roar and suddenly the two teams crashed together, the heavy clash of meaty bodies brawling on the field, team colours lost in the mud-strewn melee.

A younger Nick would have joined in, but at 26 he was a seasoned professional and knew that a punch-up didn't solve problems. Unfortunately.

He waded in, yanking bodies backwards by their shirts or shorts and getting an elbow in the ribs for his trouble.

"Wankers!" screamed Darren, spinning around to the ref. "That was a blatant knock-on! Come on, Ref! Give us a chance! Try reffing the game properly!"

The referee continued to blow the whistle impotently, but it was several minutes before order was restored, and the players leered at each other through bloody and bruised faces. Nick knew that in an hour they'd all be drinking beer together: a quiet pint, followed by 17 noisy ones.

But for now, the match became ugly with tempers fraying and flaring every other minute, and to crown the misery, Nick took a random boot to his temple during a tackle.

He sat up slowly, shaking his head to make sure it was still attached. Then he stumbled to his feet and gave a thumbs up that he was okay to play on.

As a headache bloomed behind his eyes and blood mixed with mud on his shirt, he tried to focus on some attacking play.

But at the other end of the field, Tufty, the Halfback was on his knees, cupping his balls and howling in agony.

"I got bleedin' squirrelled!" he whined, still hunched over. "I think he's ripped my nuts off!"

Without any protection, your balls were vulnerable to a sadistic squeeze or a vicious twist, as Nick knew all too well.

At least it wasn't fingers up the arse. That happened in games, too. Not often, but there was one Aussie player who was notorious for it.

Play was suspended as the paramedics sprang into action. They helped Tufty onto a stretcher, knees still clamped together. But sliding and slipping in the mud, the paramedics dropped him, and he screeched, refusing further help and shuffling from the field, his face etched with agony. Nick grimaced. The game was a bloody shambles. All they needed now was a plague of locusts or zombies wandering onto the pitch and then he'd know for sure it was the apocalypse. It would be the definition of ironic if the world ended just as he was about to be promoted to a top league club.

Despite the team's failings, he'd had the best season of his career. Without Nick, they'd have been facing certain relegation. Everyone knew it. And now Nick was leaving them behind for a starry future. He'd hoped that his last game wouldn't be such a piece of crap.

The game restarted, but the light was so poor now that it was almost impossible to see the ball. Nick flailed up and down the swampy field, yelling out instructions, backing up his captain, and chasing down every stray ball.

As the minutes ticked down to the final whistle, Nick sprinted forwards, torturing his heaving lungs for one final push, gritting his teeth ready to receive, then abruptly changing direction with the flow of play. Suddenly, he felt a sharp, shrieking pain in his right calf, and grimaced over his shoulder to see which bastard had ankle-tapped him, and ready to evade being tackled, but the space behind him was empty.

Lame, with shock setting in, fear coating his lungs, he slowed to a limping walk, hobbling as the pain settled into a dull ache that spiked with every step. It was excruciating to put his full weight on his right foot.

"Shit," he growled, and then got tackled, ploughing into the mud.

He reached for his back foot and knew something was wrong. He had two seconds to play the ball while his team were in an attacking position.

Then he turned to the bench and signalled that he needed a timeout. As he limped off the field, helped by the medical staff, Coach met him at the sideline.

"Pulled a muscle?"

"It's my ankle. I can't walk."

"Alright, Nick. Off to the physio, see what he says. Good work today."

Nick took one last look at his team, the men he'd played so many great games with, good memories, then turned and headed for the locker room in pain.

"What's up, Nick?"

Alan was the club's physio and a retired player.

"Don't know. My right calf hurts like a bitch, it doesn't feel right. I've never had this before."

He sat on the table while Alan took off his boot, examined the back of Nick's ankle, pressing all around an area that felt bruised and was beginning to swell painfully.

Alan's face was grim, the heavy jowls drooping like a bloodhound, his eyes red and watery.

Nick could smell Vicks Vapo Rub, Deep Heat and Tiger Balm mixed with nicotine and body odour—physio room and physio, combined in a familiar and overpowering fug.

He tried to breathe through his mouth and act tough. When Alan pressed harder on the injured area, he inhaled on a sharp stab of pain that made his stomach muscles contract.

He leaned back, his soaked jersey and shorts making him shiver as his body began to cool.

"I think you'll need to go to hospital with this one, Nick. Looks like Achilles tendon to me." He grabbed Nick's ankle, rotating his foot and making him gasp. "You've still got movement in your foot so I'd guess that it's not snapped, probably torn. I'll get you some gas and air."

Nick's world flipped upside down. A torn Achilles ended careers. Why now? Why in his last game before he entered the Championship league?

He swallowed and closed his eyes for a second, opening them to see quiet sympathy on the older man's face.

"Are you sure? I haven't just pulled a muscle?"

Alan shook his head.

"Sorry, lad."

So much for the end of season party. So much for leaving his club on a high note. So much for proposing to Molly—he couldn't ask her to marry him when he no longer had anything to offer her. *So much for his entire fucking life.*

He dropped his head in his hands as everything was swept away in a wave of mud and shit: all those stupid hopes and dreams, gone.

Full of misery and pain, Nick sent a text to Molly letting her know that he wouldn't make the party. He didn't say why and knowing Molly, she'd be too pissed off to ask. That gave him a few hours to hear from a doctor as well as an aging ex-Prop that his rugby career was over.

Hobbling from wall to wall as he cannoned off furniture and lockers, he managed to shower slowly, dumping his filthy kit in the laundry basket for the kit-man to take care of, and taking his boots into the shower with him to save time.

The hot water felt wonderful against his battered body and he idly rubbed his purpling ribs and swollen ankle, wondering if he'd ever need the boots again.

Dirt and blood swirled around his feet, and Nick gently fingered the cut by his eyebrow, but it was already closing, leaving another scar, another souvenir of a rough game.

Inside, his emotions whirled with barely concealed panic, but outside, his stern face was set in stoic acceptance.

Silently, he took a turn in the ice bath, letting the change from hot to freezing cold soothe his body. The rapid temperature change helped speed up healing, combatting the micro-trauma of small tears in muscle fibre caused by the game's intense physical stress. Although it wouldn't be enough to fix a torn tendon. A surgeon's knife was in his future.

He closed his eyes, enduring.

Two minutes cold-hot-cold-hot was more than enough, and his headache was worse now, then it was back in the hot shower and he tried to let the heat and steam soothe the ache he felt bone deep, brain deep, the one that came from being on the losing side—the never-ending rugby rollercoaster; the one that came from being finished. Done. Ended. Milled. Thrashed. Beaten. Broken.

"Seriously, your Achilles?" Kenny's face fell and he grimaced in sympathy. "Tough luck, pal."

The other players muttered condolences as they trailed blood and dirt into the changing room, and Nick began to feel as if he'd died out there. Maybe he had. Maybe it was his ghost sitting here. Wouldn't that be fucking pathetic? To spend eternity in a stinking locker room. He smiled grimly at the thought.

Dressing in a t-shirt and sweatpants, he could only put on one trainer. The other foot was too swollen and painful to fit, so he shoved the toes in and left it at that.

Kenny slung an arm around Nick's shoulders as he hobbled to the post-match dinner. Tradition: win or lose, you fed the team who bled on your field. Hospital would have to wait—not that there was anything they'd do for him immediately. So instead, he sat with his teammates, pretending that a black hole of desolation wasn't growing inside his chest.

Tanked up and full of curry, it was a noisy crew that headed to the waiting team bus. It was a two-hour drive back to the clubhouse, and only then would he get medical treatment. It would be different in the top league, but second division was almost nowhere when it came to fixing what they'd broken.

Eight years he'd given to this team. Eight years of success, eight years of heartbreak, just like every other professional athlete.

Nick didn't want his career to be over.

Traffic was heavy on the motorway, and rain continued to pelt the bus, clattering noisily onto the roof and falling so fast it seemed to Nick as if they were underwater. He drifted in and out of an uneasy sleep, dozing through the drunken singing of his teammates. Usually, he'd be with them, singing the bawdy songs and laughing at stupid jokes.

Tonight they left him alone, respecting his retreat into silence.

Jerking awake with a grunt of pain, Nick sat up as the bus bumped across water-filled potholes and stopped with a sudden lurch at their clubhouse.

"You want me to drive you to the hospital?"

Nick stared up at his friend's face, sickly yellow in the pale neon glow.

Nick grimaced and nodded.

Rotherham was a no-frills club. If you were conscious and vertical, you took yourself to hospital.

"Yeah, thanks, Ken. I don't think I could drive right now."

Kenny nodded.

"I'll get Tufty and Gavin to take your car home on the way to the party. No worries."

But Nick was worried.

His ankle was still swelling and trying to walk even a single step sent pain lancing up his whole leg. As Kenny drove him to the private hospital that the team paid for, Nick held a dripping bag of ice to his ankle, hoping it might help. So far, it hadn't, and he'd maxed out on the painkillers he'd been given. But he was relieved that he'd traded up from a part-time team where you had to make do with the NHS.

The last time he'd been to an Accident & Emergency department, the walls had been a dull olive colour, institutional and depressing, with old posters warning of what would happen if you assaulted a member of staff. An old guy with dementia had kept on trying to open the fire exit and his tiny, white-haired wife could do nothing to stop him. A teenage boy had vomited down the front of his t-shirt.

A typical Saturday night.

Thank God for private healthcare.

Instead, Kenny pulled up in a quiet car park outside a new-looking building.

He slung a brawny arm around Nick's waist and half carried him inside to register his name and details.

Coach had phoned ahead so they were expecting him.

Sensing he'd be here a while, Nick settled into a low, leather sofa and tried to relax.

He glanced up at his friend.

"Look, you go on to the party—no reason for us both to miss it."

Kenny shook his head.

"I'm not leaving you here by yourself. What kind of mate does that?"

"I appreciate it, seriously—but Molly hasn't replied to my text so she's probably on her way there. She'll need someone to keep an eye on her." *And to stop it turning into an episode of 'Geordie Shore'.*

"Great," muttered Kenny. "Think I'll stay here then."

Nick clenched his teeth and Kenny sighed. There was no love lost there.

"Fine," Kenny grumbled. "I'll go. Let me know if you need a lift later."

Nick waved him away.

"Nah, I'll call a taxi. I'll be fine."

He watched Kenny striding down the corridor, relieved to be free of the hospital sounds and smells.

Nick's thoughts darkened.

Best case scenario, he'd be off for at least four months, probably much longer. Worst case scenario: he'd never play again.

Pain and frustration filled him. Of all the times to get injured, why now? *Why me?*

Was he supposed to laugh or cry? Was he supposed to laugh at the irony of having his worst injury in eight years of playing rugby professionally, his final game before starting next season with a Premiership club? Was he supposed to celebrate that someone had thought him good enough? Was he supposed to sound like Marlon Brando and howl at the moon, *I coulda been a contender!*

He didn't do any of those.

He turned off his phone and closed his eyes, listening to the gurgling sound as his career disappeared down the toilet.

CHAPTER TWO

"How bad is it?"

Molly's blue eyes were tinged with red and she looked the worse for wear. She pulled the sheet tightly around her as she stared at Nick.

"Bad," he said quietly. "I need an operation—the sooner the better."

"Will the new club pay for it or do you have to go NHS?"

Nick raised his eyebrows.

"I've signed the contract with the Minotaurs, but I got injured at Rotherham. I'm honestly not sure."

She grabbed his phone from the bedside table, leaning across him as she did so. Nick drew back slightly because he was worried she'd jostle his bad leg which was hurting like a bitch, and because the smell of alcohol on her skin was overpowering.

She was probably suffering more than him right now.

Grunting with irritation, she tossed the phone to him.

"Call them. You need to know where you stand. Or call that agent of yours—he should be doing something for the amount you pay him."

"Mark's a good guy," Nick said defensively. "He got me the Minotaurs contract in the first place."

"Took him long enough," Molly grumbled, yawning and stumbling to the bathroom.

Nick sighed but did as she suggested.

"*That is damn bad luck,*" said Mark, when he answered. "*I'll check the contracts, but I think Rotherham will be picking up the tab for this—either way, you're covered. I'll make sure of it. How are you feeling?*"

"I'm gutted."

"Well, that's to be expected. But you've had a good run of luck—no reason to think it'll abandon you now."

It already has, Nick thought sourly.

~

Two days later, Nick's sister drove him to the hospital for his operation.

"Are you alright?" she asked for the third time.

Nick gave her a weary look.

"Sorry, sorry. I just ... anyway, where's her highness today?"

Nick rubbed his forehead.

"If you mean Molly, she has to work. But she's picking me up from the hospital tonight."

Trish pressed her lips together but didn't say anything else. She wasn't a fan of Molly, but then again, it was mutual. Nick knew better than to get between the two of them. He'd tried once before and had the scars to prove it.

"I can stay with you if you like," Trish offered.

"Nah, you're alright. I'll be fine."

After a bad break up, Trish had moved back in with their parents and worked from home, doing data inputting. She said it was boring, but paid okay. She'd volunteered to drive him as soon as he'd been given his appointment.

"I don't mind staying," she repeated. "Someone should be with you."

"Honestly, sis, I'll be fine. It'll just be a lot of sitting around. Don't worry about it."

She sighed and gave in, dropping him off outside the hospital, then waving and driving away.

Nick limped inside and was admitted to the day ward, where a nurse took his blood pressure, and the surgeon talked him through the procedure then made him sign on the dotted line.

He wasn't allowed to eat or drink anything before his operation, and he was hungry and thirsty. Then, in the late morning, he was escorted to the operating theatre.

His heart began to race and he prayed fervently that the operation would be a success. The anaesthetist smiled at him reassuringly and one of the nurses offered to hold his hand. Nick was rather embarrassed about that, but it was nice of her to ask.

"Count from one to ten," said the anaesthetist, giving him a professional smile.

"One, two, three...

The whole thing took just over an hour and Nick vaguely remembered talking to the same nurse when he woke up with his leg in a cast.

As he became more alert, he stared at his leg, swathed below the knee in plaster. It was the first time he'd worn a cast. His leg felt heavy and uncoordinated, but at least the pain hadn't broken through the cocktail of medication yet.

He tried to relax because there was nothing else he could do. Easier said than done.

The afternoon passed slowly, and Nick was bored sitting in his private room. He read the sports pages on his phone, played some games, then gave up and switched on the TV in the corner. He hadn't watched much daytime TV before. He soon gave up and tried to sleep, but pain was beginning to seep through, and he felt hot and uncomfortable.

When his mum walked through the door, his face lifted with a surprised smile.

"Mum! I didn't know you were coming?"

She bent down and kissed his unshaven cheek.

"Well, of course!" she grumbled, pretending to be annoyed. "My only son has had surgery. How did it go? What did the doctor say?"

Nick shrugged uneasily.

"I haven't seen him yet. He's supposed to be coming when he does his rounds."

"Do you want me to go and find him," she said, immediately standing up.

It didn't matter that he was 26 and had been living away from home for seven years, his mum still wanted to take care of him. She was the sweetest woman alive, but turned into a lioness when either him or his sister were involved.

"Nah, that's okay, thanks. I have to stay here until they've sent the meds from pharmacy anyway."

"Well, how about a cup of tea then?"

"Yeah, a cup of tea would be nice."

She sprang up and marched out of the room to find a vending machine. Even though he was in pain, Nick smiled to himself.

Finally, just as his mum was leaving, the surgeon arrived.

"The operation went well. You'll be up and walking about soon."

"Thanks, doc. I can't wait."

"I'm sure, but don't rush it."

"Listen to the doctor, Nicolas," his mum said sternly.

The doctor gave a small smile. "And the nurse will discuss aftercare with you. Good luck!"

His mum was reluctant to leave him, but Nick was worn out and promised that Molly was picking him up later.

Shortly after 6PM, Molly arrived. Nick had been waiting in the hospital's lobby for the last 45 minutes, and had a bottle of strong painkillers in his pocket.

"Hey, Nicky baby. How'd it go?"

"Okay, I think."

She gave him a quick kiss on the cheek.

"I've had the day from hell. Megan is such a bitch! I *hate* working for her. I can't wait till I can tell her to stick her lousy job."

They'd talked about the possibility of Molly giving up her position at the beauty salon when Nick was promoted, but until he knew whether or not he'd be fit to play again, they couldn't afford for her not to work.

He manoeuvred himself on his crutches and sank gratefully into the passenger seat. Not being able to drive was going to be a giant pain in the backside. It was also the least of his worries.

He listened to Molly complain about her boss until they arrived home and Nick had settled in the living room with a heavy sigh.

"Mol, I don't think that giving up work would be a good idea right now."

She looked at him sharply as she tossed her car keys onto the coffee table.

"Why not?"

He stared at her incredulously.

"Because I've just had surgery. Because I don't know if I'll be able to play again!"

"But you said you're going to be okay!"

It was true. Nick had told her that. Finally, he met her eyes.

"I'm really hoping so, but it'll be months before I know for sure. So it's not a great time to chuck in your job."

There was a long pause, and Molly looked shocked. She sat down heavily.

"You might not play again?"

"I don't know. I hope so."

"God, Nicky..." she hesitated, but whatever she was going to say died on her lips. "Sorry. Your day has been way worse than mine. Shall I order Chinese for supper?" Then she gave a wry smile. "No, probably not. You're all about healthy food, aren't you, Nicky baby?"

Nick nodded and smiled tiredly. Eating the right food was a big part of training his body as far as he was concerned. Molly loved junk food and hated cooking.

"Fine," she sighed. "I'll make something healthy for you. But I'm going to need chocolate for myself." Then she turned her innocent eyes on him. "And maybe a box of Ferrero Rocher?"

Nick groaned as Molly's smile grew wider. She knew he had a weakness for that brand of chocolate.

"Sounds great."

For the rest of the evening, Molly couldn't do enough. She arranged the food around him, brought cups of tea, and reminded him to take his painkillers. Nick felt so grateful to have her taking care of him.

So he was surprised the next day when she announced she was going to work.

"I thought you'd taken the day off."

She wouldn't meet his eyes.

"Well, we need the money, right?"

"It's not that bad, Mol."

"Gotta do my bit," she said as she searched for her car keys, then found them on the coffee table. "You'll be alright, won't you?"

15

"Yep, fine," he said, although in truth, the pain was pretty bad this morning. She gave him a bright smile and kissed him on the lips.

"I'll bring home pizza tonight."

Nick grimaced as his leg throbbed.

"Pizza? Are you trying to kill me off? I'm trying to recover from injury, not make it worse." Molly's face hardened. "Any chance of chicken, or salmon, some vegetables?"

"You want me to work all day then come home and cook?" snarled Molly. "Fine, whatever."

Nick frowned as she slammed the front door. He'd be putting on weight if he stuck with Molly's idea of home cooking. He'd cook for himself. He usually did, and a plaster cast wouldn't stop him hopping around the kitchen. He just needed something to cook with and he was regretting not stocking up more before the operation.

He limped into the kitchen using his crutches, and rummaged around in the freezer.

Finding little of interest, he sat at his laptop and ordered everything he needed from the supermarket, spending three times as long as usual. He wanted the distraction, but that simple job didn't take up enough time.

Nick was worried about bigger things than just unhealthy eating. Sitting at home all day alone with his pain ... his mind teetered toward a dark place.

He wanted to be well *now*. He wanted to know his future *now*.

Nick hopped to the kitchen and washed down two painkillers with a glass of water. Gradually, his head began to feel fuzzy as his body relaxed, but dark clouds still hovered around the edges of his vision, and he dozed uneasily.

When he woke up, groggy and feeling out of focus, the angle of the sun had changed, and the day was descending toward dusk.

Prone on the sofa, he watched spirals of dust dance in the last light of the day.

Will I play again? God, will I play again?

The house seemed to be listening, but there was no answer.

Sitting up shakily, his gaze fell on the packet of papers that the doctor had given him. He picked them up and turned on the table-side lamp, reading the instructions for post-surgery, willing the weeks to speed by, instead of dragging with dreary slowness.

The first two days you will not be able take weight after the operation but use your crutches to help you get about. You will need to rest as much as possible with your leg elevated. You should limit activity to going to the bathroom. Continue taking your painkilling tablets.

Great. The highlight of his day would be taking a piss.

He tossed the papers aside.

It was after seven when Molly walked through the front door. She was late and Nick's stomach was growling.

"Hey, Nicky," she called.

"I'm in the living room," he called out. "How was your day?"

"Same shit, different day."

She walked in and slumped next to him, her eyes closing as she kicked off her shoes.

"Did you get anything to eat?"

"Oh, no. I went out with the girls at lunchtime." There was a long pause and an aggravated huff. "I could make you a sandwich, if you like?"

"Yeah, that would be great," he said. "I put in a Tesco order—it'll be here soon. With chocolate."

"That's why I love you," she laughed, and Nick smiled.

Molly slapped a slab of cheese between two pieces of bread, then cuddled up to him on the sofa, her eyes closing. A minute later, she was asleep, and Nick was alone with his thoughts.

Nick's days began to follow a pattern. He woke up alone, with Molly already gone to work.

He spent the morning in bed, reading the sports pages on his phone, then getting up around lunchtime.

Trish stopped by a couple of times a week and filled the fridge and hung out for an hour or two, then Nick would spend the rest of the day on the sofa, watching TV.

After a week, Nick's wound was checked, then another cast applied. A week after that, the stitches were removed and Nick was given a lightweight cast to wear. He knew it was too soon to feel any improvement, but his foot felt like an immobile lump of flesh, and his heart sank.

He was bored and depressed, but too stubborn to admit it.

Inside, his hope was dying a little more each day. He knew he was being a miserable bastard, short-tempered and snapping at Molly, but he felt her pulling away, too. She was impatient with him and bored of staying at home every night.

Both their lives had changed.

They used to laugh. They used to have fun, but now the foundations of their relationship were being tested.

For once, Molly was home from work early, and Nick was relieved to see her.

"Let's go out tonight," Molly suggested, her eyes lighting up at the idea.

It was the fourth or fifth time she'd tried to persuade him to go out. But the thought of dragging himself around and watching other people drink while he stuck to water and painkillers was not his idea of a good time.

"Amelia says there's an epic new club that's opened with an awesome new DJ. It'll be fun."

Nick stared at her in disbelief.

"Wearing this?" and he waved at the plaster cast holding his Achilles tendon in place.

"You don't have to dance. You can sit in a corner or something. Come on! It'll cheer you up."

Sitting in a corner watching you drink with your sister and dance with other men? No, thanks.

"No, I'll stay here and..."

"God, you're so boring! All you do is sit in that chair and watch telly. Are you going to do that for the next month?"

"Yeah, maybe I will!" he snapped.

"Yeah, and maybe you'll do it by yourself," she shouted back. "I'm going out."

He didn't even bother to try to stop her and frankly, he couldn't take her nagging any longer.

An hour later, while Nick was brooding on the sofa, Molly walked down the stairs dressed in a short, purple dress that was sleeveless and had a plunging neckline. She looked amazing and smelled even better. But her mood definitely hadn't improved.

"Don't wait up," she said icily. "I'll be going home with Amelia tonight. She lives nearer to the club."

Nick grunted, his eyes flicking back to the TV and a biopic about the Formula One racing legend James Hunt. He'd crashed and burned, too.

"When will I see you?" he called after her as she swept into the hallway.

"When you've stopped being a boring sod!" she yelled back.

He sighed and stretched out on the sofa, his right leg aching with a dull, relentless throb.

Molly didn't come home that night, or the night after.

Molly had never officially moved in with Nick, and still had clothes at her sister's flat, but they'd been spending most of their time together. Not so much lately. They hadn't even had sex since Nick's injury. Not that he was particularly interested anyway. Being in pain was a great way to kill off a boner.

The next day, Trish came with him to his appointment.

"Everything is looking good, Mr. Renshaw," said the surgeon. "There will be some loss of muscle bulk of course, but you can begin gentle weight bearing. Your skin will be very dry, so I'd recommend moisturising. And an ice pack can be applied to your foot to ease any swelling. Of course, you'll need to wear this orthopaedic boot for the next four to six weeks, but gradually your mobility and flexibility will improve. By four months, things will be getting back to normal, but full improvements can continue for up to 12 months. However, I see no reason why you won't be playing competitive rugby again—we have every reason to be positive."

Trish gave a beaming smile.

"Thank you, doctor."

"You're welcome, Mrs. Renshaw."

"Oh no, I'm his sister!" and Trish laughed awkwardly.

"My apologies. Well, it's good to see that you have so much family support," he smiled at Nick.

Nick nodded but couldn't meet Trish's eyes. The first thing she'd asked was why Molly wasn't with him.

But the doctor said he was getting better. He could live with that.

Some of the gloom that had followed him for the last few months began to lift.

CHAPTER THREE

As she slammed the cottage door behind her, Anna felt a shadow of unease, wondering again if she'd made the second worst mistake of her life.

But she squared her shoulders and moved forward with confidence.

"This is the first day of the rest of my life," she enunciated clearly. "Each journey starts with a single step. I am the woman I am meant to be."

Then she stumbled over a cobblestone and nearly head-butted her car.

"Aagh, crap!"

She wrenched her arm muscles as she grabbed the Peugeot's handle, trying not to face-plant.

Sighing, she righted herself slowly and rubbed her sore shoulder. She'd have to ice it when she got to work, but at least it didn't feel like there was any lasting damage.

Massaging her aching arm, Anna couldn't help smiling ruefully as she gazed at her new home. Old home. Um, new old home. It was a cottage—a genuine, roses-around-the-door cottage, stone-built and nearly 200 years old. Something she'd always wanted and never thought she'd have.

True, it was small, with dark, odd-shaped rooms, and suffered from damp, but Anna was totally in love with it. It was so quaint, so English.

She even loved the cobblestone path that became dangerously slippery in damp weather—which seemed to be every day since she'd arrived in Britain.

She reversed down the short gravel driveway, exiting carefully onto the road.

Must drive on the left, she reminded herself. She'd gotten used to that over the last few weeks, mostly. When she was tired or distracted, it was too easy to make a mistake and end up on the wrong side of the road facing an angry farmer in his ten-ton tractor.

As she made the short commute to work, Anna couldn't help but make comparisons. Today, she was driving along a peaceful, tree-lined street that slowly morphed into a small, redbrick Victorian town interspersed with more modern glass buildings, a trendy suburb of Manchester.

A month ago, she'd been a resident of New York City, zipping on and off the subway, striding through the crowded streets like the native she was. But shit happens and things change. Hopefully for the better.

She pulled into the paved parking lot, no, *car park*, smiling when she saw the plaque announcing her designated spot: *Dr. Anna Scott*.

"Good morning, Belinda," she said as she walked towards her receptionist/PA/right-hand-woman.

She'd interviewed her a month ago and they'd gotten along wonderfully. Anna was smart enough to know that the success of her fledgling business would depend on a competent and caring assistant. In Belinda, she'd struck gold.

It must be a sign—everything is going to be alright.

"Morning, Anna," Belinda smiled, waving a stack of messages at her enthusiastically. "I've had two enquiries from the local athletics club already this morning, and Mr. Jewell is waiting for you in your office."

Anna glanced up from the messages, frowning.

"He's here now? There was nothing on the schedule."

"Just turned up and charmed his way in," Belinda said, raising her eyebrows. "I made him coffee. Do you want one?"

"Oh, no thanks. But could you get me a hot water with a slice of lemon instead, please?"

Belinda shook her head as she stood slowly.

"One day you'll drink my coffee."

Anna doubted it, but didn't say anything. In every other way, Belinda was fantastic, but she couldn't make coffee to save her life. In fact, she suspected that drinking Belinda's coffee could be life-threatening.

Anna opened her office door, smiling at the enormous man squashed into an easy chair that she would have sworn was big enough for two ordinary-sized people. He had a broken nose, round, thuggish face, and a surprisingly mischievous smile.

"Anna, sorry to drop in on you unannounced."

"I'm delighted to see you again, Mr. Jewell," she said sincerely. "How are you?"

He winced.

"Eh, it's Steve. I'm not nearly old enough to be your dad, and we're not so formal here either."

Anna smiled and inclined her head.

"Steve, it's good to see you."

Steve Jewell was a former professional athlete and friend of her father's. He'd been the one to lure her here with promises of plenty of work and the chance to start her own practice.

Within spitting distance—as he'd put it—were two professional rugby union teams, a rugby league team, numerous athletics clubs, and the mighty Manchester City and Manchester United premiership football teams.

Steve was the head coach for top rugby club Manchester Minotaurs.

"Settling in okay? Got everything you need?"

"My assistant just told me that I've had two enquiries from a local athletics club today, so things are starting to look up."

He grinned.

"Told you so! Once word gets out that we've got ourselves a top quality sports psychologist in the area, you'll have more work than you can shake a stick at."

Anna hoped he was right, because she was putting her professional neck on the line by making this move. Besides, rugby was a similar game to American football. Sort of. Big, burly men chasing misshapen balls across a muddy field.

Anna slid into her desk chair and folded her hands in her lap.

"So, how can I help you today, Steve?"

"Ah, nothing in particular," he said, not noticing as her hopeful expression faltered. "Just wanted to make sure you were okay. I told your dad I'd keep an eye on you."

Anna smiled, hiding a small flare of irritation.

Steve crossed one meaty ankle across a massive thigh, testing the limits of his cotton slacks.

"I've got a couple of new players who've just started this season, Dave Parks and Nick Renshaw."

Anna made a note of their names so she could Google them later.

Steve met her interested gaze, giving her the full benefit of his keen blue eyes.

"I'll want you working with them from the start. Both are coming from a lower league team, and I can tell you from experience that it's a big jump getting promoted to a top team in the Premiership. And Renshaw is coming back after a long-term injury. They'll need your help whether they know it or not."

"Sounds good," she said, trying to hide her excitement. "When do I start?"

Steve laughed.

"You're just like your dad—he could never wait to get his teeth into a scrap either. How is the old bugger?"

"Hale, hearty and still a handful, as Mom would say."

"Glad to hear it. Well, I'll be off then."

He started to rise as Anna spoke hurriedly.

"These two new players of yours?"

"Oh, yeah. Well, I have them for every day this week to meet the other lads and the rest of the team, but then they're all yours. I'll get my secretary to make the appointments. Take care, luv. Regards to your old man."

He waved as he walked out of the room, head thrust forward belligerently, already onto his next job.

Belinda peered in, a cup of hot lemon in her hand.

"How did it go? Everything okay with Mr. Jewell?"

"Yep," Anna said more brightly than she felt. "He's promised me a couple of new players to work with very soon. Something to look forward to."

"It'll be alright," Belinda said, reading Anna's anxiety as she placed the cup and saucer in front of her. "It'll just take a little time."

"Oh sure, I know. New girl on the block and all that. It's fine."

"That's the spirit," said Belinda, then frowned as she removed Steve's untouched cup of coffee and marched out of the room with an annoyed sniff.

Anna leaned back in her chair and massaged her temples. Two new players from a top league club like Manchester Minotaurs would be a real boost for her fledgling business, although she'd need more than two paying clients. She just had to have faith that it would happen. This was her new start and Jonathan was finally behind her. He couldn't hurt her anymore. She'd paid penance for that mistake. Even thinking about him caused a twist of guilt inside her.

She pulled a bag of ice from her office fridge and eased it onto her sore shoulder.

CHAPTER FOUR

NICK HAD PROPOSED TO MOLLY, AND SHE'D ACCEPTED.

"You like the ring, then?"

Since Molly was on her knees giving him an enthusiastic blowjob and it wasn't even his birthday, Nick thought that was a pretty fair guess that she did.

She mumbled something that he couldn't interpret, but the vibration sent a wave of pleasure up his dick and down into his balls.

He'd liked to have run his fingers through her hair and pulled, hard, but he knew from experience that she hated having her hair messed up and she was just as likely to bite his dick in half.

He let the sensations wash over him, forcing himself to ignore the basin digging uncomfortably into his spine.

He wasn't even close. His brain was too busy, too many thoughts and images whirling around, and he also knew that he had about 30 seconds before she complained that he was taking too long.

Exhibitionism wasn't his kink, but since Molly had followed him into the gents, he wasn't about to turn her down either.

He wondered if Kenny had worked out yet that it was Nick who'd uploaded a terrible photo to Ken's Instagram account showing him in his Minions underwear. One-hundred-and-fifty likes and counting.

Kenny hadn't congratulated Nick on his engagement, but he hadn't walked out of the surprise engagement party either. He dared to be hopeful that one day they could get along with each other.

Nick had invited his friends and family to celebrate his new job as Fullback at the Manchester Minotaurs. He hadn't told anyone that he was going to propose.

She'd said yes. What had he been worried about?

Nick glanced down at Molly who was red in the face, her eyes beginning to water; he'd counted up to 22 before she spat out his dick with a tired grumble.

"God, Nick! I think I dislocated my jaw. You'll have to finish yourself off."

Nick grinned. Like he was going to apologise for his size? He shrugged and tucked himself back in his briefs, zipping up his trousers.

"Save it for later," he said, semi-hopeful.

Molly didn't reply. She was busy pouting at the mirror, replacing her frosted pink lipstick in a perfect cupid's bow.

Nick watched her for a second, then bent down to pick up his jacket, shaking out the creases. Molly had used it as a cushion in the men's room at the fancy restaurant where they were celebrating their engagement. Probably needed dry-cleaning. Nick idly wondered whether Sir Walter Raleigh had worried about a pissy cloak when he'd laid it across a puddle for Queen Elizabeth, back in the day.

Molly finished her lipstick, flashing a practice smile then fluttered the ring at her reflection.

"You'll have to get me a matching necklace for our first anniversary, Nicky."

He liked that she was planning ahead, but a new car or a necklace to keep the wife happy? Yeah, no contest, not if he ever wanted to get laid again.

As they made their way back out to the noisy restaurant, Nick stepped aside to let a woman pass him. It wasn't like him to look twice, but this time he did. She was the polar opposite of Molly: dark where she was fair; tall where Molly was short; formal in appearance with her short, glossy hair and severe business suit, whereas Molly was all skirts and heels, hair extensions and false nails.

There was nothing about this other woman that he'd call his type, except for a set of soft, beautiful, blood-red lips.

She passed him with a quiet, "Thank you," and he caught the familiar scent of her perfume. He chuckled when he recognised it: Tiger Balm. The camphor and menthol were unmistakeable.

As he followed Molly back to their table, the noise level had risen another notch and everyone seemed to be enjoying themselves, drinking and telling bad jokes. All his old teammates were there; his parents and sister, Trish; Molly's mother and older sister Amelia, and her coven of best friends. Even his former coach had dropped in, but left early.

He missed the man. He missed his rants and his pre-game talks. He missed the swearing and camaraderie of his old team. He'd done a lot of growing up there.

He frowned, wondering why he wasn't more excited now he'd finally joined a Premiership club. He'd met all the guys at his new team that day and they were fine, but he didn't know them yet; didn't feel completely comfortable with them. He definitely didn't feel at home. He knew it would take time.

He flexed his right foot, feeling the weird drag in his ankle where a pattern of scar tissue left a ridge from his calf to his heel.

Since the surgery, he'd done everything his doctors and trainers had told him.

Two weeks wearing a cast; a month wearing a boot and using crutches; weeks and weeks of physical therapy.

But now it was all within his grasp again: and it was a scary, tantalising place. He just wanted to be good enough.

No, that was a lie.

He wanted the fire back.

~

Four in the morning, and Nick was wide awake. He stretched out in the king-size bed listening to Molly's soft snores. She'd been different lately, more distant. He wondered if she was regretting the engagement with his future still so uncertain.

With sleep further away than ever, he slid silently out of bed and padded through the house, restless and uneasy.

He hadn't admitted to anyone that he was worried. But he *knew* his body, *knew* what it was capable of ... and he knew that his ankle still hadn't healed right. Yes, he could run, but he wasn't as fast as he had been; he couldn't turn at speed the way he did before, not like 'the Rocket' could. He wasn't as strong when he kicked, the ball didn't go as far or as high. Everyone around him agreed that he was still recovering, but to Nick, it felt more than that.

And the hovering doubt threatened to choke him.

He'd never lacked for confidence before, not like this. It was a slow poison that worked its way through his heart and mind.

When he thought of not having a club to play for, his pulse started to sprint. If he had to go back to working in a factory now...

Even making love to Molly hadn't taken the edge off his fears, and his mind spiralled helplessly as he tried to force his body to relax. It was as if he was playing in fog: he couldn't see his teammates or his opponents; he just knew that they were out there, waiting for him.

He sat on the sofa, shivering slightly at the feel of the cool leather against his bare skin. Predictably, his body ached, and a spectacular bruise had blossomed on his hip despite treating it with arnica. He rubbed it tentatively, remembering the bruising tackle that he'd endured during practice today. *Another souvenir of my lifestyle*, he thought grimly.

Rugby was a hard sport, a rough game. There was no padding, no helmet, just a gum guard for your upper teeth. That was it. You hurled yourself at your opponents and sometimes the ground rushed up to meet you. And some days you were cheered and some days you were booed, and every day your body ached. But for Nick, the pride of playing, the honour of being a professional athlete, made it all worthwhile.

And he wanted that. He craved it, needed it, would endure anything to play again.

Because what am I, if I don't have rugby?

The answer hovered in the air, unspoken, threatening like the first echo of thunder in the distance.

Shaking off the feeling, he prowled into the kitchen and pawed his way past the healthy food in the fridge to a small piece of sticky toffee pudding that he'd brought back from the engagement party. He didn't have many guilty pleasures, but sticky toffee pudding with custard was hard to beat. It was one of the reasons he'd insisted having it on the menu tonight. And the reason why he'd asked the restaurant to box him up another piece to take home.

His heart sank when he saw the empty container with a few crumbs and a blob of custard. Shit, he'd been looking forward to that—Molly and her bloody diets. She'd hardly eaten anything tonight at the party, but had obviously cracked when they'd gone home. She hadn't saved him any.

He flattened the box with the palm of his hand then tossed it in the recycling.

And missed.

~

Nick jolted awake when his mobile rang.

"Answer your bloody phone," Molly grumbled, turning away and pulling a pillow over her head.

He winced at the pain in his hip as he groped around until his fingers closed over his phone before the vibrations sent it skittering across the smooth surface of the bedside table.

It was a local number, but not one that he recognised.

"'Lo?"

His voice was gruff from pain and lack of sleep, and he held the phone away from his mouth to clear his throat, so he missed what the voice said next.

"Sorry, what was that?"

There was a pause, before a man's terse voice replied.

"*I said it's Steve Jewell, your boss. I want you at the club by ten this morning. Don't be late.*"

"Who w's tha'?" Molly mumbled.

Nick blinked, now wide awake.

"My Coach."

"Oh my God, it's so friggin' early."

Nick tossed his phone on the bedside table, pushed off the duvet and headed for the bathroom.

Pulling on a pair of track pants and an old t-shirt, he made his way downstairs wondering why Coach had called him so early on a Saturday morning. It couldn't be good news because he'd have said, wouldn't he? So it must be bad news. Perhaps he was getting fired. No, they weren't allowed to fire him unless he'd been injured for more than six months—he still had two months to go. So what was it?

Cold sweat broke out across his body and he licked his lips.

"Make me a cuppa!" Molly called after him.

CHAPTER FIVE

As Nick arrived at the club, he cast a critical eye over his new team's superior facilities, feeling a twinge of disloyalty when he had to admit that everything here was bigger, better, newer.

The locker rooms had actual lockers and not just a shelf and a peg for his kit. There were two physio rooms, an ice bath shaped like a Jacuzzi and big enough for six.

Dumping his bag in a locker, he jogged up the stairs to the manager's office and knocked on the door.

"Come!" growled a voice.

Nick walked inside and found Steve Jewell parked behind a massive slab of white oak, rifling through an untidy pile of paperwork, an irritated frown tugging his bristling eyebrows together.

The walls were decorated with photographs from the team's glory days, right back to its inauguration when Queen Victoria sat on the throne. Maybe she'd been a fan.

"Nick, take a seat."

Steve Jewell shoved the paperwork away and looked up, his expression revealing nothing of his thoughts. Crossing his meaty arms, he leaned back in his chair, making it creak in protest.

"I think you need some help, Nick."

He spoke flatly, delivering his punch with no preamble as Nick sucked in a sharp breath.

"I know you've got the potential. I've seen it at your old club, but we've not seen it here. During training, you're missing easy passes and choking on the big moments."

"I'll train harder..." he began, but Coach shut him down.

"We don't need you to train harder, we need you to play smarter. No one is questioning your dedication to getting fit, but it takes more than that to come back from the kind of injury you've sustained."

He gave Nick a grim smile. Perhaps it was meant to be reassuring.

"I've made an appointment for you to see a sports psychologist that we have a relationship with. Dr. Scott comes highly recommended and has a good track record with athletes, especially men like you coming back from injury. You've got an appointment in forty minutes."

He tossed a business card across the desk, and Nick took the small rectangle of stiff card with reluctance. He'd worked with two sports psychologists before: one had been useful, the other not so much. That guy hadn't been able to take the locker-room banter and had resigned after three sessions. But those had been team-based sessions. He'd never had a one-to-one appointment before.

He rubbed his forehead. The Club's management must be really worried about him if they were shelling out for this. He wondered again if they were thinking of dropping him. He could hardly blame them. They'd paid a lot of money for his contract and all they'd got was an injured second-rate player.

Why wasn't his ankle getting better? He'd done everything the doctors and physios had asked of him. The surgeon had assured him that the repair was holding. So why did it feel like he was running through treacle? Where was the acceleration that had made his name?

He felt like a fake and a fraud, and now he was about to waste even more of the Club's time and money.

"Yes, Coach."

Steve nodded, already strewing his desk with paper. Nick stood quietly and saw himself out.

He shoved the card in his pocket, uttering a short oath and a longer prayer that this shrink would help him.

If he couldn't, Nick didn't know who could.

Following the directions from his phone, he drove to the clinic in a daze. Autumn mist rose from the fields drifting up to meet the low ceiling of cloud, making the world muffled and out of focus.

He was trying to be open-minded about this appointment, but right now everything was dragging him down.

He parked in front of an ugly two-storey building on an industrial estate a few miles from the club's training ground.

As he swung out of his car, he felt a familiar twinge in his ankle that had him holding his breath until it passed. How was he supposed to play top level rugby when it felt like every step could be the one that finished him? How could he play with no fear, when fear was a molten core that burned him from the inside out?

Walking gingerly, he pushed open the door to the clinic.

A friendly woman with a short blonde bob smiled at him.

"Good morning, can I help you?"

"Hi, my name is Nick Renshaw. I have an appointment with Dr. Scott."

"I'll let her know you're here. Please have a seat."

Her?

He hadn't expected the doctor to be a woman. There weren't many women involved in his world, although more than there used to be. Several of the physios were female.

Nick felt wary and frustrated—what had this woman been told about him? He hated going into situations where he couldn't predict the outcome.

The receptionist picked up her handset and pressed a button. "Mr. Renshaw is here ... certainly ... I'll send him in." She looked up and smiled. "Dr. Scott is ready for you—she's through the double doors and the first room on the right. Can I get you a drink of anything? Tea, coffee, water?"

"Just water, thank you."

She buzzed him through and he followed her instructions, tapping at the open door on the right.

"Come on in!"

Taking a deep breath, he walked inside, closing the door behind him with a soft click.

His eyes flicked around the room, taking in the tall bookshelves filled with rows and rows of leather-bound books and a stack of magazines, *Journal of Applied Sport Psychology*. Several pieces of furniture that looked new took up most of the room: a wide black leather sofa flanked by two large arm chairs; and a curved wooden desk that held a laptop, phone and more books.

He saw a tall woman leaning against the window, silhouetted by the opaque light outside. She walked towards him and held out her hand.

"Hello, Nick. I'm Anna Scott. It's nice to meet you."

"You're American?"

He didn't know why that surprised him, but it did.

"Yes, I am. Have you ever been there?"

Nick shook his head. "I've always wanted to."

"Well, I hope you find the time to visit," she smiled. "Please sit wherever you feel comfortable."

Nick looked around again, ignoring the sofa and armchairs, instead choosing the office chair opposite her desk. He wondered if his choice of chair was some sort of test. Maybe he'd failed already. He felt clumsy and stupid, blurting out that she was American. He must have sounded like a complete wanker.

He studied her carefully, looking for any signs that she was looking down on him. But she seemed calm and unflappable, the exact opposite of how he was feeling as his heart triple-timed. The severe black suit did its best to hide her slim curves but wasn't entirely successful. He'd never been good at telling women's ages, but bearing in mind she was a doctor, she must be older than she looked—possibly thirty?

Her hair was dark, maybe auburn in sunlight, and worn boyishly short.

Behind thick-framed glasses, her eyes appeared steely grey. He jolted when his gaze dropped to her lips: deep red lipstick. He knew those lips, but how?

"Have we met before?"

He asked the question without thinking, then cringed at such a terrible line.

She cocked her head to one side.

"I was wondering if you'd remember. Rafters Restaurant, last night."

Nick's eyebrows shot up.

"That was you!"

Her amused smile sent a faint blush to his tanned cheeks.

"I guess so."

"Nice restaurant," he croaked.

"Not really my style," she said. "I prefer something a little more relaxed, but the food was good."

Nick wholeheartedly agreed, but he didn't say anything. He was still assimilating the information that this was the woman who'd caught his attention the night before.

"And I believe congratulations are in order," she continued. "That was your engagement party?"

"Oh, yeah. Yes."

She waited a beat but Nick was still floundering in the shallow end of confusion. He'd come to this session feeling defensive, only to find that he had one of the hottest shrinks on record. If Molly found out ... he could only imagine the jealous arguments.

"So, we'd better begin. But before I do, any objections if I record this session?"

Surprised, he shrugged and shook his head.

"Great! Steve Jewell sent you to me because he thinks I can help you. But first, let me tell you a little about how I work, and then we can talk about your injury and rehabilitation."

"Okay."

"First, I'm not a shrink," and she gave a light laugh. "A lot of people think that when they come to me for the initial meetings, but it's a completely different discipline. Although, as with all aspects of our curious human minds and bodies, everything is linked.

"The simplest way to describe what I do is for you to think of me as part of your coaching team."

You're a lot sexier than any of my coaches, Nick thought wryly.

Her voice was strong and clear but had a strangely soothing effect. There was something peaceful about the way she spoke, the gentle, articulate humour. It seemed to be designed to put people at ease. It was working for Nick, and he felt himself start to relax.

"There are various ways that I can help athletes—I can teach you mental game skills to improve performance and learning. This is what I call my 'Seven Times Lucky' approach. But all of it is based on trust: I'll trust you to answer honestly and fearlessly, and you'll need to trust me to help you work through everything in the most beneficial way for you. Deal?"

Nick nodded, not really feeling like he had a choice. But the way she spoke, he liked it. It was refreshing. *She* was refreshing. And he liked watching her mouth as she talked. His body seemed to like it a lot too, and that bothered him.

"First, we'll work on your coping strategies for performance fears. Second, we'll target confidence, focus, composure, intensity, which can spill out usefully into all aspects of your life."

She smiled at him encouragingly.

Nick suspected he wouldn't have any performance fears with her, then realized how utterly inappropriate his thoughts were.

Maybe if you stop looking at her mouth, dickhead!

"Third, we'll work on some strategies to prepare for competition, specific situations on the rugby field. Fourth, and this is key for you, we'll work on your recovery from injury. You might think that the scar from your operation is the only one, but athletes are often left with mental scars long after the injury is physically healed. We'll look at methods for coping with the pressures associated with returning to a prior level of performance pre-injury."

That caught Nick's attention.

"Can you really do that, doctor?"

He was leaning forwards, trying to hide the desperation in his voice.

"Yes, of course," she answered easily. "But please, call me Anna."

"Anna, right. I'm Nick."

"I know," she smiled. "So, Nick, I'll also help you develop a pregame routine, a mental preparation that will teach you to be more proactive with your confidence. We'll also look at pre-shot routines, using mental skills to prepare for a specific motor skill, such as a dropkick, for one example. And finally, we'll work on improving the efficiency of your practices by helping you to understand principles of motor learning and performance."

She seemed so confident, so sure of her ability to help him, that Nick felt the first weak pulse of hope.

"We'll use a variety of techniques as we work: positive self-talk; you know, *I can do this!* That sort of thing. Visualisation: seeing the action before you take it, seeing yourself achieve what you want to achieve. We'll also discuss stress management and relaxation techniques. We'll look at your sport and exercise goals, and find triggers to motivate you to achieve them. And most importantly, we'll learn to evaluate the way you think and behave during a game, and how that affects your performance."

"Assuming I ever get off the bench," he said dourly.

"Positive self-talk 101: tell yourself you'll get off the darn bench."

She stared at him, a challenge in her silvery eyes.

"What, right now?"

"No better time."

"What do you want me to say?"

"*I'm going to get off the darn bench!*"

Nick repeated parrot-fashion, feeling like a knob.

"Once more with feeling, Nick. Come on! You can do this! You *want* this, right?"

"I'm not staying on that bloody hard bench any longer!"

Anna clapped.

"Nice! You made it your own. So, what do you think about what I've said?"

"Sounds great, doc— Anna."

"Terrific. Let's get to work."

They were interrupted by a knock at the door and Belinda walked in carrying a tray with a tall glass of water which she placed in front of Nick, and a cup and saucer with hot lemon next to Anna.

"Thanks, Belinda."

"You're welcome, pet."

Anna gave Nick an appraising look as Belinda left the office, closing the door gently behind her.

"You were wise not to take the coffee."

He pulled a face.

"Am I supposed to stay off caffeine?"

Anna laughed, her head tilted back, and Nick caught a glimpse of a shiny gold tongue stud. It surprised him, and damn if he didn't find it hot. She definitely wasn't like any doctor he'd ever seen before.

"God, no. I wouldn't do that to you. A couple of caffeinated beverages a day won't hurt you ... it's just that Belinda's coffee might."

"Oh, right," and he grinned at her as she smiled back.

"So, tell me how you think your rehab is going."

He folded his arms across his chest, his smile dimming.

"Yeah, good."

She raised an eyebrow, waiting.

"Really good," he lied.

"I'm happy to hear it," she smiled.

"Thanks."

"Why do you think they've sent you here?"

Ah, shit.

"To help me improve my game?"

Nick was annoyed that his voice rose at the end, making it sound like a question, like he was uncertain. Which he was, but that wasn't something he wanted to share with a stranger.

He forced a smile. That wasn't very convincing either.

"Tell me about your childhood. When did you first pick up a rugby ball?"

Nick was taken aback. He hadn't expected something so ... personal. It sounded like a shrink question.

"When you're ready..."

Her expression was so open, so warm. He thought she'd be judgmental: weighing him and finding him wanting.

She smiled encouragingly, suspecting that he wasn't used to talking about himself. She waited, keeping a small smile on her face as he cleared his throat and shifted in his seat. Finally, he began to talk.

"I don't really remember a time when I didn't play. I don't even remember the first time I held a rugby ball. My dad and uncle were always tossing a ball in the back garden. It was just a patch of grass and you had to dodge the clothesline. Mum would get annoyed if the plants got trampled."

"How old were you then?"

"Maybe four or five."

"Isn't that kind of young?"

"Not really. Some kids played football, I liked rugby. We started playing in a team at primary school when I was ten, but there was no tackling at that age."

"Did you like school?"

This time his smile was genuine.

"Not really. Playing on the rugby team was the only part I enjoyed. I left school at sixteen."

He glanced up to see if she'd look down on him for that, but she just nodded to show that she was listening and made notes in tiny, spidery handwriting.

"I never thought that I could make a career of rugby. When I left school I got a job in a paint factory. Good money, too, or that's how it seemed at the time."

Nick shook his head. It had been enough to pay for his first tattoo, an ugly, fuzzy devil that he'd had inked on the back of his shoulder. He hated it.

"How long did you work in the factory?"

"Two years. I played for an amateur club on the weekends and trained most evenings."

Everything was simpler then. He'd been happy, doing all the usual things that a kid does in his late teens: clubbing, drinking, dancing, finding a girlfriend or two.

"And what happened when you were selected to play professionally?"

"A scout for local clubs had been keeping an eye on me. I was a skinny sixteen year-old but by the time I was eighteen, I'd filled out a bit."

He paused. Was she checking him out? But then her eyes dropped back to her notebook and Nick gave a mental shrug and carried on with his story.

"Any road, I'd had enough of the paint factory and I was going to join the Marines."

"Really?"

"Yeah, maybe I'd have been fast enough to dodge a few bullets."

He laughed awkwardly, but Anna's expression was stony. He cleared his throat, hurrying on.

"I was called in for a trial at this professional club who were in the second league, Championship Division it's called. Anyway, I went in to meet the rest of the team. A week of training together followed by an actual match that was going to be televised."

Nick shook his head as if he still couldn't believe it.

"I was eighteen years old, never been paid to play, didn't know the other players, and didn't think I'd be good enough."

She made a small note on the page.

"But you were."

"Yeah, I suppose I was. I made the winning try in my first ever professional game. I think I was more surprised than anyone."

Anna made another note while Nick took a stroll down memory lane.

His salary quadrupled overnight, and while that might have messed up most eighteen year-olds, he kept his head down, worked hard, and never took any of it for granted. He rarely had a drink and he never missed a training session. Two years of working in a factory made him treasure this chance.

"I was at my old club for eight years."

"You liked it there?"

"Yeah, they're good lads."

"How do you feel about playing for the Minotaurs?"

"Surprised, pleased, happy," *worried, too.*

She gazed at him appraisingly.

"Have you ever been red-carded? Sent off during a game?"

He grinned sheepishly.

"My last red card was when I was twelve, and I'd clotheslined another player. He was a lad who was three years older and two stone heavier."

"Clotheslined?"

"I'd tackled him above the neck, which is like running into a clothesline: and I did it twice. Big no-no, because basically I could have broken his neck. I was sent off and I learned my lesson—I never made a dangerous tackle again."

Anna smiled.

"As you may have guessed, I'm more familiar with the rules for football— American Football that is. I'm still learning about Rugby Union. Tell me about the position you play. Fullback, right?"

"Yeah, that's me. Although I've played Centre and Wing, too."

His eyes lit up and he could feel the passion still inside him. He'd been humouring her before, but this, *this* was something that ignited the fire.

He leaned forward, his eyes bright and focussed.

"Fullbacks, we're the last line of defence. We catch the ball deep in our own territory and then move the ball forward, fast. There are seven Backs and eight Forwards in a rugby team, so it's not unusual for me to see all my teammates spread out in front of me during a game.

"In scrums and line-outs, it's the job of the Forwards to get the ball while the Backs find a nice wide open space, ready to receive. My position behind the backline allows me to see holes in the defensive line and I'll either cover that gap, or get the two Half-backs to do it. We have to anticipate the opposition's play.

"We have to be fast, have good catching ability under a high kick, and be able to punt the ball accurately over long distances."

She nodded.

"I've seen old game footage of you taking goal-kicks. Is that usual for a Fullback?"

"You have?"

"Of course. I need to see how you move on the field."

He snorted through his nose.

"Like an old man right now."

Her smile was comforting.

"We'll work on that. Nick, let me ask you something..."

"Why stop now?" he muttered dryly.

She flashed him a bright smile that settled inside his chest, warming him, and he found himself smiling back.

"Oh, I have no intention of stopping," she laughed. "Where do you see yourself in two years? What do you want to achieve?"

"Those are two different questions," he grumbled.

She leaned forward, her grey eyes serious.

"They don't have to be," she said. "In fact, they shouldn't be."

He sat back, surprised by her words, a thoughtful expression on his face and shadows in his eyes.

She waited, and Nick studied his hands, staring at the calluses on the palms, then folding his arms. Finally, he looked up at her.

"You want to know what I dream about?"

She nodded.

"I was a good player at my old club," he said, his voice contemplative. Then he met her gaze. "I want to be better than that. I want my new club to be proud of me. I want to help them win the Cup and..." He took a deep breath. "And I want to play for England some day."

Anna's smile was warm and Nick found himself unwinding, his hands falling loosely into his lap again.

"Then that's both our goal and our motivation."

He liked the way she said that, like they were a team.

"I'll come out and watch you train on Thursday, if that's okay with you?"

Her pen was poised above her notes and she raised her eyebrows, waiting.

"Do you usually come out and see your clients train?" Nick asked.

"It depends on the client," she said smoothly.

Nick frowned and opened his mouth to say something, but she changed direction quickly.

"But right now, I have some homework for you."

He blinked.

"Homework?"

"Yes, I want you to write down three things that you do well outside of rugby; and I want you to write down three skills that you believe define you as a rugby player. Got it?"

Nick knew that he was staring at her owlishly, his mouth open. He licked his lips and tried to look unaffected. *This woman!* She asked the damnedest questions.

"Six things I'm good at?"

She smiled and stood up, indicating that the hour-long session was over.

"It's been a pleasure meeting you, Nick. I'm looking forward to working with you."

She held out her hand and he shook it, still bemused by his 'homework'. Her hand was smaller than his, and her knuckles weren't scarred. Her fingernails were unpainted, short and blunt. He wasn't sure why that intrigued him.

"See you next week."

"Right, next week. Thank you, doc— thank you, Anna."

"You're welcome."

His head was spinning, but she'd given him a lot to think about. She was honest, but she was also optimistic. And most of all, she'd planted a kernel of hope inside him.

~

Anna followed her newest client out of her office and watched him slide into a sleek, black BMW.

Not the car she'd have picked for him. Interesting.

She'd been deliberately disingenuous during the meeting. She knew as much about rugby as she'd ever known about football, but she'd wanted Nick to tell her; she wanted to know if he still had a passion for his job. Because that had been Steve Jewell's biggest criticism—that Nick had no fire.

She was sure that Coach was very, very wrong.

On top of what she'd learned and her own instincts, when Steve Jewell mentioned that she'd be working with Nick, she'd watched as many of his old televised matches as she could find online, admiring his panther-like speed and attack. Very different from the quiet, diffident man sitting in front of her.

She'd studied his face while they talked about his rehabilitation, sad to see his passion drain away, the fire dying to a few warm embers. He didn't believe that he could improve again. That, she suspected, was the root of his problem. Of course, he could be right and he might never make it back to top level play, but Anna's job was to work on his confidence.

Anna played the recording on her phone and listened to parts of the conversation again. It had taken her a few minutes to get used to his accent. She knew from her notes that he'd been born and brought up in Yorkshire, and people from that part of Britain had distinctive accents. At least she didn't mix them up with Scottish anymore.

She listened for a few minutes, then pressed 'record', speaking her thoughts while they were still fresh in her mind.

"Nick Renshaw, 26, Fullback for the Manchester Minotaurs. Currently benched with an Achilles tendon injury—surgery was 21 weeks ago. Problem with lack of form and loss of confidence."

She leaned back, pushing her hair behind her ears, thinking about the man who'd sat in her office. They'd made a good start even though he obviously didn't like talking about himself, but he did like talking about rugby—his passion was still there. She could work with a man like that.

"He's not arrogant like some players. He has the humility of a professional who's known both good and bad luck, someone who's had to struggle. He's feeling beaten right now, worried that he might never retain his top form." She paused. "It's true that some athletes never achieve complete rehabilitation or recover to a full extent after surgery such as his; permanent loss of form is a possibility. He was also extremely reluctant to talk about the progress of his rehabilitation—definitely an uncomfortable subject for him." *What are you hiding, Nick?*

She sensed a barely restrained panic that his career might be over. If it was, then part of her job would be to help him adjust. Many athletes struggled to make the transition to retirement. They were addicted to training and dietary support—too many went off the rails. And it wasn't just that, physically, their bodies still craved the dopamine rush of competing, of winning, of being cheered by thousands of people.

She spoke into her phone recorder again.

"Belinda, make a note that I want Mr. Renshaw to have another MRI scan and a consult with an orthopaedic surgeon. Steve Jewell should know someone who specialises in athletes."

She paused again, arranging the notes in her mind.

"I haven't asked about the support he's receiving at home. He didn't mention his fiancée. Follow up in the next session."

She drummed her fingers on the table.

She'd recognised him the previous evening. It was one of the top restaurants in the area and popular with all the footballers, rugby players.

It hadn't been an instantaneous recognition. For one thing, the only photos and footage had been of him wearing his rugby uniform. Seeing him in a designer suit had thrown her. Nevertheless, her eyes had been drawn to him frequently as he celebrated what turned out to be an engagement party. After a few minutes of surreptitious ogling, Anna finally figured out why she knew his face—and was both simultaneously pleased and disappointed that he was about to become her client.

She'd been intrigued to see who he was marrying. But she was the first to admit that it took all sorts. Otherwise how could she explain Jonathan?

She frowned at the thought of her ex and their last, painful encounter.

Shaking away the memory, she stared at the photo of Nick in her file. The picture didn't do him justice, the gum guard distorting his face.

In person, she'd struggled to keep her eyes off him, his raven-dark hair, crazy curls combed away from a sculpted face with sharp cheekbones, penetrating hazel-green eyes that failed to disguise the strong emotions burning inside him, and a thick black beard hiding the softness of his lips.

The beard was a surprise. In all his rugby photographs and YouTube videos, he'd been clean shaven with military short hair, giving him a slightly boyish appearance. Now his hair had grown out, it was an unruly riot of dark curls, and with the beard, he seemed very much a man.

And his body! When he said he'd filled out, she couldn't help thinking, *More than a little*, remembering the biceps that bulged when he flexed his arms and the impressive chest that she'd seen underneath his closely fitting t-shirt. Even clothed, he exuded raw power, a sensuous magnetism that threatened to derail her thoughts.

When he shook her hand, his touch called to her in a way that was primal and unfamiliar.

It had thrown her for a loop, even though she'd spent her professional life working with many top athletes, all with hard, ripped bodies.

She slipped the photograph back inside the file and added her handwritten notes, unwilling to continue with her highly inappropriate train of thought.

He has a nice smile, too.

She shook her head wryly. He'd certainly be a testing first client.

And professionally, it would be interesting to see him in action during training on Thursday. She needed to see how his body moved post-surgery, but she also needed to understand how his mind worked. That would take more than one hour-long session. Anna wondered what he'd make of the homework she'd given him. He'd been so surprised, but he hadn't said no. She could tell that he wanted her help—he definitely needed it.

She finished reviewing her notes and put them together with the recordings for Belinda to type up. Then she spent the next two hours watching clips from his old games. He'd really been the backbone of his former team. She wondered if he'd seen how much they relied on him and how much the captain had turned to him for support on the field. It was clearly the reason that he'd been headhunted by the Minotaurs.

At six, Belinda reminded her that she had a dinner appointment, and they left together, Anna locking up behind them.

"I finished typing up the notes on your Mr. Renshaw," Belinda said. "He seems nice, very polite."

Anna smiled. *And sexy as hell.*

"I agree, and I've always thought that being nice is undervalued."

Belinda nodded.

"People tend to think it's a wishy-washy sort of word, like you're weak."

"He's definitely not weak."

Anna had glimpsed a core of something hard and determined inside Nick. But it was well buried—she needed to find ways to help him access that strength.

"He's not cocky, just nice and polite. Oh dear, there's that word again." Belinda laughed. "Handsome, too, isn't he?"

Anna smiled.

"I'm his psychologist—I'm not allowed to notice things like that."

"Of course not," Belinda said, lifting her eyebrows.

Anna waved goodbye and drove back to the cottage to get ready for her date.

All through dinner, she listened half-heartedly while her date talked animatedly about the latest applications for Artificial Intelligence in computing. It wasn't that Graham was boring, in fact she'd thought him fascinating when they'd met at a conference the week before. But now her mind was on a certain black-haired rugby player, hoping that she could give him the boost of confidence he sorely needed.

Why the hell did he have to be so attractive?

And *nice*.

CHAPTER SIX

Nick was relieved when he arrived at training on Thursday and there was no sign of Dr. Scott. He'd told Molly about his appointment earlier in the week and ignored her jibes about having his head examined, but he may also have avoided mentioning that his psychologist's first name was Anna.

He didn't analyse the reasons too closely...

Think of me as part of your coaching team. Yeah, right. He couldn't help thinking of Anna in a variety of ways that had nothing to do with coaching.

Molly was fed up with him, that was clear.

"I don't know why you don't get a job on the telly. It would pay more and you wouldn't have to get all muddy and sweaty. You're such a grouch when you're injured. You should be thinking about our future. Seriously, Nicky, you think it's fun for me to see you getting milled every week, as well as being a miserable sod when you lose all the time?"

"I love playing rugby, you know that. I don't want to just *talk* about it." He frowned, irritation making him sharp. "And I don't lose *all* the time. I'll be playing for a Premiership team any day now!"

Molly's lips trembled and she widened her eyes. "It's only because I love you."

Instead of holding her and reassuring like he usually did, he turned away, wondering what Anna would have said to him.

He felt a little guilty for that: he'd only been engaged a few days.

Nick grunted with annoyance.

Clear heart, clear mind! That's what his old Coach used to say. He understood it for the first time.

Training today was a weights workout which they did two days a week during the season, or three times a week in the off season.

He was looking forward to it, needing a brutal morning that left him too tired to think.

It was all about building strength and core stability. To some of the players, the weights room was a necessary evil—something to prevent injuries and keep the body operating at its maximum potential. Others enjoyed it, the ordered calm where the only challenge was from yourself.

Nick used to be somewhere in between, but during the weeks and months post-surgery when he hadn't been able to train at all, he'd missed it mentally and physically. He'd missed the satisfaction of working his body hard, and he'd definitely missed all those happy endorphins flooding through his body after a workout. He missed it like a drug. He was a match-day junkie, and being benched was torture. Despite the injuries he accumulated year by year, the aches, sprains, cuts, bruises and concussions were a small price to pay for doing something he loved. But this...

Molly said he'd been a grumpy git, and for a while their relationship had been rocky.

But since he'd recovered and was back with a team, they were getting along better.

He changed into his training kit, shorts, t-shirt and tracksuit and headed to the weights room with the other players, ready to push himself.

He started with the usual dynamic stretches and active mobility before moving on to endurance weights.

The metal of the bar was cool under his palms as he lay on the bench press and started to push. He felt the strain in his chest and upper body, but it felt right to be back with the group, training with the boys.

"Are you just warming up with that weight?" Trev teased. "Because my mum could lift that."

"I've seen your mum and I bet she can."

Trev laughed and moved over to the free weights.

For the next 45 minutes, Nick got in the zone, worked hard.

"Getting the gains, bro?" asked a sweaty Trev.

"You, me and your mum," replied Nick.

He sat on a bench, catching his breath, wiping his face and pushing his hair out of his eyes, but when he glanced up, he was startled to find Anna watching him.

She wasn't wearing glasses and her eyes were bright and inquisitive. Today they were the colour of a winter storm.

She gave him an easy smile, then turned to talk to their assistant coach who was watching impassively.

Ian nudged him.

"Who's that?"

"Who?"

Ian laughed.

"Like that, is it? The woman that made your eyes bulge. Maybe I'll just go and introduce myself."

Nick raised an eyebrow.

"Yeah, you do that. She's Steve Jewell's sports psychologist."

"The fuck you say?" Ian paused. "She any good?"

"Jewell says so. She's ... easy to talk to."

Ian watched appreciatively as Anna disappeared from view.

"Very nice, mate. Classy. Too good for your hairy arse. Anyway, I thought you were engaged? Just window shopping, is it?"

"Fuck off."

Ian smiled knowingly.

While Nick trained, he thought again about the homework that Anna had given him, trying to think of what he was good at. Three things non-rugby, too, she'd said. As he took a breather, he chewed his lip and tugged on his beard thoughtfully. He pulled out his phone and opened the Notes app.

He was good at sex, never had any complaints, but didn't think he should put that on Anna's list.

He could make a mean Cottage Pie—did that count? He wasn't sure, but with a shortage of other things to write, he put it at the top of his list.

He drummed his fingers on the bench. There must be something else he was good at?

Eh, he could play the guitar passably. Not that he found much time to practise these days. He'd learned to play the opening riff for 'Smoke on the Water' when he was ten—not that there were many chords involved.

He added it to the list.

Three things. Three. Surely it shouldn't be that hard to think of something? He scratched his chin, thinking about meeting up with Kenny and some of the Rotherham lads last week. He'd driven Ken home after he'd had a few too many pints. Kenny was currently nursing his own injury, a minor knee strain, but nothing that wouldn't fix itself with a couple of weeks rest.

Nick tapped on his phone, adding 'good friend' to the list.

The rugby ones were easier, or at least if he was talking about past form they would be. But what was he good at now? He could still see holes in the opponents' play, and was still strong at planning a tactical game. He could still catch and pass well. It was speed that let him down.

He closed his phone and scowled at the bench press before going back to work.

～

Anna had been watching Nick since he'd arrived. She hadn't wanted him to know, because she needed to see him being himself. Even though he'd relaxed with her a little toward the end of their first session, she knew from experience that her clients—women as well as men—would put on a show for her, pretending they felt better than they really did. She needed to see Nick candid and raw.

He'd worked hard in the gym, but she had a suspicion that he was still favouring his right leg. More than he should at this stage in his rehabilitation. She was worried.

She had two clients, two chances to impress Steve Jewell—and only Dave Parks was capable of making the grade right now. She sighed. Anna hated to fail. And there was something about Nick, a spark that excited her, a deep, burning passion—and a well disguised vulnerability.

She was determined to help him.

If she could.

"The lad's not fit."

Steve Jewell had arrived and was staring at Nick critically.

"No, he's not," Anna agreed. "And not from lack of effort in training."

"He's not backing his own talent, he's just going through the motions. He looks injured. Your thoughts?"

"I'd like him to have another MRI. I put that in my report when I emailed it to you."

"Urgent?" he barked, his expression worried.

Anna considered.

"I think it would be a sensible precaution. Sooner rather than later."

Steve gave a thin smile.

"I wanted to hear it from the horse's mouth. No offence."

"None taken," she laughed.

"Right. I'll get an appointment set up. In the meantime, keep working with him." He gave her a sharp look. "Now, tell me about Dave Parks. I need at least one of my new signings to make the grade."

Anna felt a certain amount of sympathy for Steve. Being head coach was bliss when your team was winning, and hellish when they weren't. The Minotaurs had finished low in the rankings last year, and had already lost the first two games of the new season—the Board was breathing down his neck. They wanted to see some wins.

She followed him as he led her up a flight of steps that took her to a viewing platform above the training ground's swimming pool.

Steve's phone rang and he pulled a face, muttering, "Bloody management." His heavy brows pulled together and he scowled, signalling that he was leaving.

As she hadn't a chance to ask, Anna made a note to find out if their programme included Aquafit or any hydrotherapy. Those activities were particularly good for players recovering from injury.

Her eyes were drawn to the pool door as four muscled men strode inside. She recognised Nick immediately from his inky-black hair. His body was superb: trained and honed to perfection. A lot of fit, athletic men strutted past her, but few had the lean yet powerful physique, the narrow waist, the broad shoulders, those long legs and muscular thighs. And none of them made her breath catch in her throat.

He's off limits! Get a damn grip of yourself.

Her father had drummed it into her: you don't mix business and pleasure. And here she was making exactly the same mistake again.

Anna's eyes stung with humiliation. *Why am I so bad at this?*

She forced herself to think and act like a professional. What could she learn by watching Nick and Dave swim? What clues into their psyche did the way they trained give her?

As Nick dove into the pool, she saw that he had a small tattoo on one shoulder. But from this distance, she couldn't tell what it was. Two of the other players were heavily tattooed, but Dave Parks was as unblemished as a new-born baby—if you discounted his astonishingly hairy chest.

She wouldn't be surprised if he waxed before his first match—because otherwise the opposing team wouldn't be averse to grabbing a handful of chest hair and twisting hard. The same went for excessively hairy legs.

Nick would have to shave that beard, as well. Shame.

Her eyes were irresistibly drawn back to Nick. She watched him cutting through the water with grace and economy. He really was a beautiful man *and out of bounds*.

She wasn't usually attracted to jocks; in fact, she went out of her way to find nerds to date since she was unlikely to come across them professionally. But something inside her craved the company of this tall, quiet man.

Anna watched for a moment longer, noting again a lack of flexibility in his right foot. It sickled slightly as he swam—the only ungraceful thing about him.

She jotted down some more notes then concentrated on her other client. Dave Parks was shorter and heavier. His job on the field was to be as bulky and intimidating as possible. He would only be called to the field for short periods of time: the heavy cavalry that was brought on for specific plays, a human battering ram—especially useful when the ball was near the line.

Unwillingly, her eyes were drawn back to Nick as he continued to swim lengths of the pool, water gliding sensually over his body..

She was looking forward to their next meeting.

More than she should.

～

"So, Nick. Welcome back."

"Thanks, doc. I mean, Anna."

"Either is fine. Use whatever you feel comfortable with."

Nick withheld a grimace and angled his chair so he could see out of the window instead. He exuded discomfort. Yup, the man really hated talking about himself.

"How'd you make out with your homework?" she asked, a slight smile tugging up one side of her mouth. "Three things that you're good at outside of rugby."

Nick pulled out his phone.

"You had to write it down?" she teased gently.

A faint blush rose up his cheeks making Anna regret her words, but he gave a small smile.

"No one ever asked me what else I was good at. It's only ever been rugby. Well, PE at school, but not since."

She nodded understandingly. Other athletes that she'd met were in similar positions. Many had been hot-housed as children, knowing only one way of life. It was particularly hard on them when their careers were over.

Nick's life was a little more rounded than that since he'd worked after school.

"So, hit me with it: three things that you're good at."

She wondered if he'd asked his fiancée...

Nick rubbed his hands over his jeans and read in a low monotone.

"Cottage Pie..."

"Wait, what?"

"Cottage pie."

Anna raised her eyebrows in confusion.

"I have no idea what that is!"

He stared at her aghast.

"You've never had Cottage Pie? I'll have to make you one."

He stopped abruptly.

"Would it be too much to assume it's not a pie you make in a cottage?"

He laughed, a quiet, carefree laugh, his eyes crinkling at the sides, his head thrown back. Anna wished she could hear him laugh again.

"You could," he grinned at her. "If you had a cottage, you could make a pie."

"What's in it?"

"Minced beef with onions and carrots, topped with mashed potato."

"That's it?"

"Yep."

"No pastry? No pie crust?"

"Nope."

"That's a fraud! A pie with no pie crust? I want my money back."

Nick grinned at her.

"Sorry about that."

"Eh, I'm over it. So you can make Cottage Pie."

Nick leaned forward, planting his elbows on the desk, staring directly into her eyes.

"No, I make a *fantastic* Cottage Pie."

Anna shook her head and made a note.

"Big words," she said doubtfully.

Nick's smile kicked up.

"Okay, other than your world-renowned Cottage Pie, what else are you good at?"

"I play guitar. Not very well, but I like it."

"What does 'not very well' mean? You know which way around it goes? You've counted the number of strings?"

"Yep, all four of them."

He grinned at her.

"Talent indeed. What did you do with the other two strings?"

"Used them to go fishing."

"Really?"

"No."

"Oh, funny guy! I see how it is! Now I'm in eager suspense to know what talent number three could possibly be."

He chewed his lip for a minute then finally answered.

"I'm a good friend."

Anna sat quietly in her chair, then smiled as warmth spread through her chest.

"Oh, Nick, that should go at number one."

CHAPTER SEVEN

OCTOBER 2014

For three weeks, Anna saw Nick every Tuesday for an hour. She kept her thoughts to herself and her conduct professional at all times. *God, it was hard.* But the more she learned about the quiet man of rugby, the more she liked him.

He'd turned 27 the week before, but if he'd been out partying, it hadn't had any effect on his training. Alfie, the assistant coach said that he'd never been late or turned up with a hangover, never been mouthy and always had a good attitude. He also suspected that Nick was training on his days off, too.

There was no doubt, the man was determined to win his place on the team.

His passion on the field was evident in the old tapes that she watched avidly, learning everything she could about her client. His match focus was intense, nothing was half-hearted. She watched a few blurry hand-held videos of his final game when he was still with the lower league team, and despite the blood and mud and mayhem, he'd been the steel spine, the one who kept going and kept forcing the team to play, winning a sensational try and Man of the Match at the same time. That was the game where he'd torn his Achilles tendon.

In person, the man sitting in front of her was quiet and contained, keeping his emotions tightly controlled. She couldn't help wondering what it would be like to have all of that passion unleashed. *Dammit! She was* not *supposed to think about a client like that.*

She shook her head, giving herself a pass. He was hot and she was only human.

Today's meeting with Nick started like all the others. Then took a left turn and never really got back on track.

"Hi, Nick! How are you? Have a seat. How's training going?"

"Hello, Dr. Scott," he said with a huge smile.

"You're formal today, Nick. It makes me think you haven't done your homework," she teased.

He raised an eyebrow, and she suspected that behind his glossy beard, he was suppressing a smile.

"Are you going to give me detention?" he asked in a low, gravelly voice. "Are you going to punish me, doctor?"

Anna blinked.

What the hell? Was he flirting with her?

"Depends. Do you have a guilty conscience?"

"Not yet," he mumbled.

Anna decided not to hear that. A flirty Nick was something new. He didn't say anything else even slightly off-centre, but for the rest of the hour, there was a crack and sizzle in the air, quick looks and unnerving eye contact. Anna started to sweat, feeling her armpits and the small of her back grow damp as she tried to ignore the way her body responded to his dark glances.

She was distracted when she saw a message flash up on her phone.

> I'm in the UK this week
> Let's hang out

She wished she hadn't left it in plain view on her desk, and she definitely wished she hadn't looked at it, because now she felt like throwing her phone at the wall, and she *hated* how seeing Jonathan's name pushed her buttons. As if she'd *ever* want to hang out with him, and anyway, she also suspected that was a euphemism for 'have sex'.

Anna grimaced when she realised that Nick had seen the message as well as the name she'd assigned to Jonathan on her phone.

"Douchenozzle?" he raised an eyebrow.

Anna laughed uneasily.

"My ex. And yes, he definitely was ... is a giant douchenozzle."

"Is he bothering you?"

Nick's eyes flashed with sudden anger making Anna sit back. In the weeks that she'd known him, he'd never been anything but sweet, a little flirty today, but overall a nice guy. She'd never seen *this* Nick off the field, the aggressive alpha male.

"Uh, not really. This is the first time he's contacted me in months."

"Why haven't you blocked his number?" Nick asked roughly.

Anna was flustered.

"I ... well, I didn't think I'd need to. I didn't think he'd get in touch after..."

She flushed, remembering the hideous scene.

"It's nothing."

"It's not nothing if it upsets you."

She licked her lips and Nick's gaze darted to her tongue stud.

"What were we talking about before?"

"Visualisation," he said after a lengthy pause as he dragged his eyes from her mouth.

"Oh, yes, right. So, what I think we should…"

"I've got a visualisation I want to run by you," Nick said.

"Great! Shoot!" Her voice was too bright.

"Well, Anna, what I want you to do is to visualise putting on a pair of leather work boots with steel toecaps. With me so far?"

"Um … I thought you were the client?"

"I am, and you're a great teacher. So just go with it for a moment. Close your eyes and visualise it, Anna."

His voice was low and authoritative. Anna found herself doing exactly as he instructed.

"Now imagine the douchenozzle standing in front of you. Okay?"

"Okaaay."

"Now visualise dropkicking his arse."

He said it so seriously that Anna's eyes flew open before she burst out laughing and Nick's quiet chuckle met her ears.

"Oh em gee! You really had me going there!"

"Did it work? Visualisation is a powerful tool," he grinned.

"So you *have* been listening!"

Nick's smile fell away.

"Yeah, I've been listening, and if the douchenozzle couldn't appreciate a beautiful, compassionate, sexy woman like you, then he didn't deserve you and you're better off without him."

His unexpected assertion brought tears to Anna's eyes and she looked down at her desk, rapidly trying to blink them away. She felt the heavy weight of Nick's hand on top of hers. He squeezed her fingers gently, and then the weight was gone.

Anna took a sip of lemon water, swallowing past the lump in her throat.

"Thank you," she whispered.

"You're welcome."

His words replayed on a loop in Anna's mind: *He called me sexy?!*

∿

Anna had given Nick more 'homework'. This time, she'd made an appointment for him to visit the local high school's rugby team.

Her idea was to help him remember the excitement he'd had at that age.

When you did something for a living, some of the passion could be lost. And since his surgery, he'd been so focussed on recovery, that it stopped being fun— which she totally understood. But she needed Nick to re-engage with the kid he'd been. For a twenty-seven year-old guy, he could be very serious. She'd seen glimpses of a silly, joking side—that's what he needed to find again: heart.

On the day before the visit, Nick had texted her asking if she'd like to come with him. There was nothing else on her schedule, and the chance to see Nick enjoying himself was too much to turn down. A tiny, whispering voice reminded her that this wasn't in her job description when she'd agreed to take him on as a client, but she decided it was entirely appropriate—and it would be fun.

The high school had put out the bunting for Nick. Triangles of coloured paper fluttered in the breeze, adding a jaunty air to the dull, grey building, like rouge on a great grandmother.

Nick was sitting in his black Beamer in the visitors' parking lot when Anna drove up.

He grinned through the windscreen and climbed out of his car to open her door.

When his larger hand wrapped around hers, helping her out, she smiled up at him. His old fashioned manners were sweet, and Anna was charmed.

"Ready to go back to school, Nick?"

"Yes, teacher."

She laughed, happy to see him so relaxed.

Today, he was dressed in sweats and a Minotaurs t-shirt, and carried his rugby boots in a kitbag. Anna was dressed less formally, too, opting for comfortable boots rather than her usual heels.

They made their way to reception and an excited woman phoned the headteacher who came out to greet them personally.

She had the harried, slightly distracted air of someone with too many fires to put out and not enough buckets of water.

"We're so grateful you could make the time," she said. "Our first fifteen are so excited to meet you."

"And the second team?" Nick asked, making Anna smile.

He never forgot that not everyone could be in the top grade. Not ever.

The headteacher laughed lightly.

"We only have one team, but the footballers and hockey players didn't want to miss out on meeting you, so they'll be along later."

At that moment, they were interrupted by what looked suspiciously like a picket line of teenage girls, waving banners and chanting:

"One, two, three, four
Men-only rugby, we deplore.
Five, six, seven, eight,
Rugby players are rubbish dates."

"Eloise! Will you stop that!" snapped the headmistress.

The girl leading the chanting stuck her lip out belligerently.

"It's not fair, Miss! Why is it only the boys get to play rugby? It's sexist, that's what it is! It's illegal!"

The headmistress sighed, as if this was a familiar opening bombardment in a long-running war.

"Because, as I've explained to you before, there aren't enough of your classmates who share your desire to play rugby. There simply aren't enough of you to make a team."

"You should let us play with the boys!" the girl whined.

Nick stepped forward, shaking his head.

"Eloise, is it?"

"What?" she said rudely, but not before Anna spotted her eyeing Nick closely, her gaze skating over his broad shoulders and narrow waist.

"How much do you weigh?" he asked, his voice low and steady.

"What?" she shrieked. "You're a pervert! Did you hear him, Miss?"

"I weigh 92 kilos," he said. "Two hundred and three pounds. You weigh about half that, right?"

Anna suspected that the chunky girl was considerably heavier than that, but said nothing, watching with admiration as Nick's masterplan unfolded.

The girl was flattered, fluttering her eyelashes at Nick and coyly flashing the braces on her teeth.

"About that, yeah."

"If someone my size tackled someone yours, you could get badly hurt. That's why your teacher can't have boys and girls playing a contact sport like rugby together."

"But it's not fair, Sir! Me 'ole fam'ly is rugby mad. I want to play, too!"

"That's more than enough, thank you, Miss Higginbotham. Back to class, please, Eloise. And take your ... banners with you."

Grumbling and swearing almost loudly enough to be heard, Eloise and her followers sloped off, trailing their placards in the dust.

"I'm so sorry..." the headteacher began.

"No, it's fine," said Nick. "Women's rugby is on the up—the England team is doing better than the men's team right now. It's a pity the girls can't play. Isn't there another school nearby that they could make up a team with?"

The headteacher raised her eyebrows.

"That might be possible."

Nick grinned at her.

"And the girls could do the fitness training with the boys..."

She smiled at him, and Anna could see that Nick had gained another fan.

"They could train with us today," he offered. "Just fitness stuff, no tackling. We could play touch and pass, so two hands touching your body means you've been tackled."

The headteacher snorted.

"Not an opportunity I'd like to give to Miss Higginbotham," she said tartly.

Nick tried not to smile.

"There's also a version for kids called tag rugby."

"What's that?"

"You can Velcro tags to your shorts—again, if someone manages to pull the patch off, you've been tackled. Girls can definitely play that. It's rugby, but it's not contact."

"Thank you for the suggestion, Mr. Renshaw. I'll see if I can arrange it."

He shrugged a massive shoulder.

"Just Nick."

Anna wanted to hug him. He'd easily defused a difficult situation and spread a little rugby love. But she wasn't allowed to hug him. The club's strict rules of no fraternization made that impossible. And the small fact that she was his psychologist and could be reported to the Health and Care Professions Council. She would lose her licence.

She set her face in the imitation of a smile, and he glanced at her curiously.

Did he know? Could he tell?

Anna had been aware for some weeks now that she was sexually attracted to her client. Worse still, she was emotionally attracted to him. She knew that during the therapeutic process it was inevitable that you got to know a client so deeply that many connections could arise. She cared about him more than she should.

To use a well-known sports metaphor: *she was screwed.*

She followed him around the school like the book nerd after the star quarterback, which was a closer analogy than she liked to consider. But she also knew that her plan for Nick was working. The visit had put the sparkle back in his eyes. He was excited, enthused, and this motley assortment of schoolkids had done that.

He ran up and down the school field with them, threw easy passes, let them tackle him even though it was obvious he could have outrun every single one of them. The boys grumbled a bit when the girls came out to join in the fitness section, but Nick happily reminded them that women's rugby England team had won the World Cup the previous summer. That shut the boys up, and he got them all running drills together.

Then they had a game of tag rugby, and by the end of the morning, Nick was hot and sweaty and happy.

Anna itched to touch him, to bask in his happiness for just a second. Instead, she gave him another tight smile and turned to talk to the headteacher who was discussing the possibility of setting up a combined-schools girls' rugby team with the PE staff.

When Nick was finally able to peel himself away from his new fans, he walked back to the parking lot with Anna.

"You looked like you were having fun today," she said, smiling at him.

"I was. It was a great idea of yours. Nice bit of reverse psychology," he teased.

"Oh, there was nothing reverse about it—seeing kids enjoying themselves can rejuvenate the most jaded athlete."

He frowned slightly.

"You think I'm jaded?"

"A little, yes. But that's inevitable when you've had a run of bad luck or when you're injured."

He thought about this, shoving his hands in his pockets and frowning.

"And," she said gently, "kids do it for the love of it. In the hothouse atmosphere of a club, salary negotiations, sponsorship and contracts, it's easy to lose sight of that." She paused. "Maybe even more so now you're in a top-tier club."

"Yeah, I suppose so. I had a sponsorship contract once."

"Really? I didn't know that. What for?"

"Shaving products."

Anna goggled, staring at his thick black beard.

"Seriously?"

He laughed happily, his eyes crinkling at the corners.

"They might want their money back," Anna muttered, raising her eyebrows.

"Nah, I don't have that contract anymore. And anyway, I'll have to shave before my first game or some git will try to see if it's detachable."

Anna smiled but didn't comment.

He turned his intense hazel-green eyes on hers.

"Are *you* okay? You seemed a bit … off, today. Has the douchenozzle been in touch again?"

She blinked, remembering their previous conversation. She hadn't thought about Jonathan all morning, although she'd had a few sleepless nights wondering whether to ignore him or to reply to his text. What she really wanted to say was that it would be a cold day in hell before she willingly set eyes on him again, but she didn't want to get into anything resembling a conversation. In the end she'd simply texted back that she was busy. He hadn't replied.

"No, I haven't heard anything. I'm fine."

"Okay," he said, still looking worried. "Er, can I buy you lunch today? To say thank you for setting this up?"

He looked so hopeful, Anna was dying to say yes. For a second she hesitated, her heart ruling her head. Which was the exact reason she had to say no.

"Thanks for the offer," she smiled politely, regretting her decision already. "But I have to get back to the office. Other clients, you know?"

He took a step back, rocking on his heels.

"Sure, no problem. See you next week, Anna."

~

Nick watched Anna drive away. He could tell that something was bothering her. All those sessions in her office hadn't been one way; he'd started to get to know her, too. All her mannerisms, how she spoke; the way her lips twitched when she was amused but trying to hide it; the way she settled her hands on the desk before she hit with a one-two punch of steely insight; the way she met his initial scepticism with tolerance and persistence.

And today had been fantastic. It would never have occurred to him that going back to his roots could fire him up like this. The way the kids had responded to him and his suggestions. Yeah, definitely good for his soul, and definitely good for his ego. He smiled at the memory of brazen Eloise—a little tank of a girl who might even have a future in women's rugby. If she did, he'd like to think he had played a small part in that.

He climbed in his car and drove to the training ground, wishing Anna had taken him up on his offer of lunch, but at the same time knowing Molly would have hated that he was spending time with another woman, no matter how platonic.

Except Nick wasn't sure how much longer he could go on kidding himself—a lot of his thoughts about the sexy doctor were far from platonic.

He could guess what Ken would say—he'd tell him to go for it, to enjoy himself with Anna before he got hitched and promised to sleep with just one woman for the rest of his life. But Nick wasn't Kenny, and he wouldn't disrespect either woman that way.

But lunch would have been nice.

CHAPTER EIGHT

The pub was busier than Anna was expecting, and she pushed her way through slowly, scanning each table in the hope that Graham would be there—so far, no luck. And she didn't think a table would be freeing up any time soon.

"What's a nice doctor like you doing in a place like this?"

She spun around to see Nick's grinning face. Even in four-inch heels, she had to tilt her chin up to meet his amused gaze.

"Looking for a place to park her weary ass," she smiled.

"Are you here by yourself?"

"Yes, I thought it was women-only night. My mistake."

His eyebrows shot up. The whole team was there, so the pub was filled with burly men. Then he laughed at her amused expression, and she grinned at him.

"Can I buy you a drink?"

"Um..."

"You're off duty. That's allowed, isn't it?" He leaned closer. "Crowded pub, nothing shady ... and I won't tell if you won't."

He was so close, she could feel his warm breath on her cheek. He was wearing a light cologne, cinnamon, maybe a hint of cedar, something that she couldn't identify, something that was all man, all Nick. She swallowed and glanced around quickly. *No harm in it*, said the devil on her shoulder.

The pub was crowded and they shuffled closer together, his arm steadying her when she was jostled. Up close, in her personal space, he smelled even better, and she had to resist breathing in deeply as her body was briefly pressed against his.

By sheer willpower alone, she managed to inch backwards, even as she longed to move closer still.

Anna realised that he was watching her with confusion, probably wondering why she was acting so weird ... or maybe just wondering if she wanted a drink or not.

"In that case, thank you," she answered, giving him a bright smile. "I'll have a scotch on the rocks."

He winced.

"What's wrong with that?"

"You can't put ice in a good whiskey—that's just wrong. It spoils the flavour."

Anna smiled at him, her eyes lighting with challenge.

"First, I didn't ask for a single malt, I asked for scotch—blended whiskey. And second, you're wrong. A little dilution makes it more flavourful. That's been scientifically proven. You need to thank guaiacol for that—it's an aromatic herb, and it has a smoky aroma, some think it has a scent of creosote," and she pulled a face. "Guaiacol tends to sink, so diluting it a little moves it closer to the surface —more flavour, more taste." She smiled at his stupefied expression. "And it's rather warm in here, so I'll have it with ice."

"That is ... how do you know this stuff?"

"I read," she said with a hint of a smile. "Plus, memory like an elephant."

He shook his head, still smiling.

"Scotch on the rocks coming up."

He waded through the crowd in front of the bar, and with a nod of his head, was served immediately. Anna was jealous—she wished she had that effect on bartenders.

Nick returned a minute later with her drink, and a bottle of water for himself, she noted.

"You look ... different tonight," he said cautiously.

"You're missing the cape and superhero outfit I wear for work?"

He slapped his forehead.

"That's it! I knew it was something."

"Ten out of ten for observation."

Then he spoke more seriously. "You look really nice, Anna."

She paused before answering. "Thank you."

They stared at each other and Anna's pulse started to race. *Damn, the man was intense.* His eyes were narrowed as if he was about to say something important. She glanced away and took a sip of her scotch, enjoying the bite and slow burn, feeling as if this was dangerous territory. There was an attraction, a pull, a magnetism that seduced her.

Anna held the glass in front of her, a weak defence against a battle she didn't want to fight.

"I'm hoping to get some match time on Saturday," said Nick, leaning back, his expression relaxed again as he gestured with the bottle of water.

Whatever he was going to say, he'd thought better of it. *And now she was really curious.*

"So I've heard. Good for you," she said with a neutral expression. "You've worked hard and..."

"Hey, Nicky baby, where've you been?"

They were interrupted by Molly who latched onto Nick's free arm as if it was made of solid gold. She stared questioningly at Nick, her gaze turning hostile as she swung toward Anna.

"Mol, this is Anna. Anna, this is my girlfriend, Molly."

She shot him a furious look and then smiled sweetly at Anna.

"Fiancée."

"Yeah, of course. Fiancée," Nick amended quickly, his eyes darting between them.

"Hello," Anna said pleasantly.

Nick hadn't introduced her as his psychologist, so Anna wasn't sure if Molly knew about her. She decided to err on the side of caution since she was getting the *keep off* vibe.

"How do you guys know each other?" Molly asked, jealousy glinting in her gaze.

"We work together," Nick answered shortly. "Anna's a sports psychologist. She's been helping me with aspects of my game."

Molly's eyes narrowed.

"*You're* Dr. Scott?"

"Yes, I am. How nice to meet you," Anna said politely.

She was curious about this woman—Nick had mentioned his fiancée a grand total of three times in all their meetings.

"Nick's told me about you, *Dr. Scott*. Although I don't remember him mentioning that you're female." She tossed her long hair over slim shoulders. "He probably doesn't think of you as a woman."

Anna's eyebrows shot up, wondering how Nick had gotten involved with someone so rude.

"Mol! Jesus!"

Behind Molly, Anna was relieved to see that Graham had arrived, because by her reckoning, Nick and his fiancée were about twenty seconds from a full-scale argument.

"Well, it was ... nice ... chatting with you both, but if you'll excuse me, my date has arrived. Thanks for the drink, Nick."

She walked away, but not before she heard Molly's strident tones and Nick's low, angry response.

~

The day after seeing Anna at the pub, Nick arrived for a day of training.

He'd been surprised to see her, but enjoyed talking to her out of office hours. Shame the evening had ended in another row with Molly.

She'd accused him of lying. *Not true.*

Of not telling her that Dr. Scott was female. *True.*

That he fancied the pants off Dr. Scott. *Also true, but strongly denied.*

That he'd disrespected Molly. *False.*

That he had to promise to stop seeing Anna. *No way.*

He'd slept in the spare room. In his own house.

But his edginess was about more than another irritating row with Molly. He loved her, but he had to admit that since he'd met Anna, he was wondering if Mol really was the woman he wanted to spend the rest of his life with. Since he'd just got engaged, his timing sucked. She was also still nagging him about trying to be a TV pundit. He wasn't totally against the idea, just not yet. Rugby was his passion, his life: Molly had never understood that.

He also knew that something was happening between him and Anna, but neither of them were in a position to acknowledge it. And he wasn't sure how he felt about that. He was drawn to her, strongly, but he wasn't a cheater and never had been. With an older sister and a mum he respected, he'd have had seven bells knocked out of him by both of them if he'd tried anything like that. And he'd been with Molly for three years. It was confusing and disconcerting to find himself attracted to another woman just a few weeks after he'd asked Molly to marry him.

Even so, Anna was very much on his mind when he walked into the locker room, only to find a post-it note with an instruction to see Steve Jewell. Nick's heart kicked up a gear.

Today was decision day for who'd be playing on Saturday. Nick was aching for the chance to prove himself.

With some trepidation and a lot of expectation, he jogged up a flight of stairs to the head coach's office.

"Come in, Nick. Take a seat."

Steve's voice was gruff and the frown lines on his face had deepened since the start of the season.

"You're not training today. I want you to take yourself down to the clinic. You're booked in for an MRI scan on that Achilles tendon."

Nick was stunned. This wasn't what he'd expected to hear.

"Why's that then, Coach?" he asked, feeling uneasy. "Why now? I thought ... I hoped I'd made the pick for Saturday."

"Doctor's orders," came the reply. "Just a check-up. We want to make sure everything's healing as it should. Right?"

"Right," Nick echoed doubtfully.

The only doctor Nick had seen lately was Anna. He felt a small stab of betrayal—that she was sending him for this scan without discussing it first. Obviously he knew that she was reporting back—that was her job—but still, she should have mentioned it.

Nick knew he wasn't as fit as he could be; definitely not as fast as he'd been. But he was so much better than at the start of the season. He wanted to be out there, playing for his club.

Feeling numb, he took the appointment letter that Coach held out to him, seeing the address of a private clinic that the Club used.

When he arrived, he was ushered into a plush waiting area. Wide, comfortable sofas were arranged around a small coffee table that carried glossy brochures describing the clinic's services. He scanned through one then quickly dropped it back onto the table with a heavy sigh.

Thank God he didn't have a prostate problem.

Growing bored as he waited, he sent a text to Molly, telling her where he was on the off chance that she might actually care. They still weren't speaking, but surely she'd want to know that he was seeing a doctor?

Yes, things were rocky between them, but that didn't mean they didn't love each other. Nick's injury had been a rough patch, but they'd survived, and it had made him stronger. Nick knew how worried Molly had been, but they were getting married next year and this was just a stupid argument.

Right now, he needed her. With this new uncertainty hanging over his head, he needed to know that he and Molly were still good.

She was working today, so he hoped she'd text back and he could kill some time, but she didn't.

He waited a few more minutes with growing disappointment, then pocketed his phone and scowled at his wristwatch, but a short while later, he was taken in for his appointment.

Dressed in a hospital gown, the kind that left your arse hanging out, he slid onto the cold plastic of the scanner tray and put the earphones over his head, listening to classical music playing. It was relaxing in a weird sort of way.

The heavy, rhythmic thumping of the MRI scanner rolled through him. Somehow, this huge metal tube was taking pictures of the inside of his body. It was a pity it wasn't doing his brain as well—it would have been interesting to see the mess inside his head.

Twenty minutes later, he was out, dressed and sitting in the consultant's office. Definitely not as much waiting around as in an NHS hospital.

"Well, Mr. Renshaw, I have the results of your MRI scan."

The doctor glanced at his computer screen then up at Nick, small round glasses perched on the end of a long nose that bristled with nasal hair.

"I'm afraid the tear in your Achilles tendon has not been successfully repaired. It's going to require further surgery. In fact, the tear is at 90 percent, you're lucky it hasn't snapped completely. It's hanging on by a thread. It could go at any moment, even if you weren't playing a physical sport like rugby. Frankly, it's a miracle," and he smiled broadly so Nick could share his appreciation. "We'll need to schedule surgery as soon as possible. This week."

Nick felt the blood drain from his body then replaced with ice. The shock of the doctor's prognosis felt like a life sentence ... or a death sentence. He'd suspected that something wasn't right because he wasn't moving like he used to. But he'd just assumed he needed to train harder, not ... not *this*.

He swallowed a bitter taste as all those hopes that Anna had given him disappeared in the smoking remains of his career.

It was all over this time. He couldn't think of a single athlete who'd come back from two surgeries like that and play top level rugby. It was no coincidence that most careers ended in injury rather than retirement.

He remembered the release form he'd signed before he had the last surgery. He'd waived pretty much all his rights then, it seemed.

"I can't say I'd have done it like that myself," said the consultant, frowning. "Too much chance of dead material being left in—as is the case here. You really can't partially keyhole an Achilles tendon repair. Of course, the wound heals more quickly, however..."

The consultant continued talking, but Nick barely heard a word of what he said about scheduling surgery and rehabilitation. All he could think was, *it's over*.

When the doctor stopped talking, *if, maybe, could, perhaps,* he shook hands wordlessly and drove home.

The house echoed with his footsteps as he paced through the living room and out to the kitchen, staring at the narrow back garden that he'd never got around to planting out.

It was too empty and he couldn't bear to be around so much silence when the voices in his head were threatening to deafen him. He pulled his phone from his pocket, his first instinct to talk to Anna. He needed her quiet reassurance, but he hesitated. Anything he said could be reported to Steve Jewell.

He stuffed the phone back and jumped into his car, driving too fast to see the only other person who'd understand.

Kenny was still on the injury list and had physio most afternoons, so Nick knew he'd be home at this time of day.

The thirty minute drive usually gave Nick time to think, but today the time filled a great well of depression that had sunk inside him.

He pulled up outside a redbrick, semi-detached house of the type that Manchester suburbs specialised in. Except for the flashy car parked outside the garage.

But then he saw another car on the short driveway, and his stomach plummeted. It was the Mini Cooper that he'd bought for Molly last year.

Why was Molly visiting Kenny at this time of day? An answer sprang to mind, but it seemed too improbable because they hated each other. That's what they'd always told him...

Nick gripped the steering wheel, his knuckles whitening as sheer rage filled him.

He was out of the car before he knew what he was doing and he strode up Kenny's short driveway.

Music was blaring through the house, blocking out the sound of his approach. He glanced through the front window and exhaled slowly.

It was the knee brace that clued him in.

Kenny had been wearing a knee brace for weeks now.

A woman was bent over an armchair, and Nick watched as his best friend slapped the plump backside while he pumped inside her, his hairy white arse pistoning roughly.

Nick's heart stumbled.

He didn't want to believe what he was seeing, but he knew it was her, knew it was Molly. He recognised the dress that was pushed up around her waist and the shoes that she'd worn when she walked off in a huff this morning.

She turned slightly, and Nick could see the soft curve of her cheek, flushed and sweating.

I've got to be at work early today, Nicky baby. Lie Number One.

Your girlfriend, sorry, fiancée, does my head in. Lie Number Two.

I'm supporting you all the way, Nicky baby. Lie Number Three.

I've got your back, mate. Lie Number Four.

Love you, Nicky baby! Lie Number Five.

Nick's stomach turned over when Molly's mouth dropped open with pleasure.

It was supposed to be *him* who made her cry out like that, not Ken. Never Ken.

How long? How long since his fiancée and his best friend had been fucking? How long had he been a naïve, trusting fool? *How long? How long? How long!*

As if someone had lit a match, his blood began to boil in his veins. Flames of rage fanned by the fires of humiliation consumed him.

He burned.

He ran back to his car, grabbing a wrench from the toolbox in the boot. The cool metal felt right against his hot skin.

Nick swung the wrench like a baseball player, shattering the large pane of glass in the front window. Molly screamed and Kenny yelled obscenities. Nick charged at the front door, *BAM! BAM! BAM!* Then shoulder barged the door and booted it open.

Molly screamed again when she saw him and cowered on the floor.

Kenny was still trying to pull sweatpants over his knee brace, his now flaccid dick swinging wildly.

"Nick! Mate! It's not what it looks like!"

Nick ignored the words, more lies, and moved around the room methodically smashing everything in there.

SMASH! The TV screen shattered and sparked.

CRACK! The tall reading light was bent in half.

CRASH! The Bluetooth speaker met a bitter end.

Kenny grabbed his arm, trying to stop him, but Nick didn't even think as he hooked Kenny around the neck, the clothesline manoeuvre that he'd so graphically described to Anna all those weeks ago.

Kenny was yanked backwards, shrieking as his bad knee buckled, and then the scream was cut off as Nick gripped his windpipe and squeezed.

His rage was so huge, so overwhelming, so filled with blinding fury that he stared wordlessly at the two people he'd trusted most. He couldn't stop, couldn't...

Kenny's face was turning blue and his eyes were bulging. Nick threw a punch at Kenny, catching him on the jaw, hoping that there was still some fight in him, but he just slipped to the shag pile carpet. Nick barely realised that Molly was clawing at his arm until he shook her off, accidentally elbowing her in the face. She sat down heavily, holding her streaming nose.

Suddenly, Nick's awareness flooded back, and he was appalled when he saw what he'd done. There was shattered glass and splatters of blood everywhere.

Nick was panting as he watched Molly crawl to Kenny on her hands and knees, wailing that he'd killed him.

He hadn't, but for a moment...

Did she really care about that arsehole? Molly had always said that Kenny was a moronic dickhead with the brain the size of a gnat and the social skills of a badly trained, incontinent Labrador. Un-fucking-believable! He'd defended Kenny, stood up for him. Now, she was kneeling next to him as tears blackened with mascara stained her cheeks.

Nauseous with disgust, Nick turned away.

His trust, his love had been betrayed, treated as worthless, butchered and tossed away.

It's all gone.

He left the door wide open as he strode from the house, but when he saw Molly's car, the one she'd nagged him to buy, the one he'd paid for, he lost control again.

He was still beating the fuck out of the bright red Mini Cooper when the police arrived.

"Drop it, mate!" ordered one of the police officers.

It took a moment for the words to penetrate his rage-flooded brain, but when the officer repeated the order, Nick dropped the wrench obediently and waited, panting as sweat coated his body. Molly was screaming and crying, pointing a shaking finger at Nick as blood dripped onto her dress.

Nick wondered if she'd taken the time to find her underwear.

The police didn't hesitate, pushing him against the remnants of Molly's car and fastening his hands behind him.

"You are under arrest on suspicion of assault and criminal damage. You do not have to say anything but it may harm your defence if you do not mention when questioned something which you later rely on in court. Anything you do say may be given in evidence."

Nick hadn't spoken since he arrived at Kenny's house. Not once.

Not a word.

The police officer glanced at him to see if he'd understood, then continued.

"It is necessary to arrest you for preservation of evidence and immediate safety of others under Code G of the Police and Criminal Evidence Act 1984. Do you understand?"

Nick nodded.

He watched as paramedics helped Molly and Kenny into an ambulance. Kenny's throat was purple and his eyes bloodshot.

"He's a fucking nutter! Have you seen what he's done to my house! He wants locking up!"

Kenny's voice was hoarse, but Nick just stared, wondering if everything Ken had ever said to him was a lie. He'd put up with laddish, dickhead way for years, thinking that there was a decent man underneath.

Ken's betrayal was hard to understand, hard to take.

And as for Molly...

Love had turned to dust.

His eyes turned to her, screaming and wailing as the paramedics tried to calm her down. *She should be enjoying this,* he thought dispassionately. *She always loved being the centre of attention.*

A little worm of guilt worked its way inside him as he noticed her purple eyes and swelling nose. Looked like it was broken. He tried to swallow past a hard chunk of disgust. You didn't hit women: that wasn't how he'd been brought up.

The rage had burned itself out, leaving him numb, as yet unable to reach the deep emotional well of misery, shame and despair.

CHAPTER NINE

"NICK RENSHAW HAS BEEN ARRESTED!"

Anna stared as Belinda delivered the news.

"What? Are you sure? Why?"

"Assault and criminal damage. Apparently, he caught his fiancée in a compromising position with another man, and then smashed up her car and the fella's house. Can you believe it?"

For a moment, she was speechless. Poor Nick. Poor, poor Nick. She knew only too well the deep, fierce pain of betrayal.

But she wondered ... could she imagine him beating up his best friend? Could she imagine that? She'd seen the passion for his game, sensed the deep waters that flowed through him, but this sort of violence?

There was a long pause.

"They say he hit her, too." Belinda's voice dropped to a whisper.

"No!"

Anna's automatic denial was immediate.

"That's what they're saying. It's already all over the internet."

Revulsion flickered, spreading a wildfire of horror throughout Anna's body. She pressed her fingers against her forehead, trying to erase the mental images Belinda had unwittingly set loose.

How could he do that? How could a man like Nick hit a woman? It seemed impossible. But he'd been arrested for it. How had she gotten it so wrong again? She really didn't know him at all.

Disappointment stole her breath, and her stomach churned.

An hour later she received an email from Steve Jewell's assistant cancelling all future appointments for Nick Renshaw.

So that was that.

~

"Time for your phone call."

Nick followed the police officer who pointed to a cheap-looking plastic phone on the desk.

"I can't use my mobile?"

"Just the landline, sir."

"Okay."

He took a deep breath and called his agent.

"Mark, it's Nick Renshaw. I've fucked up..."

After that, he sat quietly in the police cell, stretched out on the thin, lumpy mattress as the wheels of justice ground a path through his life. His thoughts were sluggish and spinning at the same time. He knew that he'd just detonated a bomb under his career. Or his whole life.

Shouldn't he feel *something?*

The police had given him a breath test when he'd arrived at the police station, although he wasn't sure why. Maybe because he'd driven to Kenny's house before losing his rag and going terminator on the fixtures and fittings. Maybe *drunken rage* was easier to understand than sober rage.

He breathed in slowly, trying to filter out the smell of piss and bleach, and the slurred rambling from the cell next door. For a moment, the muttering stopped, and then Nick heard the sound of vomiting.

He studied the bandage over the knuckles on his right hand, still slowly oozing blood. *When had it started? Had they been together all along, laughing at him behind his back?* Or maybe it was new? All those nights when he'd been too tired or too sore while he recovered from his surgery, too much of a miserable git to go out with her, had it happened then?

And then he wondered if it mattered, wondered if he cared.

The emptiness inside numbed him.

He'd been booked in by the Custody Sergeant and been checked over for any injuries as well as having a short mental health assessment, his hands were bandaged, and then he'd been put in a cell.

All he could do now was wait it out. He'd been told that the police had 24 hours to collect evidence, which included statements from the injured parties, photographs of bruises and the damage, and a search for witnesses. Kenny's neighbours were probably lining up for that one.

Pain and despair slowly filled the vacuum where love and friendship had lived. And he realised that nothing about his life had been real.

Eleven hours later, Nick had been interviewed, charged, and released on bail with the conditions not to approach the injured parties, Kenny's house, Molly's mother's house, or Molly's sister's flat.

The solicitor his agent had found for him was a brisk, well-dressed woman, with the clipped tones of someone who was perpetually busy. Mark probably had Miranda Wilson-Smith on speed dial because altercations between belligerent rugby players wasn't unusual. She was the go-to guy when you'd got "in a spot of bother" as Mark put it.

"We'll need to meet as quickly as possible to start planning your defence, Mr. Renshaw. Given that the assault included a weapon..."

A wrench from a tool box was a weapon? Yeah, probably, when you swung it the way Al Capone swung a baseball bat.

"You'll appear in court at the first available opportunity, probably within one or two days, to enter a plea of guilty or not guilty. I would advise you to plead guilty; if you plead not guilty, the case will be referred to crown court for a trial. And that could drag on for six months or more."

Nick dropped his head into his hands.

"I didn't mean to hurt her. It was an accident—I'll cop for the rest."

"But you agree you assaulted your fiancée?"

Shame burned him—he was dreading telling his mum, his sister.

"Ex-fiancée," he said softly. "Yeah."

"The magistrate will hear the evidence, then adjourn for sentencing."

"As quick as that?"

"Yes."

Nick felt an odd sense of disconnection. The man who'd raged around Kenny's house hours ago felt as though it had happened to someone else; as if he'd watched through the wrong end of a telescope as some maniac systematically destroyed his former friend's house. All that fury, overtaken by a frenzy of destruction, it seemed so remote from him now. The pulse of pain and betrayal beat weakly deep, deep inside him.

He ought to care that everything had gone to shit. But he didn't. He didn't care about anything.

Miranda Wilson-Smith packed all her papers away in her briefcase and left him with a severe warning to stay away from Ken and Molly. He had no problem with that. Seeing them even once more in his lifetime would be too much.

The desk sergeant handed back his phone, shoelaces, car keys and wallet with polite indifference. Not much seemed to ruffle the police officers. There was that disconnection again: his life had imploded messily, bleakly, and it was just another twelve-hour shift for them.

When Nick looked up, his dad was standing there, watching him with so much love and pity. Nick swallowed several times before he could speak; the weight of how he'd disappointed the man who'd given him everything left him wordless.

His father wrapped his arms around him and hugged him tightly.

"I'm sorry, Dad."

"It'll be alright, son."

Nick stepped back, grateful for the undiluted love he saw on his father's face. He didn't think of his dad as old, but today he saw the grey flecks in his hair and the lines of life and love, grief and happiness all leaving their mark over the years.

He slumped wearily into his old man's battered Volvo, and it was only when they'd driven for ten minutes in silence through the late evening traffic that he realised they weren't going to Nick's house.

"Dad? Where are we going?"

"Trish has gone to pick up your car from Kenny's," he sighed, "and your mother wants you home."

"Oh."

His dad glanced at him but didn't say anything else.

Home. He hadn't lived under his parents' roof since he was 19, but it seemed right to go there now.

His mum threw open the front door and hugged him tightly, talking quickly and wiping tell-tale tears.

Nick hated to see his mother upset, hated to see the worry and regret on her face. And when Trish arrived back with his car, she was furious, torn between threatening to beat the shit out of Kenny even though Nick knew that she'd always had a bit of a crush on him, and trash-talking Molly. Either way, he didn't want to hear it.

His dad handed him a can of Stella and his mum made his favourite cottage pie, as if food and drink could make it all better. If he was ten, it might have worked, but he appreciated the effort.

He ate mechanically without tasting anything, drank the beer and then a second and a third as they watched with the anxious, tortured faces of people who loved you but didn't have the power to make it all better.

"Alright if I kip here tonight, Mum?"

He knew his mum would like that and he couldn't face going home just yet. At some point he'd have to go back; if nothing else, to find out how much Molly had taken since she still had a key. Right now, he didn't give a tuppenny fuck.

"Of course you can stay. I'll go and put fresh sheets on the bed for you."

"I'll clear up in the kitchen," muttered his dad.

Trish came and sat beside him, his big sister who hadn't been bigger than him for 14 years.

"Do you want to talk about it?"

"Nah, you're alright."

"Is there anything I can do? Slash her tyres? Slash *his* tyres? Post ugly-drunk photos of them on Twitter? I've got loads."

Nick gave half a smile and leaned back on the settee.

"No thanks, sis. My brief says I can't go near them or it'll make things worse."

There was a long silence, then Trish spoke softly.

"Did you really hit her?"

He opened his eyes and met her worried gaze.

"It was an accident."

"Really? You can tell me, Nick. I'd understand."

He sat up straight, staring at her tight expression as understanding rushed through him.

"You don't believe me! Jesus!"

"I do! I'm sorry. I had to ask."

"Did you? You couldn't just believe I'm not like that? I'm your *brother!*"

Trish bit her lip.

"I thought maybe, in the heat of the moment, you just lost your temper. It happens."

"Fuck, Trish! If you don't believe me, I've got no fucking chance of convincing anyone else. I can't believe this is happening. My own *sister!*"

"Oh God, Nick! *Of course* I believe you! I know you wouldn't lift your hand to a woman. It's not in your DNA. I hate that the mardy cow has done this to you!"

He stood up, glaring at her.

"Where are you going?"

"Out. Home. Away from here."

The idea that his family thought he was the kind of man who battered women made him physically sick.

"Don't go! Not like this!"

He brushed past his mum who was holding two mugs of tea.

"Nick?"

He kissed her cheek quickly.

"Sorry, Mum," he muttered.

He ignored his car keys, knowing he was too lit to drive. Instead, he walked quickly, shoulders hunched and hands shoved in his pockets, his expression bleak.

The dark streets were quiet and Nick was utterly alone with his thoughts. On the way, he stopped at an off licence, studying the brightly-lit rows of spirits, wine and beer. Oblivion in a bottle. Cheap at the price.

As he neared home, his footsteps slowed, the emptiness spreading inside to fill every part of him.

The street was silent when he reached his house but in the orange glow of the streetlamp, he could easily read the red paint sprayed across the front door in foot-high letters.

WOMAN BEATER!!

He touched the paint but it had already dried. Whenever this had been done, it was hours ago.

He turned the key in the lock, pushing open the door slowly, then stood staring at the wreckage inside.

Everything had been trashed, pretty much the way he'd trashed Kenny's house. He wandered through his home, staring at the graffiti sprayed across the walls, wading through shards of broken glass. All Molly's stupid throw cushions had been gutted, and he was followed by a cloud of feathers as he moved from room to room.

The worst devastation was in his bedroom. All his clothes had been slashed or had paint poured on them, and the duvet looked as though wild animals had torn it apart.

He slumped on the settee, angling himself to avoid lumps of foam protruding through the ripped material, and opened the first of two bottles of Scotch that he'd bought, tipping the burning alcohol down his throat. He paused, wiping his mouth and remembering the night Anna had drunk Scotch and the clever stuff she'd said about the flavour—guacamole? Whatever. Nick took another swig, enjoying the burn in his throat and his belly as the amber liquid made its way south.

He sat in the unlit room, drinking until the darkness consumed him.

~

The next morning, the shit hit the fan.

Nick's phone buzzed continually as the alerts and notifications started to flood in.

Online news sites had picked up the story, and were enjoying the real-life soap opera:

Rugby Renegade in Police Custody!

Top Player in Vicious Assault

Minotaurs' Fullback Charged

Battered Girlfriend Tells All!!

Nick struggled to sit up, feathers caught like snow in his black hair. His body ached and his tongue felt as if it had been at the bottom of a parrot's cage all night.

His phone was full of dozens of messages and missed calls. He jabbed at it with bleary eyes, sitting up a little straighter as he read the accusations against him.

Shit, this was bad. Really bad. He realised he'd made a serious mistake by letting Molly get the PR upper hand. But now it was too late. There was no way he was coming back from this, not for a man who had the reputation of being a bullying abuser. Not that he had anything to come back to.

His stomach was sour with whiskey and grief, and he wondered how he'd go on. What would life be like now? Where would he go? What would he do?

Someone thumped on his front door and he heard voices yelling. He hadn't bothered to pull the curtains last night, so he could see camera flashes and realised that there were reporters outside.

Then he heard a key in the lock and tensed. Molly?

But it was Trish. She marched into the room and slapped him across the face.

Fuck, that stung!

"What the hell, Trish?"

"That's for walking out last night and making Mum cry. And this," she slapped him across his other cheek, "is for not answering your phone and generally behaving like a knob."

"Bleedin' hell, sis! Is this your idea of sympathy?"

"No," she said grimly. "It's me telling you to get your arse in gear." Then she seemed to become aware of the destruction around him. "Oh my God! Did Molly do this?"

He shrugged and Trish shuddered.

"Thank God you're not marrying into that family. They're all bonkers." She glanced at his chagrined face. "Sorry. But you're better off without her. What did the police say?"

Nick almost laughed.

"I haven't reported it."

Trish's eyes widened.

"For God's sake! Why not?"

"Seriously? You think I want anything more to do with the police?"

"But ... you can't let Molly get away with this!"

Nick shook his head and rubbed his throbbing temples.

His sister looked as though she was about to argue, but then pressed her lips together in a hard line and didn't say anything.

Nick thought about his ex-fiancée. It hadn't all been bad, had it?

A memory of silver-grey eyes and Anna's ready smile flashed into his mind. What would she think of him now?

"Nick, you have to get up!"

Nick ignored his sister, too tired, depressed and hungover to function.

Then Trisha grabbed his hands and attempted to pull him off the settee.

"Oouf! How much do you weigh?" she asked, giving up the unequal struggle and slumping down next to him.

"Twice as much as you, shrimp."

"Bog off, you great heathen. God, you stink of whiskey. Take pity on my sense of smell and go and have a shower."

"What for? I've got nowhere to be."

She raised her eyebrows.

"Check your messages, Einstein. Steve Jewell wants to see you. He phoned our place first thing when he couldn't get through to you. And I've brought your car back. Again."

"Thanks, Trish," he said, touched that she'd bothered with him after their fight the night before.

She stared at him seriously, crossing her arms.

"Just because you've behaved like a dickhead doesn't mean that I don't love you, little brother. And you're not alone."

He gave a weak smile, because whatever she said and however much his family cared, the problems were his and no one else's.

"Thanks, sis."

"Thank me with an amazing present at Christmas."

She hustled him up the stairs and he took a long shower, washing away the sour smell of whiskey and failure, then dried himself with a shredded towel.

The only wearable clothes were in his kitbag, slightly wrinkled sweatpants and t-shirt, but clean.

When he came down again, feeling like a bad photocopy of himself, he found that Trish had called the police about the vandalism.

He was too tired to be angry with her. Besides, the police couldn't say when an officer would become available—it wasn't the kind of crime that was a priority. Trish had even taken photographs of the damage, but Nick wasn't going to hold his breath.

She had a guilty expression and was busy sliding her phone back in her pocket.

He raised an eyebrow.

"Are you looking at the news pages?"

"Don't read them, Nick," she said, her voice pleading. "You know they only print lies."

Nick took her phone and flicked through the pages she'd bookmarked. The trouble was, as far as Nick could see, they'd all told the truth, or a version of it.

"It'll blow over," said Trish quietly, squeezing his arm.

He couldn't bear any more sympathy and he hadn't even told his family yet that he needed another surgery.

"You'd better get going."

"Yeah."

She handed him his car keys and he pulled a dark blue beanie over his damp hair and slipped on a pair of sunglasses, trying to ignore the camera flashes and questions from the two journalists standing outside.

"How long you been knocking her about, Nick?"

"Did you know they were having an affair? Did you do threesomes?"

"Give us a quote, Nick!"

He climbed into his car, carefully reversing down the driveway so he didn't run them over, even though he really, really wanted to.

One of them pressed the lens up against his window and nearly blinded him with another camera flash.

"Wanker!" shouted one of the journalists as Nick drove away.

An hour later, he arrived at the Minotaurs' HQ for what he strongly suspected would be the last time.

"Morning, Sally," he said to the woman on the front desk who'd smiled at him every day for the last three months.

She stared stonily at her computer screen, refusing to meet his eyes.

"Mr. Jewell is waiting for you. In the boardroom."

The boardroom? Yeah, that didn't sound good.

"Thanks," he said shortly.

She acted as if he didn't exist.

Steve Jewell wasn't alone. He was sitting with the assistant coach, the club's manager, Sadie from PR, and Ernie Carter, the club's owner. Nick was relieved to see that on the other side of the table was his agent, Mark Lipman.

"Take a seat, Nick," said Steve, grimacing slightly as Ernie blew cigar smoke and stared impassively.

Nick's heart beat faster but his face remained blank. He wished he was better dressed.

"This is a bad business," said Steve Jewell, shaking his head. "Very bad. But we've thrashed out a deal," and he nodded at Mark to take over.

"You're being released from your contract, Nick."

The blow fell soundlessly, but all Nick could hear was the death knell of his career.

"The club is willing to pay you a third of your annual salary," Mark continued carefully. "You can't talk about this to the Press. That's the deal."

"Released?"

Nick's heart slammed against his ribs. *This was it. It was really happening.*

Steve Jewell leaned forward. "You're not being sacked. It'll look better for you this way."

"We ought to bloody well sack you!" snorted Ernie, teeth fastened around his cigar like a Bond villain. "Men like you make me chuffin' sick and..."

Sadie tapped her pen on the table, effectively halting what would have been an unpleasant tirade.

"We feel it's best for everyone..." *meaning the club* "if you leave quietly." She pushed a piece of paper towards him. Sign here."

Mechanically, Nick took the pen, then stared up at the ring of faces.

"The orthopaedic consultant you sent me to says I need another operation on my Achilles tendon."

Steve Jewell nodded slowly.

"We know, son."

Ernie spat out his cigar.

"We're not chuffin' paying for it. You shouldn't have lammed your lass!"

Nick signed and stood up to leave the room, looking around for one last time.

His moment of playing for a top team had come and gone and left him in the dust. He nodded at the grim faces and walked out.

~

Nick tried to concentrate while his solicitor went through the charges against him.

"I'm not going to sugar-coat this," she said. "It doesn't look good. As I said, I'm recommending you plead guilty, because if you don't, it'll be six months of negative publicity before the case even gets to court. Then they'll paint you as a woman-beater with no remorse. The prosecution are going to whip out a photograph of your fiancée with a black eye, and you'll be finished. You used a weapon—the fact that you had to go and get it out of the tool box in the boot of your car looks bad. Not quite as bad as a premeditated assault, but bad nonetheless. Nick, are you even listening to me?"

Nick heard the exasperation in her voice, but still felt like he was watching a badly-written soap opera, all melodrama and facial tics.

"Hitting Molly was an accident."

"So you said. Given the circumstances, a magistrate will take one look at you, a six foot, fourteen stone rugby player, then take a long hard look at her, all five foot nothing and a hundred pounds after binge-eating a litre of Haagen-Dazs ice cream, and you won't like the answer."

"There's sod-all I can do about that."

Ms. Wilson-Smith nodded.

"We need lots of women—credible women—to come forward and say that you've never lifted a hand to them, not even during a bit of slap and tickle..."

Nick grimaced, feeling like the soap opera had turned into a 1970s sitcom.

"...I'm talking ex-girlfriends, significant women in your life—and I don't mean family. So let's hear it."

She stared at Nick expectantly, a fountain pen with green ink, poised over a yellow legal pad.

"I was with Molly for three years..." *Three wasted years.*

"Nothing on the side?"

"No!"

"Sure?"

"Very."

"Because I need to know where the hits will be coming from."

Nick gritted his teeth.

"I was faithful." *Like a stupid, trusting fool. Unlike Molly.*

"Right, well ... before Molly?"

Nick sighed and then listed all the girlfriends he'd ever had, and the solicitor wrote careful notes.

"That's it? That's all of them?"

"Yeah, I think so."

"No one-night stands?"

Nick ran a hand through his hair, making the curls even wilder.

"A couple. I don't remember their names—it was a long time ago."

Ms. Wilson-Smith tapped her pen.

"It's, er, quite a short list ... sure you haven't left anyone out?"

"Bloody hell! How many times are you going to ask me that? No, that's it!"

"Alright, you've made your point. But let me give you a tip, don't lose your temper like that in court—it'll be exactly what the prosecution will want. They're going to portray you as an aggressive, laddish thug with violent tendencies. Got it?"

"Yes," Nick seethed.

She adjusted her glasses and pursed her lips.

"You're paying me to represent you, Mr. Renshaw. I'm just doing my job."

"Yeah, sorry."

"Okay. So, you and Molly, anything kinky in bed? Handcuffs, punishment, any rough stuff?"

Nick's mouth dropped open.

"What?!"

The solicitor sighed again.

"These are the kind of questions you could be asked. They'll try to show that you have ... tendencies, like I said. So, once more..."

"No, nothing like that."

The solicitor raised her eyebrows as if expecting more, and Nick felt his anger start to build again. When the fuck had his sex life become important in a criminal trial?

"Ah, well, okay. So ... you're saying the whole incident was out of character?"

Nick wasn't sure how to answer that—he barely knew who he was anymore. He didn't have a fiancée, didn't have a career, and now his reputation was in shreds, too. The newspapers were reporting it as a nasty piece of domestic violence, in a *what can you expect from a rugby player* sort of way. It made him sick. Ironically, it made him want to punch someone.

"Yeah, it was out of character."

"Have you ever been arrested before?"

"No."

"Ever been involved in any drinking-related incidents? Any trouble at all?"

"No. I kept my head down, worked hard, trained hard. I didn't want to go back."

The solicitor looked up.

"Back to what?"

Nick shifted in his chair.

"Back to working in a paint factory." *Back to being nothing.*

There was another pause.

"We'll need to bring in some character witnesses—people who can say what a great guy you are, wouldn't hurt a fly ... off the rugby field. Anyone come to mind?"

"Not my best friend ... former best friend."

"No, indeed ... but we might be able to work in some deep-seated jealousy of your promotion to the Premiership that led to his ... the affair."

Nick wondered about that. Could it be true? He'd always thought that he and Ken were mates, solid.

"I'd asked him to be my Best Man."

The solicitor's eyes brightened. "Excellent! That'll show how much you trusted him. Good ... anyone else who'd speak up for you?"

"Um, my old coach at Rotherham, Henry Selby, he might."

"Anyone else?"

Nick scratched his beard. Why was it so hard to think of people who'd stand up for him?

"Steve Jewell might."

"Hmm, he might ... as he hired you in the first place. And then fired you."

"I was released from my contract."

"I'll put him on the list. Next?"

Nick named a couple of former teammates, knowing that he was putting them in the awkward position of having to choose between him and Ken: a teammate and a former teammate.

"We need some women—other than your sister and mother, of course. All this testosterone isn't going to play well when you're accused of hitting your ex."

One name flashed to Nick's mind, but he hesitated. The solicitor caught it at once.

"Yes?"

"Uh, well, I was seeing a sports psychologist to help me with my game. She might speak for me."

"How exactly did she help you?"

The solicitor's gaze was sceptical, and Nick felt irritated on Anna's behalf.

"She works on confidence, visualisation techniques, stuff like that. Dave Parks, one of the Props, was seeing her, as well. The Minotaurs sent us both."

"Excellent, I can use that. Name?"

"Dr. Anna Scott."

"A doctor? Even better. How close were you and this Dr. Scott?"

"I had appointments with her weekly since September..."

Would Anna speak for him or would she walk away? The thought disturbed him more than it should.

"Did you ever socialise with her?"

"No. Uh, once she turned up at the same pub as me. But I was with Molly, and Anna ... Dr. Scott was meeting someone. That's everything."

The solicitor wrote it all down, looking pleased, then placed her pen on the yellow jotter filled with tiny notes.

"I'll be honest, Mr. Renshaw. I'm looking for potential factors that could reduce blame and ultimately help you to achieve a fair, just and positive outcome."

"Such as?"

"A nominal fine, a couple of hundred hours community service. That's the best case scenario."

Nick swallowed.

"And the worst case scenario?"

"Let's focus on the positive."

"Tell me."

The solicitor folded her arms, looking grave.

"Well, court listings are matter of public record, so the media will know everything…"

"I don't care about that."

"You should. It will affect your future career."

That seemed unlikely since there was no chance of a club signing him now, injured and in trouble.

"What's the worst case scenario."

"Upwards of six months in custody, possibly a year."

Nick's mouth dried and he felt a cold sweat break out across his body.

"Shit."

The solicitor gave him a hard stare.

"You used a weapon—that makes it a lot more serious. I have to show that it wasn't premeditated and that you were under extreme stress. If the wrench had been on the passenger seat, that would have been better. But by your own admission, you got it out of the boot of the car. That's why we have to show how out of character it is for you." She paused. "However, the courts look closely at the specific factors of the case and the individuals involved and, on occasions, the conduct of the victim. The fact that your fiancée was caught *in flagrante delicto* with your best friend and Best-Man-to-be is in your favour…"

Nick grimaced.

"… because one factor that is relevant to sentencing is whether the victim provoked the assault—and that can be construed in many different ways."

She gave Nick a chilly smile that was meant to be reassuring.

Nick's heart sank.

CHAPTER TEN

Anna had never been in a court before. She'd been surprised to be called as a character witness for Nick's defence, and wasn't sure how she felt about that.

She hadn't seen Nick since his last appointment, only his photograph in the *Manchester Evening News* as well as several national newspapers. She suspected the trial would put the story on the front page again, locally at least.

She clutched her purse more tightly and stared up at the grand Victorian building of the Magistrates' Court. It reminded her of a redbrick version of New York Public Library, somewhat swaggering and self-satisfied.

Belinda was already at the courthouse, waiting for her.

"Thank goodness they decided to call you," she said cheerfully. "It was awful this morning—the prosecution lawyer interviewed the ex-fiancée and her hideous family. He had to get them off the stand as quickly as possible. What on earth did he ever see in her?"

Anna had asked herself the same question.

"And I'm sure she's lying when she says he deliberately hit her. That man doesn't have a violent bone in his body."

Anna raised her eyebrows and Belinda gave an apologetic smile.

"I mean ... well, um. But honestly, that woman! She's already been caught in one lie. She said that the bonking was a one-off thing, but then Nick's lawyer brought up her phone records and they'd been at it for months. Sexting, too."

Belinda was definitely Team Nick.

"He looks so tired. Still a hunk, of course. Then the defence brought in two of his ex-girlfriends who both said that he'd never laid a hand on them and they couldn't imagine it. You should have seen the other piece when they said that—face like a smacked bottom."

Anna winced. Probably not the best analogy.

Belinda filled Anna in on the rest of the case that she'd been watching avidly from the public gallery, then hurried off to find a seat, "before all the good ones are taken."

Bored, but too on edge to read, Anna sat on an uncomfortable plastic chair in the witnesses' waiting room, wondering what the cross-examination would be like.

She'd been surprised when Nick's solicitor had approached her, but after carefully re-reading her confidentiality contract with the Minotaurs and checking with Steve Jewell, she agreed to do it. She didn't feel comfortable about speaking up for a man who hit women—one woman—but she could be candid about his appointments. After what Belinda said, she felt a lot better about it.

She read over the statement that she'd given to the police, barely able to understand her own words as nerves jumbled her brain.

Finally, an usher came to take her in, and Anna tried to breathe calmly. The Magistrate wore a rumpled suit and had the sour expression of a vegetarian at a hog roast.

As Anna took her place on the stand, trying to keep calm and use visualisation techniques to get her through this, she glanced across at Nick.

He was wearing a charcoal grey suit and dark blue tie, and he sat silent and stoic next to his lawyer.

He looks so lost.

His cheekbones seemed even sharper now and Anna felt a prickle of concern as she took in the dark shadows that ringed his eyes. There was a tightness about his expression and the way he held himself. His downcast eyes met hers briefly and she thought she saw a flicker of emotion before he turned his head away again.

He looked shattered.

When she glanced across at the prosecution bench, she had to look twice before she recognised Molly. The bottle-blonde hair had been dyed a more gentle dark gold, and the clinging micro mini had been replaced with a pale grey shift dress and a green silk scarf. Her nose was swollen and she had two black eyes. The man she assumed was Kenny also looked like he'd been badly beaten.

Anna swallowed and reminded herself that she was being objective and only telling the truth—until she met Molly's hate-filled stare.

Anna was slightly taken aback, but then again she was speaking for the defence.

She studied the Magistrate's face, but despite her expertise in body language, she couldn't guess which way he'd go, and she knew that a clever lawyer could sway him one way or another.

She rubbed her suddenly sweaty hands against her dark suit pants and tried to appear unaffected as she stood, placing one hand on the Bible.

"I swear by Almighty God that the evidence I shall give shall be the truth the whole truth and nothing but the truth."

After she'd been sworn in, Ms. Wilson-Smith introduced her and asked her to list her credentials and qualifications.

Anna spoke clearly and authoritatively, gaining confidence as the lawyer led her through the rehearsed questions.

"No, I've never had reason to worry about being alone with my client. I always found him polite and professional. No, he never exhibited any signs of anger. He was frustrated that his injury was holding him back, but that was all. We didn't talk about his personal life in so far as I knew that he was engaged, and I also knew that he had an older sister and parents living nearby."

Anna was careful to put her answers in context, but she wasn't prepared for the prosecutor's questions during the cross-examination.

"So, Dr. Scott, during this *polite* and *professional* relationship, there was no hint of anything more?"

"Excuse me?"

The lawyer smiled coldly.

"No hint of impropriety, Dr. Scott?"

Anna's mouth fell open, and Ms. Wilson-Smith was on her feet.

"Objection!"

"Sustained."

"Credibility of the witness, Your Honour."

The Magistrate peered down at the oily prosecution lawyer for a long moment.

"Continue, but be careful Mr. O'Keefe."

Anna seethed, hoping that Ms. Wilson-Smith would say something, offer a rebuttal. She stumbled on the next few questions and knew it made her look guilty.

He smiled snidely. "I'm sure he enjoyed talking to you about himself as the sole focus."

Anna stayed silent.

"Miss Scott?"

"It's *Doctor* Scott, and I was waiting for a question."

A murmur of amusement rippled through the public gallery and Anna glanced across to see Belinda giving her a thumbs up.

"Did you like your client, *Doctor* Scott? After all, he's a good looking man and you're a single woman." He paused then stared over his shoulder at Anna. "Did you like Mr. Renshaw?"

"I found him very pleasant," Anna said guardedly.

"So pleasant that you escorted him on a publicity trip to a local school—wholly beyond your contracted employment—and were seen getting into a car with the accused later?"

"I didn't get into his car; we arrived and left separately. Visiting the school was part of his therapy," Anna said icily.

"But not yours," the lawyer said nastily. "Am I right?"

I wanted to see him happy, wasn't much of a defence. She remembered the mild flirtation that they'd enjoyed that day, hating that this poisonous toad was making her think of it with guilt. It was like watching a pristine white snowy street turn to slush.

Anna kept glancing at the defence lawyer, waiting for her to stop this line of questioning. So far, she hadn't.

The prosecuting lawyer leered at her.

"Ha! I put it to you, *Doctor* Scott, that you became infatuated with your client and deliberately engineered *meetings* out of the office, plus orchestrating an *occasion* when he'd be with his fiancée—his girlfriend of *three years*, a public house that *you knew* he visited regularly! Did you have a relationship with the accused?"

"No! It wasn't like that!"

"Objection! Badgering the witness."

Finally! Anna thought shakily.

"Sustained. Final warning Mr. O'Keefe."

But the damage had been done, and by the time the defence lawyer returned for a rebuttal, half the jury were looking at Anna as if she was some sort of scarlet woman who'd been instrumental in breaking up Nick's engagement. It was so unfair! Was this how the *justice* system worked? Silver-tongued lawyers who could twist everything you said.

Anna left the courtroom close to tears. Belinda was waiting for her.

"I can't believe that scumbag said those things!" She paused, her eyes flicking to Anna's distraught face. "You didn't go out with Nick, did you?"

"Oh my God! Even *you* don't believe me!"

"No, no, of course I believe you, luv. I'm being silly. It's just…"

"What?!"

"I know you liked him."

"Yes, I liked him. He's a nice man! You said so yourself! Oh my God, I can't believe this. I haven't done anything wrong! I haven't been unprofessional *ever*."

Although Anna knew in her deepest thoughts that she *had* been attracted to Nick. But she'd never acted on it. Not once.

She put her head in her hands.

"If this gets reported, I'll be ruined."

Belinda put her arms around her and hugged tightly.

"It won't come to that, luv. That lawyer was just trying it on. Everyone could see that. Everyone."

Anna stared at her helplessly. It was all so horrible and brought back bad memories of being with Jonathan.

And what a clusterfuck that had turned out to be.

CHAPTER ELEVEN

THE MAGISTRATE GLOWERED DOWN AT NICK.

"You need to understand," he said ponderously, "that a prison sentence is what I have in mind at the moment for these offences."

Nick's whole body went cold, but he stood without showing any expression, focussing on the magistrate's left shoulder.

"Whilst I accept that your assault of Miss McKinney was accidental, the same cannot be said of Mr. Johnson, who suffered a sustained and violent assault at your hands. I also have to take into account the considerable damage done to his property and Miss McKinney's car. It is clear that Miss McKinney and Mr. Johnson were terrified. I take a very serious view of this."

The court was adjourned for pre-sentence reports and Nick sat heavily in his seat as the magistrate left the room to a low murmur.

"Don't worry about that," said Miranda Wilson-Smith. "He's just trying to put the fear of God into you. You're not going to prison. We've done enough to discredit the testimony of both of them, you'll be fine."

Nick rubbed his aching neck, and glanced over his shoulder to see the wan, anxious faces of his parents and sister. Trish gave a small wave but looked as if she was about to faint. Nick was surprised to see Anna's receptionist sitting behind his family, and she gave him a quick smile. He checked, his eyes darting around the room, but couldn't see Anna anywhere.

He wanted a drink—whiskey, preferably—but Miranda said the magistrate would come to a decision imminently.

"He's just an old peacock—loves being the centre of attention." She leaned closer. "Rumour is, he wears women's silk knickers when he's in court."

Nick choked on a laugh as the magistrate reappeared looking grim.

His heart sank. He wouldn't have been completely surprised if the magistrate had placed a square of black cloth on his head and instructed the ushers to take him out and hang him.

"All rise."

Nick stood up, hopping on his good foot as he gripped the wooden sides of the bench.

The magistrate unbuttoned his jacket, glaring about with beady eyes like a giant bird, and everyone sat down again.

"The accused will stand."

For a second time, Nick shuffled to his feet, and the magistrate frowned.

~

Anna's phone rang just as she'd finished a long and difficult session with a teenage soccer prodigy who had a problem with mouthing off to referees. Anna had been coaching him on techniques for keeping calm—and to avoid being sent off.

But she'd been waiting for this call, and she snatched up her cell phone so quickly, she almost dropped it.

"What's the verdict?"

"They went easy on him, which surprised me after everything that had been said."

"Did he get jail time?"

"Twelve-week suspended sentence, 200 hours unpaid work, £5,250 for the cost of breakages and £350 court costs. But get this, the 'compensation' he was ordered to pay to the victims," Belinda almost spat the word, *"just £150 for each of them. You should have seen their faces!"*

Anna breathed a sigh of relief.

"Did you get a chance to talk to him at all?"

"Only a word. His family was there and a couple of his rugby friends, but he said to thank you."

Anna smiled, feeling as if the cold stone in the pit of her stomach had dissolved.

~

Nick left the courtroom in a daze. Despite his lawyer's optimism, he really thought he'd have been banged up in prison by now. He felt hollow with relief.

His father slapped him on the back, and his mum and sister were smiling and crying and hugging him. But Nick wasn't sure how he was supposed to feel. He had the weight of a criminal conviction attached to his name—nothing would ever be the same again.

Nick loosened his tie and wished again that he had a drink.

Ms. Wilson-Smith looked pleased and stacked away her papers with a flourish.

Nick shook hands with her.

"Thank you for everything."

"Congratulations, Mr. Renshaw. I do hope we don't meet again, professionally, that is."

Nick gave her a weak smile.

"Come on. Let's go home and ... celebrate," said his dad quietly.

Nick didn't feel like celebrating anything, but his family had stood by him and it had been a difficult time for them, too.

As if to underline his shame and disgust, Molly stalked towards him, hissing and spitting like an alley-cat, claws out.

"You bastard! You won't get away with this!"

Trish was in her face immediately.

"You stupid cow! He wasn't trying to get away with anything—that's what a guilty plea means. Now he's paying for *you* fucking around on him with bollock-face!"

Molly ignored Trish, sticking her finger in Nick's chest.

"They should have sent you to prison and thrown away the key."

"Oh my God, you're such a drama queen," Trish replied as Nick turned away, unable to look at the venomous expression on Molly's face, contorted with rage.

"Stay out of this, you ugly bint!" Molly screeched.

Nick spun around, his voice a low growl.

"Don't you dare have a go at Trish! You cheated for months! You took my ring, and you cheated with *him!* You're a cheap liar. You don't have an honest bone in your body, and I'm well shot of you."

Molly tried to slap him, but Kenny marched over, scowling as he grabbed her arm and dragged her away still screaming.

"This isn't over, Nick! You'll be sorry you ever met me!"

"I already am," he said.

The silence hung heavily and the people around them averted their eyes, embarrassed by the ugly scene.

"What an evil little bitch," said Trish, summing up for everyone.

They were subdued as Nick's father drove them home. The weariness of worry had been overwhelming, and now they didn't have to fight it, silence reigned.

As they parked, Nick's mum spoke.

"I'll make a nice cup of tea for us all."

"I think I might want something a wee bit stronger than that, luv," said Nick's dad.

"Too bloody right," Trish muttered wearily.

Nick didn't care. He still had the best part of a bottle of whiskey at his own place and he planned on walking home and drinking that later.

He trudged up the stairs and stripped off his suit. It was new, but he didn't ever want to wear it again.

The sting of failure burned inside his chest, a physical ache that throbbed with every breath he took.

Reluctantly, he made his way downstairs. His mum had bought a Marks & Spencer chocolate gateau; his dad had opened a bottle of Glenmorangie single malt that he saved for special occasions.

Nick threw himself on the settee and downed a whole glass in one gulp, wiping his lips on the sleeve of his sweatshirt and reaching for a slice of cake when his phone lit up with an incoming text message, then another and another.

With a sinking feeling, Nick tried to ignore them, pouring himself another whiskey, so Trish snatched up his phone and flipped through the messages, her forehead wrinkling as she read them.

"Oh, that's horrible," she said softly.

"What is it, luv?" asked Nick's mum, looking worried.

Trish bit her lip.

"Um, nothing. Just a lot of rubbish."

Nick grabbed the phone from Trish's hands and scrolled through the messages. They were all from numbers he didn't recognise, calling him a *lying, wife-beating scum, fucking rapist* and other charming names, along with the hope that he'd get his balls ripped off, or that he'd be fed to pigs. One particularly long-winded text ended up with the wish, *get cancer and die.*

Whiskey churned in his stomach and he knew he couldn't face food. Right now, he couldn't face anything.

"I think I'll get off home now," he said as he stood slowly.

"But..." Nick's mum started to protest.

"Let him go, luv," said Nick's dad. "He's a grown man. Let him go."

His family stood and hugged him one by one.

"You'll phone if you need us?" his mum called after him.

Nick didn't reply.

He walked home, stopping at the same off licence and stocking up with more alcohol.

It was difficult to fathom that he now had a criminal record. A single moment of madness would haunt him for the rest of his life. He'd lost everything he'd worked for. He was weighed down by the guilt and shame.

He still hadn't told his family that his playing career was over.

As he opened the door to his house, there wasn't much left to look at. His dad had hired a dumpster, and together they'd tossed out everything that had been trashed. Trish had insisted on taking photographs of the damage, but the insurers wouldn't touch it without involving the police. Nick had refused to press charges—he'd had enough of Molly and the police to last a lifetime.

Trish had started to paint over the graffiti, but it would take more than a couple of coats to completely cover the red paint, and the ugly words ghosted through, a grim reminder.

He picked up the bag of booze, and headed for the stairs.

The messages continued all night as Nick sat in the dark drinking whiskey and watching his phone light up with another notification or alert. As if to punish himself even more, he read the posts on his Facebook page, Twitter and

Instagram accounts. Molly had tagged him in a post that showed her bloody nose and black eye, along with Nick's mobile number.

It looked like the post had gone viral. Hundreds of people had commented—none of it was good.

As his phone started to die, Nick deleted all his social media accounts one by one, saying goodbye to the memories, the friends who were unfriending him by the bucket-load. Then he tossed his phone aside, and let the whiskey medicate his mind and numb his body.

~

Thin shafts of light pierced the curtains, making Nick groan and throw an arm over his eyes. His skull throbbed as if his brain was trying to batter its way out of his head, and his muscles ached.

Swaying with nausea, he staggered to the bathroom and stared at his bloodshot eyes and rumpled face.

Welcome to the rest of your life.

He heard the front door slam, and the echo pounded through his tortured brain. Trish's voice carried up the stairs but he ignored her. Instead, he stuck his head in the sink and turned on the cold water tap, gasping as icy water sluiced over his head.

His stomach coiled into a tight knot, then exploded as Nick retched into the toilet.

When he'd finished throwing up, he rinsed his mouth, flushed the toilet, and shuffled downstairs.

When he staggered downstairs, Trish was in the kitchen with two take-out coffees from Starbucks on the table.

"I've brought the newspapers. Mum said I shouldn't, but you'll find out anyway. I thought ... I thought you'd want to know. I can get rid of them if you don't?"

She stared at him questioningly, her hands hovering over the pile of newsprint.

His stomach curled and tightened.

"I want to see."

Nodding slowly, she laid them out for him.

GUILTY! RUGBY THUG SENTENCED
[Read the full story on page 7]

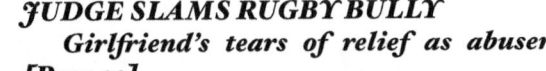
JUDGE SLAMS RUGBY BULLY
Girlfriend's tears of relief as abuser is found guilty
[Page 23]

"It's not as bad as it looks," she said, her eyes glassy with tears. "It's reported quite fairly inside, quoting the magistrate that you didn't mean to hurt Molly. I'm sure people will…"

"Remember the headlines," Nick finished wearily.

There was a painful silence.

"It'll get better."

Nick turned slumped into a chair and rubbed his head.

Trish slid one of the paper coffee cups toward him.

"Do you want some breakfast?" She took one look at his face. "Maybe not."

Trish stayed for a while, not wanting to leave him alone, but with nothing else to say and nothing to do, Nick's silence and sullen indifference, she left shortly after.

Nick spent the day in bed, staring at the ceiling. Depression settled over him like a thick fog. No matter what he did, he just couldn't see a way forward. Everything he'd worked for was gone.

He rolled face down on the bed, burying his head under a pillow.

He knew that he should return his agent's calls. Hell, he should probably take a shower and brush his teeth. But he didn't. Instead, he opened another bottle of whiskey and drank steadily.

For the next week, Nick brooded in his room. He'd long ago stopped charging his phone, let alone answering it, and only left the house once to buy more whiskey.

The single good piece of news was that Steve Jewell had phoned his parents and left the name of a top orthopaedic surgeon who could fit in Nick's operation in the New Year. They'd been shocked, not realising that a further surgery was required. Nick had shrugged it off, and kept everything locked inside, then slowly numbed himself. He intended to spend every day before the operation drunk out of his skull.

If he bothered to have the operation.

The days passed in a blur. Nick knew he needed to do something, something to fix himself, but the effort of moving from his bed seemed too much. He'd stopped shaving after his court appearance, and the thick scruff on his face was turning into a full beard, dark and untamed.

He'd stopped exercising and was beginning to lose muscle tone, but he'd also stopped eating. Right now, all his calories came from whiskey.

He was slowly and methodically falling apart.

Maybe for some people breakdowns came quickly, shatteringly fast. For Nick, it was a slow descent, like walking through swampy ground. Each footstep sucked you down, deeper and deeper, sucking the life out of you, one slow step at a time, until you couldn't move.

Visualize it, plan for it, make it happen.

Anna would be appalled if she knew what he was doing, but he pushed away the creeping guilt … and opened another bottle.

He didn't think he could have sunk any lower, but every day seemed to prove him wrong. Something about hiding away and drinking himself into a coma appealed, but he knew, *he knew* it wasn't an answer.

His dad threatened to pour the whiskey down the sink, but Nick just locked his front door and carried on drinking. His parents didn't know what to say or what to do.

He ignored every attempt from his family to help him. *A guilty conscience needs no accuser.*

December arrived with the first snowfall of the year.

Nick watched the world turn white and sat shivering in the ruins of his house. He hadn't paid the electricity or the gas bill and both had been cut off. His court fines had all been paid, but that left only enough money to pay his mortgage for the next two months. The letters that came through the door all seemed to be printed in red. So Nick ignored them.

The house had been his refuge but it had become his prison.

One day, he thought he was dreaming because he heard someone singing outside his window. His whiskey-soaked brain slowly comprehended that it was people going door to door, singing Christmas carols for charity. Christmas? He hadn't known. Didn't realise. Didn't care.

He reached for another bottle of whiskey, but Nick hadn't eaten for three days and as he staggered to the bathroom, a thin stream of stomach acid spilled from his mouth.

He wiped his face, then stumbled back to the rank-smelling bedroom and picked up the first bottle he could find. His hands shook and it was hard to focus. But that was okay because whiskey would make everything easier.

The harsh bite wiped away the taste of vomit and his thoughts became hazy. As he slumped against the headboard, he started singing to himself, an anthem that he'd heard in many rugby grounds, sung loudly, sung badly, sung loyally, but never had the words seemed more poignant, now when he couldn't seem to find the strength to go on.

Swing low, sweet chariot,
Coming for to carry me home....

As Nick drifted into an alcohol-induced sleep, he felt a certain satisfaction in hitting rock bottom, a quiver of relief that it was nearly all over. No more raging against the dying of the night. Just a cool, quiet room inside your head where a voice whispered,

"It's alright, lad. You did your best. Not your fault you weren't good enough. No harm in failing. It's what people expect anyway. You've lost everything. Best get on with it now. Erase yourself from the world, nice and tidy. No one will miss you. No harm done."

I believe in you, Nick.

Who said that? Who? Was it real or did he imagine it? Real or not...

His last thought before he passed out was that living was harder than dying.

~

Nick woke up coughing, unable to breathe, unable to drag air into his heaving lungs. He was choking on his own vomit, drowning as his airways clogged with regurgitated whiskey.

Voices, somewhere, shouting. Voices had woken him.

He was choking to death.

Below, more shouts and loud banging, and his front door exploded inward, footsteps pounding up the stairs.

Screaming his name, Trish crashed through his bedroom door, falling on her hands and knees before she scrambled onto the bed, rolling him onto his side.

His dad gripped his shoulders, holding firmly as Trish fought to clear his airway.

Finally, he coughed up the vomit he'd inhaled and sat with tears dripping down his flushed face, shivers running through his body as the surge of adrenaline ebbed.

Trish ran to the bathroom to bring him a glass of water and sat on the bed next to him, her eyes wide, her skin ghostly and grey. His dad looked as if he'd aged a hundred years. Nick sagged against the headboard, a crushing pain in his chest and the realisation that he was still here, still alive. He hadn't even managed to get the ending right.

He sipped some water held in Trish's trembling hands.

Or maybe it was Nick's hands that were trembling. He wasn't sure. He wasn't sure of anything.

Only that someone was holding him. Someone who cared.

"Oh God, Nick! What have you done? What have you done!"

Trish slid off the bed, swiping furiously at the tears running down her cheeks.

She pushed open the window and breathed deeply, letting a frigid blast of cleansing air whip through the room.

"Are you happy now?" she cried. "You're such a selfish arsehole! Don't you think you've worried us enough without *this*? Mum's been a mess all this time and Dad hasn't been much better. Don't you care about us at all?"

Nick was silent. His vomit covered clothes clung to him and he suspected it was in his hair, too. The weight of Trish's disgust and disappointment was drenched with fear.

He'd been so lost in his own misery for the past weeks, he hadn't thought about how it had affected his family. He'd honestly thought they'd be better off without him.

His plan to slip away quietly without a fuss had ended up in a pool of vomit with an elephant-sized headache, a sour stomach, aching ribs, bad breath and the shakes. All that was missing was a quick trip to the psych ward.

Trish's voice lowered to a sob.

"What if we hadn't made it here in time, Nick? You could have died! I can't believe you'd do this. If you don't care about yourself, at least think about us, your *family!*"

"I'm so—"

"What about all the people who spoke for you at your trial? Is this any way to thank them?"

Anna's face flashed into Nick's mind.

"Trish, I..."

She held up her hand.

"Don't even talk to me. I'm so angry with you right now. Get your act together, Nick." She bit her lip and turned away. "We can't lose you. We can't!"

She slammed out of the room and he cringed.

His dad sat on the edge of the bed, his shoulders slumped and tears brimming in his eyes, those eyes that were the mirror image of Nick's.

"I want to help you, son. But I don't know how. Your mum and I ... we love you very much."

He stood slowly, as if the effort was almost too much for him. He opened his mouth to speak again, then shook his head and left the room.

Nick rested his head on the greasy pillow.

Every angry word that Trish had spat at him rattled through his brain, her outrage and disappointment lashing him. His father's quiet desolation hit him harder. Hell, he was disappointed enough in himself—he didn't need his family piling on the guilt, too.

Then prove them wrong, a voice whispered to him. And in his mind, that voice had an American accent.

Anna.

He hadn't even thanked her for speaking up for him.

CHAPTER TWELVE

New Year's Eve, 2014

Nick had quit cold turkey. What a fucking stupid idea.

Trish had warned him. She'd Googled the dangers of stopping suddenly after binge drinking for over a month. She'd been right about all the withdrawal symptoms.

The tremors and anxiety had started almost immediately, followed by a blinding headache, prolonged nausea and vomiting

Now, his heart was racing, he was sweating constantly even though the room was cool, he was irritable and confused. He paced his room the whole night, suffering acute insomnia, and when he did manage to fall asleep in the hours before dawn, nightmares plagued him.

Over the next three days, the symptoms worsened. Trish wanted to call a doctor, but Nick didn't want to be medicated—he wanted ... he didn't know what he wanted. He just wanted it all to end.

His skin itched or felt like it was burning, and he scratched mercilessly until bloody weals appeared on his arms and legs. He started seeing things, hallucinating for hours at a time. His mum cried and his dad was at his wits' end. Trish sat with him, talking to him, reading to him, sometimes just holding his hand.

And finally, nine days after his last drink, the fever broke.

Nick cried with relief.

~

February 2015

"Breathe deeply and count back from ten ... nine ... eight..."

As the cool anaesthetic took him, Nick couldn't help thinking, *What's the point of any of this?*

The darkness closed in, the walls shrinking around him, and his body fell limp.

The surgeon peered at the anaesthetist.

"Douglas?"

"BP is 120 over 80; pulse ox is 99; looks good. Yep, you can tee-off now, Gerald."

The surgeon followed the black pen mark down Nick's right calf, the scalpel slicing through the tough outer epidermis, leaving a red, bloody trail behind.

"Vertical and medial incision ... good God! Look at this mess," said the surgeon, poking with his scalpel. "The ruptured tendon looks like the head of a mop. There's rotten tissue in here—I'll have to cut it out. There's only a tiny string of good tendon to work with. I don't know what butcher performed the last operation ... very shoddy. What did you say this fellow does again? Footballer?"

"Rugby," replied Douglas. "Or he was. Had a bit of a hiatus."

"Hummph," said Gerald, cutting into the frayed tendon. "Poor sod should have come to me in the first place."

"He got here in the end," said Douglas, watching the monitor closely, his round spectacles sparkling in the light from above the operating table.

"Retractor!"

A surgical nurse slapped the Gullis hook retractor into Gerald's waiting palm, watching as he tugged Nick's skin and tissue out of the way then squinted at the wound and sighed.

An hour later, Nick was wheeled into recovery, his bandaged foot adjusted to hang above his prone body. As he started to come around, he couldn't feel his feet and some bastard had stuffed his head with cotton wool.

He heard the sounds of people moving around him.

"Is he famous?"

"Don't think so. I don't know. I don't watch rugby."

A woman laughed.

"I might if they all looked like him."

More laughter.

"He's waking up. Nick! Nick, can you hear me? That's it, you're doing really well. Just breathe normally. That's it, that's it. Can you open your eyes for me, Nick?"

Nick breathed deeply, listening to the nurse's calm voice. He peeled open one eyelid, trying to remember ... he had an important question to ask ... what was it...?

"That's it, Nick. Both eyes. The surgery went well."

Oh yeah. That was it, the important question.

"Okaay?" he slurred.

"Yes, you're going to be fine."

His eyes closed again and he drifted, a tiny ship in the middle of the ocean, rudderless, powerless, in danger of sinking. Drifting ... drifting...

~

The next time he woke up, Nick knew exactly where he was: flat on his back in a hospital bed with a raging thirst, a fiery pain in his right leg, and a cloud of depression settling over him like a cold mist.

"Hello, luv. How are you?"

His mum's voice was close by, and he opened his eyes to see her leaning over him, her anxious gaze belying the smile on her face.

"Alright," he said hoarsely. "Thirsty."

She helped him take a sip of water.

"Dad and Trish send their love. They'll visit this evening. Everything's going to be fine."

Nick loved his mum. But she was a terrible liar.

~

Nick was back at his parents' house again, back in his old bedroom.

He stared moodily at the pale blue walls of his childhood, still covered with posters of sporting greats Sugar Ray Leonard, Chris Eubank, and Nigel Benn— all boxers—and the obligatory Pirelli calendar from seven years earlier. He couldn't even smile at the 'improvements' Trish had doodled on every busty model.

He knew the routine and was trying not to feel daunted by the recovery regime. Trish had also told him point blank that every drop of alcohol in the house had been removed, even his mum's Amontillado dry sherry.

Trish was also strictly monitoring his use of painkillers. The last hour before he got his next fix was excruciating and worse than after his previous operation. Trish was worried that he'd become addicted to painkillers. Nick was worried that the pain would drive him crazy—crazier.

"You'd better be a model patient," she said, leaning over him threateningly. "It's been a shit Christmas and New Year."

Nick sighed as Trish eventually sat down next to him.

"And stop being all mardy, it's giving me a headache."

Nick cracked an eye and scowled at his sister.

"Is this what they call tough love?"

"Who says I love you? Yeah, fine, call it whatever you like. You're going to get better."

Nick looked away.

"You don't know that."

"You've got to think positive!" she snapped, her patience waning. "And the surgeon said the operation was a success."

"So did the last one," Nick pointed out.

Trisha was silenced. She smoothed the duvet and avoided his eyes.

"Nick, have you thought about what you might do if you're right and you can't play rugby?" She hesitated as he closed his eyes. "I'm not trying to be mean, but after ... well, you know. Do I have to worry about that ... again?"

He opened his eyes to meet her worried gaze.

"I won't try to drink myself to an early grave again."

"Promise."

"Yeah."

"Promise you won't ... try anything else either?"

Nick sighed.

"I can't promise I'm going to be all sunshine and rainbows. But ... I won't try to off myself. Okay?"

Trish didn't look completely reassured but nodded.

"Well, seeing as you've decided to join the land of the living again," and she gave him a weak smile, "I've got you a new phone with a new number. The only people who've got it are us and Mark Lipman."

Nick glanced up.

"Has he called?"

"Yes, he wanted to know how the operation went. I told him what your surgeon told us. He was pleased. He said he'd be sending out your CV to a few clubs."

Nick grunted.

"Good luck with that. No one will touch me—post-surgery, criminal record."

Trish slapped him lightly across the head.

"You're supposed to be thinking positive."

Nick shook his head, irritated.

"I'm supposed to be realistic."

Trish grimaced.

"What?" Nick asked, anger and frustration leaking into his voice.

"I went to your house to pick up any letters."

"And?"

"I opened them."

Nick frowned.

"You're overdrawn at the bank, you know that, right?"

Nick shrugged, finding it hard to care.

"All the money you got from the Minotaurs went on paying the fine and your

95

operation. There's nothing left. You won't be able to pay next month's mortgage."

A cold trickle of fear made him sit up straighter and lancing pain shot through his leg.

"I didn't realise it was that bad. I could sell my car, but that would only help for a few months then I'd be back to square one."

"Mum and Dad said that they'd..."

"No!" Nick's voice was sharp. "I'm not having them using their savings. This is *my* problem."

Trish's eyes were bright with unshed tears.

"I told them you'd say that. I'd help you if I could..."

"I know that, sis."

He reached out and held her hand, and she gave him a watery smile, squeezing his fingers.

"So," she said after a long pause, "I talked to an estate agent. He said that it's not a good time to sell..."

"Fuck."

"But he thinks you'd do better renting out the place. It would cover your mortgage—just. There wouldn't be anything left over. What do you think?"

"I think I don't have any choice," Nick said tiredly.

Trish's smile was brief.

"Okay, well, I'll help you get that sorted. You'd better get some rest. And, um, maybe make an appointment to go to the Job Centre and..."

Nick's heart missed a beat.

"Go on benefits? No."

Trish grimaced.

"Don't rule it out."

Nick closed his eyes. If he had to apply for welfare now ... he felt Trish's hand on his arm and looked up to see the sympathy and love on her face, the pain that matched his.

She didn't need to tell him that his family cared about him, he could see it in everything they did.

Trish cleared her throat.

"I've brought my laptop up in case you want to watch Netflix or anything later."

She turned to leave the room, but he stopped her.

"Thanks, Trish. I mean it. Thank you."

"You're my brother," she said simply.

～

Life carried on for everyone but Nick.

No one came to see him. During two months of drinking, he'd pushed away all his old teammates, the whiskey and paranoia making him feel as though he couldn't trust them. He suspected some of them of having known about Ken and Molly. He had no proof of that, so maybe in truth he was just too ashamed to see them.

A few of the lads had been in touch, the ones he was closest to, but now they were getting on with their lives, training hard, and he wasn't part of the team anymore.

When Nick stopped answering messages, the calls became fewer and fewer.

So, when his parents were out at work and his sister was doing data entry in the kitchen, the radio playing softly in the background, Nick was utterly alone.

He'd deleted his social media accounts and had to change his email address. The media interest in him had died down, thank God, and there'd only been one short article about his operation.

The parole board had given him a month before he had to start his community service. He'd told them that he'd still be wearing a surgical boot, but they'd promised to find him "something suitable", whatever that might be.

The thought rolled over and over in his head: *what if this is it? What if my rugby days are over?* Trish had asked him what he'd do and the choices were bleak. He could probably go back to the paint factory, a thought that he could hardly bear. He couldn't imagine trying to go to evening classes—he'd hated school the first time around. He honestly didn't know what he'd do.

Mark Lipman had been working hard, keeping his ear to the ground, finding out if anyone was looking for a new Fullback next season. But no club would touch Nick—no one was willing to take a risk. Either on his fitness ... or anything else. He'd pleaded guilty to assault: club managers looked at their insurance policies, then looked away; publicity departments stamped any potential interest with a big fat NO.

"I'm sorry, son. I'll keep looking. It'll be a different story once you're fit again, but..."

"What is it?"

"I won't be able to get you anything nearby. If you're prepared to travel ... there are clubs in the south that might take you, or what about France? Italy, perhaps?"

Nick sighed.

"I'll take anything," he admitted with humiliating honesty.

Alone with his thoughts, Nick stared at Trish's laptop. And he remembered something she'd said before, about him thanking the people who'd helped him.

She was right: there had been a few people who'd stood up for him. Maybe he wasn't as alone as he thought.

He balanced the laptop across his thighs, thinking about what he wanted to say. He stared at the blank screen for a long time, and then he started to type.

CHAPTER THIRTEEN

1ST MARCH 2015

Dear Anna,

Can I still call you Anna? If not...

Dear Dr. Scott,

I'm sorry it's taken me so long to get in touch. Everything has been ... well, you know. But I wanted to thank you for speaking up for me in court. It meant a lot to me and I was really sorry that the other lawyer was such a douchenozzle to you.

Anna smiled as she read Nick's email. He'd remembered that she'd used that term to describe Jonathan.

She'd been surprised to hear from him three months after the case. She'd wondered about him, read in the newspapers that he'd been in hospital again, but after that—nothing. She was glad he'd had the operation; she could only hope that it had been successful.

She continued to read, curious as to what he might have to say.

He was bang out of order and I wanted to punch him, but that probably wouldn't have been a good idea as the magistrate looked like he wanted my guts for garters. (Is that a saying Americans use?) Er, he looked like he wanted to take me outside and have me flogged. Luckily, that's not allowed these days.

You've probably heard the verdict by now, but I hope you know that I'm not really like that. I don't have any excuse and part of me isn't sorry for trashing Ken's house. But the stuff they said about me in the papers isn't true. Molly knows the truth of what happened that day, and she knows it was an accident. But it doesn't change the fact that I did hurt her, and I'll have to live with that.

I had to pay to replace Kenny's windows and TV, but otherwise it's not too bad. I don't mind the community service. They'll probably have me painting park benches for the first couple of sessions, but I'm going to ask if I can work with schools. I don't know if they'll let me, but something sport-related would be good. (Remember that kid who wanted to start a girl's rugby team? She was a mad sort—funny, as well.) But I don't care if they make me sweep the streets. I'm not going to prison so anything else is fine by me.

It was a real surprise to see your receptionist in court. (Sorry, I can't remember her name—Linda?) Please say hi to her and thank her for coming. It was good to have a friendly face there.

Thank you, Anna, for everything that you said, and for all the stuff before. It really helped me, and if I ever get out of this effing plaster cast/surgical boot and get a job in rugby, I know it will come in handy.

Even if I don't make it back on the rugby field, I'm going to use what's happened to try and make myself a better man. Or at least a work in progress.

Thank you for speaking up for me—it means more than I could ever say and more than you'll ever know.

Best,

Nick

She read the email three times, then started to type.

2nd March 2015

Dear Nick,

May I call you Nick, or should I call you Mr. Renshaw, or maybe even Prisoner 7435? Well, thankfully not that last one.

I was happy to receive your email. It seems your sense of humor is intact, if not your foot. Steve Jewell spoke very highly of your surgeon, so I'm crossing my fingers and toes that the operation went well. Are you jealous that I can cross my toes? Scratch that—gloating is never nice.

I know we've talked about this, but Achilles tendon injuries are *not* career-ending. I'll repeat that because you never seemed to hear me when I said it before: Achilles tendon injuries are *not* career-ending. You have every chance of coming back and picking up your career where you left off. Visualize it, believe it, make it happen.

You've been through a really tough time, but it will get better. I was happy I could help a little in the court case, but I only said what I knew to be true.

I have a mantra that I used at a low point in my life. I think you might like it.

When your world crashes down...
When they say you're all out...
When your mind is broken...
I will rise...
I will return...
And I will be undefeated.

Catchy, huh? Although since you're returning from injury, you might want to substitute 'body' for 'mind'. Anyway, I hope it helps you.
Think positive, Nick.
Kind regards,
Anna

Nick smiled as he read the first part of her email, but his smile faded when he came to the mantra. He read the words, feeling the pain that Anna must have felt to have written them, reading the determination to survive, the refusal to be destroyed.

He wondered what had happened to her. Was it something to do with the douchenozzle?

He looked up at the mirror in his bedroom, studying himself.

He looked like shit. He'd lost weight and a lot of muscle tone. His hair was getting long and curling wildly, and his beard was thick and bushy.

He wanted a drink. Badly.

It was a struggle each day and sometimes the need to disappear into a bottle of whiskey was overwhelming. But he was trying.

He stared into his own eyes, repeating the words she'd given him.

"I will be undefeated."

He wanted to believe it. He needed to.

29th March 2015

Dear Anna,

I'm using your mantra. I really like it, although my sister thinks I'm a nutter. She's afraid I'm about to run off and join a cult. Not that I can run anywhere right now. But you said I have to think positive so I'm trying to do that.

I'm trying, but I can't help thinking that I won't play professionally again. I've seen injury end more careers than guys retiring and hanging up their boots. I know no one goes on forever, but I'm 27 and I thought I had another five or six years, so it's hard.

If I don't have rugby, I don't know what I'll do. I'm not all that brainy and I didn't do well at school.

Sorry, didn't mean to dump all that on you. I got used to talking to you when I was with the Minotaurs. I'm just feeling sorry for myself.

It turns out I'm going to prison after all. Yeah, that's not a joke, but not as bad as it sounds. They wouldn't let me work with schools for my community service, but they did say I could coach a bunch of kids in a Young Offender Institution. I'm a bit nervous about it. Hopefully I'll have a couple of prison officers with me, or maybe ten. Do you think they'd beat up a guy wearing a surgical boot?

I did a couple of weeks in a charity shop first, working with some really sweet older ladies. It was okay, sorting out charity clothes and that, but in the YOI, I'll be able to do something that's more me, if you know what I mean.

I'm actually looking forward to it. Trish, my sister, says it'll be a laugh. But then again she laughs at all the gory bits in 'Game of Thrones', especially when someone gets a sword through them. I'm glad that magistrate didn't meet her—it would have been like a rematch of 'Alien Vs Predator'.

How's work going? Okay, I hope. I heard that Steve Jewell got the boot (that sounded funnier in my head). It's a bummer for him. He was a good guy. I reckon he'll get a new club soon. We need blokes like him in the game.

I saw Dave Parks on TV scoring a try last Saturday. I heard he was seeing a really great sports psychologist. Who knew that hocus pocus really worked? (kidding!)

Anyway, hope you're well. Say hi to Belinda for me (I looked up her name on your website).

Cheers!

Nick

3rd April 2015

Hi Nick,

How are you? Did you get rid of the boot yet? Maybe it's a little too early, but soon, I think.

You can tell me whatever you like. Just because you're not my official client now, I'm still a doctor and still a sports psychologist, so if talking to me, or typing it out helps, then please do.

It's hard for a sportsman not knowing what's next, when all you've known finishes, or when injury makes you think life isn't worth living, never mind all the bullshit you've had to deal with, the court case, negative publicity and accusations.

But let's look at this objectively.

I really take issue with you saying just because you don't have qualifications you're not smart. You're very wrong. You think deeply on many subjects and have some really great ideas. Smart is not about qualifications, it's about the ability to learn from mistakes.

So let's look at this. If you can't play professional rugby again, you could coach, right? I think the thought of leaving it all behind completely would be really hard for you anyway. But it would also give you time to work out what you want to do.

Or you could easily get the certification you need to be a personal trainer. I think you'd get a lot of satisfaction from helping people to attain fitness goals. Just something to think about.

Anyway, how did it go with the young offenders? Did you survive? (If I don't get a reply to this email, I'll assume that you got shanked during a tackle. Is that funny? Ugh, not really. Sorry, I'm so tired. Busy work stuff.)

You might like to know that I heard from the headteacher of the high school we visited. She's managed to find another school who want to start a girls' rugby team so they're going to be working together to make that happen. She asked me if I'd pass on the good news and to thank you for your support and encouragement. She says the kids still talk about you—especially Eloise!

Dave did great and I'm really proud of him. YES! The 'hocus pocus' does work!! And if you say anything else, I'll put a spell on you—and not in a good way.

Gotta run. Stay positive!

Anna

4th April 2015

Hi Anna,

No, I haven't got rid of the boot yet, but it won't be much longer—maybe another three weeks. Each week my physio changes the angle to stretch the tendon. It's murder, but he says it's improving so I have to trust him. I want to believe the op worked this time, but it's not always easy.

Thank you for what you said. I really appreciate it. And I'll think about it. Promise!

That's really great news about the girls' rugby team! It feels good to think I had something to do with that, although it was your idea to visit in the first place. I wish I could go over there and say hi, but I'm still keeping my head down.

Yes, I went to my first coaching session with the youth offenders. They were a tough bunch but I think they enjoyed it. Mouthy, you know? Maybe you don't—you were probably a good girl!

The newspapers are leaving me alone now and Molly's already told everyone her 'story'. I'm going to try and put it all behind me.

My agent is also telling me to keep positive, so between you and him and Trish kicking my arse, I think it's starting to work. Maybe.

Why are you so busy at work? Lots of new clients? Just remember, all work and no play makes Anna a dull girl. (I don't think you're dull, by the way.)

Nick

17th April 2015

Hi Nick,

Sorry for the delay in replying. I haven't been in the office that much lately. I know that's not a very good excuse when our cell phones make us all 24/7, but

I've been super busy. And yes, lots of new clients which is great, but the main reason is that I'm opening another clinic in London!

It was a bit slow going when I started in Manchester nine months ago, but then it really took off. I've hired a keen young guy to run things with Belinda up here, and I'll be in London setting up the new office. I'd love to take Belinda with me, but she's settled 'up north' and couldn't take the journey. Really? You Brits don't travel much. It's only two hours by train—you'd think I was asking her to fly to the moon. But yeah, I get it. She has family here and doesn't want to spend all her time commuting. A friend told me that the difference between Brits and Americans is that the British think a hundred miles is a long way, and Americans think that a hundred years is a long time. Anyway, she's going to help me set up the new office and hire a Belinda #2. I'm happy to let her handle that. Fingers crossed she finds me someone as great as she is.

Keep going with the physio—it sounds like he knows what he's doing. You can't rush these things.

Anyway, hope you're well, and that your family are well, too.

Anna

17th April 2015

Congratulations! That's fantastic news. I'm a bit jealous that the players down south (and it is a long way south of the Watford Gap) appreciate you. They're lucky to have you. Do you know which teams you'll be working with yet, or doesn't it work like that? Or do you help whoever needs you (like the Gryffindor Sword)?

I'm really glad to hear from you. I thought I must have said something to annoy you. That's what I hate about text and emails—you never know if you've been a dickhead. Not you, obviously. I meant me.

I'm surviving 'prison'. That's what the kids call it even though officially it's a 'Youth Offender Institution'. It's turning out to be pretty interesting. They're so crazed with boredom that anything new is appreciated. I think they just liked having someone from 'outside' to talk to. I'd go mad locked up in a place like that. I feel sick when I think I could have been one of them. Well, the adult version, which is probably way worse. It's been life-changing, Anna. I was so down that I ended up drinking too much and passing out, more than once. Trish made me clear up the vomit the next day—not my finest hour. But I've decided that I'm not going to let this break me. (I'm still using your mantra—it helps ... even though Trish laughs her arse off when she hears me.)

But you know what they say: what doesn't kill you makes you stronger. I am feeling stronger now.

I decided to get a tattoo—something that symbolizes change or a new start or something like that. It's hard to explain. I've been thinking about it for a while, but now seems the right time. Who'd have thought I'd want to be around more needles! Does it sound weird that the pride in my new ink is helping me get through the injury and everything? It's part tribal Samoan and part Maori. I explained what I wanted to the tattoo artist and he got it right away. It's a lot of work though, a lot of hours being inked. Probably not the cleverest way to spend money right now when I'm out of work, but I wanted to do something for me —something I could be proud of. It takes my mind off all the bad stuff I stress about.

I've probably learned this a bit late, but giving up only accomplishes one thing: failure.

Anyway, you're leaving us! The North won't be the same without you. Any chance I can buy you a goodbye drink before you go (I know you drink whiskey with water, but I'll wear dark glasses when I have to ask the bartender for that ... assuming you say yes, of course)? Maybe that pub we met before? Any time that suits you. I have a lot of free time!
Nick

Anna read and re-read Nick's latest email. He was funny in print, not as shy as he'd been in their sessions. It would be nice to have a farewell drink with him. He wasn't her client anymore, so she didn't see any reason why not.

Although he was an ex-client ... did that matter?

She decided not to worry about it. Through their emails they'd become friends, sort of. There was nothing wrong having a drink with a friend.

18th April 2015

Sounds good. I'm not 'up north' again until the week after next, so how about Monday 27th? 8PM okay?
Anna
PS I never thought I'd fit in at Gryffindor, I'm more of a Ravenclaw. I'll leave you to figure that out.

18th April 2015

Brilliant! See you there!
Nick x
PS "Ravenclaw values intelligence, knowledge and wit." I looked it up ;)

Anna smiled as Nick's reply dropped into her inbox four minutes after she'd sent hers. She pictured him googling the Hogwarts' houses and typing on his phone. In any case, he was wrong about her reasons for choosing Ravenclaw, but it was sweet of him to look it up. The truth was, she identified with Luna 'Looney' Lovegood—she'd always felt like the outsider.

Her pulse gave a little hop when she saw that he'd put a kiss at the end of his email, but she squashed that thought immediately.

He was just being friendly.

CHAPTER FOURTEEN

NICK WATCHED ANNA AS SHE MADE HER WAY THROUGH THE PUB, TAKING A few seconds to appreciate her tall, slim figure before she saw him.

He'd never seen her in jeans before or anything other than her classy trouser suits. Even on the day they'd visited the school together, she'd been in her work clothes.

She looked good, younger maybe, and her hair was longer. He wondered again how old she was. Not that it mattered. Some days he felt ancient.

When she looked in his direction, he raised his hand and waved her over.

She smiled, but he saw the nervous twitch of her shoulders and the self-conscious way she tucked her hair behind her ear, let it fall free, then tucked it back again.

He stood up, balancing on his good foot. *Just one more week in this damn boot.*

"Hey, Anna."

"Nick."

He wondered if she was going to shake his hand, but he resolved the problem by leaning in and giving her a fleeting kiss on the cheek.

He caught the scent of her perfume and had to hold back an urge to kiss her again more fully.

"It's good to see you. What can I get you to drink?"

She glanced pointedly at the clumsy boot.

"I think I'd better do the drink getting."

Nick grinned at her.

"Nope, I have my methods. Prepare to be amazed. Scotch on the rocks?"

Anna raised an eyebrow.

"You remembered?"

"Yep."

Her cheeks warmed and she smiled at him.

"I'm impressed, but as I drove tonight, just a soda, please."

"Soda? Oh, okay. Anything in particular? Coke? Lemonade? Have you tried the ginger beer?"

"Is that alcoholic?"

"No, just ... gingery."

"Sounds like something I should try," she smiled.

Nick swung toward the bar using just one crutch, ordered the drink, then carefully limped back to the table, the bottle of Fentimans in his pocket, holding the glass in his other hand, frowning as he navigated the barstools, tables and chairs.

"Impressive! Mad skills you've got there."

She laughed, and once again Nick caught a glimpse of that tongue stud. It was sexy as hell.

"Could come in useful if I end up being a bartender," he joked, but the reality of his situation made it all too likely, and his smile slipped a little.

"I don't know, can you do Tom Cruise bottle juggling? Because otherwise, you're out of luck, my friend."

"Damn! I thought I'd found a new career!"

He was joking but Anna didn't join in, thoughtfully sipping her drink.

"This is just temporary, Nick. Every professional athlete ... and I do mean *every* athlete ... they've all been through what you're going through now. It's because you use your bodies so aggressively. They're imperfect, they're not machines and they break down, but where you have the advantage over ordinary people like me is that you're disciplined and you know how to train. You *will* get better." She gave him a rueful smile. "Sorry, didn't mean to go into work mode."

"Nah, it's fine. I was being a mardy sod and didn't even know it. I need my arse kicking from time to time."

She smiled more broadly.

"Then I'm happy I could help."

There was a short pause while they both thought of what to say next.

"How's the London clinic going?"

Her eyes brightened.

"It's going great! I have quite a few clients lined up already, and not just rugby players, although you guys are my specialty. I've got a couple of soccer players and I took a call from the British American Football League last week."

"Soccer!" Nick grumbled. "Bunch of wimps. They call on a trainer when their hair gets ruffled. The medics probably keep a can of hairspray in their first aid kit."

"Oh, harsh!"

Nick shrugged, a smile twitching at the corner of his mouth.

"Same as your American footballers with all that padding, helmets and body armour."

"Hmm, I'd love to see you go up against Peyton Manning saying that."

"Who's he?"

"Oh my God, seriously? Only the greatest quarterback of 2014! Also, 6' 5" and weighs 230 pounds. Still want to call him a wimp?"

"Sure, as long as I'm not in the same room with him at the time."

Anna laughed. "Who's the wimp now?"

They exchanged cheesy grins.

Nick's smile faded and his expression became intense and serious.

"Look, I just wanted to thank you again for what you said in court, and I'm really sorry that cockwomble tried to make you look bad."

Anna's expression was comical.

"That's okay ... wait, what? What is a *cockwomble*? I mean, I think I can guess, given the context, but really, what is that?"

Nick felt himself blushing.

"Er, well, someone who's a bit of a prick."

"Yeaaah, I got that part. But what's a womble?"

"You don't have wombles in America?"

"I don't think so. I have no idea."

"Well," Nick scratched his beard aware that he was stalling as he tried to dig himself out of a hole. "A womble is a small creature that picks up litter ... a made-up character on kids' TV."

Anna blinked. "They pick up litter?"

"Yeah, it's their thing. Kind of like Greenpeace, but with fur."

"They're furry?"

"And they have pointed noses."

"That makes everything clear."

"Great!"

Anna fixed him with a smile that said, *Gotcha!*

"So a cockwomble is ... what exactly?"

Nick grimaced. "You're enjoying this, aren't you?"

"You bet! An exchange of cultural views—fascinating."

"You're winding me up."

Anna laughed.

"Just a little. It was fun to see you try to define 'cockwomble'. I'll definitely have to add that to my dictionary of British English. I think it might be my new favourite, even better than 'wanker', or 'codswallop' which I've since learned means 'baloney'."

She winked at him and sipped at her ginger beer, sucking on one of the ice cubes.

A spark of excitement shocked Nick as her cheeks hollowed and her eyes half closed.

Not good! his brain said.

You definitely want some of that, his body argued.

His body was more honest. Stupid fucker.

"So, will you be moving down to London permanently?"

Anna pulled a face.

"Yes, I am. I'll come up here every now and again to make sure that my new associate is settled in, but I'll miss my cottage."

"You have a cottage? I thought Americans preferred apartments."

She rolled her eyes.

"Stereotype much? I rent an eighteenth century cottage in Hale. It's so pretty, roses around the door and everything. I think it's what most Americans dream about when they think of England. What about you?"

Nick could have kicked himself with his bad leg. He should have seen that this was the obvious follow up question. He decided to be honest rather than try to pretend. Pretending everything was okay in his relationship with Molly had got him exactly less than nowhere. He'd been papering over cracks that had turned into the Grand Canyon.

"I'm back with my parents at the moment."

"Oh, because of your leg?"

It would have been so easy to agree and she'd never have known the difference, but over their sessions together, he'd developed an annoying habit of honesty.

"Er, well, not exactly. I couldn't afford to keep up the mortgage on my house without a job. So I rented it out."

"Oh, I see."

Nick saw the pity on her face and hated it. He didn't want to be the object of anyone's pity, even when the dictionary definition of pathetic had his picture next to it.

Anna seemed to read his mind.

"Nick, you'll get another club, I know you will. Is your agent sending out your résumé?"

"Yeah, but until I can pass a fitness test, no club will sign me."

She leaned back in her chair, her eyes soft and sympathetic.

"It'll happen for you. You just have to believe."

He glanced down at his beer.

"I hope so ... it's just hard, after everything that's happened."

He was so surprised when she laid her hand over his that he reacted too slowly, and it was gone before he could...

Before he could what? Hold hands with his psychologist in a crowded pub.

"Can I ask you something?"

She looked surprised by the intensity in his voice.

"Sure, of course."

"The mantra ... I was just wondering ... you said you'd come up with it when you'd had a really bad time in your life..."

He grimaced when he realised that her open expression had closed down and the gates were clanging shut. Looked like the honesty habit was a one-way street.

"Sorry, I shouldn't have asked."

She fidgeted, playing with her drink.

"No, it's okay. It's just not something I'm very proud of. I don't like talking about it."

"Christ, I know how that feels."

She met his eyes and something passed between them.

"Yes, I think you do know." She gave a tense smile. "At the time it felt like I'd never ... live it down, but time blurs everything and I was able to figure out that I wasn't wholly at fault. I mean, I was in the wrong, but I wasn't the only one."

Nick was bursting with curiosity, but just nodded.

"The thing is," and she cringed, "I had an affair with a married man." She glanced up then looked away quickly. "I knew he was married, but I didn't care. Oh, he said all the usual crap, that they were separated but staying together for the kids," and she pulled a face. "He'd leave her, he just needed some time. I believed all his bullshit. But really, it makes me as bad as ... as Molly."

Nick didn't know what to say and the silence stretched out between them.

"Ugh, years later, it still sounds terrible. I can guess what you must think of me."

Nick shook his head.

"No, he told you he was separated. It's not your fault that you believed him."

"That's sweet of you, but he told me exactly what I wanted to hear. I knew he had a wife and kids, but I didn't stop."

"What happened?"

One corner of her mouth pulled down.

"What always happens—we were found out."

"His wife?"

"No, it was worse than that."

"Worse than his wife finding out?"

"God, that sounds bad, I know." She ran her finger around the rim of her glass. "He was my supervisor while I was doing my PhD. He was always so sympathetic when I was struggling, always knew the right things to say. I felt special, you know?"

Nick wasn't sure he did know, but the blast of jealousy held his voice hostage.

"Turns out I was just a cliché—the ingénue student falling for her professor. And it wasn't the first time for him."

"What do you mean?"

"Another student, a Senior, admitted to sleeping with him for better grades."

"Blimey."

"She was hustled away before graduation. They still gave her the degree."

"Why wasn't he fired then?"

Anna shrugged.

"He's something of a star in the department—knows the right people, gets money coming in. They can't afford to get rid of him, so they get rid of the students instead."

"Wow, that's a bit rugged."

"Yeah, big wakeup call. I nearly got kicked off the program. I only had one semester left, so they let me finish my thesis online. I slunk back to my parents' in NYC. Sound familiar?"

Nick's lips pressed together in a hard line.

"What happened to the guy?"

She gave a grim laugh.

"Sent to a sister college for a 'sabbatical' and then study leave for a year. He's back now with his wife, and only a faint stain on his academic record. It turns out it was pretty easy to paint me as a clingy homewrecker, who only needed a kind word and sympathetic shoulder to me turn into Glenn Close. Truthfully, he was the one who made the first move ... but by then, I was more than ready for whatever he wanted." She sighed. "I have terrible taste in men."

A lightbulb went off in Nick's head.

"Is this the douchenozzle?"

"The very one."

"And he still texts you?"

Anna flushed bright red.

"Yes, sometimes. Maybe three or four times since."

"You could report him for that! It would prove that it wasn't all you."

"It was years ago. Anyway, I'd really rather just forget it ever happened."

Nick was silent. Wanting to forget—he knew what that felt like.

"So that's when you came up with the mantra?"

She nodded, but wouldn't meet his eyes. Instead, she drained her glass and looked as if she was about to make an excuse and leave. Nick really, really didn't want her to go or this evening to end.

Tonight might not be a date to her—just two friends having a drink together —but Nick couldn't kid himself anymore. He wanted this to be a date. He just had to get Anna on the same page first.

"Are you hungry?" he blurted out.

Anna blinked then smiled. "I could eat."

"Do you like curry?"

She laughed quietly, a low, husky laugh that resonated inside Nick.

"I've lived in Manchester for nine months—liking curry is a rite of passage."

He grinned, pulling out his phone to call a cab. "Yeah, that's true. I know a good place a couple of miles away. I'll just phone for a taxi..."

Anna stopped him.

"I'll drive us. My car's outside."

CHAPTER FIFTEEN

ONCE THEY WERE SETTLED IN THE CAR AND NICK HAD GIVEN HER directions, the silence felt awkward, as if there was too much unsaid between them. And yet, Anna wished she could take back everything she'd told him.

She *never* discussed what happened with Jonathan, but something about Nick's own suffering had made her honest. It had also brought back all those feelings.

All that self-flagellation—she'd seen it in his eyes. He felt guilty and at some level, thought he deserved everything that had happened. She'd felt like that at one time, but with hindsight, recognised that she was only partially to blame.

So when he'd asked about the mantra, she'd told him everything.

"I don't think you're like Molly. I don't think you're anything like her."

Nick's voice interrupted Anna's grim thoughts, and she glanced at him before returning to stare at the road.

"I am though."

"You didn't cheat on anyone!" Nick said hotly. "The douchenozzle was the cheat."

"I'm the same," Anna said quietly, "because I didn't care who was hurt so long as I got what I wanted."

And that was the ugly truth that shamed her.

Nick sighed but didn't try to contradict her again. The honesty seemed to weigh them down, another brick in the wall of truth that they used to keep others out.

"You're a good person, Anna."

"Well, I ... thank you."

His refusal to blame her warmed something in Anna's heart.

"You're a good person, too, Nick."

He grimaced and stared out of the window.

"I'm trying to be."

"And that's all we can do."

They arrived at the curry house and hurried inside, blanching as the freezing air snapped at their faces and the icy wind whipped through their clothes.

Nick stumped across the car park, pausing to hold open the restaurant's door for Anna.

They were seated quickly and Anna sighed with pleasure as warmth flowed through her again, the spicy air making her empty stomach rumble.

"What's good here?" she asked, studying the menu.

"Everything, but probably best avoid the vindaloo, unless you want to lose a layer of skin from your tongue."

She raised an eyebrow. "The voice of experience?"

"The voice of someone who thought it sounded like a good idea after nine pints on a night out with the lads—for a bet."

"It went bad?"

"My eyes watered, my nose swelled up, and my tongue nearly fell off."

"Wow! In that case, I'll stick to the chicken korma with naan bread and one of those cucumber yoghurt dishes on the side, just in case."

He grinned at her disarmingly. His hazel-green eyes sparkled with humour and she felt herself relaxing in his company. *I like this man*, she thought to herself.

They placed their orders and Nick sipped a mineral water while Anna asked for a herbal tea.

Anna broke the silence.

"So, your tattoo sounds pretty awesome—do I get to see it? Uh, unless it's somewhere really embarrassing!"

Nick laughed.

"Nah, but I'd have to take my shirt off and I don't think the restaurant's owner would be very happy.

No, but I would. Anna dismissed the random thought quickly. They weren't on a date, they were just ... having a friendly meal. Although, sometimes it had seemed like there was a spark in the air, but then one or both of them would pull back.

The food started to arrive and they dug in hungrily, sharing the many dishes and talking, talking, talking, about their families and growing up, about work and the things they did to relax, about music they liked and movies they loved, about everything and nothing, about life. Anna admitted that she was hard on technology and had to buy replacement phones, tablets and laptops regularly. Nick admitted that he could be really messy but had trained himself to keep all the chaos under control.

It was the connection of people who just *fit*, for no particular reason. They differed and yet they were alike—changed, altered by events from their past.

The evening sped by too quickly, and despite the hours they'd talked, there seemed so much still unspoken between them.

Nick stared at his hands, large and rough compared to Anna's, then looked up, meeting her enquiring gaze.

"I never meant to hurt Molly."

Anna met his pained gaze.

"I know."

"Really? You believe me?"

"I do."

He closed his eyes in relief. She'd said it in emails, but he needed to hear the answer from her own lips.

"Thank you."

She nodded slightly, an expression of sympathy and understanding on her face.

Nick took a sip of water, embarrassed by the rush of gratitude he felt. He needed to know that he didn't disgust her, that she hadn't just been humouring him because she was kind.

When he looked up again, he could see goodbye in her eyes.

"Tonight's been fun," she said, brushing her fingers over the back of his knuckles, before leaning over to pick up her bag. "I don't take nearly enough breaks. I'm very bad at taking the advice I give out."

"We can do this again any time," Nick said quickly, not wanting her to leave. "As friends ... or as a date."

Her mouth popped open.

"Oh, wow, um ... I don't think that would be a good idea—dating, I mean."

Nick waited for the sting of disappointment to fade before he spoke again.

"I think it's the best idea I've had for a long time," he said carefully.

Anna frowned, twisting her bag's strap in her hands.

"Nick, you're my client. There are rules about this. What Molly's lawyer said in court..."

He scowled, his eyes darkening.

"That bastard was slinging mud, hoping some of it would stick. He has nothing to say about who you do or don't date. And anyway, I'm not your client. I haven't been your client for months. There's nothing stopping us—if you want to."

Having laid his cards on the table, he leaned back, watching her, his gaze intense.

Her eyes studied his face, sucking her bottom lip between her teeth, contemplating him as he sat waiting for her verdict.

"I guess it couldn't do any harm," she said at last. "Just friends. My reputation —I can't risk anymore scandal. You understand?"

Nick's body sagged with disappointment, but he nodded half-heartedly. Friends was better than nothing. She'd been there for him at a time when friends were hard to come by. He wanted her in his life.

"Yeah, I can do friends."

She smiled and Nick thought he could see relief in her expression. He had no idea what his own face showed.

"I guess we've kind of nailed the getting-to-know-you questions," Anna smiled at Nick. "All that stuff you ask when you first meet someone."

"Nah, you know way more about me than I do about you."

"You think?"

"I spent hours talking about myself," he smiled sadly. "My favourite subject."

"Hardly!" she snorted. "Getting you to talk about yourself was worse than pulling teeth. The only times you really enjoyed it was when I asked a rugby question. Then you lit up. It was kind of amazing. Those were the best sessions."

Nick's cheeks flushed. Molly said rugby was boring, but she'd enjoyed being a WAG. If he'd tried to talk to her about training or a match, she quickly changed the subject. He wondered now why he'd ever thought they should get married.

He shook his head—he didn't want to think about the bitch with Anna in front of him.

"Why did you want to be a sports psychologist?"

"Oh, wow, the big questions," she said, sitting up straighter and losing her smile.

Nick was surprised. Of everything he could have asked her, he didn't think *that* would upset her. But she sat stiffly, her expression tense, her body rigid.

"You don't have to..." he trailed off lamely.

"No, that's fair. I don't mind, it's just ... kind of hard to talk about. Well, not so much with you."

He was surprised by her comment but wasn't sure what to say. But then Anna began speaking again.

"My father was a big shot football player—American football, NFL hall of fame. It was practically all we ever talked about in our house when I was a kid. He read me game-plays to get me to sleep. True story!" She looked down. "My dad's a great guy, but football always came first. I was kind of a typical daddy's girl—always wanting to please him. I trained to be a doctor because it impressed him. But I guess all of that football had seeped into my blood. One day, a guy came into the hospital with a ruptured C7 vertebrae. He was a Running Back for a college team and became one of my long-term patients—we talked a lot. I even visited with him when I was off duty. He admitted how scared he was about the possibility of football being over for him, but also scared to go back on the field and risk getting injured again. It got me interested in the mental blocks that stop athletes from achieving their full potential. I wanted to help guys like him, so I decided to specialize as a sports psychologist with a specific interest in football." She paused. "Dad wanted me to be a surgeon—get to the top in a male-dominated career. He was really disappointed." She gave a small laugh. "Although I did choose another male-dominated career. It's part of the reason I came to the UK. I just couldn't get the kind of work I wanted over there. But here, sports psychology is much less established, and Steve Jewell was a friend of Dad's, so it was the natural place for me to come. I think Dad's kind of over it now, I guess. I think he's proud of me. I hope so."

"How could he not be?" Nick said, shaking his head. "You're really good at your job. It's helped me a lot. I saw how you helped Dave, too. You were the one who spotted that I needed another operation." Nick winced. "Without it, the surgeon said the tendon could have snapped at any time. I never thanked you for that."

They stared at each other across the table until Anna dropped her eyes.

"Wow, that was some getting-to-know you conversation," and she gave a brittle laugh. "But I have an early train to catch in the morning, so fun as this has been, I really need to get home."

Nick signalled the waiter and dropped his credit card on top of the bill.

Anna started to offer to pay half, then stalled halfway through the sentence when Nick's eyebrows drew together in a frown. He was a proud man and he'd asked her to come out tonight so he could thank her. Even though he'd had to move back into his parents' home and didn't have much money, she should be graceful and let him pay.

"Thank you," she said simply.

They walked out to the car together, the wind cutting through their bulky coats and snowflakes settling in a thin blanket. Anna shivered as she pulled out her keys.

"I didn't think you'd get snow this late in the year."

"It's rare, but it happens. This probably won't stick. Bloody freezing though, isn't it!"

"Can I give you a ride somewhere?"

Nick shook his head.

"That's okay, thanks. I'll call an Uber."

"Well, at least wait in my car. You'll turn into a popsicle otherwise."

Nick pulled out his phone, frowning when he saw that it was at least a ninety minute wait.

"Shit, I should have booked earlier."

"Can I drive you instead?"

Nick grimaced.

"It's a forty minute drive each way. I won't ask you to do that." *And he really didn't want his mum or sister opening the door and asking questions.*

Anna sucked her teeth, then made a decision.

"Look, I'm only five minutes away. Come back for a coffee and tell the Uber to pick you up from my place."

"Are you sure you don't mind? You said you had an early start..."

"It's no problem. And I can't leave you out here."

The drive was short, and soon Anna was pulling up outside her cottage. She was happy that she'd left a light on. It was one of the things she hated about living alone—coming back to a dark, empty house. And it felt good to have some company for a change. She'd been so busy establishing herself in Manchester that Nick would be her first guest. Not that she was going to tell him that.

"Be careful on the cobbles," she advised, second-guessing her impulsive decision to invite him home. "They're real pretty to look at, but very slippery, especially in weather like this."

Nick wasn't looking at the cottage but the snowflakes that clung to her lashes and her breath that frosted in the night air. As she spoke, he swung around to study her home. The cottage looked like a Christmas card, the stonework feathered with snow and warm glimmers of light peeping from a gap in the curtains.

Nick made his careful way up the snowy path and through the heavy wooden door, glancing around Anna's hallway. A vase of cut flowers stood on a side-table and a Tiffany lamp sent a warm glow of coloured light across the walls and ceiling. It was upmarket and sophisticated, just like her, but also warm and inviting. Just like her.

He shrugged off his heavy coat and followed her into the living room.

He had to duck as he walked inside, avoiding the low beams that told of the cottage's age. Walking slowly, glancing at the antique furniture and *olde worlde* charm, he found Anna kneeling on a rug in front of the grate. She held a lit match in her hand and a hint of sulphur hung in the air.

She hadn't turned on the lights and the only illumination came from a small lamp with a red shade that gave a soft, romantic glow.

Nick's heart rate kicked up.

"I love having central heating," Anna murmured, preoccupied, "but there's something about a real fire, don't you think?"

She still hadn't turned around, coaxing the small flames that licked up the shredded newspaper and kindling.

Nick imagined making love to Anna on that sheepskin rug in front of the fire, then had to look away. *This friends shit was going to be hard.*

The flames threw dancing shadows across her cheeks, and when she glanced up at him, a lock of shiny hair slipped across her face.

He stood in the doorway, admiring the long curve of her neck and the bunched muscles of her legs tucked up underneath her.

"You're staring," she said uneasily, glancing around at him.

He took a pace forward and hesitated. Anna's heart stumbled at the intensity of his gaze, and something in her body woke up, alert.

This beautiful, honourable man was in her home, looking at her as if she was his next meal.

"I'm sorry. I can't help it. You're so..."

Nick stopped, worried that he was going to scare her. He was in her home, taller, stronger and heavier than her, with a criminal record of violence against women. *One woman.* Another second, and she'd be freaking out or throwing him out. He should have kept his damn mouth shut.

Anna continued to stare up at him, her eyes shadowed by the low light of the flickering flames now dancing along the logs stacked in the fireplace.

What was he saying? What did he mean? Could she do this? Could she risk everything again. She had all the reasons to retreat at her fingertips.

But she didn't.

"I'm so what?"

Her voice was low and husky, her expression hidden. Nick swallowed.

"I shouldn't have said anything."

Anna stood up in a single, fluid motion, moving closer to him.

"I'm so what?" she repeated.

"Sexy," he coughed out, his throat contracting on the word.

She paused, her head cocked on one side.

"You think I'm sexy?"

"Jesus, that tongue stud," he croaked. "I've had dreams about that, what you can do with it."

A slow, amused smile spread across her face.

"Yeah?"

"Fuck, yeah!"

The smile died away and her lips parted.

She still hadn't taken a step toward him and Nick waited, his heart beating furiously in anticipation of her touch.

Her silver-grey eyes darted over him, his hair, his beard, then came to rest on his mouth. She stepped forward cupping his cheeks with cold hands, then kissing him lightly on the lips.

It was the permission he'd needed.

Nick shuddered, a deep tremor triggering a tsunami of emotion.

His large hands wrapped around her waist, tugging her toward him, pressing his lips against hers as the wind howled around the chimney, whining and ravenous.

Her mouth opened and he tasted mint from the herbal tea she'd been drinking as well as something spicier and darker.

She kissed him back hungrily and for the first time he felt the metal of her piercing against his own tongue, hard and erotic, totally unexpected from someone like her. It was such a turn-on.

She gripped his beard to angle his head to suit the slant of her mouth. Her aggression sent shockwaves through Nick, and his hands travelled along the length of her back—one up to cup her neck, one lower, stroking down her spine then wrapping around her hip.

A moan rolled out of her, and she sounded like she was in pain, drowning and lost, and all the protective core of Nick bristled with pride and lust.

His cock thickened in his jeans and he tore his mouth from hers, kissing and biting her neck, his beard soft and rough against her skin.

Her hands skittered under his sweater, pushing the thick cable knit upward so it bunched uncomfortably under his arms.

He swore, tearing himself free and yanking the Aran over his head together with the grey Henley he'd been wearing, and tossing them away.

Anna's eyes widened at the black ink scrolling across his heart, across his left shoulder and arm.

Her hands reached out to touch him, his smooth skin bronze in the firelight, the flat masculine nipples, pebbling slightly.

"Beautiful," she breathed, warming his skin as her fingers trailed over the ink. "So strong, so vivid ... like you."

Nick stood as still as stone as her fingers travelled over his body, but everywhere she touched him, his skin tingled and his blood ignited.

"It's so intricate. Does it mean anything?"

Nick had to swallow before he could speak, and when he did, he hardly recognised the strangled tightness of his voice.

"*Ta moko*—the ancient Maori art. The marks showed your achievements— and a warrior didn't cry out while he was being tattooed. Withstanding the pain was a matter of pride."

She paused in her exploration, her eyes locking with his.

"And you? What does your tattoo mean?"

Nick hesitated, the answer more revealing than his naked flesh.

"That I've survived. That I've gone through the pain, through the trial by fire." A wry grin tugged at the corners of his mouth although he didn't feel like smiling. "I was so down on myself after everything that had happened—the injury, the surgeries, the court case—I needed something for me, something to show I'd survived and come through it stronger."

There was the smallest upward curve of Anna's lips before she spoke.

"A warrior."

Nick gave a small nod. *She understood.*

She didn't speak again, but ran her hands over his chest, her short nails scratching lightly on his skin. Then she leaned forward and dragged her tongue-stud across the broad swathe of ink covering his heart.

Nick longed to reach for her, to touch her, to take her, but he knew Anna well enough to let her set the pace. She'd already shot him down once this evening—he didn't think he could take it if she stopped now.

He clenched his teeth and clamped his arms at his sides. Her hands were anchored on his hips as she continued to lick her way down his body.

Glancing up quickly, she slipped free of his hands, then gave a brief, devilish smile as she sank to her knees and snapped open the top button of his jeans. She worked the zipper down with painful slowness, pushing the worn denim out of the way.

Nick exhaled slowly, his lungs shuddering as they emptied, his eyes closing with pleasure. He'd thought about this for so long, even when he'd still been engaged to Molly—thought about it but would never have acted on it.

Anna kissed him softly through the material of his briefs, and as she dragged the tongue stud across his belly, he could feel the smooth metal. His arms ached, tensing with the need to hold her.

She rested her cheek against his flat stomach, her hands moving around to grip the back of his thighs, and her warm breath fanned over his skin.

His hands crept up to cradle the back of her head, tangling in her glossy hair, the shiny strands slipping between his fingers.

"I want you," she said, her eyes closed, her cheek still resting on his stomach.

"I'm here, Anna."

Her mouth widened with a smile and her eyes opened, flaring with intent.

"I know. My bedroom is..."

"No, here. On the rug."

Her eyebrows rose and she tipped her face upwards, her expression intrigued.

"In front of the fire," he said, taking her hand, coaxing her forwards.

"Ah," she smiled.

She sat on the rug, long legs stretched out in front of her, cheeks ruddy in the firelight, hair gleaming as she waited for him.

They'd stepped over a line—way over it, and they both knew what this meant, what they were going to do. Lust and arousal thickened in the air, tension that was sexual boiling between them.

Nick's surgical boot made him clumsy as he lowered himself to the floor, and a wisp of concern swept across Anna's face.

"Are you okay?"

"I will be when I get this damned boot off," he grimaced. *So much for smooth moves, Renshaw.*

She seemed to be holding back a smile.

"Can I help?"

"I'm fine."

She watched impatiently as he unstrapped the Velcro with a ripping sound, easing his foot out and sighing with relief.

"Does it hurt?"

"Only when I laugh."

Anna snorted with amusement and Nick grinned at her.

"Yeah? I have a cure for that," and Anna yanked off her sweater and sat in front of him wearing her skinny jeans, thick boots, and a dark green bra.

Her breasts were small and high, but when she reached behind and tossed the bra aside, her nipples were the colour of cinnamon, puckering in the cooler air.

But she was right—Nick wasn't laughing anymore.

He reached for her hands, pulling her towards him so she was straddling his thighs. Then he leaned up to capture a nipple in his mouth, sucking hard, his beard tickling her, the over-sensitised skin sending sparks of pleasure racing across her body.

She touched his cheek, her fingers drifting across a small, white scar.

"How did you get this?"

"Rugby."

"Of course. And this?"

She traced another scar running through his eyebrow.

"Rugby. I have a lot of scars."

"Really? Where else, or maybe I'll just explore."

Nick smiled and lay back, his arms above his head, inviting her to look and touch wherever she liked.

Injuries during matches ended more careers than simply retiring when you got to thirty-five. There was a lot for her to explore.

The flames flickered and flared in the fireplace, the scent of wood smoke hung in the air.

Anna yanked off her boots and shimmied out of her skinny jeans while Nick watched her with the expression of a starving man.

Free of her clothes, she stood naked before him, strong and confident in her own skin. She let him look, let him drink her in, her body gleaming in the firelight, the glow from the hearth casting intriguing shadows. And then she knelt across him, her knees sinking into the sheepskin rug, the flickering light dancing across her pale skin as her breasts pressed against his chest. They kissed with violent urgency, intensity, desire and need held in check for too long.

Anna felt bold and empowered, wondering why doing the wrong thing felt so good, but not caring anymore. She licked, bit and kissed the ridges and valleys of his carved abs, honed by years of dedicated training that told their own story. She dragged her piercing over every salty inch of them while Nick vibrated with intense pleasure and barely controlled need.

His hands stroked and moulded her body, and when those long, strong, scarred fingers pressed inside her, pleasuring her roughly, she lit up like a Fourth of July rocket, her spine snapping and arching as she cried out.

She collapsed onto his bare chest and his strong arms wrapped around her, warming her and holding her.

Nick ignored the pulsing need in his own body, tried to ignore it as Anna lay against him, her heart racing wildly, her breaths coming in harsh gasps.

When her eyes opened, dark and feral, she leaned forward and licked up his throat, pulling his earlobe with her teeth.

"Again."

Nick broke, all restraint gone, and he rolled them over until he was on top of her, flames in his eyes as he ignored the sharp tug in his healing ankle and the edge of his jeans pressing painfully into her soft, vulnerable thighs.

His mouth dragged across her lips, her chin, her neck, kissing and biting everywhere with hunger and need, unable to get enough of her scent, her taste, the arousal he could smell in the air.

She scrabbled against his jeans, then hooked her fingers into the material of his briefs, yanking them over the curve of his ass, her nails sinking into the firm globes of flesh.

His cock leapt free, bouncing against her leg as it jutted from his body, the tip glistening and dark with arousal.

Nick's brain was so flooded with sensation he couldn't think, could hardly breathe, his heart thudding against his ribs, cock pulsing and throbbing.

"I'm protected," she whispered against his heated skin.

He hesitated, his thoughts moving like tar, but then he shook his head and grabbed a condom from his jeans, his body shaking with tension as he sheathed himself.

The rug was thick and soft beneath her and Nick was hot and hard above her.

He thrust inside, a long groan, and exquisite relief shooting up his spine. Unable to slow the racing need inside, he set a frantic rhythm as their bodies slammed together, the sound of flesh on flesh echoing through the empty house as sweat beaded on his magnificent body.

Deep, hard, deeper, harder, it wasn't enough.

Pleasure filled her belly, rolling in faster as Nick's hips swivelled and jerked. More and more, and his rhythm faltered, shattering spectacularly as he flew apart.

Anna felt him stiffen and tense, his cock jerking inside her as she crossed her ankles under his ass, pulling him closer when he came with a desperate moan. The wave broke over her body and Anna cried out, spots of light exploding behind her eyes as sensation poured over her, almost too much to bear.

Slowly, the tide of sensation receded and as Nick's body softened, his damp forehead leaned against hers, a private, intimate gesture that threatened to crack her heart. Then he rolled off her, tucking her against his burning body as the flames leapt and soared, waves of heat washing over them.

Anna's eyes closed, her body throbbing as the shudders quietened gradually.

"You're so beautiful," he said.

And she smiled.

~

When Nick woke up the next morning, he felt stiff and sore but wonderfully relaxed. The blanket covering him was soft. But when he opened his eyes, the fire had gone out, leaving a pile of grey ash in the grate.

"Anna?"

The house was silent, just the whisper of wind in the eaves to answer him.

He sat up frowning and tugged on his jeans, shivering slightly in the cooling house. Dressing quickly, he pulled back the curtains letting a shaft of blue-white light filter into the room. Outside the world was coated with a brilliant blanket of crystalline snow, fresh and new.

Nick strapped on his surgical boot and limped into the kitchen, frowning at a large, cream coloured Aga that took up a quarter of the space. On a scrubbed pine table was a cold cup of coffee and a note.

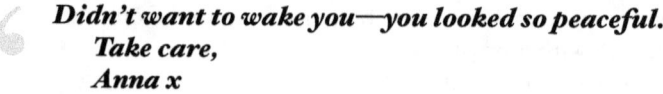

> *Didn't want to wake you—you looked so peaceful.*
> *Take care,*
> *Anna x*

He read the note twice then left it under the cold coffee as he slammed out of the cottage. She hadn't left a number.

She'd gone, and he was alone.

CHAPTER SIXTEEN

Sweat poured down Nick's face and he grimaced.

Leg day.

Most guys hated leg day at the gym. It was the biggest muscle group and therefore meant the most work. Yep, guys bitched about it, but Nick wasn't one of them. He relished the stress on his muscles, knowing that each day was making a difference. Reps of back squats, front squats, dumbbell-walking lunges, hip thrusters with a 140 Kg bar across the top of his thighs, arching his back to strengthen the glutes and lower back. It was draining, but his body was strong. And more importantly, he had confidence that his right ankle wasn't going to let him down either. Every time he asked for more, his body responded. He almost dared to hope that match-fitness was within reach.

His surgeon, Sir Gerald Whitworth, had been worth the exorbitant sum he'd charged. Nick knew his body and now he could trust it again.

Months and months of work, days filled with sweat and strain, aching muscles and nights of Tiger Balm and Deep Heat.

Since he'd had the all-clear on his tendon repair, he'd been working-out every day, hoping that he'd get signed by a club.

So far, nothing.

But there was more to it than just playing rugby. He was an athlete and he wasn't a quitter. He *needed* to prove himself after everything that had happened.

Shaking his head, he refused to let the negative thought take root. *When* he was signed, he'd be ready. Ironically, it was Anna who'd taught him to turn his thoughts around like that. He frowned. Thinking about her unsettled him. He'd long given up hoping that he'd hear from her. A short reply to an email he'd sent had made it clear that it was just a one-time thing for her.

He'd had to let it go.

But still, it hurt. He thought they'd made a connection. He didn't like the feeling that he'd been used, even though he knew that was unfair. She'd told him she wouldn't date him. It was stupid to hope for more.

On the bench next to him, his mobile rang. He glanced down to see that it was his agent checking in for their weekly catch up.

"Hi, Mark. How's it going?"

"Excellent, my friend. How are you? No, don't answer that, because in thirty seconds you're going to tell me that this is a fantastic day. Where are you?"

Nick stared at his phone bemused, wondering when Mark had started taking the happy pills.

"Uh, I'm at the gym."

"Of course you are. Do you ever go anywhere else? Never mind. I have news, good news, the best news. I've been in negotiations with Sim Andrews, the new Head Coach for Finchley Phoenixes in North London. I didn't want to say anything until I was sure ... he wants to sign you. At the start of next season, you'll be their new Fullback!"

Nick froze, the news shocking, slicing his mind wide open. Finally, after all the work, after all the setbacks, the injuries, everything he'd endured, he had a chance of playing for a club again. Not just a chance—a firm offer. He closed his eyes, his hopes soaring, flying higher and further.

His throat burned and he realised that he was choking back emotions that threatened to unman him.

Finally. Finally, he could breathe again.

He opened his eyes and noticed that his left hand was balled into a fist. He forced it open, still trying to take in the news.

The Phoenixes were a good club with a long pedigree, although currently on the slide, finishing at the bottom of the table this season, one point from relegation—but the bottom of the *Premiership* table.

They were perfect for Nick's comeback, a chance to reboot his career. Perfect in every way.

Except one.

They were in London.

Near Anna.

Nick hated the thought that she'd be so close and still out of reach.

"Nick? Nick! I'm not feeling the love!" Mark called out, his voice tinny through the speakerphone. *"Hello?"*

"Ah, sorry, Mark. I'm just ... surprised, you know? They've made a real offer?"

"A solid-gold, American Express Platinum Card offer."

"A London club."

Mark huffed in frustration.

"I know your preference is to stay up north, but no one is interested. I know it's not right or fair, but you've burned your bridges up there for now. That will change, but you need

some wins under your belt, and you won't get that when you're benched, sitting on your arse. Bloody hell, Nick! You could sound a bit more grateful. I've worked my backside off to get this chance for you, you ungrateful sod! I need my percentage or the children won't eat this month."

Nick chuckled quietly. Mark had five grownup girls, and each of them had received a brand new Mercedes on their 18th birthday. He couldn't imagine Mark denying his princesses anything.

"Don't tell me you're going to turn it down?!"

He could almost hear Mark's eyes popping.

"Shit, I'm sorry. It's a great opportunity. Of course I'll take it. Thanks, Mark. You've been..." *a good friend, someone I could trust, someone who believed in me* "... great."

It took several more minutes of Nick brown-nosing before Mark was mollified.

"Contracts are being signed at the club next week. Get yourself on a train to the Big Smoke. You'll do your fitness test and they'll want a new scan of your ankle. Then we'll go over the small print. Standard contract." He paused. *"There is one clause I should mention,"* and he cleared his throat. *"If your Achilles tendon goes again, the contract is void."*

Nick's stomach clenched. The aching fear of getting injured again haunted him.

"Other than that, there's nothing to worry about," said Mark.

His agent rang off on Nick's promise that he'd be in London in seven days.

Nope, nothing to worry about. It was what he wanted, so he was going to make the most of it. Anna had taught him that.

***

A week later, Nick's train pulled into St. Pancras station. He was wearing 'smart casual' because his mum insisted that he only had one chance to impress his new club. She'd even ironed his shirt for him. Nick thought that playing well would impress them more, but he wasn't going to argue with her and spoil her excitement for him. Both of his parents had been quietly happy, even his dad wiping a manly tear when he thought no one was looking.

They'd stuck by him and he'd never forget that, but being 27, nearly 28, and living at home with his parents was beginning to wear on him. He was ready to live his life again.

As the train slowed to a stop, he glanced down at the Underground map on his phone, even though he already knew the route by heart: seven stops on the Northern line. Just follow the white rabbit.

He let all the other passengers off first, then hoisted his kitbag down from the luggage rack and made his way from the platform, flashing his ticket at the gate barrier.

The Northern line was one of the deepest sections of the Underground in London, and it took Nick three sets of escalators to reach the northbound section. The air was warmer down here, and a bead of sweat trickled down his temple, and his shirt became damp, moulding to his body. The platform filled quickly, but more and more people squeezed on, waiting for the scent of burnt paper and the rush of warm air that meant a Tube train was coming.

Nick was trying to be polite and respectful of people's space, but everyone around treated him with the indifference of a rock. No one smiled, no one made eye contact, each lost in their own little world, the daily toil of commuting in a city.

Finally, a train arrived, with only a little shoving and pushing as everyone tried to get on at the same time. Nick was squeezed up against one of the upright supports, the metal pressing into his spine.

At each stop the congestion eased a little. Nick jumped in surprise when someone pinched his bum, but couldn't tell if it had been a man or a woman. He glanced around quickly, but no one was owning up. Sighing, he pressed himself further into the train, keeping his back to the wall and his kitbag in front of him until he arrived at Finchley Central.

As he walked along the high street, he could see the towering floodlights of the club's stadium in the distance and excitement began to drum through his veins. Known locally as the Birds Nest, the Hangar Lane arena had a capacity crowd of 29,000, which was one of the largest rugby grounds in London, except for the mighty Twickenham that held 82,000 and was where all the finals and internationals took place.

Nick had been there a couple of times, but only as a spectator. He couldn't imagine what it would be like stepping out in front of that many people. So far, the largest ever crowd he'd ever played for was 3,500 and that had felt like walking into a wall of sound.

He grabbed a bottle of water from his bag and took a long drink.

Anna had taught him that looking confident went a long way to feeling confident. She'd explained how the body could trick the mind and how he could use those techniques.

Thinking of her teaching ideas started to stir up deeper thoughts, ones he'd worked hard to suppress. And he knew the location of her London office—she was less than 13 miles away across the city.

He wished he didn't care.

Shaking the thought away, Nick stepped up to the entrance, knowing that this day, this moment could change the rest of his life.

Pushing open the door, he walked inside.

He was met by one of the assistant coaches, given a brief tour of the ground and facilities, then ushered into the training room, where the newly appointed head coach, Sim Andrews, was waiting for him.

"Good to meet you, Nick," he said, shaking hands. "Now, let's see you smash this fitness test."

As Nick changed into his workout clothes, he sent up a small prayer that everything would go well. It should do, he knew he was fit, but there was that small niggle of doubt. He shoved the thought away.

Taking a deep breath, he followed the coach into the training room.

One chance. I have one chance to nail this.

Nick's determination was a living thing, pushing him on, needing success. He would do this: *no fear.*

Think it.

See it.

Believe it.

Do it.

The club's doctor took him through his paces, checking his weight, heart, blood pressure, lungs and basic flexibility. Then he was bundled into a taxi and sent to a private clinic for yet another MRI scan.

Three hours later, Nick was back at the club staring at the sheet of paper, his eyebrows drawing together in a deep frown.

He studied the statistics that the Phoenixes' assistant coach had given him. In black and white, it described the minimum fitness standard he had to achieve to get through the front door.

- ***Test for Inside/Outside Backs***
- Body fat sum of 7 Skinfolds (mm) <56
- Vertical Jump (cm) 65
- Sprint 10m (sec) on grass 1.65
- Spring 40m (sec) on grass 5.25
- Max Bench Press (Kg lifted/Kg of body weight) 1.3
- Max Squat (Kg/Kg.bw) 1.3
- Repeat Spring Ability (m) on grass 780
- Bleep Test (Level) 13.5
- 3 Km run (min/sec) on track 11.15

It wasn't anything unexpected, but it wasn't going to be easy either.

"This is today's target," explained the coach. "In six weeks, you'll need to have improved your scores, and again six weeks after that. We want to see you training hard."

He stuck out his hand, a big grin on his face.

"Welcome to Finchley Phoenixes!"

***

Anna finished the call with a satisfied smile. Business was going well and she'd just picked up another new client. Moving to London had been the right decision.

Her smile dimmed slightly as she thought of the man she'd left behind.

No, London was definitely the best place for her. Nick was too damn tempting. She knew that their one night together had been a mistake, but it had also been a wonderful night. The best she'd ever experienced.

Guilt tugged at her. Running out on him had been an act of cowardice. She knew it. He knew it.

He'd emailed her once, asking if she was okay. She'd sent a short response. He hadn't replied.

Never mix business and pleasure. There was a reason people said that.

Smug assholes.

She sighed. Months later, and she could still remember the way he tasted, the way his eyes darkened when he touched her, the way he moved inside her.

Those memories were her own special hell, and now she was living with the consequences. Again.

The night was still so vivid in her memory, memories that haunted her.

She closed her eyes, the images rushing and tumbling through her mind.

They'd made love, beautifully, powerfully, erotically, and for a few minutes, Anna lay peacefully, but as Nick's body relaxed into sleep, she sat up slowly, staring down at him as the horror of what she'd done woke her more thoroughly.

Primum non nocere—First do no harm.

It was a basic tenet of all medical training. And she'd violated that. She knew with every female instinct, every minute of medical training that sleeping with Nick was wrong. He'd been her client; with her he'd shared his secrets, his hopes and dreams; an intimate relationship was wrong, wrong, wrong.

Sickened at her loss of control, Anna had crept from the room, gathering her clothes in shameful silence even as her thighs clenched at the memory of Nick moving inside her.

It had felt so right and been so wrong.

If it ever got out that she'd had a liaison with a former client, she'd be screwed. And not in a good way where you were given breakfast in the morning.

And in the highly competitive world of sports psychology—a male-dominated world, particularly when it came to rugby—she'd be finished, her reputation ruined.

She'd decided that it would be better to end it with Nick before it started ... or before they took it any further.

Even knowing all this, regret was a shadow that never left her.

In her bedroom, she'd washed herself quickly, afraid that using the shower would wake him, then dressed in warm clothes, her suitcase already packed and ready. Leaving like a thief in the night, she could catch the late train.

Tiptoeing down the stairs, her arms had strained so her suitcase wouldn't bang against the narrow, wooden newels.

Standing at the kitchen table, she'd hesitated, but in the end left a brief note, scrawling that short message. Then, shivering slightly, she'd risked making a quick cup of coffee, leaving another for Nick, certain that he'd wake soon. But when she'd peeked into the living room, he was still deeply asleep, his chest rising and falling rhythmically, a lock of hair curling across his forehead.

As emotion tightened her chest, she picked up the blanket from the sofa and draped it over him tenderly.

"I'm sorry," she whispered.

And with guilt prickling her skin, she stole from the house.

And now, all this time later, in her dreams they were together again, and each night she dreamed of making a different decision, one where she didn't walk away.

But then, anything is possible in dreams.

What was it about this man that had made her forget all her ethics training, her professionalism, even her own ghastly history with Jonathan? Was she doomed to repeat the same mistake over and over?

Yes, coming to London was definitely the right thing to do.

Slamming the door on a quiet voice of emotion, she concentrated on her work. There were contracts to draw up, training sessions to be scheduled and client files to be reviewed.

She stood up and stretched, walking next door to her new assistant's office. She missed Belinda, but Brendan was turning out to be another lucky choice. He was late-twenties, exceptionally efficient, and very good-looking in a skinny, nerdish sort of way. He wore thick-rimmed black glasses and a Hoxton quiff that was sculpted with liberal amounts of hair gel every morning and, in his own words, he was as camp as a row of tents.

He looked up from the computer, his eyes slightly enlarged behind the thick lenses.

"Ooh, someone looks happy! Either you've been bonking in your lunchbreak or we have another new client. Sex and money—both put a smile on my face too, honey."

Brendan had waltzed across the employer-employee line on his first day and hadn't stopped since. He seemed fascinated by Anna's love life, or lack of it.

She shook her head, smiling.

"New client."

"Pity. You're totally babelicious—for someone who dresses like a nun on a day trip to Skegness. You could do with someone revving your engine before it seizes up."

"I'm ignoring you, Brendan. Yes, we have a new client. A rugby club in North London."

"Yum! Buxom men with brawny thighs. My favourite."

"Can men be buxom?"

He rolled his eyes.

"Have you seen the size of their pecs? That's where it's at, Annie. No pecs, no sex."

She raised an eyebrow, glancing at his narrow shoulders and boyishly slim frame.

"Unless you're as gorgeous as me, of course," he grinned at her.

"Of course. What was I thinking? Okay, so I need you to work a three-hour session into my schedule for six weeks from August 1st, and prepare the usual paperwork. The contracts will be emailed to you today. Print them out and I'll sign them later."

"Gotcha. And the name of our new pay cheque is?"

"Finchley Phoenixes."

"Catchy."

"And I'll need a preliminary appointment with the manager and head coach to find out exactly what they need from me."

"On it like fleas on a dog's scrotum."

He turned back to the computer and started typing furiously.

CHAPTER SEVENTEEN

AUGUST 2015

Brendan handed Anna her schedule for the week, along with a file on her new clients, Finchley Phoenixes. Her mind half on her emails, she scanned through it, then choked on her drink, spitting a mouthful of hot lemon over her keyboard.

Her eyes watered and her face turned red as she fought to clear her airways. Brendan thumped her on the back and attempted to perform the Heimlich manoeuvre, but Anna waved him away, standing to catch her breath.

When he was certain she wasn't about to expire, Brendan flopped down into the chair opposite her and pressed a hand to his chest.

"You know, boss," he said thoughtfully when she sat down again cautiously, "I like to think of myself as pretty low rent—mostly on Friday nights at Heaven—but sometimes you really make me look classy."

Anna pulled a sour face, and Brendan laughed hysterically with relief and delayed shock.

"So what caused that little vom? Your eyes bulged and then ... bleurgh!"

"My drink went down the wrong way, that's all. I'm fine. Thanks for asking."

"If you say so," he tossed over his shoulder as he stood up and walked away. "I'll get the truth out of you."

That's what Anna was afraid of.

Her choking fit had been caused by reading through the Phoenixes' file and coming across the names of four new team members. Nick Renshaw was listed as the new Fullback, wearing the number 17 shirt.

"How did I not know this?" she groaned shaking her head. "Why is this my life? Of all the clubs in all the world, you had to walk into mine. Ugh!"

Anna knew that every Thursday afternoon for the next six weeks, maybe longer, she'd be seeing the man she fucked and dumped. Nope, not even a little bit awkward. Just hugely, enormously, cosmically awkward.

"I am a professional. I can do this!" Anna put her head in her hands. "I can't do this!"

The thought of seeing him across the team meeting room every week knowing what he looked like naked, knowing what he *felt* like naked—no, it was too awful to contemplate. But even if she could cancel the contract—which she wouldn't—this was her business. Pulling out now would not help her to build her client base.

So she decided to face it head on. Well, slightly head on. Head on as in completely not facing him while she did it.

She logged into her email and sent a message.

3ʳᵈ August 2015, 8.45AM

Dear Nick,

So, it's been a while. I hear that you'll be wearing the number 17 shirt with Finchley Phoenixes this season. I'm really happy for you. I always knew that you'd get a club.

By now, you'll probably also know that I've been hired by your team to work with the players over the next few weeks before the new season kicks off. I want you to know that I'll be totally professional and do my best to help you all have a really good season.

I also know that I owe you an apology for the way I behaved in April. It was rude and cowardly and I'm really sorry. I could have dealt with the situation much better. I should have. And I'm sorry that I didn't.

But what I said then still stands—even more so now we'll be working together again. I know that we can both be professional, but I hope that we can be friendly, too. Despite how I behaved, I have the greatest respect for you and what you've achieved.

Warm regards,

Anna Scott.

Then she scowled at the screen, realising that admitting she'd crossed a line, putting her guilt into writing wasn't smart. Sighing, she hit *delete* and started again.

3ʳᵈ August 2015, 8.52AM

Dear Nick,

So, it's been a while. I hear that you'll be wearing the number 17 shirt with Finchley Phoenixes this season. I'm really happy for you. I always knew that you'd get a club.

By now, you'll probably also know that I've been hired by your team to work with the players over the next few weeks before the new season kicks off. I want you to know that I'll do my best to help you all have a really good season.

I have the greatest respect for you and what you've achieved.

Warm regards,

Anna Scott.

She re-read it four times, hesitated, then pressed *send* and waited. And waited. And waited.

Then she sighed, and went to make herself a fresh cup of hot lemon, since her last one had cooled—what was left after she'd spat most it over her keyboard.

But when she returned to her desk, Nick had replied.

3rd August 2015, 9.16AM

Dear Anna,

It won't be a problem.

Nick

When Anna read his terse reply, she winced. He obviously wasn't happy with her. Maybe she shouldn't have put that bit about being friends. It probably sounded … hell, she had no idea how it sounded. Like a brush off? Like it had just been a meaningless fuck to her?

The problem was she'd liked it too much. Far too much to be seeing the man every week. It hadn't been meaningless.

She rested her head in her hands. What a clusterfuck.

"I've just got to get through the next six weeks," she muttered to herself. "How the hell do I do that?"

～

It was all very polite.

Very British, Anna decided.

When Sim Andrews introduced her to the team, Nick nodded, shook her hand and said, "Nice to see you again, Dr. Scott."

Nice. *Nice?* Suddenly, she didn't like the word anymore.

Surreptitiously, she studied his face, but nothing in his stoic expression revealed what he was thinking.

Nick looked good—really well, fit, broader in the shoulders than he had been, tanned, and his thick thighs seemed more muscled, his sweatpants clinging to his legs as he moved. But his eyes were harder and colder than before.

He'd cut his hair and shaved his beard, too, and she'd bet her last dime that he'd waxed his chest, as well. For half a second, she had to close her eyes as the memories of that chiselled chest pressing over her leapt to the front of her mind.

She caught the faintest scent of soap and his cologne as he walked past. Why was this the most evocative of the five senses. Five? She felt that at least a dozen had woken, simply from being in the same room with Nick.

But other than greeting her politely, he hadn't acknowledged her again.

Once, maybe twice, she thought she detected something in his eyes, a flash of emotion, but it was gone so quickly, it could well have been wishful thinking.

Was he still angry with her? Maybe even hurt? She couldn't get a read on him. Or was it just wounded pride that he'd been humped and dumped?

Sim Andrews walked to the front of the room and began his pre-season motivational pep talk.

"Good morning, everyone, and welcome. I'm Sim Andrews, Head Coach. Most of my playing career was with Bath and Bristol. I've been a Cup winner seven times and been capped for England twelve times. I was assistant coach with the Saracens for nine years. This season, I want to take the Phoenixes back to the top of the league table, where we belong.

"Joining us we have Giovanni Simone from ASR Milano playing Fly-Half, Bernard Dubois from the Stade Toulousain playing Scrum-Half, Fetuao Tui from Apia West in Samoa as our new Tighthead Prop, and Nick Renshaw from Manchester Minotaurs playing Fullback.

"I hope you've all had a good rest over the summer and have come back fit, because we'll be training hard from now on. We've got our work cut out for us, and I want to see the Phoenixes back on top, where we belong!

"I'm going to talk about our goals for this season and about the values we have here at Hangar Lane. I know some of you have heard this before, but it's worth repeating. We play hard, we play fair and we don't give in. Ever. How you conduct yourselves off the field is as important as on it. I don't want anyone here getting in the newspapers other than for playing bloody well."

He looked around him, making sure he met the eyes of every player. Over the summer, two England football players had been caught paying prostitutes, and one had been taking cocaine at the time. For a few days, it was a big scandal —there'd been heavy fines and suspensions; there was talk that they'd all be dropped from the national team.

Once Sim was satisfied that he'd made his point, he turned to introduce Anna.

"Part of our new team is Anna Scott. Dr. Scott is an experienced sports psychologist and it'll pay you to listen to what she has to say. She'll be working with you in groups this afternoon.

"We'll be going over specific goals in a few minutes, but you know what I'm going to ask of you: let's keep those missed tackles to less than ten per cent, and mistakes or tries conceded to two or three a game or we'll fall behind quickly.

"We've got a great team here, and if you keep your heads down and your noses clean, we'll be bringing home the Cup this year. We can have fun along the way, but we've all got a job to do. It's a long season and we want to have fewer injuries. So here's to a successful year."

Nick forced himself to concentrate, but as the morning wore on, he found it impossible to be in the same room with Anna. He caught himself looking at her every few seconds, even though he'd sworn to himself that he wouldn't. And he'd been irrationally furious when Giovanni Simone, the Italian player sitting next to him, had taken one look at Anna and smiled appreciatively, murmuring, *"Ciao, bella!"*

Sim's voice droned on as he made the players write down their personal goals for the season, as well as those of the team.

Nick pulled a pencil and piece of paper toward him reluctantly, and scratched his neck. He glanced around, seeing that everyone else was squinting over their own work, scribbling away. He sighed, and wrote down some thoughts.

What I'm going to do
- *nomistakes*
- *play better than my oppositenumber*
- *help myteammates*
- *score*
- *give it all Ihave*

Anna leaned over to read what he'd written, and his spine stiffened as he caught the all too familiar scent of her shampoo so close to him.

"That's good, Nick, but you need to be more specific. Is it realistic to say you'll make no mistakes? That's probably not achievable. What would be more realistic? Think about that."

He scowled as she walked away, and Giovanni raised his eyebrows questioningly.

Nick shook his head and tried again.

1. Less than two mistakes
2. No missed tackles
3. Be loud, be confident
4. I'm here to do my job and help my team
5. Stick to the game plan
6. Give it all I've got
7. Leave everything on the field
8. Enjoy this moment, enjoy the game and be grateful for being in this position to do what I do.

. . .

Anna passed by again, paused to read his words and smiled. But it was her professional smile. Nick was angry that he could tell the difference.

Later that day, when the lecture became interactive, he found it impossible to speak to her naturally, so he didn't. Even when they broke into smaller groups to practise some of the techniques she'd suggested to help with their focus, Nick couldn't concentrate. His energy was spent on trying to avoid looking at her, but his traitorous eyes continually sought her out, and he found himself listening for her voice, drawn by her laughter. It was a fucking nightmare.

His silence was obvious and noted with concern by his new head coach. Nick wanted to kick himself for giving the impression that he wasn't interested, that he couldn't get involved like the other team members. But just shaking hands with Anna had sent flames leaping across his skin. She didn't appear to have noticed anything, but sometimes he felt her eyes on him as she talked, soft and questioning, then hard and irritated.

In every other way, he was back in the groove, training like his life depended on it, even on his off days, and ready to take his place on the team.

"What's up with you and the psych woman, Anna something?" asked Jason Oduba, a Winger, as they filed out of the lecture room.

"What do you mean?"

"You know her from before, right?"

Nick glanced at Jason uneasily.

"Yeah, from when I was with the Minotaurs."

"Yeah, right. So what's your problem with her? I think she's pretty good—I'm definitely going to try out her ideas. But you..."

"What about me?"

"You look like you want to kill her or fuck her. I dunno, man, you just seem to have an issue with her. You never joined in any of the group discussions." He lowered his voice, "Sim asked if there was something up with you, I heard him. Man, you gotta shape up! Or you'll be benched before you get a chance. Know what I'm saying?"

Nick's stomach twisted. Jason was a straight up kind of guy, so what he said was on the level. And in any case, Nick knew exactly what Jason was saying. He'd done his best to fly under the radar with Anna, but it wasn't working. He'd have to try harder. A lot harder.

Sim Andrews was of the same opinion when he pulled Anna to one side.

"You knew Nick Renshaw when he was with the Minotaurs, didn't you?"

"Yes, I did."

"Hmm. And how did he seem to you?"

Hot, sexy, amazing in bed.

"Determined, very keen to improve his game. But he was being dragged down by a persistent injury, so that coloured his judgement at the time."

Sim tapped his fingers against his thigh impatiently.

"Is he a team player?"

"From what I can see, yes. Although he never got to play for the Minotaurs, as you know. But I studied a lot of footage of his games with his previous team..."

"And?"

"He wasn't the captain, but he was the spine of the team. They all looked to him in matches. He *was* that team."

Sim Andrews sighed and shook his head.

"Then why isn't he engaging with your sessions? The man turns into a block of stone as soon as you speak. What's his problem?"

Anna felt her cheeks heat up. *Me, I'm his problem.* "I'm not sure. Probably just getting acclimated."

Sim Andrews frowned in annoyance. "Talk to him. Get him engaged. I need every team member 100 percent committed, or they're out."

A rush of guilt made Anna feel nauseous. "I'll talk to him."

Sim gave a sharp nod of his head, glaring at Nick's broad back, then stalked away.

As if he'd felt the angry stare, Nick swung around to watch Sim, then his gaze fell on Anna, and his eyes narrowed.

She smiled weakly, but he turned away, heading to the locker room to change for the team's cardio workout.

During her next session, Nick avoided interacting with Anna and sat conveniently near the door so he could be first out of the team meeting room. Sim Andrews wasn't the only one who noticed his behaviour. But it was another ten days before Anna finally had the chance to talk to Nick alone.

This time she was prepared. She'd simply wait him out.

So while Nick joined his teammates in ninety minutes of cardio, Anna completed paperwork, then leaned against the wall outside the training room.

The players streamed back to the locker room, hot and sweaty and chatting animatedly. Some headed for the showers, others for the ice bath, but Anna caught Nick before he did either.

"Can I talk to you?"

He folded his arms across his broad chest, his damp t-shirt clinging to him, and he stared down at her, his expression guarded.

"Sure."

"Not here," she licked her lips and Nick's hard stare darted to her mouth.

"I have to get a shower," he said coldly, his lip curling slightly as he spoke.

Anna straightened her shoulders and took half a step back when she realised how close she was standing to him, close enough to smell the salt and sweat on his skin.

She licked her lips again nervously.

"Sim Andrews asked me to talk to you."

Nick's stony stare became worried.

"Let's just step inside the physio room for a minute so we can talk privately," Anna said firmly.

Nick followed her down to the corridor to the second of the two physio rooms.

It was a smallish space crammed with two massage beds, three chairs and a medicine cabinet that held bandages, anti-inflammatory gels and a range of treatments for sprains, grazes and other minor injuries.

With Nick glowering down at her, the room felt even smaller.

"What do you want to talk to me about?" he asked, his body language defensive, his tone terse.

Anna cleared her throat.

"Let's sit down," she suggested, pointing at two of the chairs.

Oozing reluctance, Nick sat.

"It's been noticed," she began carefully, "that you're not engaging with the team or ... or with me during my teaching sessions."

His lips pressed together and his scowl deepened.

"Look, I know this is all kinds of awkward," she sighed, "but your behaviour is already giving Sim concerns. It's making him wonder about your commitment to the team."

Nick exploded, his anger filling the space as he leapt to his feet and began to pace up and down, hands scrubbing over his face roughly.

"He's questioning *my* commitment?! I train harder than anyone! I train on my off-days," he spat furiously, his voice tight with emotion.

"Nick..."

"I'm out there, slogging my fucking guts out harder and longer than anyone else during practices!"

"Nick..."

"I've *fought* to come back from injury. I'm fit! I'm ready! I..."

"NICK!" Anna slapped her hand down on the massage table. "Will you listen to me!"

His jaw snapped shut and his stormy eyes narrowed on hers.

"Sim didn't see that commitment during *my* sessions."

"And we both know why that is," he sneered. "You don't want any commitment from me."

Anna's eyebrows shot up and Nick looked as though he was already regretting his words. He took a deep breath and looked away while Anna chose her next words carefully.

"You assured me that you could be professional and..."

"Yeah, well excuse me if seeing you again is fucking with my head! Not everyone can be as cold and calculating as you!"

She knew she deserved his anger, but her own frustration was rising to meet his. The volcanic pressure inside started to build, searching for an exit, searching for weakness.

"I cannot have any sort of relationship with a client!" she hissed, her body rigid. "You know that!"

"Didn't stop you before," he taunted.

"You weren't a client then," she choked. "But you're right—I should have stopped. Oh boy, am I regretting it now!"

And she tossed her clipboard onto the table, pointing a finger in his face.

"Are you trying to ruin this for me? Is that what this is? Your ego can't bear it, so you're going to make sure I lose this contract? Or maybe ruining my reputation forever will settle the score. You tell me, Nick! What do you want from me?"

She was breathing rapidly, and two points of colour marked her cheeks in an otherwise chalky complexion.

He prowled toward her, his jaw clenched, his hands balled into fists.

"What do I want? I want to fuck you so hard you'll never forget it's my cock that's been inside you. I want you screaming *my* name. I want you to say it wasn't a mistake. That's what I want, Anna, and it's fucking killing me to not even touch you!"

He was so close, she could see the flecks of gold in his angry eyes, smell the salty sweat on his skin, and feel the heat from his large body.

She remembered. She remembered it all. The way they'd moved together, the way his neck corded and his eyes squeezed shut when he came, the way he'd tucked his face into her neck, his breaths racing.

Her body filled with heat.

"Oh, God! I..."

Nick didn't let her finish the sentence, although it seemed unlikely that words would come to her.

One large hand wrapped around her waist, jerking her toward him, and his lips covered hers possessively, his tongue invading her mouth.

Her head screamed no, but her body was in the driving seat.

Anna's hands scraped over Nick's short hair, and when her fingers scrabbled futilely against the bristles, she wrapped her hands in his damp t-shirt, tugging him forward so their bodies were pressed together.

She lapped the salt at his neck, dragging her tongue stud over his skin in a way she knew that made him crazy.

He half growled, half groaned as she yanked the t-shirt over his head and he ripped her blouse open, the buttons popping and skittering across the floor in all directions.

His hard cock was tenting the front of his shorts, lodging itself hot and thick between Anna's thighs. She moaned and bit his throat. Nick swore and snapped open her bra, squeezing her breasts and twisting her nipples almost painfully.

She retaliated by shoving her hand down the front of his shorts and wrapping her fingers around him, making him grunt and curse, goading him.

He smacked her backside, making her gasp, then forced her pants and panties down her legs.

Without a word, he spun her around so she was wedged against the massage table, and he pressed his hand between her shoulder blades, forcing her down.

"Yessss!" she hissed.

Nick's face was a grim mask as he freed his cock, pushing his shorts and briefs over the curve of his arse.

He gasped a ragged breath, then drove inside her hard.

Anna screamed into the table, then bit a seam in the plastic covering, a muffled shriek rolling out as Nick's thighs slammed against her, his cock ramming inside her ruthlessly.

He gritted his teeth as their skin slapped together, his hands gripping her hips, his sweat dripping onto her torn blouse. All the anger and frustration and longing were combined in a brutal fuck that sent him spiralling out of control.

Within seconds, his sac was drawn up tight and when Anna gave another muffled cry, clenching around him, he exploded, pouring himself inside her as he collapsed, pressing her even harder into the table.

His breath was harsh and his thighs trembled when he pulled out of her, his dick glistening.

Swearing to himself, he tucked his still hard dick away, yanked up his shorts and strode from the room, slamming the door behind him.

Anna didn't move.

She felt a trickle of warm cum slide down her thigh, and she forced herself to stand on shaky legs. Her hands trembled as she plucked a paper towel from the dispenser and cleaned herself up as best she could, but when she caught her reflection in the mirror, her face was bright red with an imprint of a seam down her cheek. Her lips were swollen and bruised, and her hair clung sweatily to her scalp.

She raised a trembling hand to her mouth. She could still taste him.

Anna stumbled to the washbasin and splashed water on her face, combing her hair with her fingers.

Slowly, she pulled up her panties and tried to smooth out the wrinkles in her dress pants, but there was nothing she could do about her torn blouse. She tucked it into the waistband and buttoned her suit jacket tightly over the top.

Her reflection mocked her. No matter how she tried to repair herself, she looked guilty.

And freshly fucked.

CHAPTER EIGHTEEN

NICK STORMED INTO THE LOCKER ROOM, EARNING SURPRISED LOOKS FROM HIS
new teammates, but he didn't care.

What had they done? What had he *done?* He'd fucked her like an animal, and
bloody hell, it had been the hottest thing ever. He was still half-aroused, but
wholly disgusted with himself. There was no excuse for his behaviour. None.

God, he'd wanted her.

And now he'd had another taste, he wanted even more. He was hanging on
by his fingernails, only his revulsion at the way he'd used her was keeping him
from running back into the physio room and taking her again.

He threw himself in the shower, turning the water to cool as he shivered
under the powerful stream. It helped him to think, and helped to ease the raging
need inside him.

As the adrenaline dissipated in his blood, he began to think more rationally.
And he was appalled.

He needed to apologise. Would she demand he was kicked off the team? The
way he'd used her, mauled her.

Yeah, he'd start with an apology then try begging.

Nick dressed slowly, and something about his demeanour kept his teammates
from asking questions. They all knew that he'd been alone with Anna—they
assumed he was in a foul mood because he'd had his balls in a blender with Anna
turning the handle.

Sitting on the bench, his bare feet resting on the tiled floor, he pulled out his
phone and googled Anna's address. Her office was listed on her website. That
was a start. He'd send ... no, he'd take her some flowers, and go from there.

He packed his kit away and muttered to his housemate, Fetuao, that he'd be back later. The huge Samoan Prop gave him a look and shrugged his massive shoulders.

"No wuckers, mate."

Along with Giovanni and Bernard Dubois, they shared a house that the club owned. Mostly, it was for overseas players, but anyone who had accommodation issues could use it. Nick was still renting out his house near his parents, so this suited him.

Nick was furious with himself. He'd never, *never* treated a woman like that. He needed to ... he had no fucking idea what could put this right. Flowers? Chocolates? He shook his head, despair filling him.

It took him the best part of an hour to drive across London to Anna's office. He passed a florist on the way and stood outside indecisively, wondering if this was a bad idea in a long day of bad ideas.

He wanted to trust her, but it was hard. He definitely needed to apologise for how he'd behaved.

What sort of flowers said, *sorry for fucking you like a wild animal?*

He settled on white tulips, the most virginal of flowers.

When he reached her office, he realised that it was after hours and the building was shut. But since her office suite was on the second floor of a three-storey building, he wondered whether she lived above the shop. Taking a punt, he pressed the buzzer.

There was a short pause, then he heard her voice through the intercom.

"Hello?"

"It's Nick."

There was no reply, just static air, so Nick hurried on.

"I'm sorry, Anna. So fucking sorry. That shouldn't have happened. I ... I'm sorry." He paused, but there was still no answer. "I didn't mean to hurt you. I'd never want to hurt you. I don't want you to lose your job, I promise."

There was another long pause and Nick squeezed his eyes shut, half praying.

"Apology accepted. Goodbye."

His shoulders sagged.

"Anna, please. Can we talk?"

There was another long pause.

"I don't know. Can we?"

"I promise I won't even touch you. I'll stand on the doorstep. Whatever you want. I don't want you to be scared of me. Christ, Anna..."

He leaned his head against the door, stumbling when the buzzer sounded and it opened suddenly.

A nervous energy took over his body and he jogged up two flights of steps and knocked on the door.

She opened it a crack, and it killed him to see that she'd put the chain across the door.

"What do you want, Nick?"

His face fell.

"To give you these," he said, gesturing with the tulips, "and to apologise. Again."

She hesitated, then slowly unchained the door.

They stood staring at each other for a beat, before Nick remembered that he was holding the tulips.

Again she hesitated, then finally accepted the flowers, her fingers brushing against his.

Nick shoved his hands in his pockets and rocked on his heels, uncertain what to say next.

Anna glanced up at his face and sighed.

"You'd better come in."

The flat was a complete contrast to her cottage. There, it had been quirky and cosy, old fashioned and quaint. Now, the walls were painted white and the furniture in the lounge was sleek and modern; bright, abstract paintings hung on the walls.

"It's ... different," Nick said, stumbling over his words.

She shrugged her narrow shoulders.

"You've gotta work with what you're given, right?"

Nick wasn't sure how to answer, so he stayed silent.

Anna spent several minutes arranging the flowers in a vase and placed them on a small coffee table in her living room.

"They're beautiful. Thank you."

She slumped onto the leather sofa, her face defeated.

"I don't know how to do this, Nick," she said brokenly. "I didn't contact you before because I was afraid of ... this. I *can't* be involved with you." She looked down. "But I can't *not* be involved with you either."

He sat next to her, tentatively taking her hand between his own until she pulled free and moved to sit at the other end of the sofa.

Nick followed her with his eyes then began to speak quietly.

"I don't know what this is, Anna. But I want to find out. With you I feel ... shit, I don't know—alive. Like I have no choice in this, but I do. After everything that's happened—before and now—I want ... no, I need to find out if there's something here. I think there is."

"We *can't!*"

He rubbed his hands over his cropped hair in frustration.

"Do you honestly think we can go another month or longer like this? Andrews thinks I'm not committed because I'm trying so damn hard not to look at you and risk showing how I feel."

She shook her head.

"Exactly! That's why we have to ... control ourselves."

"I don't want to *control* this! And if you'd just be honest with yourself, neither do you."

They stared at each other across the expanse of the sofa.

"I'm not sure..."

Nick was frustrated. He understood her resistance, but didn't know what to do about it. He stood up slowly, prepared to retreat. For now.

"I really like you, Anna."

She gave a defeated smile.

"I like you, too. More than I should."

"And I'll wait for you. I'm not Jonathan and I don't want to hurt you. So I'll wait for you."

Myriad emotions reflected in her eyes and her lips turned down.

"Will you just hold me?"

Nick stepped toward her and opened his arms. With a sigh, Anna leaned against him, feeling the gentle weight of his hands on her waist as his warmth and solidity surrounded her.

"This is all wrong," she whispered, "but it still feels right."

Tears pricked her eyes and she clung to him more tightly, pressing her face against his broad chest.

Nick shook his head, lightly stroking the curve of her back, his lips brushing her forehead.

"It's not wrong. We're both single, we're not hurting anyone."

She looked up, giving him a thin smile.

"Our contracts don't permit fraternization."

Nick scoffed. "We were involved before we signed those. If you want, I'll go to Andrews tomorrow and tell him exactly that."

Anna looked horrified. "You can't! You'll ruin me!"

"We've done *nothing* wrong!" he cried out in frustration.

"They won't see it like that," she sighed.

"Anna!" he gripped her shoulders and stared into her eyes. "Do you want to be with me?"

She stared back at him, her eyes roving across his face, weighing his sincerity.

"Yes," she said, at last. "I shouldn't, but I do."

His arms tightened around her and he leaned down so his face was buried in her neck.

"Then that's all that matters."

They stood together silently, just feeling, just being. It was simple and intimate in its simplicity.

Then the moment was broken as Nick's stomach rumbled loudly and Anna gave a soft chuckle at the chagrined expression on his face.

"Sorry," he mumbled.

"Nah, it's fine. I'm hungry, too."

"Are there any good restaurants around here?"

Her closed expression returned.

"We can't be seen out together! Not while I'm still working for the Phoenixes."

He sighed. "Fine. How about ordering takeout?"

For the first time she gave him a wide smile.

"Nope! I'm going to cook for you. Well, I'll be the chef, you can chop stuff. Deal?"

Nick grinned. "Deal."

He took off his jacket and draped it over the back of a chair, then followed Anna into the kitchen. It looked as though he'd interrupted her part way through the food prep. Assorted salad vegetables were heaped next to a cutting board, and a pair of salmon steaks was still sealed in a packet.

"Eating healthy?" Nick grinned at her.

"I do take my own advice sometimes," she smirked, flipping him with a pair of oven gloves as she took a baking pan out of the pre-heated oven. "See if you can do something creative with the salad."

It felt right. Working together quietly, standing together to prepare a meal, without tension, without expectation, it was the most relaxed Nick had felt in months. And it exceeded every hope he'd had when he'd trod with heavy steps towards her home earlier that evening.

The white tulips had been arranged in a frosted glass vase and looked beautiful, if fragile. Just like Anna, Nick mused.

They ate together, talked together, and later that night, made love together, soft and tender, heated and passionate. And it was right.

～

The preparations leading up to the Phoenixes' first game of the season were intense. It was a home game and the fans' expectations were riding high. After the nail-biting final weeks of the previous season when they'd nearly been relegated, the pressure was already building.

Nick had been selected to play in the opening match. He felt proud of the responsibility, determined to play his best, itching to get out onto the field and show what he could really do, show that he'd earned his place on the team.

They'd spent their mornings in training and their afternoons analysing video tapes of last season's games as well as tapes of their opponents. It gave Nick a chance to see how his style of play would fit into the team, although as there were three other new members, there were bound to be some significant changes, as well.

Wednesday was a day off, but Nick went for a long run and booked himself in for a sports massage after.

Thursday and Friday morning were run-throughs of the plays, practising together. The training focussed on making last minute improvements, as well as learning to read each other as much as was possible for the new team structure. Calvin, the team captain dictated game scenarios as well as plays in different parts of the fields, almost like a dress rehearsal for the forthcoming match.

Nick felt strong and confident, as if he was finally being allowed to become the man he knew he should be.

But the best part was that every morning, Nick woke up with Anna wrapped around him. He loved that she slept naked. He loved feeling her silky warmth curled up next to him, the softness in her eyes that turned to glittering heat as they made slow, intense love, their bodies sliding together in a tumble of grunts and sighs, sheets and pillows tossed to the floor.

The night before his first match as the Finchley Phoenixes Fullback, Nick had joined the rest of the boys for a light training session, massages and ice baths, followed by a movie marathon afternoon and a dinner of steak, rice and broccoli—high in carbs and a little protein. Sim Andrews had arranged it but not attended, knowing that the team needed to chill out and relax both their bodies and minds.

After that, he'd gone home to Anna's, dodging questions about what he was doing and who he was seeing. His evasiveness had led to speculation that his girlfriend must be married. Nick hated that anyone would think it, but decided that saying nothing was best. For now.

"I'm not supposed to have sex the night before a match," he sighed, as Anna greeted him at her front door dressed in skimpy boy shorts and a tank top.

She laughed happily.

"You'll be relieved to know that is complete nonsense. Studies show that there is no significant difference in performance between athletes who abstain and those who indulge, provided the coitus takes place at least twelve hours prior to the game. Although two hours before a match decreases performance. I can find you the reference if you want, McGlone and Shrier, I believe."

Nick gazed at her in amazement, then swept her up in a full body tackle, ran through the flat and threw her on the bed.

～

The next morning, he cracked an eye as Anna slipped from the sheets, and he watched her pull on a thin robe.

He stretched out in bed, a smile on his face as the stars aligned. After a miserable year, he was back, better and stronger, and a hell of a lot happier.

It had been so long since he'd had a match day that his routine seemed unfamiliar, but the aroma of strong coffee percolated through to the bedroom and he heard the ding of the microwave. Anna poked her head around the bedroom door.

"Get your lazy ass up. I've made breakfast."

Nick raised his arms over his head, stretching slowly again, then stood up, feeling the roll and play of his muscles as he sauntered buck naked into the kitchen, his dick semi-erect.

Anna shook her head.

"That beast needs a leash!"

"Feeling a bit kinky, doc," he teased. "You're staring at me again."

Amusement coloured his voice.

"Don't blame me. You're the one walking around naked, being all sexy. I'm only human."

She smiled as she plunked a bowl of porridge in front of him, and passed over a jar of honey.

It had been months ago when he'd told Anna about his porridge cravings on match-day and his preferred routine, but she hadn't forgotten.

"It's good for you," she said softly, and Nick saw the care and concern in her eyes, in everything she did.

He felt the familiar pinch of match-day nerves, but ate everything he was given, and drank down two cups of coffee, discreetly washing down a couple of Ibuprofen, something he'd being doing pretty regularly.

Then he hit the shower.

Anna was waiting for him when he climbed out, freshly washed and clean shaven.

She was holding a bottle of massage oil.

"Did you know," she said suggestively, "that I took a class on how to give a deep tissue massage?"

Nick groaned.

"I don't know. I'll get too turned on with your hands all over me."

Nick looked longingly at the bottle of massage oil, and realised that he was already growing hard. He sighed, knowing it was a losing battle either way.

"Yeah, I'd love a massage. Thank you."

Nick lay naked face down on the bed, his head turned to one side, watching as Anna kneeled across the rounded globes of his glutes.

"Nice ass, Renshaw. I could bounce quarters off of those buns."

"We could try that later," he grinned.

She dug her thumbs into twin knots in his shoulders and Nick moaned softly, the pain exquisite. She really knew what she was doing.

Twenty minutes later, he felt liquid and weightless, all the knots and tightness had vanished, and he was relaxed, yet deeply focussed.

As he lay there, missing her body covering him, he heard her in the kitchen and then she reappeared with a large glass of water.

"I've mixed in some rehydration salts—they'll help keep your hydration levels high. And I've brought your stretch-bands—you'd left them in the living room."

Nick sat up, blinking with surprise.

"I thought you'd want them…" she said softly.

He'd never had anyone take care of him like this on match day—never thought anyone would. But Anna knew exactly what he needed before he'd even asked for it. She'd remembered every part of the routine, the structure that supported him on one of the most important days of his playing career.

The cold space in his chest that Molly had created, finally thawed, filling with a gentle warmth, like sun creeping across a frozen field.

He felt the deep contentment that came from being cared for.

Her gaze caught on the packet of painkillers that he'd forgotten to put away.

147

"What are these?" He could tell by her tone that she already knew. "Are you in pain?"

"Not right now, but..."

"Do you take them often?"

"No, not really," he said uncomfortably.

"Nick, you know these are addictive, right?"

"I'm not addicted, don't worry."

But her forehead was creased with concern.

"How often do you take them?"

"Not often. Now and then. Before a game."

She frowned, still holding the packet.

"If you're not in pain, don't take them. If you're in pain, you should see the Club's doctor."

Nick forced a smile.

"You're my own private doc."

"Nick, I'm serious."

"Okay, I'll stop. I promise. Honestly, it's not a problem."

Whatever her thoughts, Anna accepted him at face value and Nick felt a twinge of guilt. He had been meaning to stop taking the pills. It was just nerves, in case his ankle got fucked up again. But he'd stop. No problem.

"I just worry about you," she said softly.

"Thank you," he said, because he didn't have words that adequately conveyed how much her caring meant to him.

Even so, Anna heard it in his tone and her smile softened.

"You're welcome."

"Anna..."

"Yes?"

"I love you."

Her mouth popped open.

He walked around to her chair and clasped her face in his hands.

"I fucking love you. Everything about you."

He kissed her gently, his soft lips pressing against hers.

"I love you, too," she whispered.

"I know," he said, his voice hushed. "You show me every day."

∼

Two hours before kick-off, Nick was at the club. Anna was there, too, but he'd dropped her off a quarter of a mile down the road so that they didn't arrive together.

The stewards and supporters had already arrived, and Nick could hear the incredible sound of thousands of voices rising in the Autumn air.

A few fans were also gathered outside the players' entrance, calling out words of encouragement:

"Make the fuckers bleed!"

"Good luck, mate! Make us proud."

His heart clenched, and he said a silent prayer of thanks for being here today, for getting his second chance. A quiet wave of pride washed over him as he walked into the locker room and saw his number 17 shirt hanging up on a peg.

He greeted his teammates, seeing the suppressed energy and excitement in all of them. But when he opened his kitbag, he found that Anna had packed a huge bag of snacks, including a protein shake, granola, oats, a lunch box containing cold pasta, two bananas and a packet of sweets so he could load up on sugar.

And there was something else. Nick pulled out a small parcel wrapped in fancy paper and ripped it open. Inside was a brand new pair of Speedos in the team colours of burgundy and gold, and a handwritten note.

> *These are your new lucky Speedos. I know that they're lucky, because I believe in you. You are strong, you are fit, and you are an amazing man. You mean the world to me. Now show the world what you can do.*
> *A x*

Holding the Speedos in his hand, Nick's heart expanded as he read her words. There was nothing special about them—except that she had bought them for him. It was the best gift he'd ever received.

Still smiling to himself, he drank down a bottle of water, pulled out his headphones, listening to his favourite playlist as he stretched out his muscles again, then stripped down to his briefs, taking his turn as the club doctor strapped him up.

He glanced at the motivational quotes that Anna had placed around the room.

> *Champions believe in themselves.*

> *Fitness is not about being better than someone else. It's about being better than you used to be.*

> *Look in the mirror—that's your competition.*

> *Talent + teammates!*

> *I do it because I can. I can because I want to.*

> *We scrum for possession. Run for the try zone. Bleed for the team & live for the game.*

That was one of Sim's, not Anna's. She didn't want anyone bleeding, especially not Nick, although she knew it was a likely probability.

Nick finished dressing, drank more water and salts to stop himself from getting a cramp during the game, then pulled on his lucky Speedos as if they were body armour, feeling safe and protected because he was wearing them. He knew it was stupid—they were just briefs—but with Anna's belief behind him, he felt invincible.

Finally, he laced up his boots and stood ready with the rest of the team for the referee and assistants to do a boot check, as well as talk to the Captain and the front rows.

He wasn't nervous, he was eager. He had a lot to prove.

A team meeting with Sim Andrews and the assistant coaches followed, meaning another re-cap of tactics.

Then Sim stood in front of the team, his eyes bright, pride on his face.

"Well, here we are, lads. First game of the season. You've worked hard to get here. We've got some new players and it's time to show what you can do. Everything we've worked on, it's time to put it into practice. The Club's invested a lot of money in the lads we've got here and we've had a great pre-season. Remember your individual goals and your team goals. You need to go and outplay your opposite number—do that and there's no way we'll lose! The fans are here, you need to show them what we're made of. We're going to play *our* game not their game, and I expect you all to be respectful of the referee. I've done all I can," and he paused, looking each of them in the eye, "now it's time to show me what you boys can do. Go out there and do your best and I'll see you at half-time."

As Sim left the locker room, Nick's blood roared. He wanted to pound his chest like Tarzan and take on the opposition single-handed as they went into warmup drills, then hitting the pads, preparing their bodies for the flesh on flesh collisions that were a key element of a rough sport.

His blood thundered and he saw the grim determination on the faces of his teammates.

They finished the warmup with a quick lap of the field, and for the first time Nick experienced the heady feeling of hearing tens of thousands of people cheering him on. It was the most extraordinary, powerful feeling.

Back in the locker room, they had a few moments of personal time, and Nick studied the goals he'd written down for this game, the tackle counts and hit-ups.

The seconds ticked down toward the kick-off and each man inserted their mouth guards as Calvin rose to give his Captain's speech.

"You heard what Coach said. We don't want to let him down and we don't want to let the fans down. We know how good we can be if we play well. If we stick to the game-plan, we'll win this game. We all know what we've got to do, don't we?"

The team roared as one.

"YEEEEEAH!"

Game time.

CHAPTER NINETEEN

23RD SEPTEMBER

23RD *SEPTEMBER*

Surreptitiously, Nick picked up his phone and texted Anna.

Nick: I have to see you.
    Anna: You should be training right now!
    Nick: I'm taking a break.
    Anna: You have a match on Sunday.
    Nick: Yeah. I don't have one tonight. Can I come over?
    Anna: Of course. I miss you.

25th *September*
    Anna: It was so hard seeing you at the Club today. I wanted to take you into the physio room and have my wicked way with you.
    Nick: How wicked?
    Anna: Use your imagination.
    Nick: Fuck, I'm walking around with a chubby now.
    Anna: Dead puppies. Dead puppies.
    Nick: What?!
    Anna: I was trying to help with your little problem.
    Nick: There's nothing little about my problem.
    Anna: #truth

. . .

30th September

Nick: I'm coming over tonight.

Anna: Aren't the guys at the house getting suspicious?

Nick: Yeah.

Anna: What do you tell them?

Nick: Nothing. It's none of their business.

Anna: I hate this.

Nick: I know.

Anna: Where do they think you go at night?

Anna: Nick?

Nick: They think I'm seeing a married woman.

Anna: WTF? Why would they think that? Oh, because you're always sneaking around. Ugh. I reeeeally hate this.

Nick: If we went to Sim and explained...

Anna: No. I'd be fired. And you'd be benched.

Nick: I wish I could hold you right now.

Anna: Me 2.

3rd October

Anna: OMG!!!!!! MAN OF THE FREAKIN' MATCH! I'M SO PROUD OF YOU!!!

Nick: It's insane here. I've got paps taking photos of me.

Anna: That's because you're insanely sexy.

Nick: Haha.

Anna: You are!

Nick: You're the sexy one.

Anna: We'll have to agree to disagree. Enjoy your post-match dinner!

Nick: I wish you could be here.

Anna: I know. Have fun.

Nick: I have more fun with you.

15th October

Anna: They're renewing my contract with the Phoenixes.

Nick: Shit!

Nick: Sorry, I don't mean that. I just hate that we have to hide this.

Anna: I know.

21st October

Nick: Training was shit today.

Anna: What's up?

Nick: Sim Andrews was being a right bastard. The guy needs to get laid.

Anna: Definitely not your problem!

Nick: LOL!

Nick: Show us yer tits!

Anna: Very mature.

Nick: Sorry. Would you show me your gorgeous breasts?

Anna: Yeah, that's not gonna work.

Nick: [*sends photo of chest*]

Anna: Very nice. I'm still not sending you a photo of my boobs.

Nick: Spoilsport.

Anna: [*sends photo of one boob*]

Nick: You only have one boob?

Anna: You only just noticed?

Nick: Both boobs. Please!

Anna: No.

Nick: Spoilsport.

Anna: You already said that.

Nick: I thought you might change your mind.

Anna: Nope. But you can see in person later.

Nick: I'm on my way home now!

Anna: Can you bring Thai? I'm starving.

Nick: Will do.

Anna: Love you!

Nick: 🩶🩶🩶

14ᵗʰ November

Anna: Nick! Why are you sending me dick pics!

Nick: That fucker!

Anna: What?

Nick: Gio stole my phone.

Anna: OMG! Is that Giovanni's dick?

Nick: Yup.

Anna: Yuk.

Anna: Should I be worried? What name am I stored under on your phone?

Nick: Doctor.

Anna: You're kidding me!

Nick: Nope.

Nick: What name do you store me under?

Anna: Seventeen. Like your jersey.

Nick: Nice.

Anna: And because you gave me 17 orgasms our first weekend together.

Nick: I thought only guys kept score.

Anna: Who told you that?

Nick: An ex-girlfriend.

Anna: She lied.

Nick: Oh shit!

Anna: It's okay. You have a good overall average.

Nick: Do you seriously keep score?!

Anna: Are you worried?

Nick: No!

Anna: Not even a little bit?

Nick: I am now!

14th November

Anna: I love you. I miss you when you're away.

Nick: I love you too. The bed's too big without you. And Jason snores.

Anna: So do you.

Nick: I don't!

Anna: Yes, you do.

Nick: Really?

Anna: Only a little bit. It's more like a sort of soft snuffling. It's quite cute.

Nick: You snore.

Anna: No way!

Nick: I thought there was a herd of water buffalo in the room.

Anna: That is so mean!!!

Nick: Kidding!

Nick: Mostly.

Anna: Do I really snore?

Nick: Yeah, a bit.

Anna: I'm so embarrassed.

Nick: Don't be. I love everything about you.

Anna: I think that's the nicest thing anyone has ever said to me.

Nick: Does that mean you'll send me a photo of your boobs?

Anna: [*sends photo of boobs, no face*]

Nick: Shit, I've got a dong like a donkey now!

Anna: Furry?!

Anna: You asked for it!

Nick: You're fucking killing me!

Anna: I have to go. I'm having dinner with Brendan.

Nick: 'kay. Have fun. Not too much fun. Call me later?

Anna: Will do! Love ya!

Nick: 🤍🤍🤍

19th November

Nick: Meet me in Physio Room 2 in 10 mins.

Anna: I can't. I'm working.

Nick: 7 mins.

Anna: I can't!

Nick: Do you want me to beg? I'll beg. I want to be inside you!

Anna: On my way.

Nick: That was so fucking hot!

Anna: Shh! Sim is looking at me!

Nick: That thing you did with your tongue stud was insane!

Anna: Go away!

Nick: I can't stop thinking about you.

Anna: I'm working!

Nick: You are so fucking sexy. I'm a lucky bastard.

Anna: Ditto.

Nick: See you at home.

Anna: :)

20th November

Nick: Do you want me to get takeout for tea, or are we cooking tonight?

Nick: Are you there?

Nick: You're freaking me out here! You're not answering your phone. Are you ok?

Anna: Sorry. I was talking to my dad.

Nick: Shit! I nearly had a heart attack.

Nick: Is everything ok?

Anna: Not really?

Nick: ?

Anna: We just had a massive fight. He kept telling me I was being a fool for dating you because of the no-fraternization policy. He kept going on and on. He doesn't understand.

Nick: He's just worried about you. He loves you.

Anna: I know. But he really hurt me.

Nick: I'll kick his arse.

Anna: He's 6' 5" and weighs 290 pounds.

Nick: I'll kick his arse then run really fast.

Anna: I love you.

Nick: You're the best thing that ever happened to me.

Anna: Better than playing for the Phoenixes?
Nick: Always.
Anna: When did you get to be so sweet?
Nick: I mean it.
Anna: Thank you.
Anna: I love you.
Nick: :)
Nick: Thai?
Anna: Yes, please.

CHAPTER TWENTY

"*Usually people are a bit more excited when I call them. I am speaking to Nick Renshaw?*"

Excited? Nick's brain wasn't firing on all cylinders. He rubbed his eyes as Anna stirred sleepily next to him.

"Who is it?" she asked, her morning voice so husky it sent a bolt of lust through Nick.

As least it woke him up, and he put the phone back to his ear.

"Yep, this is Nick Renshaw. Sorry, who's this again?"

"*Eddie Jones, Head Coach for the England Rugby Union team.*"

Nick grunted disbelievingly.

"Yeah, right. Who put you up to this? Because you've got the voice really well."

"*I spoke to Mark Lipman this morning. Perhaps you'd like to talk to him.*"

For a moment, Nick paused.

"Oh, you're good, mate, throwing in Mark's name. Seriously, who put you up to this? Was it Giovanni? No, hang on, was it Jason? Or Bernard?"

The reply was sharp with irritation.

"*I suggest you talk to your agent and when he's stopped cacking himself laughing, he'll tell you to find your passport and pull your head out of your arse. You've been called to play for your country—although I'm beginning to doubt that decision. Have a nice day. Mate.*"

By now, Nick was wide awake and Anna was sitting up next to him looking concerned.

A hot flash of embarrassment coloured Nick's cheeks as he dialled his agent with shaking hands. Had he just made a right royal tit of himself with Eddie Jones? *The* Eddie Jones, the newly appointed Head Coach of the Rugby Union England team?

Mark answered on the first ring.

"I've been sitting by this bloody phone waiting for you to ring me," he said acidly. *"Eddie Jones called at 7.30 this morning. Did he tell you that Alex Bruce is out with a broken femur? Congratulations, Nick, your first cap for England. I always said it would happen. Well done, lad."*

"Thanks," Nick said, and then more faintly, "Shit!"

"Pardon?"

Nick groaned as he ran through every stupid word that he'd said to England's Head Coach.

"Everything alright?" Mark asked.

"Yep, fine. All good. Great. Never better. Wow."

"Well ... I'll email over the details, but you'll be playing in the side against Ireland at Twickenham on 13ᵗʰ February. Okay?"

Twickenham—the home of English rugby—82,000 fans. *Holy shit!*

"Yep, all good. Bloody fantastic! Thanks, Mark. Sorry to disturb your Sunday."

"Not a problem, son. I don't mind being disturbed for news like this. Well done. You've worked hard."

"What's going on?" asked Anna.

Nick dropped his phone on the bed, a huge grin lighting up his face, pride swelling inside him. *I'm good enough to play for my country.*

His throat dried as he tried to find the words—the most amazing feelings of achievement, hope and success washed through him.

"I've been selected to play for England."

"Oh my God!"

Anna shrieked and threw herself at him so suddenly, he fell backwards against the headboard.

"Oh my God! Oh my God! This is the best news ever! I'm so proud of you! I knew you'd do it! All your hard work, I knew it! I love you!"

She kissed him hard then leaned back. Tears sparkled in her serious grey eyes. Gently, he swiped a thumb under her eyes, then kissed the tears away.

An hour later, he picked up his phone again to call his parents with the good news.

His mum was the second woman he'd made cry that morning.

Happy tears.

~

Four days later, Anna finished reading *The Independent*'s double-page spread with satisfaction. There was a similar feature with a splashier headline in the tabloid newspaper *The Sun*.

RENSURE! Nick picked for England team!

Nick Renshaw is the shooting star of Finchley Phoenixes, resurrecting his career with an angelic host of fantastic tries and devilishly delightful footwork that has put the formerly ailing team at the top of the Championship table.

Nick, dubbed 'the hunky honey of Hangar Lane', has now added to his accolades by being picked to play for England by new Head Coach Eddie Jones.

"Nick is quick on the ball and has a good eye for the game. I've been impressed with how he's played for the Phoenixes."

"Hey, did you know they're calling you 'the hunky honey of Hangar Lane'?"

Nick rolled his eyes as he walked into the kitchen, just a towel slung low around his waist, droplets of water glistening on his shoulders and chest.

"I don't know why you read that stuff."

Anna laughed.

"Are you kidding me? I'm having it framed so I can look at my own 'hunky honey' every day."

Nick growled as he bent down and kissed her neck.

"If you put it up anywhere, I'll use it for a dartboard."

"I was going to put it in the bathroom," she teased him.

"Yeah, shove it in the bog. Best place for it."

She eyed him thoughtfully.

"How does it feel, being picked to play for your country?"

Nick closed his eyes briefly, a small smile playing on his face. When he opened them again, she saw the calmness inside. He'd weathered the storm and come out stronger.

"I feel proud, honoured. I know the hard work it's taken to get me here."

He knelt down in front of her, his arms encircling her waist as he buried his head in her chest.

"I couldn't have done it without you."

She smiled and kissed his damp hair.

"Yes you could. You were already doing it before I came along. You would have made it with or without me. I'm so proud of you, Nick."

He lifted his head, his eyes solemn.

"I love you, Anna."

"I love you, too. Hunky honey."

His eyes darkened and he swept her up, slung her over his shoulder, and sprinted to the bedroom.

Anna shrieked, pulling his towel free and swatting his bare ass.

"Put me down! I can't be late for work!"

Nick didn't listen. He tossed her onto the bed and ripped open her robe, making fast and furious love to her.

Already hard, he thrust inside, loving the feeling as her heels dug into his backside.

Minutes later, she sat up panting and Nick checked the bedside clock as he rolled onto his side.

"Got you off in four minutes," he said with a huge, satisfied smile on his face.

"That's not necessarily a recommendation," Anna laughed, still gasping. "Although it could be another reason your nickname is the Rocket."

Nick grinned up at her. "You said you didn't want to be late for work."

She couldn't argue with that.

"That was an awesome orgasm," she said sleepily.

She saw the smug grin of satisfaction on Nick's face.

"Hey, that wasn't all you!" she protested. "I'm responsible for at least half of the awesomeness, buster!"

"So you said. Hey, I'm going to cook for you tonight! Cottage Pie with garden peas."

"Aha! The world famous Cottage Pie that isn't a pie! I can't wait. Sounds good to me. Maybe I'll bring home some sticky toffee pudding for you."

Nick's eyes turned misty.

"And custard," he said in a dreamy voice.

Anna laughed. She was happy to indulge his sweet tooth. She was happy to indulge him, period.

As she showered slowly—and alone—Anna's thoughts turned to this time last year and how different her life had been. Her business was doing well and she was all but living with this amazing man who cared for her, who loved her, and told her so every day.

She should be happy that the Phoenixes had kept her on a retainer because they were so pleased with the positive effect she'd had on the team. She should be, but part of her was saddened, because it meant that she and Nick were still a secret.

Wild rumours flew around the locker room about where Nick spent most of his nights. Once or twice a week he'd put in an appearance to spend time with his flatmates, but the team was incredibly gossipy and had speculated that he was a secret tranny and lived as a woman, that he must be dating a married woman, that he was dating a guy. Since the team's captain was gay and nobody gave a damn, that rumour died pretty quickly, but still, they were intrigued.

Nick wanted to be able to tell them, but he couldn't. On the nights when wives and girlfriends were invited to team events or evenings when the Press were there, he attended by himself, hanging with the other guys who weren't currently dating. Several times he'd been asked to escort someone's sister or wife's best friend, and he felt a fraud doing it. He particularly hated it when Anna saw the pictures and read the speculation in the newspapers the next day. He hated the shadows in her eyes.

The secrecy ate away at him, and although he wouldn't have said he was famous, the newspapers were starting to take an interest. He and Anna had to be even more careful. He was frustrated that simply taking her out to a nice restaurant was a risk. On his birthday, they'd ordered pizza. They ate in every night because they had to, but he'd thought of a way to spoil her and show her how much he cared.

He'd overheard Anna talking to her dad and realised that it was Thanksgiving and that she'd be missing it for a second year running. She'd played it down, but he knew that she must be feeling sad, homesick for her family.

He couldn't do anything about that. But if she couldn't go to Thanksgiving, he could bring Thanksgiving to her.

Anna came home after a long day spent with a young female soccer player who had a history of suffering from depression. She had the chance of a scholarship in the US, but the university had asked Anna to give her professional opinion on whether the young woman would be able to handle the stress.

It had been a difficult decision, but Anna believed that the young woman was too vulnerable to be separated from her family right now. She suggested that the offer be held over for a year to give the player time to mature and prepare for a major upheaval in her life. Her recommendation hadn't gone over well with the girl or her family.

So when she opened the door of her apartment and caught the delicious aroma of roasting turkey, she thought she was hallucinating. But no, there was Nick in her kitchen, mashing potatoes with the ferocity of a man who hadn't eaten for a month.

He'd even decorated the table with two miniature pumpkin-shaped candles and tea lights on the window ledge.

"If you have pumpkin pie with whipped cream as well, I might have to marry you."

Nick spun around, his eyes wide. With shock or surprise, Anna wasn't sure, but she wished she could call back the words.

Instead, she forced a smile.

"It all looks wonderful! Thank you so much. This is amazing."

Nick relaxed but his eyes held a wariness that she hadn't seen since they'd gotten back together again.

He gathered her into a hug and kissed her hair.

"Happy Thanksgiving, babe."

"Thank you so much," she mumbled into his broad chest.

He gave a quiet laugh, then unbuttoned her coat and slipped it from her shoulders.

"Tea's in five minutes," he said.

Anna still couldn't get used to the way mealtimes seemed to be interchangeable. 'Lunch' could also be 'dinner' if it was served in the middle of the day, but 'dinner' was also an evening meal, which could also be 'tea'. Or 'tea' could be a cup of tea, or an invitation to enjoy a pot of tea and a slice of cake at four o'clock. At least breakfast and brunch had the same meaning as in the US, although she did like elevenses which meant coffee and a biscuit mid-morning. On the other hand, one of her Australian clients said that the mid-morning break was smoke-oh, even though he didn't smoke.

"Divided by a common language," she smiled, as she washed and dried her hands in the bathroom.

"What's that, luv?"

"I was just thinking how different British English is from American English."

"Yeah, you lot talk funny," he teased, putting a plate in front of her piled with thick slices of turkey breast, peas and broccoli, and a veritable Everest of mashed potatoes.

A ready argument sprang to her lips, but then her eyes feasted on the plate and she breathed in the aroma of roast turkey and gravy.

Nick smiled as his clever, argumentative woman was silenced. And yes, he did have pumpkin pie with certain plans in mind for the whipped cream.

Full of great food and a couple of glasses of wine, Anna sprawled on the sofa, her head resting on Nick's thighs. She'd almost embarrassed herself by becoming teary when he flipped to the children's movie section and *A Charlie Brown Thanksgiving* started playing.

When her phone rang from the kitchen, she was too full and sleepy to move, and waved her hand vaguely in the direction of the annoying ringing.

"I'll get that then, shall I?" Nick chuckled quietly.

She heard him walk to the kitchen and answer her cell.

"It's your dad," he said, handing it over to her. "I'll be clearing up in the kitchen."

"Hi, Dad! Happy Thanksgiving!"

There was a long pause.

"Hello?"

"How's my favourite daughter?"

She felt a swell of emotion at hearing his voice across the miles.

"Dad! I'm an only child! But I'm good, really good! How are you and Mom?"

"She'll talk to you in a minute." He paused. *"Who answered the phone just now?"*

Anna sat up.

"That's Nick."

"The man you told us about. One of the players."

"Yes," she said in a clipped tone.

"You're still seeing him, despite everything I said?"

Her brain couldn't come up with an answer quickly enough and her silence spoke louder than the words she choked on.

She could hear her dad swearing in the background as he passed the phone to her mother.

"Anna, it's Mom. What's going on? Why is your father so mad?"

"I ... I'm still seeing Nick," she whispered, clutching the phone tightly in her hand. "He wasn't a client when we met."

It was stretching the truth, but she *had* first seen him when she was out having dinner. She cringed at her own words and her mother's disappointed sigh.

"Not again, Anna."

"It's not like that! Well, it is, but ... I'm sorry, Mom." *Why am I apologizing?*

I'm thirty years old! "You'd like him. He's really great! He cooked me Thanksgiving dinner."

"I hope he's good to you because you know the risk you're taking. Is he worth it?"

"I love him."

Her mother sighed again.

"Please think carefully, sweetheart. We discussed this months ago. You didn't tell us you were still seeing him. I can't help thinking that's because you know it's a bad idea." She sighed softly. *"I'm not sure your father could go through it all a second time."*

"I'm sorry."

"I know you are."

As the call ended, tears tracked down Anna's cheeks. She hated disappointing her parents. She felt disgusted with herself, upset by the worry she heard in their voices, her father's anger.

Her mother's allusion to the affair with Jonathan stung deeply. She knew that in their eyes she was making the same mistake again. It had been one hell of a truth-bomb.

But this *wasn't* a mistake! She and Nick loved each other! He told her every day that he loved her.

The tears came faster.

Was Nick worth her job? Undoubtedly.

Was he worth her job, her reputation, and her parents' disappointment and pain?

She hurried to the bathroom splashing cold water on her face, trying to reduce the unhappy flush in her cheeks, but it was a losing battle.

When she trudged back into the living room, Nick was sitting on the sofa waiting for her.

It was obvious to Nick that Anna had been crying. She tried to deny it, saying she'd eaten too much and felt a little queasy, but he knew her well enough to read the misery on her face. It frustrated the hell out of him that she wouldn't tell him what had upset her. Although he could made a damn good guess.

It scared him that the continued secrecy was poisoning their relationship. They couldn't go on like this.

Two days later, Nick dragged the truth out of her. He was angry at her old man, but couldn't blame him either. The whole thing left him feeling like the world's biggest arsehole. Because of the spat, she'd decided to stay in London for Christmas and as he was going to his parents, she'd be alone. He wasn't about to let that happen.

"Come with me when I go home at Christmas," he said as she started to make a grocery list.

"I don't know if it's a good idea," she said, dropping the pen and crossing her arms across her chest.

Nick was momentarily distracted as his eyes followed the movement of her breasts, then brought his brain back online.

"Why not?"

"Because!"

She swept the air between them with her hands.

Nick just stared at her, a puzzled frown on his face. Anna huffed in frustration.

"Because no one can know about us!"

Nick laughed. He absolutely laughed and Anna wanted to smack his smug face. Then kiss it better.

"I told Mum and Dad about you months ago. They're looking forward to meeting you. And Trish."

"You ... you *told* them?"

"Course I did."

"But..."

He took her hands and wrapped them around his waist, then pulled her against his chest.

"You're important to me. I love you. Of course I told my family about you. They know how much you've helped me. And they know why we have to keep it quiet for now."

"Oh."

Worry hung in the air like fog.

"We'll drive up on Christmas Eve. If we leave it late enough, the traffic shouldn't be too bad."

"Oh."

He grinned and kissed her on the forehead.

"Time to meet the in-laws," and he released her with a wink.

Wait, what? In-laws?!

CHAPTER TWENTY-ONE

Nick was happy to be going home. Even happier that Anna was sitting beside him as he drove north.

Sheffield's pavements glittered with a hard frost, and cars at traffic lights trailed clouds of vapour.

Despite the biting cold and the late hour, crowds of revellers ambled along the streets, waving cheerfully at the passing vehicles.

"You know, I never figured you for the kind of guy who'd drive a Beamer."

"Yeah, why's that?"

"It's a nice car but..."

"Spit it out, luv."

"Well, it's kind of flashy!"

Nick laughed but didn't mention the BMW had been Molly's choice. He'd thought about selling it, but, well, it was a great drive.

He glanced across at Anna. She was anxious but trying not to show it. She'd definitely gone overboard on presents for his family, and the back seat was piled with parcels of various sizes, all professionally wrapped in colourful Christmas paper.

"It'll be fine. They'll love you."

Nick's reassurances were unheard and Anna sat ramrod straight in her seat.

He pressed his lips together but didn't try to convince her again. If she was really uncomfortable, he could try to find a hotel. Although he wasn't sure how easy that would be on Christmas Eve.

He pulled up outside his parents' semi-detached in a quiet suburban street and turned to Anna. He didn't speak, just kissed her quickly. Sometimes their kisses were so hot, the soft furnishings were in danger of catching light, but this kiss was meant to reassure and to remind her that whatever happened, they were together.

Nick wasn't worried about his parents. He knew they'd like her, and felt certain they'd grow to love her. Anna's anxiety came because of her own parents' reaction to their relationship. That still pissed him off.

He climbed from the car, stretching out the kinks in his spine as he walked to her side to open the passenger door, but she was already out and pulling packages from the backseat.

A broad beam of yellow light spilled across the doorstep as Nick's mum barrelled toward them.

"Nick! Merry Christmas, luv."

He laughed as his tiny mother pulled him down for a hug.

"And you must be Anna."

Anna froze as Nick's mother walked towards her determinedly, her carpet slippers leaving faint prints in the snow. And then she was embraced in a warm hug.

"Oh, she's lovely, Nick! Come on in out of the cold, luv. Leave the men to unpack the car. You must be perished."

Protesting weakly, Anna was led inside. Nick's dad shook her hand on his way out to help Nick unload the car, and then Trish was squeezing her tightly.

"I'm Nick's big sister," she smiled. "It's great to meet you at last. You'd think we all had mange the way he's been avoiding this."

Anna felt guilty.

"Oh, I'm sorry. That's probably because ... well, me ... and, um..."

Trish waved a hand.

"Yeah, he said you have to keep it on the QT. But not *family*."

Anna wasn't sure what to say to that, so she stayed silent.

"Cup of tea?" offered Nick's mum.

"Mum! She's just driven up from London and faced with us lot! She'd probably prefer a glass of wine. Or maybe a bottle of vodka if Nick's driven her to drink yet."

Anna smiled. "Tea's fine, thank you. It's pretty cold out there."

She'd have loved a glass of wine but hadn't eaten since lunch and it was nearly 9PM. Definitely not the time to get sloppy drunk when meeting Nick's family for the first time.

Nick's mum shot Trish a triumphant look.

"How do you take it? Milk and sugar?"

"Uh, black and weak, please. Do you have any lemon?"

Nick's mum looked desperately disappointed.

"Sorry, luv, we don't. Just black and weak alright? Or a coffee? What about a hot chocolate?"

"Mum!" snorted Trish. "Leave her alone. She said tea's fine."

"I'm just being hospitable, Miss Bossyboots!"

Anna smiled, but their warmth made her miss her own family. She hated fighting with her dad.

"Anything hot and wet is perfect," she said.

When she realised how that sounded, her eyes widened and her cheeks flushed bright red.

Trish burst out laughing.

"Oh my God! I completely agree!"

Nick's mum just smiled and shook her head.

Anna was mortified.

"I can't believe I said that!" she croaked.

"Said what?" Nick asked, filling the small living room with his large presence as he dumped suitcases, bags and parcels in a messy pile.

"Your girlfriend told Mum she likes it hot and wet!" Trish crowed. "God, she's fab, Nick. Can we keep her?"

Nick laughed, then squeezed himself between Trish and Anna on the sofa, ignoring his sister's annoyed squeaks as he squashed her into the corner.

"I know you like it hot and wet, babe," he whispered into the shell of her ear, "but maybe just stick to 'hello' for the first five minutes."

"I hate you," she mumbled, her cheeks still burning.

"Nah, you love me," he laughed. "Can't help yourself, can you?"

She gave him a reluctant smile.

Nick's mum arrived with cups of tea all around, and plates of sandwiches and mini sausage rolls. Eyeing all the bags in the middle of the room, she told Nick off and he was sent to take their luggage upstairs. Anna could hear him thumping through the house. The walls seemed very thin, she thought ruefully.

Trish passed her a plate of food and a paper napkin with reindeer on it.

"Thank you for putting a smile on my brother's face," she said, her voice soft and sincere.

Christmas Day 2015

It was the best Christmas for years, Nick decided. His parents loved Anna, just as he knew they would, and Trish and Anna had been chatting away like old friends.

On Christmas Eve, they'd cuddled in his narrow bed and listened to the church bells ringing out Midnight Mass. They'd made slow, quiet love, and Anna had held a pillow over her face to stop herself from making too much noise, but her body had still quivered around his, sending him over the edge, followed by a deep sleep.

They'd woken on Christmas morning, feeling giggly and childish as they snuggled under the duvet and made lightning trips to the bathroom, waiting for the central heating to come on.

And when they had lunch, Nick didn't care that his mum's turkey was dry or the roast potatoes burnt, and that his grandparents got tipsy on sweet Sherry and fell asleep in front of the telly during the Queen's Christmas Speech. He didn't care that Trish had given him the ugliest novelty jumper ever with a knitted reindeer who had a rugby ball for a nose and seemed cross-eyed. He was happier than he could ever remember.

Anna's presents to Nick had included downloading some great chill-out tunes to his phone so he could listen to them before matches, a gift certificate to drive an Aston Martin at Silverstone race track—something she knew he'd always wanted to do, Roget et Gallet bath products, and—his favourite—IOUs for more massages. His present to her had been a delicate gold necklace with a tiny rugby ball on it. He'd wanted to give her a ring, but sensed it was too soon for that. But definitely one day.

She'd also given him a bottle of aromatherapy massage oil and promised with a wink that she'd use it on him later.

By six o'clock, they'd gorged themselves on Christmas cake and more cups of tea, and Nick was very ready to stretch his legs.

"We're just going for a walk," he said. "You coming, Trish?"

"No, I'm going to stay and massage my stomach," she groaned. "Have fun, children."

Nick muttered something under his breath, then helped Anna bundle herself into a thick scarf and warm coat.

The air felt clean and crisp, and stars glittered in the inky sky as their breath curled like smoke. Their footsteps crunched over frozen snow and their noses turned pink.

As they passed the White Rose pub Nick turned up his collar, hoping he wouldn't see anyone he knew. Up until a year ago, the pub had been an old fashioned local, with a wooden floor, hard leather bench seats, and served six different real ales. Now it was a popular wine bar, furnished with black vinyl bar stools and decorated with gleaming chrome.

It was also packed, everyone else having decided that they needed a break from family time, too.

Nick stepped off the pavement to make room for a group of people about to enter the pub, but Anna was nearly knocked off her feet by a drunken woman.

"I know you. How do I know you?"

Anna's head jerked, and she peered up as she caught her balance, the slurred voice sending shivers racing along her spine, then she heard Nick's soft curse.

Staring at her, a puzzled and belligerent expression on her face was Nick's ex-fiancée: Molly.

Her hair was a brassy blonde again and the bandage dress she was wearing pushed her breasts up so high it was as if she was serving them on a plate. Only a pink denim jacket protected her from the bitter cold.

"I'm talking to you!"

Molly staggered closer. She didn't seem to notice that Nick was still standing in the road.

"I'm aware," Anna replied dryly, leaning away from Molly's alcoholic fumes and glancing warily at Nick.

Molly saw him immediately, one hand going to her hair as she pushed a hip out, striking a pose.

"Well, well, well, look what the cat dragged in!"

Molly smiled smugly as his gaze darted to her breasts then to her face.

"Hello, Nicky," she purred. "Did you miss me?"

"Yep, as much as a case of herpes."

Molly's eyes flashed with anger, then she laughed loudly.

"You couldn't help copping a look though, could you?"

"Fascination of the horrible," he grunted, shooting a worried look at Anna who seemed frozen.

Molly followed his gaze, her eyes narrowing malevolently.

"You've got to be fucking kidding me! I recognise you now, you slut!" and she turned to Nick. "What the fuck is *she* doing here?"

Molly glared at Anna who was shocked and upset.

"We're just walking off Christmas dinner," Nick said calmly, even though his heart was racing. "And the only slut here is you. Now sod off."

Of all the people he hoped never to see again in his whole life, Molly took the number one spot.

"I knew it!" she hissed, her eyes glittering with malice. "I knew you'd been shagging her all along. I could tell!" she snarled, pointing her inch long fingernail at Anna.

"The only person here who cheated is you, you sad cow. Now go away and annoy someone else," said Nick firmly, his stance protective as he stood between the two women.

Molly straightened up, no longer seeming drunk.

"You won't get away with this!" she snapped. "Fuckin' bitch."

To Anna, it sounded like a threat.

Molly reeled away, swearing at everyone who was in her path.

"Sorry about that," Nick muttered as Molly disappeared inside, his good mood punctured.

Anna was quiet, staring at the ground.

"I'd like to go back now," she said, her voice a hoarse whisper that spoke of unshed tears.

"Come on, luv," Nick pleaded. "Don't let the likes of her drive you away."

Anna turned and started to walk back the way they'd come.

Nick followed, uncertain what to say. But nothing seemed to help, and Anna wasn't talking. After ten minutes of continuing silence, Nick was tired of being ignored. He stepped in front of her and brought his arms around her stiff body, pulling her against him. She was cold and unyielding.

"Anna, she was drunk. She probably won't even remember this in the morning."

Anna's eyes lit with fury and she shrugged out of his embrace.

"That's your brilliant summation of the situation, is it?"

"What?"

"That she'll be too drunk to remember she met her ex-fiancé with a woman who spoke against her in court, whom she believes cheated with said fiancé? If you think this is just going to go away you're either stupid or incredibly naïve."

Nick's temper flared.

"Don't call me stupid!

Anna's voice grew louder.

"Then stop being so dumb! Don't you get how serious this is? She could *finish* me!"

"She won't."

"Aaagh! You don't know that! You heard what she said—we're not getting away with this!"

Nick tried to catch her flailing hands but she turned on her heel and started striding along the icy street.

"Fuck," Nick said softly, then jogged after her.

"Anna, it's going to be okay, I promise."

Her voice was as cold as the piercing air.

"And how could you possibly promise that, Nick?"

"Because I love you!" he shouted in frustration. "We're in this together! Whatever happens, we'll deal!"

"So love solves everything?" she sneered. "Oh, why didn't I think of that? Wait, the answer is coming to me ... because *love doesn't make any difference!*"

Nick felt as if he'd been punched in the chest.

"Of course it makes a fucking difference!" he shouted.

Anna shook her head furiously and stalked away.

"I knew this would happen," she muttered. "I *knew it* and I did it anyway. I'm such a fool."

"Woah! Slow down! Nothing's happened," Nick insisted, matching her fast pace.

"*Yet*. Nothing's happened *yet*."

"Look, if it makes you feel better, I'll talk to Molly."

Anna laughed mirthlessly.

"Oddly enough, no, that wouldn't make me feel better. You'll just be giving her more ammunition."

"You're blowing this out of proportion," he said testily.

Anna threw him a look that should have frozen his 'nads off.

"Am I? Well, I guess we'll find out how smart your ex-fiancée is. And then we'll see how smart *you* are."

"Stop being a fucking bitch!"

She whirled around, all composure gone.

"Don't you get it?! It's over! I'll be finished!"

"Anna..."

"She won't let this drop, Nick! I will lose *everything!*"

"You won't lose me."

She burst into tears, all the fight leaching out of her.

Nick pulled her against him and held her tightly, whispering into her hair that he'd look after her, that he'd protect her, and all the while his blood boiled with rage as his heart froze with fear. So many emotions rushed through him that he felt like he was choking.

Instead, he focussed on the woman in front of him that he loved more than his own life, and he held her.

Their footsteps were slow as they made their way back to the house. Trish took one look at them and opened her mouth to ask questions, but Nick beat her to it.

"Molly was at the pub."

"Oh shit. What did the bitch say to her?"

"I'll tell you later. I'm going to take Anna upstairs."

They lay fully-clothed on Nick's narrow double-bed, his arms around her as she sagged limp and lifeless against his chest.

He thought she was wrong to worry about Molly, and felt sure that the Phoenixes' management would give them a pass if Nick could tell them that he and Anna were engaged. But he wasn't stupid enough to ask her to marry him there and then. Besides, he had a feeling she'd say no. She trembled in his arms, and Nick felt a chill breath of fear. Would she bolt? Would she run from him? Back to America? Or would she finish with him instead to save her career?

He was desperate to ask her, desperate to know, but he just held her.

They stayed that way all night, and in the morning they said their goodbyes to Nick's parents, quiet and muted.

Nick told Trish about Molly's threats. Unlike him, she took them very seriously.

"You need to watch out for her, Nick. She's a devious psycho bitch and vindictive, too. Look at the way she got trashed your house—which you should have prosecuted her for, by the way."

"Drop it, Trish."

"I'm just saying. The woman holds a grudge and she's bitter."

"She's the one who cheated! I'm the one who got fined, community service and a criminal record."

"Yes, you did, but you're also playing for a Premiership club and have been selected to play for England. Meanwhile, she's been dumped by Kenny, and knows that she screwed up by cheating on you. Everything she ever wanted is what Anna's got right now. You should be worried about Molly. I mean it."

His sister's words reverberated through his brain, giving him a foul headache.

Anna was morose and uncommunicative, answering his few questions with one word answers.

Nick wasn't sure what to do.

So he did nothing.

CHAPTER TWENTY-TWO

ANNA'S ANXIETY GREW, BURROWING DEEP INSIDE, GNAWING AT HER GUT, whispering spiteful words, pouring poison in her ears. A bomb was ticking under her life and she was running out of time.

They drove back to London the following day, Boxing Day, and there was nothing in the newspapers or online.

Nick's confidence returned quickly, certain that Molly was all talk and wouldn't do anything.

But for the next few days, Anna scoured the tabloids and online news site each morning, her stomach churning with apprehension.

All it would take was a single phone call to the news desk at one of those papers, a few questions, a photograph of Nick coming out of her apartment and it would all be over. So far, there hadn't been a breath of intrigue, but Anna couldn't relax. She'd hadn't eaten for the last three days and had gone from slender to skinny, her collarbone protruding through its thin case of skin.

She couldn't talk to Nick about it because he was so laidback he just assumed the problem would go away; she couldn't talk to her parents since they'd disapproved of the relationship from the beginning; and her friends were far away and she wasn't sure they'd understand.

Belinda might have helped, but she was immersed in the joys of a new grandchild and was busy celebrating the festive season.

Instead, it was Brendan who noticed the change in her.

"What's crawled up your shiny new suit, Miss Positivity?" he asked sarcastically, clearly ticked off that she'd been miserable and bad tempered since they'd returned to work.

"I'm sorry," she sighed. "I've got a lot on my mind."

Brendan gave her a sassy look and put a hand on his hip.

"You're not fobbing me off with that, Annie Get-Your-Gun-and-shoot-yourself. Tell Auntie Brendan what's wrong. And don't even think of saying 'nothing'."

"I..."

"I mean it!"

She took a deep breath, desperate to share with another human being.

"I've been seeing someone ... a man..."

"Nick Renshaw, yes, I know. Very studly."

Anna blinked, her mouth popping open with surprise.

"You ... you know?"

Brendan rolled his eyes.

"You didn't hire me just for my outrageous good looks, you know!"

"But..."

"Honey, your eyes light up like Piccadilly Circus when someone even mentions his name. Totes emosh when you're in the same room together, even *I* feel like jumping your bones—which I'm seeing a lot more of these days, by the way."

Anna's head was spinning. If Brendan had figured it out, who else might know?

He seemed to read her mind.

"Don't worry, your little in-lust secret is safe with me. Not everyone is gifted with my incredible insight. I'm a *personal* assistant, Miss Smartypants. I am all-seeing, all-knowing."

"Oh," she said weakly.

"So you've been practising the beast with two backs on Mr. Downright-Sinfully-Dark-and-Deliciously-Dangerous and you're obviously worried someone will find out." He fanned his face. "Soooo obvious."

Anna lowered her eyes.

"Someone has found out."

"Not from me!" Brendan said sharply.

She glanced up, touching his arm briefly.

"No, Bren, not from you. It was at Christmas. I ... we ... were staying with Nick's parents and ran into his ex-fiancée. She wasn't happy, to put it mildly."

"The bimbo who cheated on him."

"The very one."

"Ah."

"Yep."

Brendan tapped a pen against his newly whitened teeth.

"Just out of interest, when did this whole love-malarkey start?"

Anna sighed.

"The night before I interviewed you, as it happens."

"Seriously?"

"Yes, one time, that's all."

"Hmm, one night of unbridled passion with a man who has buns of steel. Lucky you. No wonder you were in such a good mood for my interview."

Anna gave a weak smile.

"And then we met again when he started playing for the Phoenixes. The ... attraction was still there."

"Understatement," Brendan coughed, rolling his eyes so hard he nearly sprained his eyelids.

He sat on the edge of the desk and crossed his legs.

"Pre-emptive strike."

"Excuse me?"

"You need to go to Sim Andrews. He likes you, worships the ground your Manolos walk on since the Phoenixes are doing so well. And he rates your boy-toy. Throw yourself on his mercy. Fess up. It'll go much better than seeing it as front page news in *The Daily Sleaze*."

"But..."

"Please!" he sighed, flapping a hand in her face. "I've confessed to more sins than the average Playboy Bunny. I know how this works. Besides, you're both too valuable to lose. Trust me. It'll be fine," and he yawned. "And better than hiding away and pretending blind indifference to each other."

"You really think so?"

Brendan stared at her seriously.

"You're the best boss I've ever had, Annie. I don't want you to fuck this up for either of us."

He picked up the office phone from the desk, dialled a number, and turned to leave.

"Speak to him now. Start the New Year with a clear conscience. Well, that's what other people do. I like to start the New Year in the arms of a nice piece of rough trade—bikers, sailors, Ethan from the tattoo parlour. But that's just me."

The phone rang four times, then Anna heard Sim's curt voice.

"This is Sim Andrews. Leave a message."

She took a deep breath and was about to speak when her cell phone dinged with an incoming alert, and the words she'd dreaded flashed in her face.

She slammed down the landline phone, her heart hammering wildly.

"Brendan!"

He came hurrying in.

"Did you call Sim already?"

"No. Look!"

And she handed him her cell phone with shaking hands.

NAUGHTY NICK PLAYS DOCTORS AND NURSES!

And there was a photograph of them kissing and, oh God! It must have been taken from outside!

Anna stumbled to the window and whipped the drapes together, while Brendan watched her with compassion in his eyes.

"What does it say?" she whispered. "I can't bear to look."

"Uh, well, not too bad, really. Just that, um, Nick is, um, involved with the club's doctor—they got that part wrong—and that you're a hot totty from America."

Anna blinked.

"I'm a hot *what?*"

Brendan waved a hand.

"Don't worry about that—they caught your best side. You do look hot, and I must say, that's a steamy clinch I wouldn't mind sharing with your Nick."

"Brendan!"

"Sorry."

"Is it just that one news site?"

Brendan scrolled through her phone.

"Ah, no, there are mentions on others, but they've only got stock images, nothing else like ... well, nothing else."

Anna's heart was skipping and she couldn't catch her breath.

"Oh, fuck! Come and sit down, Annie! You look like you're about to pass out! Where are the smelling salts?"

He lowered her into a chair and ran to the office, returning with a bottle of brandy and two glasses.

"Take a sip, it's good for shock."

Anna did as she was told, even though the tiny part of her brain that was still rational knew that hot tea with sugar was better for shock than alcohol.

She sipped the brandy and coughed.

"I need to tell Nick."

"Where is he?"

"At the Club, probably in the gym."

"You'd better call him before the shit hits the fan."

"I know. Oh God, I know!"

It took her three attempts to find his name in her contacts and press the right button. The phone rang once and went to voicemail.

"Nick, it's me. They know. It's all over the online news sites about us. Call me when you get this."

"Are you going to phone Sim Andrews?"

Anna bit her lip.

"I want to talk to Nick first."

The office phone rang, and Anna jumped.

Brendan grabbed it and answered in his most officious voice.

"Scott's Sports Psychology, Brendan speaking..."

He listened for a moment then gently replaced the phone in the cradle.

"Who was it?"

He pressed his lips together.

"*The Daily Express*, looking for a quote."

The phone rang again and Brendan picked it up, listened for a second, then slammed it down. Without speaking, he unplugged it from the socket in the wall.

"I think you should phone Sim again right now. If they're calling you, they'll be calling him."

Anna gulped and nodded slowly.

Sim's office line was engaged repeatedly, and Anna could only guess why. In the end, she used his private cell phone number.

He answered immediately, his voice curt.

"Anna."

"Sim, I'm so sorry!"

"It's true then?"

"Yes and no."

"You'd better explain that, Anna, because the Board is busting my balls about having brought you to the Club in the first place!"

"I'm so, so sorry, Sim."

"Sorry doesn't cut it!"

"I know," Anna whispered brokenly. "The truth is, Nick and I were completely professional at the Minotaurs. Nothing happened there, I swear it. I spoke at his court case, as you know. Later, he sent an email to thank me for speaking, and we started chatting online. By then he was no longer employed by the Minotaurs and I was setting up my London office. The night before I interviewed my assistant, Brendan, Nick and I ... we spent the night together. That was the first and last time until..."

"Until?" Sim's voice was a low growl.

"Until I walked into the meeting at the Phoenixes and saw him there with you. I knew he'd be there from your briefing notes. He was hurt and upset, so we talked."

"I think you did a lot more than talking, Dr. Scott."

Anna's face flushed.

"It's not just ... we're in a relationship. We love each other."

She heard Sim's long-suffering sigh.

"I take it you were both aware of the Club's no-fraternization policy?"

"Yes."

"I'm sorry, Anna. You've been good for the team, but I can't let this go. You'll be informed of the Board's decision, but it's looking pretty cut and dried."

"I know. I'm sorry ... that I let you down, Sim."

"You let yourself down, Anna."

The call ended and Anna put her head in her hands. But there was still one more unpleasant call to make.

Telling her parents was the hardest thing she'd ever done. It hadn't hit the newspapers in the US yet, but it was all over the internet. She also knew that with her father's fame, it would get a lot more airtime than would otherwise have been the case.

Even though it was only just noon, they already knew. 'Friends' had been eager to tell them.

"I'm so sorry, Mom," she whispered.

"Is it true what they're saying?"

"Some of it," she said tiredly. "Only that we're in a relationship. The rest is lies. Can I talk to Dad?"

There was a long pause and muffled voices in the background. Finally, her mother returned to the line.

"I don't think that's a good idea right now, sweetheart. Dad's not feeling great. You know how he gets these days. We'll talk to you this evening. You know we're supporting you."

Anna ended the call feeling even worse. For five minutes, she sat unseeing, unhearing, wondering again how she'd managed to fuck up her life so thoroughly. Stupidity. It was the dictionary definition: making the same mistake twice and expecting a different result.

Her own father wouldn't talk to her. She didn't think she could sink any lower.

When she listened to the messages on her phone, she was assaulted with over thirty texts and voicemails. Most seemed to be from newspapers and journalists, but others were from unknown numbers and were just plain nasty.

She texted Nick once to say that she was okay but insisted that he stay away. Her heart fractured at the thought of not seeing him, not having him there to hold her.

Brendan saw the look on her face then leaned down and hugged her. It was the only comfort she'd receive.

~

Nick had just finished a punishing workout and was being massaged by one of the Club's physios when Jason walked in with his phone in his hand.

"'Sup, Jason?"

Jason glanced at Ben, the physiotherapist.

"Could you give us a minute, mate?"

"Sure. I was just finishing up here anyway."

The physiotherapist gave them a curious look as he slung a towel over his shoulders and closed the door behind him.

"You haven't heard?"

"Heard what?"

Jason passed his phone to Nick.

As he scrolled through the news page, his face tightened.

"Shit! I have to call Anna."

Jason sighed and pushed his hands through his hair.

"This is why you wouldn't tell us who you've been dating. Is this who you've been seeing all this time?"

"Yes."

"Well, I hope it's serious, buddy, because the shit is about to hit the fan. You'll be fined and benched for a couple of games, and Anna..."

"Fuck! I know! I have to call her!"

He stormed out and the locker room fell silent.

Giovanni walked across and slung an arm around his shoulders.

"Tough break, *amico*."

Nick shrugged off the arm and picked up his phone to call Anna. He groaned when he saw that she'd already tried to call him several times, but there were also a lot of numbers that he didn't recognise. He was appalled when he read some of the texts from journalists, and wondered how they'd all found his number so quickly. It was a fucking nightmare! He read through Anna's texts, upset and angry that she was telling him to stay away. What difference could it make now? He tried to call her back, but all he got was her voicemail.

"I've just heard. I'm on my way home. Call me when you get this."

He yanked on his clothes, dressing hurriedly, and was still zipping up his jeans when his phone rang again.

"Anna, thank God! I'm so sorry!"

Her voice was faint and distant.

"I don't think you should come here tonight."

"What? Of course I'm coming over. We need to..."

"Nick, no! There are journalists outside now. I can't risk more pictures of us together being in the newspapers."

"But ... they already know!"

"I can't give them more ammunition. I've spoken to Sim," she took a deep breath and Nick's heart somersaulted. *"I'm going to lose the contract. He's said as much."*

"Anna..."

"Right now I have a chance of keeping my other contracts, but I need this story to drop out of the papers as soon as possible. I can't see you. I can't be seen with you."

Nick's mouth went dry.

"Okay. Okay, I get it. For how long?"

"I don't know. A while."

"Jesus. I'll call you later, okay?"

"I'm going to turn my phone off. Journalists have gotten the number..."

"Me, too."

"So I might not answer. Don't worry about me. I'll be fine." She gave a hollow laugh. *"I've been through it all before."*

"Anna, don't."

"I'll be fine, Nick."

"Yeah, *we'll* be fine. I love y— "

But she'd already hung up.

Giovanni came and sat next to him.

"Are you coming back to the house tonight?"

"Looks like it," Nick sighed.

"Good. I'm making *pasta con pomodoro e basilico*—pasta with tomatoes and basil to you."

"Thanks, Gio."

They bumped fists and stood up to leave.

"Renshaw! My office now!"

Sim Andrews was purple in the face and roaring like a bull.

"I think I will see you later, *amico*," Giovanni said quietly.

"If I live that long," Nick muttered out of the corner of his mouth.

Nick plodded behind Sim and dropped into a chair opposite the cluttered desk.

"You fucked up, Nick. You could have your contract terminated for this."

Nick gritted his teeth, waiting for the axe to fall.

"I took a chance on you: injured, in the division below us. But I've followed your career for a long time and I like that you were loyal to Rotherham for so long. But *this!* This makes me look bad to the Board, and I don't like looking bad. What have you got to say for yourself?"

"I love her."

Sim blinked, not having expected that answer. Then his gaze hardened again.

"And how long has this been going on?"

Nick cleared his throat.

"Since August, Coach."

Sim squinted at him. "Not before?"

"Not really."

"And what does that mean?"

"I'd been dropped by the Minotaurs and Anna was moving to London. The night before she moved down here full time, we ... um, got together. But it wasn't until I was in London, as well..."

"Did any of your teammates know?"

"No, Coach."

"Hmm."

Sim stared at Nick, his eyes dark and angry. Finally, he spoke.

"Consider yourself benched for the next two games. The Board will determine your fine—that's out of my hands. You'd better keep your nose clean from now on or you're out, no matter how well you play. And I wouldn't be surprised if Eddie Jones doesn't have something to say about this. You've been a fucking idiot, costing me a damn good sports psychologist and brought the Club into disrepute."

"It's not fair that Anna..."

Sim stood up and roared, the veins in his forehead popping ominously.

"I'm talking! You don't talk when I talk! When I finish talking, that's when you talk!" His face turned purple. "She's finished here. Out of my hands. Now get out of my sight!"

Nick swallowed but knew that arguing further wouldn't help.
"Yes, Coach."

∼

The Phoenixes' game the next day was torture for Nick. He'd never been benched when he was fit before, never had to sit and watch his team lose when he knew that if he'd been out there it could have been a different story.

So he sat and fumed, enduring the harsh looks and harsher words from the fans who all said something along lines of, "Shoulda kept yer cock in yer pocket not hers, Naughty Nick!"

Worse still, Anna wouldn't return his calls or reply to his emails. He'd had a short conversation with her P.A. Brendan, but other than that, no contact.

Brendan said Anna was "coping". It didn't sound very encouraging, and Brendan, who was normally so upbeat and snarky, had been short-tempered and edgy.

He'd also had to endure the tabloids' photographs of Molly looking sad and demure, presenting herself as a slighted woman, manipulating the truth and managing to make herself appear as the injured party.

Nick lay alone in his bed at the team house, listening to the unfamiliar sounds of the house and the orchestral snores of Bernard, Fetuao and Giovanni.

For the next two days, the stories continued until finally it seemed like interest was dying away, but then one of the newspapers picked up the thread that if Anna and Nick had been together at the time of his court case, Anna would have committed perjury by denying that they were in a relationship.

Nick smelled the sulphurous machinations of Molly in that story. It was all so ridiculous, but it kept the story in the newspapers and on the gossip sites, and as they approached the New Year, it showed no signs of slowing down.

NICK ON THE NAUGHTY BENCH!

ANNA RAISES NAUGHTY NICK'S PULSE!

DID THEY LIE?
Naughty Nick's fiancée tells all [pictures on pages 2, 5, 6 and 7]

Eddie Jones, the England Coach, had called Nick to yell for a few minutes, then calmly said it wouldn't affect his place on the England team, so that was something.

And right now, Nick would grab at any straw he could.

CHAPTER TWENTY-THREE

New Year's Eve 2015

The newspaper headline was an inch high above a photograph of Anna and Nick kissing. The photo was blurry and hard to see. The headline stood out like a traffic beacon.

DID SHE LIE?

Anna's hands shook as she read the article beneath, scrutinising every word, hurting herself but unable to stop.

When there was nothing more to read, she read it again.

It was midday on New Year's Eve and Anna hadn't gotten any work done at all.

She was missing Nick desperately, but besieged by journalists, she'd decided that staying apart was the best thing for them to do—certainly the best thing for him. Right now, she was media poison.

Brendan was in the office next door, answering the ringing phones with brisk efficiency, cutting off the journalists with a few words. Calls from clients were few and far between, and although only one football club had asked to see her early in the New Year about "certain regrettable newspaper allegations", so far no one else had tried to terminate their contracts with her. Whether or not they'd renew them the following season was another question.

"Look, it's nearly lunchtime on New Year's Eve," Anna said tiredly. "We're not going to get any work done today. Why don't you go home early? You said you have a party to go to."

"Of course I have a party to go to!" Brendan said grumpily. "Who *doesn't* have a party to go to on New Year's Eve?"

Anna gave him a wry smile.

Brendan shook his head and went back to work. Anna was touched by his loyalty to her.

Nick had a team party to attend. Anna was planning a quiet night in with a bottle of Prosecco, a bag of Reese's Peanut Butter Cups and Netflix.

It was just after 1PM when the buzzer on the office front door sounded and Anna jumped a foot in the air, spilling hot tea over the desk and part of her keyboard.

"Shit!"

Brendan poked his head around the office door.

"Probably more journalists. I'll answer it."

"Thanks, Brendan."

"Anything for you, Annie," and he winked at her.

A moment later, Brendan re-entered her office, his eyes wide and worried.

"Annie, it's the police. They want to talk to you! They're on their way up now!"

"Oh my God! Something must have happened to Nick!"

Anna grabbed the edge of her desk as the world tilted.

Two plainclothes police officers entered and flashed their Warrant Cards, followed by two more officers in uniform. The woman officer in charge spoke first.

"Dr. Anna Scott?"

"Yes?"

"Anna Scott, you are under arrest on suspicion of perjury. You do not have to say anything but it may harm your defence if you do not mention when questioned something which you later rely on in court. Anything you do say may be given in evidence."

Anna heard the words but couldn't understand them. She'd been expecting to hear bad news about Nick, not ... what was this?

"I don't understand. What are you saying?"

She threw a pleading glance at Brendan who stood frozen in shock by the door.

The police officer barely took a breath.

"It is necessary to arrest you to preserve evidence under Code G of the Police and Criminal Evidence Act 1984. Do you understand?"

The second officer stepped forward.

"You need to accompany us to the station to be interviewed."

Perjury: the offence of wilfully telling an untruth or making a misrepresentation under oath.

And the only court case that Anna had ever been involved with was Nick's.

Suddenly it all fell into place. She'd sworn under oath that she and Nick weren't in a relationship at the time: Molly must have told the newspapers otherwise. Media interest had then have forced the police to investigate.

Anna swayed and Brendan stepped forward to catch her elbow.

"Oh my God," she whispered. "I'm going to be sick."

Brendan gripped her shoulders.

"No, you're not. You've done nothing wrong, Annie. Take a deep breath. I'll phone Sim Andrews and get the Club's lawyers onto it."

"But..."

"Let me help you, Annie! God knows you need it! I'll do what's necessary. Everything," and he gave her a telling look.

Anna could only agree as she collected her coat but was instructed to leave her purse, then was escorted from the building.

Curious bystanders turned to watch her being led to the back of a waiting police van. Several people had their phones out and camera flashes blinded her as the waiting journalists got their money shot. God, the humiliation. At least they hadn't cuffed her.

The van doors were opened and she stepped into the cage with a metal floor and hard wooden bench to sit on. There were no windows, no lights and no seatbelt.

Brendan watched as Anna was driven away. The two uniformed officers stayed behind and started taking the office apart methodically. They confiscated Anna's cell phone and tablet, unplugged her laptop and took that away, too. They rifled through desk drawers and papers while Brendan stood helpless, videoing proceedings on his cell phone until he'd used up all the memory.

Frustrated, he followed them as they started on the upstairs flat, systematically searching room by room. When he asked them what they were looking for, they gave the stock answer: they had "reasonable suspicion that a crime has been committed and had the authority to search and seize, preserving evidence of any possible offence."

With nothing more he could do, no way of protecting Anna, Brendan called Sim's office. But Sim had left for the day and his assistant said that the Club's solicitor wasn't available to Miss Scott because she was self-employed and not a salaried Club employee.

Worried, upset, and more than a little desperate, he tried to call Nick's number, but had to leave a voicemail.

In the end, he Googled solicitors who might be able to help Anna, but no one wanted to go to a police station on New Year's Eve. It took him two hours to find someone who agreed to help her. Two hours while Brendan wondered what was happening to Anna. Two hours while the police offices questioned the neighbours on either side of the property and those opposite: how long had Nick Renshaw been visiting Anna, what had they seen.

Brendan believed what Anna had told him, but it didn't seem that the truth would help her now.

~

During the short ride to the police station, Anna stared at the side of the van. There were no windows, but she knew that all around her, the day was winding down, people preparing for the end of year party. They would be passing the fountains in Trafalgar Square, already covered with boards to stop people dancing in the icy water and catching hypothermia. The ambulance services would be busy enough as it was.

Anna was desperate to see Nick, but ironically, his appearance at the police station would simply make her look guilty, guiltier. Tried by the media and already condemned. It was all so unfair. She wanted to cry, but the tears were locked away inside. She felt icy cold and her pulse was weak but racing; her skin felt clammy and she was dizzy. Anna's medical training warned her that she was going into shock.

She put her head between her knees and forced herself to breathe deeply.

After a considerable wait at the police station, Anna was booked in, then taken to a custody cell. At various stages she completed a medical and mental health questionnaire, and was informed that the police could detain her for up to 24 hours.

"Do you have a solicitor?"

"Yes, no, I'm not sure."

The police officer seemed stoic, trudging through the paperwork.

"If you have your own, it's quicker. Once the officers have finished searching your premises, they'll come back and question you."

Yes, Anna could have a duty solicitor, but it might take a while, especially on New Year's Eve, especially when there were seven other people before her who required legal assistance. She didn't know, couldn't know, that the Club had already washed its hands of her—no help would be coming from them.

Anna's cell was cold and uncomfortable. There was a metal toilet and an inch thick, blue plastic mat on the bench. She sat shivering, unable to stop the tremors that wracked her body. All along the corridor she could hear the sound of drunks yelling and fighting and swearing. It felt like the grimmest place in the world.

Fear settled inside her, a stone in the pit of her stomach. It wasn't even uncertainty—it was a cold, hard knowledge that her life, as it had been, was over. The photographs of her arrest would last forever, longer than her own lifetime. Her name would forever be associated with the doctor who fucked her patient. Those puny little details of truth—who cared about those?

Anna's future scrolled in front of her: humiliation, public shame, disgrace, dishonour. Her integrity, gone. Her livelihood, gone. Everything she'd worked for, gone.

Someone yelled close to her cell and she startled. The shrieks grew louder as if someone was maddened by pain. On and on they went until Anna felt like screaming with them. It was terrifying and raw and she was so scared.

The screams cut off suddenly, replaced by wild sobbing. Tears slipped down Anna's cheeks and she didn't know if she was crying for herself or the wretched man in the next cell. The noise increased as more drunks were brought in and it felt like she'd fallen into an insane asylum from two hundred years ago.

How could these police officers stand it? The noise, the smell, the stench of despair and defeat?

When she thought she couldn't stand it any longer, an older lady in a Custody Detention Officer uniform brought her a cup of tea in a polystyrene cup.

Such a normal, ordinary thing to do.

Anna hated milky tea, but she was so cold and miserable that she was pathetically grateful.

"Do you think I could have a blanket?" she asked politely, her face haggard, her hands shaking.

The CDO gave her a sympathetic look.

"I could get you one, but I'm not sure you'd want it."

"Why wouldn't I?" Anna asked, wrapping her cold hands around the flimsy white cup.

"Well, they're riddled with scabies and impetigo, but it's your choice."

Anna's eyes widened as she cringed and shook her head.

"You'll be alright, luv," the woman said in a kindly way as the metal door closed with a clang.

But Anna wasn't alright; she was barely holding it together. Tears continued to trickle down her cheeks hopelessly, and she was too tried and despairing to wipe them away. She'd held onto her bladder for hours until she was crying with the pain before she could bring herself to use the disgusting toilet. There was no paper.

She wondered what Nick was doing and where he was. She wanted nothing more than to see him, to hold him, but also prayed that he wouldn't come here.

Her tired brain was tormented by the shrieks and wails surrounding her, the sound of retching and swearing as more and more drunks were brought in to sober up safely.

There were no windows and her wristwatch had been removed, but when a small pre-prepared tray of supper arrived, Anna knew that she must have been there five or six hours. But still, no solicitor came and no one had any news for her.

It was cold and dark, she was scared and alone. So scared, so alone.

The misery was overwhelming.

She wept.

~

Nick grabbed his phone the moment the message came in. But it wasn't from

Anna, and his hope died. Instead, Brendan's name flashed up again with an urgent warning.

He'd been shocked and furious when he'd received the voicemail a short time before. Ignoring his teammates questions, he'd stormed out of the party and had texted Brendan immediately, saying that he was on his way.

But Brendan's message was clear.

> **DO NOT, repeat DO NOT go to the police station!**
> **Do NOT go to Anna's flat.**
> **You'll make things worse.**
> **I need to meet you. Where's safe?**
> **Brendan**

Desperate, Nick tapped out a message, arranging to meet Brendan at a small pub around the corner from the house he shared with the other players, but the place was packed and noisy. Reluctantly, he texted Brendan the address for the house instead, hoping that the journalists had given up and gone to do something more interesting than stalk his house on New Year's Eve.

There was one journalist lurking in a car, but he paid scant attention to Brendan, snapping a couple of photographs that were poorly lit, and simply showed a well-dressed man frowning. Not exactly a money shot.

"How's Anna?" Nick asked, grabbing Brendan's arm.

"Off the cloth!" Brendan snapped, slapping Nick's hands away and shrugging out of his coat. "I've managed to find her a solicitor..."

"What about the Club's solicitor?"

"Doesn't cover her since she's technically self-employed, and don't interrupt. God, I need a drink."

Tense enough to punch a wall, Nick led Brendan into the kitchen-diner and poured him a gin and tonic, even adding a slice of lime. He'd drunk two of these already: low calorie, high kick.

Brendan took a large gulp and slumped into a chair.

"It was murder trying to find a solicitor on New Year's Eve. I've got one, but he can't be there until the morning. Still, marginally better than waiting for the duty solicitor, although I'm beginning to wonder."

"Are you joking? Anna has to stay in a cell all night?"

Brendan's eyes flashed with anger.

"Do you think I like it? You're not the only who cares about her. *You* try finding someone on New Year's Eve."

"Sorry, it's just..."

"I know. The police took her phone, tablet, laptop and searched the flat and office. They're saying that she perjured herself during your court case."

"She didn't!"

"So there's no incriminating evidence to find on any of her devices."

Nick flushed.

"We ... um ... shared some photographs..."

Brendan slapped his hand against his forehead.

"Seriously? Sexting? What is wrong with you? When did it start?"

"It was just a bit of fun while I was playing an away-game. And no, nothing happened until we met again in London."

"Well, that's something. I have receipts for what the police took, but from what I'm told, there's not much chance of getting them back in working order."

"Why not?"

Brendan sighed.

"Well, as I understand it, they'll be given to the police super-hackers to get to any incriminating evidence and then tossed into an evidence room until the next millennium. Apparently, they send all the electronic devices to the hi-tech crime unit, Cy-comms or whatever it's called. They'll access every image, every message, every email. But that could take up to six weeks."

"Six weeks! It's going to take six weeks to clear her name?"

"At least."

"Shit!"

"They'll be able to read any deleted files, too."

Nick frowned.

"That will only prove that she's telling the truth. So that's a good thing."

Brendan looked at him as if he was a rather dim student.

"Nick, her reputation is already ruined. Have you even looked at the gossip sites?"

He huffed impatiently as Nick shook his head.

"Of course you haven't. They've found out about her ex, Jonathan, the married professor; and *your* ex has been mouthing off, too. She's having fun painting Anna as a homewrecker, and the newspapers are lapping it up. They've started describing Anna as someone with a track record of sleeping with inappropriate people. No offence."

"Shit, they know about her ex?"

"Here, read this."

Doctor Heartbreak

Home-wrecking doc, Anna Scott, has a bad track record of sleeping with men who are married or involved with other people. It's been widely reported that she had intimate relations with rugby star Nick Renshaw while he was engaged to his long-term girlfriend, Molly McKinney. Dr. Scott is currently awaiting trial for perjuring herself about the nature of her relationship with the England Fullback while she was "coaching" him at his previous club.

The sexy doc has also been caught on camera with Naughty Nick at his new club, Finchley Phoenixes, breaking a strict no-fraternization policy.

"Rules don't seem to mean much to either of them," a source has been quoted as saying.

It has since been revealed that Dr. Scott had an affair with a married man while he was mentoring her during her college years. Professor Jonathan Frankle, father of three, supervised Anna Scott when she was a student at Boston University. When their affair became public knowledge, the posh Prof was sent on a 'research sabbatical' for a year, while Dr. Scott was banned from the campus and forced to finish her PhD from home. Friends of Professor Frankle described Dr. Scott as 'attractive but manipulative—a dangerous woman who slept her way to the top.' Staff at Boston University were approached, but declined to comment."

Other headlines were on a similar theme:

Love Sick! Sports Psychologist's Shocking Past

Rugby Doctor's Secret Shame

Well, it wasn't secret anymore.

And three other sites had already picked up the news of Anna's arrest.

LIAR! Sports Doc in Arrest Shock!

Anna's a Goner! Naughty Nick's Girlfriend Arrested

Nick tossed Brendan's phone aside in disgust.

"This is such bullshit!"

"With just enough shreds of truth to make it plausible," Brendan added, picking up his phone.

Nick threw him a furious look.

"Hey! I didn't say I believed it, but other people will. For now, at least."

"This is crazy! What can I do?"

Brendan sighed and shook his head.

"The story has already gone viral: sex, sport and celebrities. They're probably hacking *your* phone as we speak."

"Who? The police?"

"No, you muppet! Journalists! Hackers! Newspapers have hackers on call to get into 'phones of interest'. Don't you ever *read* the tabloids?"

Nick pulled his phone from his pocket, staring at the device as if it might bite him. His eyes became angry as he re-read the last message he'd had from Anna hours earlier, before she was arrested:

They know. There are photographers outside

Don't come home tonight. Please.
I love you.

"Have you still got any, you know, *private* pictures or messages or voicemails from Anna on there?"

Nick looked flustered and Brendan had his answer.

"Delete them," he advised. "It's all you can do for her right now."

Nick's heart sank as one by one he deleted all the sexy selfies that she'd sent him, all the pictures he'd sent her, all their sweet and funny text conversations were erased. He even memorized her number before deleting it. It was as if she'd never been in his life.

And the thought of Anna being locked up all night killed him.

"There must be something I can do?"

Brendan shook his head sadly.

"You've done everything you can. Just hope the hackers haven't got hold of your sexting pics."

But Nick was too late, and once again the ghosts were coming back to haunt him.

Before the police had even bagged and tagged the evidence, Nick's second worst nightmare came true and the nude photos started showing up on websites. Nick felt sick as he saw the intimate photographs that Anna had shared with him and him alone, now available for anyone to see.

Molly had done the same, except that she'd received a large pay-out for her tit pics. Along with a rumour that she'd be appearing on the next season of *I'm a Celebrity, Get Me Out of Here*.

CHAPTER TWENTY-FOUR

New Year's Day 2016

Breakfast arrived, another pre-packed airplane meal. Anna choked down as much of it as she could, because even though her stomach attempted to climb out of her throat, she felt weak and dizzy and knew that she needed to eat.

She was relieved beyond words when she was told that her Brief had arrived and was waiting for her in an interview room.

She felt grubby, soiled and defiled when she met her solicitor, an older man wearing a navy three-piece suit and an avuncular smile.

"Miss Scott, I'm Damian Harris. I've been retained on your behalf by Brendan Massey."

"Oh? But you work for the Finchley Phoenixes?"

"No, I'm from the law firm of Weston, Harris and Dempsey." He cleared his throat. "As I understand it, the rugby club's legal cover doesn't stretch to those classed as self-employed."

A cold shudder went through Anna. The Phoenixes had cut her loose. She should have expected that.

The interview began, and Anna was hyper-aware that it was being digitally recorded. Two police officers interviewed her. There was no good cop/bad cop, just two people who looked like they'd had a long night.

The questions went on, going over and over the same ground:

"How long have you known Nick Renshaw? When did you become intimate? Could anybody else vouch for that? Do you have an alibi?"

An alibi for love? What did that look like? Anna had no idea.

After ninety minutes of question and answer, Anna was left alone with her solicitor.

"What will happen now?"

"You'll be released on bail with conditions. They'll be deciding what those conditions are now. If there's no evidence to find..." and he gave her a hard look, "there'll be no case to answer and the charges will be dropped."

"They won't find anything because there's nothing to find." Anna sighed. "How long will it all take?"

"I would imagine two to three months?"

Anna gasped.

"That long?"

"That's quite fast for the justice system. With a high profile case like this, they'll want to get it done and dusted."

"My business will be ruined by then," she cried softly.

"You'll be permitted to go about your business although there'll be restrictions on any travel abroad, I'd imagine."

Anna shook her head.

"I'm finished. I know it."

He patted her hand kindly.

"What if they find me guilty?" she gulped.

"As you've said, there's no evidence to find."

"But what if ... I mean, we had private sessions when he was with the Minotaurs. I didn't record all of them!"

"They need *evidence*," he said, his voice gentle. "A custodial sentence is highly unlikely."

Anna felt faint.

"What happens next, with the investigation, I mean?"

"They'll interview witnesses, neighbours in London, your neighbours in Manchester, and ask whether Mr. Renshaw ever visited you there; they'll speak to your work colleagues and his; they'll analyse your electronic devices as the police explained. Right now, we'll concentrate on getting you out of here, Miss Scott."

"Did they say who told them that I'd committed perjury?"

He shook his head.

"They wouldn't disclose who the informant was, but given what you've told me, I would suggest your partner's ex-girlfriend is a likely candidate. Looking at the reports in the gutter press, I'd say she also seems as if she believes what she's saying."

"How can she?!"

"Hard to say. Delusional? Simply jealous?"

Or just a bitter, scheming bitch.

"Is Nick in any trouble?"

"Unlikely. There's no suggestion that he committed perjury as he wasn't asked during the court case about his relationship with you. You say you had no communication with him prior to the trial and that it was his lawyer who asked you to appear as a character witness. Correct?"

"Yes," Anna whispered.

She'd been caught in a horrendous nightmare, but she couldn't wake up and shake it off. It had ensnared her, dragging her down, down, down, until she couldn't think, couldn't breathe.

The police officers returned thirty minutes later with a sheaf of paperwork.

"You're being released on bail with conditions not to contact Mr. Renshaw."

Anna's mouth dropped open as the police officer continued. All pride gone, she began to sob quietly, hopelessly.

"Should you breach those conditions, you may be liable for further arrest. You're being bailed for two months. If you need to travel abroad, you must notify the police through your solicitor."

Anna stood on shaky feet as Damian Harris escorted her from the room.

"I can't see him *at all?* I can't see Nick?" she pleaded.

Her solicitor's gaze was severe.

"You're to have no contact with him. If you do, you'd be in clear breach of your bail conditions and could be re-interviewed or even re-arrested."

A pit of darkness opened at Anna's feet and she wanted to howl.

"There are photographers outside," he said, more gently. "I have a taxi waiting."

The nightmare continued as Anna stepped from the police station. The shouting and yelling started immediately.

"Did you lie, Anna?"

"How long have you and Nick been seeing each other?"

"Did you do it for the publicity, Anna?"

"Do you feel bad about breaking up Nick's wedding to Molly, Anna?"

"Prefer married men, do you, Anna?"

She ignored them all, keeping her eyes fixed on the ground as Damian moved her toward the taxi as quickly as possible.

Once inside, she sank into the leather seat, exhausted, her body aching, her brain numb.

She knew that she'd have to run the gauntlet again at her apartment, with Damian reminding her not to talk to any journalists.

"Why would I do that?" she muttered.

He gave her a pitying look.

"In my experience, some clients think that giving their side of the story will help. It won't."

Anna's lips turned down.

She longed to see Nick but she couldn't.

She had nothing and no one.

When she walked through her front door, her apartment would be as dark and empty as her heart.

~

Nick was fuming. He paced his small kitchen, fury radiating off him, a murderous look on his face that had Brendan stepping away and putting a table between them.

"What do you mean I can't see her?! This is bloody ridiculous!"

"It's the conditions of bail," Brendan repeated nervously.

"How can they say that I can't see my own girlfriend? Who the fuck do they think they are?!"

"Um, the police?"

"I can't believe this is happening!"

Nick fisted his hair and screwed his eyes shut.

He wanted to hit something, break something, destroy something the way he was feeling destroyed inside.

Despair was mixing with rage. There was no one to fight. There was no way to win.

"It won't be forever," Brendan offered tentatively.

"I need to be there for her!" Nick yelled, making Brendan cringe. Then more quietly, "She was there for me when I needed someone. Fuck! What do I do?"

Brendan chewed his lip anxiously.

"Right now, the only way to help her is to leave her alone."

Nick turned wrathful eyes on Brendan.

"She needs me!"

"Actually, Nick, you're the last thing she needs right now."

"I have to see her!"

Brendan lost his temper.

"This is your fault!" he shouted, stabbing Nick in the chest with his finger. "I'd bet anything that it's your ex-bimbo who leaked all these lies to the newspapers. It's because of *your* court case that this whole fiasco has ended up with Annie being accused of perjury! It's all because of you! And now you want to be a macho man and ignore her bail conditions. Isn't her having to spend one night in the cells enough for you? Do you want to see her end up in prison, too?"

Nick felt as if he'd been kicked in the chest, and he couldn't breathe.

"You have to leave her alone," Brendan said firmly.

Nick was defeated. Brendan was right—it was all Nick's fault.

"Tell her ... tell her I'm sorry. Tell her I love her, that I'll wait for her. And we'll get through this."

"I will, I'll tell her."

Nick rubbed his forehead as he slumped into a hard wooden chair, resting his elbows on the kitchen table.

"This can't be happening!"

But it was.

~

Stony faced, Anna ignored the reporters who clamoured outside her apartment. She wanted to yell at them, scream at them, *You've already had your pound of flesh! Go away! Go away! Leave me alone!* But she couldn't. Silence was her only defence.

She hurried inside, slamming the door behind her.

But she wasn't by herself after all—there was someone waiting for her.

"Brendan!"

"Oh, Annie!"

She fell into his arms and sobbed, letting out the tears that she'd tried so hard to hold inside.

He led her to the sofa where she and Nick had sat together so many times.

"He wanted to be here, Annie, but he's not allowed to, you know that. He told me to tell you that he's sorry, that he loves you and that he'll wait for you. I'm not allowed to take or receive any further messages, but he means it, Annie, I know he does. He was beside himself. We waited at his flat all night for news." He paused. "And there's something else you should know..."

"Oh God! What now?"

"Uh, well, they've started printing stories about your ex ... some professor guy named Jonathan Frankle."

"Oh my God! What are they saying?"

Brendan grimaced.

"That it's your M.O.—find a married man, well, an unavailable guy and ... you know..."

His words trailed off.

"I can't believe this! When will it end?"

"I'll make you a cup of tea before I tell you the rest," he said, patting her arm soothingly.

Anna blanched. "There's more."

Brendan closed his eyes as if in pain.

"Tell me!"

"Your ... um ... phones have been hacked."

"Oh no! The police warned me ... I can't believe it's happened already?"

"'Fraid so."

"The *private* photographs?"

"Yes."

Anna looked away, hurt and ashamed. Now she was a victim as well as a suspect. What else would the world throw at her?

Brendan stayed for an hour, but there was nothing for him to do and Anna was craving the sanctuary of her bedroom.

Brendan unplugged her landline and gave her a cheap pay-as-you-go for emergencies. He really was the best P.A. a woman could want, the best friend.

Once he'd gone, the apartment was eerily silent. No phones ringing, no Nick laughing or singing in the shower, no emails to check, no work to do. No one to help her through the agonising misery.

She took a long, hot bath, collapsed into bed and cried herself to sleep.

But Anna didn't sleep well. She tossed and turned, chased by nightmares and nameless, faceless threats. When she finally gave up trying to rest, she plodded into the kitchen to make coffee, feeling tired and stripped raw. Peering out of the window, she saw that there was a different reporter's car parked outside. Surely they had something better to do on a public holiday? Apparently not.

Wondering if it was a good idea, she plugged the landline back in and jumped when it rang immediately, sighing with relief when she saw her mother's name pop up; she longed to hear her voice.

"Mom! It's so good to hear from you. How are you? How's Dad?"

"Oh, Anna, sweetheart!"

"I'm so sorry about the photographs. I don't know how they hacked them, but, oh God, I'm so sorry! Has Dad seen them?"

Her mother's voice soft and broken, the words interrupted by muffled sobs.

"Mom! Are you okay? Where's Dad?"

Her words jarred to a halt as her mother continued to cry quietly.

"Mom, please!"

Her mother took a gasping breath.

"Your father ... he's had a stroke."

"What? Oh my God!"

Guilt clamped a cold hand around Anna's heart. Because of the photographs? *Because of me?*

"All that red meat, and butter on everything. I kept telling him, but he wouldn't listen. You know your father."

"Mom?" Anna's voice cracked. "Is he...? Is he...?"

"We're at Phelps Memorial Hospital. I don't know, Anna. It was a major stroke. I don't know..."

Tears streaked Anna's face as she fought to stay calm for her mother's sake, but the shock was too great, and she took great gulps of air before she tried to speak again.

"I'll get the first flight home."

Her mother didn't even try to argue with her.

She didn't care that she wasn't allowed to leave the country. She didn't care that she might be committing another crime. All she cared about was getting to her dad as quickly as she could.

While she waited impatiently for the first available flight, she emailed her plans to her lawyer. If the British police wanted her, they could damn well come and find her.

It was fifteen hours before Anna arrived at the 236-bed hospital of Tarrytown, an hour north of New York City.

By then, the nude photographs of her had gone viral, but she didn't have it in her to care.

～

"Can I stop more of the photographs being published?" Nick asked the Club's solicitor.

The man sighed.

"Once the images are out there, it's very hard to get them taken down for good. You can try, but they tend to pop up on other websites. You'll be chasing your tail ... and it's expensive to pursue."

"I don't care about that! Just do it!"

Both Nick and Anna's phones had been hacked. Even though they'd had security passwords, it hadn't slowed the hackers for even a minute. It was a wakeup call to realise how easily an expert hacker could gain access without even having to touch the devices. It had all been done remotely.

Giovanni's 'dick pic' that he'd taken with Nick's phone did the rounds of some of the gossip sites but with all of them attributing the shot to Nick. That pissed him for another reason—Giovanni's dick was nowhere as impressive as his own.

But it was the photographs of Anna posing for him that made him slam his locker door and swear loudly as the other players tried to calm him down.

"At least she looks hot, mate," Jason grinned, which was *not* the best thing to say.

Nick grabbed him by his shirt.

"Don't! Just ... don't!"

Jason raised his hands in the air, looking about him worriedly.

"I'm just saying..."

"Shut up!"

"I would listen to him, *amico*," Giovanni said quietly.

The team supported him and the Club stood by him, but none of that helped Anna.

Molly was loving the publicity. As much as possible, she was trying to keep it focussed on her and not Anna. There were photographs of her in skimpy outfits, doing Page Three 'glamour' shots, and she appeared on a couple of cheap online talk shows. She was enjoying her fifteen minutes of fame, and eking out every additional second she could.

Jonathan was also basking in the attention, describing himself in several articles as a "committed family man", making Anna sound like a stalker who'd blackmailed him into a relationship. He also managed to phrase it to seem as if he'd taken pity on her because she was "unstable".

In the same way that possession is nine-tenths of the law, getting out your version of events first played best in social media.

Nick vented his fury in the gym, beating the shit out of a punch bag.

Late one evening, he called Molly.

"Nicky, this is a surprise—not a particularly pleasant one."

"Why did you do it, Mol?"

Her tone was wary.

"Are you recording this?"

Nick laughed unhappily.

"No, just you and me. Unless *you're* recording it. Going to make a few more bob, are you, Mol?"

"Fuck off!"

"I will, when I've said what I want to say. I never cheated on you. Never. Not once. Not even when chances were right in front of me and I knew you wouldn't find out. Not with Anna, not with anyone. You and me were long over when I started seeing Anna. And you know me well enough—you know I'm telling the truth. So I'm asking you again, why did you do it?"

He listened to her breathing, wondering if he'd ever get an answer.

"You deserved it."

"Hitting you was an accident, you know that."

"You broke my fucking nose!"

Nick hung his head.

"I am sorry about that. But did I deserve you cheating on me with Kenny? I was good to you. I treated you well."

"You never loved me."

"What?! I did everything for you! Everything! I was going to marry you!"

"I was an afterthought. You only cared about rugby. You were so moody and miserable when you were injured. I was sick of you feeling sorry for yourself."

Nick was shocked.

"I thought I'd never play again! Yeah, you could say I wasn't exactly happy about that! It was supposed to be for better or worse."

"It seemed like worse to me," she snapped back.

"You didn't care what harm it would do?"

"You've got to look out for yourself, because no one else will."

Her voice was hard and cold.

"That's where you're wrong, Mol."

"Don't be so fucking holier than thou! You're just the same as me, only you won't admit it! You've got your fancy car and your fancy woman, and what have I got? Nothing! It isn't fair!"

Nick didn't bother to reply. He simply ended the call. It hadn't made him feel any better; it hadn't really answered any questions. Molly was a jealous bitch, and she'd never admit she did anything wrong. But it did make him wonder: how the hell could he have ever wanted to marry her? When he thought about how Anna made him feel, he knew that Molly was right—he'd never really loved her.

Great. Something else to feel guilty about.

~

Anna peeled off some bills and thrust them at the cab driver, yelling, "Keep the change!" as she ran toward the hospital entrance.

The driver had stared at her like he couldn't figure out why he knew her face.

Anna had ignored all his attempts at conversation during the drive from the airport.

It was almost ridiculous to run now, but she had to. For her own sanity, she needed the momentum, she needed her father to know that she'd gotten to him as fast as she could.

Her new cell phone had been turned on since she stepped off the plane at JFK, but her mother hadn't replied to her texts and Anna had been too scared to call her.

Adrenaline made her shake as she waited breathlessly for the hospital's receptionist to tell her where they were keeping her father, and then she ran up two flights of stairs and down a long corridor until she skidded to a halt outside his room.

Unable to stop her hands from trembling, she peered through the window and saw her mother sitting next to a hospital bed.

Anna pushed open the door gently.

"Mom?"

Her mother spoke without turning her head.

"Anna's here, Gary. Open your eyes for her, please, baby."

Anna stared down at her father's grey face, sagging on the right side, his right hand curled into a claw.

"Oh, Daddy!"

She knelt on the hard floor and put one arm around her mother's waist, resting her free hand on top of her father's.

"I'm here, Daddy. Please wake up now. I love you so much. Please, Daddy!"

His left eye twitched and Anna's mother took it for a sign, squeezing her daughter's hand.

"He knows you're here! Talk to him again, sweetheart."

"I've missed you so much, Daddy. If I'd known you'd be laying around in bed..." but she couldn't finish the joke and tears came again. "I'm so sorry, Daddy. I'm so sorry I disappointed you." Her sobs came faster now. "All I've ever wanted to do is to make you proud. Please wake up, Daddy."

"He can hear you, honey. I'm sure he can hear you," and her mother turned to Anna, wiping the tears on her cheeks. "He's *always* been proud of you. Always. We both have. He missed you so much while you were away, but he was proud of everything you achieved." Then her eyes turned back to her husband. "Gary, Anna's here. Time to wake up now."

Gary Scott was a big man, an ex-pro footballer, tall and broad with a tendency to gain weight once he'd passed fifty. But he was a fine-looking man; everyone said so. Seeing him in that hospital bed, pale and diminished, it was the worst feeling in the world.

Anna pulled up a chair and sat on the opposite side of the bed from her mother, each of them holding one of his hands. They spoke quietly through the still of the night, and each hour they watched the man who was their rock slip away from them.

Dawn came quietly, a whisper of light on the horizon, and Anna rubbed her eyes. She gazed down at her father and stroked his hand.

"I love you, Daddy. So much. Please wake up. Please wake up, Daddy."

But there would be no more waking up for Gary Scott, and an hour later, on January 4th, he slipped away.

Anna and her mother clung to each other with the stunned faces of shipwreck survivors. And when they couldn't cry anymore, a kindly nurse led them to a quiet room and took them through the paperwork, telling them what to expect now, who to contact and what to do about the funeral.

Anna could barely take it in. Neither she nor her mother had slept more than a handful of hours in the last two days. The nurse understood that and calmly, gently told them to take their time.

All that they had left was time. And each other.

After a while, there was no point staying at the hospital. Gary Scott's body might still be there, but his spirit was gone; the beautiful soul that made him the energetic vital man he'd always been was gone.

Anna's mother stared at the watery sun struggling to climb in the sky.

"He would have hated it, you know," she said. "He wouldn't have wanted to survive that. He hated any sort of illness. He never stopped complaining about the ache in his knees on damp days, or the cold in his bones in the winter. He was talking about moving to Florida, but he'd never have done it." She turned to face Anna. "He didn't want to grow old. Now he never will."

Anna wrapped her arms around her mother, and they held each other as the grey clouds hung dark and ominous above them. But what are clouds when the worst has already happened?

Anna took her mother's car keys and drove them both home. During that short, twenty minute drive, their roles reversed, and Anna became the parent.

She guided her mother through the house, knelt to take off her shoes, quietly bringing her hot tea, then undressing her and putting her to bed.

She sat alone in the kitchen, staring out at the trees stripped bare in the back yard. Their skeletal arms, dark and black, waved at her in the bitter wind.

She sipped her tea, clasping the mug until it grew cold.

The radiators ticked softly, the pipes humming and rumbling. Her dad never had gotten around to draining the air out of them.

Her head dropped into her hands and her hopeless tears came again.

14th January 2016

There's so much to do to organise a funeral. So many things to think about. And the last thing you want to do is discuss catering or flowers or any of those thousand things you have to decide on. And when the person who has passed has been well known in his time, there's double the work.

The Health and Care Professions Council didn't let this get in the way of the wheels of their justice. The investigation must have been unusually rapid, because on the day before her father's funeral, Anna woke up to read an email from them.

She should care what they said, knowing they had the power to end her career, but she didn't.

She read the words slowly, misery dragging her down.

> *Dear Dr. Scott,*
>
> *As you were unable to attend a ruling on your relationship with a former client, we have taken the unusual step of informing you of our decision by electronic mail.*
>
> *You have admitted breaching professional boundaries by engaging in a personal and sexual relationship with the service user. You have further acknowledged that your actions constituted misconduct and as such, we conclude that your fitness to practise was impaired as a result.*
>
> *Dating former patients is flawed and risks undermining the public's trust in the profession. Further, you have breached the HCPC's ethical guidelines and we are therefore withdrawing your licence to practise forthwith.*
>
> *Yours sincerely,*

More than once Anna wished she'd never met Nick Renshaw. But Fate wasn't paying much attention to what she wished or what she wanted. She didn't believe that 'things happen for a reason'. That's just what people told themselves to feel better.

But I did meet him and I made a lot of wrong decisions.

Her life had changed for good, for bad—changed permanently and irrevocably.

Damn his beautiful face. Damn his beautiful body. Been there, done that, got the scars to prove it.

Anna read the email twice more, then quietly deleted it.

She had work to do.

She put a notice in the local newspaper and sent emails to news desks and city sports desks, announcing her father's passing. The florist had to be contacted, a menu finalized with the caterer for the gathering after the funeral, the minister briefed, the guest list updated.

Anna took charge of the paperwork, notifying her father's insurers, pension, bank, clients and clubs—so many people, all sad, all sorry, all moving on with their lives. And then there was Anna, with no clue how to do that. Just another day to get through. Another day to fall asleep at the kitchen table because half a bottle of vodka was the only peace you could find in your life.

The day of the funeral was bitterly cold, an icy wind feathering the ground with flurries of snow that hung on trees and branches, and drifted into soft, silent mounds.

The small church was packed, people standing at the back, and even a local TV crew attended because her father had been somebody. The minister talked about the impact he had as an NFL player, the years as a coach, and his charity work with young athletes from disadvantaged backgrounds. If anyone knew of the scandal surrounding Anna, it wasn't obvious.

Her father's drinking buddies arrived, awkward in out-of-date suits and sober ties, and his football friends filled the aisle with their broad shoulders and broader bellies. Her mother's friends wore navy or black, and whispered that they'd bring food later.

Her father had been loved and admired, and that was something. But it felt as if her hands were empty even as she wrapped them around her mother, who was graceful in her grief, offering brave smiles to friends and distant cousins that Anna didn't recognise.

There was one other person there, and Anna felt him before she saw him.

She felt a prickle on her skin, and turned. From the corner of her eye, she saw Nick watching her, his expression troubled. He nodded, but didn't move towards her, and for that she was grateful. She didn't have the strength to talk to him, even if she'd had anything to say, but something about his silent presence soothed her.

The service ran over time because so many people wanted to share their memories of the great Gary Scott. Anna smiled through her tears, knowing it was exactly what her dad would have wanted—laughter and slightly off-colour locker room jokes. Her mom smiled sometimes but seemed absent, except for the moments when tears slid down her rouged cheeks.

When they finally faced the interment, the ground was iron hard and the weather deteriorating. The minister rushed through the words as the mourners turned blue with cold and stamped their feet.

Anna's mother placed a bouquet of black-eyed-Susie's on the coffin, because those had been his favourites—bright yellow and full of sunshine, just like her, he used to say. Anna laid a single sunflower on top and held her mother as their tears froze and their teeth chattered.

When the coffin was lowered into the ground, it didn't seem possible that such a large presence had left the world, and Anna felt her father's absence bitterly.

Everyone else was grateful to leave the grim and grey churchyard for the warmth of Anna's mother's house. They drank toasts to Gary Scott's memory and ate the sandwiches and quiches, and forked pie into their mouths that opened and closed like hungry birds.

Nick had disappeared into the crowds of people without speaking, but Anna knew that he'd be back. He wasn't a man who gave in without a fight. She hadn't spoken to him since that terrible day—the thought of starting now was too much. Too much. And her throat closed with horror.

As the last stragglers left, a town car pulled up outside the house, and Anna's heart began to beat wildly. She stood with her back pressed against the door as if her thin, stick-like arms could keep him out. When he knocked, it reverberated through her fragile frame. She didn't want to answer, but knew her mother would hear and ask questions that Anna would rather not answer.

Slowly, reluctantly, she opened the door and stared.

"Anna."

He wore a heavy overcoat, but his hands were bare. Those long fingers with the blunt nails that had touched her so many times, seemed vulnerable in the icy grip of winter.

She hardened her heart, her breath misting in front of her.

"I'm sorry for your loss. He sounded like a great guy. I wish I'd known him."

"Thank you."

"Can we talk?" his eyes pleaded with her.

"You know we can't. You shouldn't even be here."

His head drooped.

"I had to. I couldn't let you go through this alone," he said softly. "I miss you."

She'd missed him, too. Missed his soft Yorkshire accent, those flattened, drawn-out vowels. Missed his warmth. Missed his kindness. Missed his body wrapped around hers, pressing down on her, inside her. Above all, she missed his love. And here he was, offering it to her again. But it was too late to heal the wounds.

"Please, Anna. We need to talk."

She lifted her chin and forced herself to meet his gaze.

"I'm *not allowed* to have any contact with you. Those are the conditions of my bail. You know this."

"That won't be forever. They'll see from the phone records that we weren't lying. It's just a matter of time. I'll wait for you."

"Don't."

"Of course I'm going to wait for you!" he cried out in frustration.

"I don't even know if I'll go back to London. It's not like I have a career left. I've lost every client. Brendan did his best, but they all cited broken contracts because of the morality clause." She laughed bitterly.

Nick took a shocked breath and his eyes filled with sympathy.

"They didn't even wait for the police to finish investigating. I'm guilty—judged by the public and the Press."

"It's all my fault. Let me make it better!"

"You're going to make it better?" her voice was as cold as the wind that whipped Nick's coat around him and cut through Anna's thin black dress.

He saw a delicate gold chain around her neck and hoped that she was wearing the gold rugby pendant that he'd given her. Hoped, but couldn't be sure.

"How exactly are you going to make it better?"

Ice in her heart, ice in her words. Nick blanched.

"Well, I..."

"No, let me guess," she folded her arms and glanced over his shoulder, staring at the scudding clouds with a ferocity that chilled him. "Did you know that the Health and Care Professions Council revoked my licence to practise?"

Nick sucked in a breath and closed his eyes.

"But if we tell them the truth..."

"Really? I only broke the morality/no-fraternization clause a little? You'll go to them and tell them we're sorry and we won't do it again, then ask them nicely if they'll give me back my licence to practise. Is that what you were going to do? No?"

She knew she was being a bitch but she couldn't stop the juggernaut of emotions. She felt overwhelmed one minute, empty and lost the next. Seeing Nick was too much, just too much.

"Anna..."

He saw the moment that she started shutting down, closing him out. Her eyes drifted across the familiar planes and angles of his beautiful face with the blankness of a stranger, then she met his eyes.

She knew exactly what to say.

"There's nothing for me in London now."

Nick's gaze turned fierce, and Anna could see the determination in his eyes. He wanted her to fight, not give up.

And she couldn't do that to him.

She lifted her chin and met his heated gaze.

"I wish I'd never met you."

And then she closed the door, a soft click as she locked it.

Disbelieving, Nick leaned his head against the door, then turned on his heel, a curse dropping from his lips as he strode back to the waiting car.

CHAPTER TWENTY-FIVE

FEBRUARY 2016

Nick had moved on.

It hurt Anna to admit that, but it was true. She'd told him to go, practically thrown him out after her father's funeral, so what could she expect?

But it didn't stop tears hovering in her eyes.

Unable to help herself, she searched for all the evidence she could find that Nick had returned to his so-called bad boy ways.

There were photographs of him at three different events with four different women—all attractive, all blondes, and two of them were married.

The newspapers were enjoying their lurid headlines.

PLAYING THE FIELD!
Wife-swapping scandal of top rugby players
Notorious womanising bad boy Nick Renshaw raised eyebrows when he was seen at Soho House last night with a bevy of blonde beauties.

"He arrived with one woman, but soon after another joined them. They were flirting with him all night and Nick was definitely enjoying himself," said an eyewitness. "He disappeared with one of them for ages. Everyone was talking about it."

The mystery blonde has been identified as Madeleine Dubois, wife of Naughty Nick's teammate, Bernard Dubois. Astonishingly, the second woman on the arm of the rugby bad boy was soap actress Kimmy Clayton, new wife of footballer Alan Clayton.

Since Nick cheated on his fiancée, reality star Molly McKinney, with his former club doctor, the star Fullback has been seen with a string of different women. [See page 7, 8 and 9 for photographs.]

Anna closed the laptop and rubbed her arms. She was cold, so cold. Cold inside.

～

It was the night before the big match, Nick's first international cap for England. He should have been excited and happy, the promise of all those years fulfilled.

But he was still reeling from the outrageous newspaper allegations and the implication that he was a womanising bastard who couldn't keep it in his pants.

It was such a distortion of the truth that it should have been laughable. Instead, he'd been hauled into a meeting with the Club's management for disciplinary proceedings. It was only after Bernard backed him up that the Club's PR team retained a libel lawyer to sue the newspapers who'd run the story. But these things took time. Most people believed there was no smoke without fire.

Was this his life now? Anyone could make up lies about him and it was published as Gospel truth?

Bernard had apologised over and over, but the damage had been done. Besides, it wasn't Bernard's fault that he'd been delayed and was late getting to the party, so had asked Nick to look after Madeleine. And it definitely wasn't Madeleine's fault that her new pregnancy made her nauseous and Nick had been worried enough to hang around outside the ladies' bathroom when she became sick. It wasn't even Kimmy Clayton's fault because they'd only met that evening when she'd spent five minutes advising Madeleine on the best way to get through morning sickness.

For some reason, the newspapers seemed determined to portray him as a hole-chasing playboy. They liked their bad boys, and when they couldn't find them, enjoyed manufacturing them. Jason had told him to go with the flow and make the most of the opportunities it threw Nick's way. He certainly had a lot more chances for one-night stands.

But he missed Anna, the ache of a phantom limb: the pain was acute, even though the limb was no longer there.

He hoped like hell that she hadn't read any of the fake news reports.

Moodily, he rubbed his ankle, feeling the thicker scar tissue, faded to white now. Imagining a twinge, he popped a couple of painkillers, ignoring the memory of Anna's face when she'd found him doing that months ago.

Irritated with his own company, he picked up his long neglected guitar and experimentally strummed the strings. It was horribly out of tune and Nick winced.

He spent several minutes tweaking the pegs, getting it to the right pitch. There was only one song that he felt in his heart when he was feeling blue.

At half-speed, he sang the lyrics of Tracy Chapman's *Talkin' 'Bout A Revolution*.

The words meant a lot to him. He was still afraid he'd be one of those guys standing in a welfare line. The image haunted him; it could still happen.

There was no Anna to talk him out of his funk. He could have called Trish, but she'd done enough for him already. She wasn't there just to drag him from depression yet again.

He sang alone in his room, his voice low and melodic, but when he looked up Giovanni was watching him, sympathy and understanding in his eyes.

"But of course you sing about love. A revolution of the heart perhaps, *mi amico*. What else is there? We Italians understand this."

Nick didn't answer and went back to playing his guitar, alone in his room, alone with his thoughts.

England V Ireland, Rugby World Cup, Qualifier Match

Dear Nick Renshaw,

My name is Eloise Higginbotham and we met at my school, St. Aubyn's High School in Cheshire when you was with the Manchester Minotaurs.

You was well cool and told our Head, Mrs. Herman, that us girls should be allowed to play rugby if we wanted to. It took ages, but we got together with another school, Hale Secondary School, and started a team with the girls there. They was a bit up themselves at first, but now they're ok. We're in a proper league and everything and Malcolm, the Coach, he says I'm really good and could get into the County team.

My mum is a big fan of yours as well. She saw them photos of you and your missus in the paper and thought they was well hot. She told me that you're going to be playing for England and I read an article about you. That's what I want to do. I want to play for the Women's Rugby Team for England. I'm going to do it one day.

If you hadn't come to my school, none of this would have happened. Well, it might, but maybe not. That's a bit scary, because I love playing rugby. I effing love it. Everyone always told me that girls can't play it, but you didn't. You were all like, yeah, she can play if she wants.

Thank you for everything.

Play awesome for your match against the Irish. I'll be cheering for you.

Your friend,

Eloise xoxoxoxox

Nick read the letter again. It had been delivered to the Phoenixes' clubhouse, and had only just now reached him. It was written on a piece of paper torn from a notebook and drenched in strong perfume. Eloise had used a glittery pen and decorated the paper with tiny hearts and big, loopy flowers.

He remembered her, remembered the day he met her. Visiting the high school had been Anna's idea. She'd accused him of being jaded, and thinking back, she'd been right.

Being with the kids and watching their excitement and passion for the game had given him the kick he needed at the time.

And even though she didn't know it, little Eloise had given him another kick today. He could see her in his mind's eye, thundering up and down the field, legs like tree trunks, looking as if she'd run right over anyone who got in her way given half a chance, and then she'd smiled so big when he'd praised her speed and drop kick.

Nick's mood was determined.

It had been a month since he'd spoken to Anna, a whole month since her father's funeral. She'd looked so fragile, so broken and nothing he'd done had helped. He'd wanted to be with her, to support her. He loathed those stupid, cruel bail conditions that meant he couldn't. Nick couldn't even hold her when she needed him most.

He knew Brendan had heard from her but was under strict instructions not to pass anything on to Nick. In desperation, he'd phoned Anna's mother. She'd been distant, polite, but had made it very clear that his call wasn't welcome.

He'd almost believed Anna when she said she wished she'd never met him. Almost, but the emptiness in her eyes had been betrayed by a quiver in her pale lips, a convulsion of her hands as if she was reaching for him.

As soon as the police realised that she'd told the truth, he was going to her, he'd force her to listen.

Fury darkened his vision and he fought to bring his breathing under control. Fucking up was not an option.

The police case was dragging on, and although the Press interest had died down, Nick felt like he was living on a knife edge. The nude photographs had continued to crop up on different websites and although the police had filed his complaint, they didn't hold out much hope that anyone would ever be prosecuted. They'd wearily informed him not to keep 'private' images on his phone anymore. That horse had bolted, jumped a fence, and won a couple of derbies since he'd locked the stable door on the police's advice.

Sim Andrews had benched him for two games for breaking the no-fraternization clause and fined him £5,000, but since then, he'd been allowed to play again. Not that he cared about the money, but he did care about the damage he'd done to Anna's reputation. It had been reported with relish by all the newspapers that her licence to practise had been revoked. Without that, she seemed to have given up. At least, that's what Brendan said. She'd also been forced to pass all of her business and few remaining contracts to the man who'd taken over her Manchester branch. He'd also taken over her lease on the office building and apartment, and had kept Brendan on, too.

To everyone else, it was as if Anna had never existed, and Nick hated that. Hated that everything she'd done, all her work, all her hours of helping teams and different players appeared to have been forgotten and erased. She'd been airbrushed from the Club's history.

But Nick's aching loneliness was sharp and painful. He forced himself on, forced himself each day to choose the path that would make her proud, even as he died a little inside.

He wasn't sure when he'd fallen in love with her, he was only sure that he had. Each smile, every hour he'd spent with her—they'd been the best of his life. Although he hadn't really *fallen* into love. It hadn't been a wild tumble, a jump over a cliff; it had been a slow, sweet warmth stealing through his body, like the rising sun.

He hated that Molly had won. Whatever her twisted game had been, she'd ruined Anna's life, nearly destroyed Nick, and then waltzed away with money in the bank, a new career as a reality TV 'star', and a squeaky-clean image as a woman betrayed. The fucking irony.

But Nick wasn't destroyed and he wasn't defeated.

He'd achieved his dream—he was representing his country, he was playing for England. Today should have been one of the best days of his life. But the woman he loved more than his next breath was 3,000 miles away and a world apart.

He had a message for her.

~

All across Britain, millions of people were tuning in their TVs to the BBC's World Cup coverage.

[Rugby World Cup: Titles and music, cue VT of England team]

BBC Studio Head: We're going live in five, four, *[gestures: three, two, one]*

Jimmy Smith: Welcome to *Rugby Today*! We're here, live, at Twickenham along with 82,000 fans, and it's a big day for England's rugby team as they begin their World Cup bid against a strong team fielded by the Irish. The sun is out but it's a frosty day. It's not stopping the fans though, and we can hear them singing from the commentary box. To talk us through the match, I'm here with a man who's been there himself, known as 'the Rocket' when he played for Bradford Bulls, and he'll know exactly how the players are feeling right now. Stuart Reardon, you were a professional player for sixteen years, notably with the Bulls and AS Carcasonne, and you were capped for your country fifteen times. Stuart, welcome.

Stuart Reardon: Thanks, Jimmy. It's good to be here.

Jimmy Smith: You must have a lot of memories at Twickenham.

Stuart Reardon: Yes, some of the best days of my life have been on match days here. It's the home of rugby.

Jimmy Smith: So, Stuart, talk us through England's chances today. They're a young team with a new coach. I think we need to talk about Eddie Jones' choices for the team. As a new manager, he obviously wants to put his stamp on things, but eyebrows have definitely been raised by his choice of Fullback, Nick Renshaw wearing the number 17 jersey. This time last year, Renshaw was on a long-term injury list, then he was dropped by his club, and he'd never played in the Premiership. True, he's had a terrific run this season with the Finchley Phoenixes, but is it enough to make him a useful part of the England team? Talk us through what Eddie Jones might have been thinking in picking Renshaw?

Stuart Reardon: Well, Jimmy, I think Eddie Jones must have seen something in Nick a while back. He watched him coming up as a young player. Although he's not had much Premiership experience, it could well be because he had chances to move up the leagues in the past, but chose to stay loyal to the club where he started.
He's had a tough injury, but he's been determined to come back. Before the injury he was outstanding for Rotherham, easily the best player, year in, year out. Everyone deserves a second chance. He's fully fit now. I like what I see in him and it's a new club, new start. He's in a good headspace so it's a prime time to give him a chance. I like his style of play; he's very fast, sees openings, so I don't think Eddie Jones sees it as a gamble. He thinks Nick Renshaw can show us what he can do. This is the Coach changing things up, he wants to see them playing his way. Bringing in new players is how you do it.
As you know, Jimmy, anyone can get injured in this game, and many of them come back stronger and tougher than they were before because they've been through the pain. And don't forget, a lot of teams sign up players coming back from injury because they can get them a little cheaper than what they would have gone for otherwise.

Jimmy Smith: That's a bit cynical, Stuart.

Stuart Reardon: It's just the way it is, we all know it. It's a tough

game. And there's no reason that Nick Renshaw won't play amazing today and in the rest of his Premiership season.
I know Eddie Jones personally and I've spoken to him about this. I know there's been a lot of media speculation. Eddie Jones rates Nick as a player and has followed his career for years, that's why he's given him a shot as starting Fullback—they've got a good bond.

Jimmy Smith: Nick Renshaw's personal problems have been all over social media lately. Will that affect his game?

Stuart Reardon: He'll be putting all that out of his head and concentrating on what he's got to do today. When you're in a match situation, you can't let anything else mess around with your head. He'll be getting in the zone, making sure he's in the right head space.

Jimmy Smith: Well, we certainly wish Nick good luck. Now, how do you rate England's chances against the Ireland team?

Stuart Reardon: The ground looks frosty, so there'll be slippery conditions. It'll change the way they play: they'll keep the game tight, keep the passes short. The team that keeps the mistakes down to the minimum and controls the ball will win the game. We must complete the sets, which means it's more of a Forwards game when the field's frosty or there's wet conditions. It makes it a tighter game, rather than a free-flowing, passing game. [*smiles big*] Yeah, we'll beat the Irish easy!

Nick was focussed and intense as he followed his teammates out onto the field. A great roar went up and it felt like walking into a wall of sound, so loud he couldn't hear Jason speak, even though he was standing next to him. Half of the stands were shamrock green and the other half were white and red, the flag of St. George waving everywhere.

Nick knew what he had to do. A sense of calm descended on him and he barely saw the fans singing and yelling in the stadium.

As the National Anthem rang out, he stood tall and proud as he sang the dignified words, determined to prove himself—to his teammates, to his Club, to his country, to himself. And to Anna. He had to prove himself to Anna. He had to prove his love.

As the words died away and the roar of the crowd shook the air, Nick jogged into position, his heart thundering as the whistle blew and he flew forwards, as fast and direct as an arrow.

"The young guns in the back have a lot to prove, but look at Nick Renshaw go! He doesn't know that this match is 80 minutes long! He thinks he's got to win it in the first minute! Look at him go! And he's scored a try with just 32 seconds on the clock! I've never seen anything like that. Do you think he'll crack a smile? Not today! Jason Oduba makes a conversion from that amazing run. The try-scorer calls for the re-start and takes it.

"The set pieces are going to be important. If you can't get the line-out right, Ireland will be in trouble. They're going to struggle. Dylan Hartley, his first throw. Danny Care, to Farrell, a chance here for England! Johnny May coming up his left wing. Holt passes. Dan Cole, the Prop, takes the inside left ... it's loose! Hartley scoops it up ... well picked up. Farrell again ... that's what they want the powerful number 8 to do, take out two defenders. Farrell ... good pass away to Renshaw. Another chance for Renshaw in his first capped game. Renshaw's passing to ... no, he's faked it, he's going to run, he's going all the way ... he's going to make it ... no, the Irish defence is ... yes, he's through, he's going all the way! Renshaw scores his second try! And the crowd are on their feet! England are in the lead! They're in the lead!"

Later, Nick would only remember flashes of the game, but he didn't put a foot wrong and England won 47-23, putting them through as one of the qualifying countries for the World Cup.

He only looked up to acknowledge the crowd at the end, raising his hands in the air and applauding them as they yelled his name.

His white kit was streaked with mud and the red rose, the symbol of England, had taken a battering. Sweat soaked his body but the myriad aches and pains were something he'd only feel later.

The BBC commentator strode forward with a microphone in his hand.

"Nick Renshaw! Man of the Match, three tries and a dropkick goal! You must be feeling pretty good about now!"

Nick turned to gaze at the interviewer whose wide smile matched his excited expression. Nick drew his eyebrows together in a small frown. Then he turned his head to stare straight at the camera...

When your world crashes down...
When they say you're all out...
When your mind is broken...
I will rise...
I will return...
And I will be undefeated."

The TV presenter stared dumbfounded as Nick walked out of camera shot.

"Um, well, that was Nick Renshaw, Man of the Match, and clearly a man of few words."

"You know, Jimmy, that must be the strangest post-match interview since

Eric Cantona said in a press conference, 'When the seagulls follow the trawler, it's because they think sardines will be thrown into the sea'."

"Yes, Roy, it's definitely up there."

Three thousand miles away, Anna gasped, her heart pounding as she watched the match on her mother's laptop. Because she knew *exactly* what Nick meant—it was a message to her. It had to be!

He was telling her not to give up, and that he still loved her.

Anna's mother lowered her book and peered at Anna over her glasses.

"What was all that about?"

Anna closed the laptop, her face flushed.

"You remember what I was like after ... after Jonathan?"

Her mother raised her eyebrows and nodded.

"Of course I do."

"Yes, sorry. It's just when I was trying to put my life back together, I came up with a mantra, words that meant something to me; something to remind me that I'm stronger than I think I am." She turned around to meet her mother's eyes. "I shared those words with Nick when he was at a low point in his life. He liked them. But I didn't know..."

Tears glistened on her long lashes as she dropped her gaze.

"I didn't know that he'd remembered them."

She wiped a stray tear and glanced up at her mother.

"Anna, honey, come here!"

Willingly, she went to her mother, kneeling at her feet and wrapping her arms around her mother's waist, just like she had when she was a child, drawing comfort from her mother's softness and warmth.

"Oh sweetheart, it's been so wonderful having you here. I couldn't have done all of this without you."

"You don't have to, Mom. I'll be here and..."

"No, that's not what I'm saying. Having you here has helped more than you'll ever know, but it's time for you to go home now."

Anna's head shot up.

"What are you talking about? I *am* home."

Her mother stroked her hair.

"No, sweetheart, you're not. Home is with your young man, not here."

Anna's eyes widened in shock.

"But ... but you don't even like Nick!"

"Whatever gave you that idea?" her mother asked, bemused.

"You and Dad, you were so disapproving!"

"Well, of course we were! Your contract made it impossible for you. But you made your choice and you chose him, not your work. And he's made it very obvious that he cares deeply for you. Very publicly, in fact."

"I ... I can't go back to London!"

"Why not?"

"I don't have a job! I definitely don't have a reputation! I don't even have an apartment anymore. What would I do?"

"You're a bright young woman, Anna. You're my daughter and your father's daughter. You can do anything you want. But I think you'd be miserable if you don't find out if things could work with Nick first. And I know there's nothing else stopping you."

That was true.

Anna had received a short email from her solicitor explaining:

"The police do not consider that you have reached the threshold test for prosecution. Therefore you are not being charged. There is no case to answer."

At the bottom of the email was an invitation by the Metropolitan Police to come and retrieve her cell phone, iPad and laptop.

After all the heartache, all the worry and angst, it had boiled down to their ability to check her old texts and emails. She wasn't exactly innocent in the whole mess, but she wasn't guilty of perjury, and that was all the police cared about.

With no police case hanging over, she could do what she wanted. Well, she could do anything but work; anything but have her old life back.

Anna bit her lip.

"I can't leave you here by yourself!"

"And I can't expect you to stay. Sooner or later I'll have to figure things out for myself. I can't and won't stop you from living your life. Having you here has been wonderful, but now it's time for us both to move on."

Anna's lips trembled.

"I don't know how to do that."

Her mother's eyes turned glassy.

"Neither do I. I miss your father so much!"

They held each other and cried: tears for the past, what had been; tears for the fear of the future.

"I'll come visit you in London," said her mom at last. "We'll go to Harrods and Liberty's and Selfridges!"

"Mom, I hate shopping!" Anna laughed and cried.

"I know you do, but I love it, and I'm your mother!" she smiled, wiping her tears. "And I'm looking forward to meeting your young man."

She cupped her hands around Anna's face.

"You're so much like your father. He wasn't a quitter either. Now, go be with Nick."

CHAPTER TWENTY-SIX

MARCH 2016

The studio lights were unbearably hot, but Nick didn't appear to notice them. He sat upright, his long legs crossed at the ankle, his gaze distant.

He hadn't heard from Anna since his very public declaration, but it had sent the media into a frenzy: there was nothing they loved more than an enigmatic hero and unrequited love. Besides, Nick was flavour of the month after the way he'd helped the England rugby team to a comprehensive mauling of the team from Ireland.

"Well, Nick, it's been quite an eventful couple of years for you."

The interviewer gave a soft, diffident chuckle that the audience echoed.

She'd been excited about this, interviewing the famously private Nick Renshaw, golden boy of English rugby, but he was making her work for it, giving polite, one-word answers.

In truth, 'eventful' didn't even begin to cover the beautiful, terrible chaos of the last twenty-two months of his life.

He leaned back in his chair, increasing the distance between them as he continued to stare at the interviewer while she waited expectantly for his answer.

The silence lengthened and she licked her lips, glancing at the producer as the studio lights drew beads of sweat on her heavily powdered forehead.

"How would you describe the last two years, Nick?"

The Team England publicist was staring at him wide-eyed from behind the cameraman, willing him to say something, praying that Nick didn't freeze on national TV.

His fingers drummed quietly on the arm of his chair as if he was choosing his words carefully. He wasn't.

"Yes, Jasmine, you could say it's been eventful."

The words rolled out in Nick's distinctive Yorkshire accent—taciturn, economical, the flat vowels making him sound bored.

The interviewer's eyes tightened and she clutched her clipboard harder.

"There have been highs and lows..." she said encouragingly, giving him another lead-in. "Perhaps you could tell me how those have been, from your perspective?"

She wasn't wrong, but her questions weren't tapping into the well of emotion that she sensed underlay his weary answers. She knew it was there; she sensed it.

Physically, he'd never looked stronger, his athlete's body draped in a designer suit and crisp white shirt, his raven-dark hair combed away from a sculpted face, penetrating hazel-green eyes now shuttered, and a newly grown, thick, black beard hiding the softness of his lips.

But it was there, barely perceptible, an undefinable something. To the interviewer's experienced gaze, he looked ... defeated.

Nick closed his eyes momentarily. Yes, there had been incredible highs, flying so far he thought he'd never come back to earth. But he did. He crashed and burned, shattering spectacularly.

Broken in body and spirit, he'd clawed his way back, step by painful step. And *she* had been there. For every time when it seemed too hard and he wanted to give up, Anna had kept him going. For every time the shadows threatened to choke him, she'd driven them back, her brightness blazing.

And when she'd needed him most, he'd watched her fall.

"Playing for your country, that must have been an incredible feeling," the interviewer urged, becoming more agitated as Nick choked on the words crowding at the back of his throat. "How does it feel to stand in front of 82,000 people all chanting your name?"

He glanced up at her, frowning slightly, as if offended by her question. It revealed her basic misunderstanding of why he played rugby at an international level or any level for that matter. It wasn't for adulation. When he played, he focussed on the game, on the white lines painted on the field. He rarely looked up at the people in the first tier, let alone higher. So how the hell could he answer her? Not that it was a bad question—everyone said it was the greatest moment of his life. He didn't agree, but that's what they said.

How had Jonny Wilkinson felt when he scored the winning drop goal in the last ninety seconds of extra time during the Final of the 2003 Rugby World Cup?

She may as well have asked how Neil Armstrong felt when he took his first step on the moon? Or how Michael Collins felt when he didn't and was left behind in Apollo 11? Unless you've walked in those men's shoes, you can't know.

But how did *he* feel? How had he felt? Stunned, overwhelmed, invincible? Lost, broken, destroyed?

He shrugged his shoulders and gave her a wide, meaningless smile.

"You had to be there."

"I was!" she said enthusiastically. "I was there cheering my head off in front of the TV along with everyone else in the country. I'm sure people will remember that day, where they were at that actual moment, for the rest of their lives! And after everything that you've been through, after being told you'd never play again, it must have been an extraordinary moment."

"Yes, extraordinary," he said quietly, lost in the memories.

He'd played for Anna that day. He'd played for her every day since.

"I'm told that you recently got a tattoo," the journalist said, trying a different tack to get him talking, to unlock the story and save the interview from being a car crash. "...A phoenix. I think I can guess the relevance of that: not just for the Finchley Phoenixes, but rebirth and renewal, recovery from injury, rising from the ashes?"

A photo of his new ink was shown on the screen behind him, the camera scrolling pornographically across smooth tanned skin, swooping over muscles and polished flesh, dipping erotically low. Several of the women in the studio audience whooped and cheered, wolf-whistles piercing through his fog of despair, making him smile despite himself.

The interviewer felt a blast of euphoria. Of course! The fans! They'd always been Nick's weak spot. He was always kind to them.

As his fame had grown, his natural boy-next-door friendliness had morphed into a wariness of strangers, and he'd learned that self-deprecating way of the superstar to smile and slide away without causing offence.

"Your fans are important to you," said the interviewer. "Have they been part of your recovery?"

His eyes flickered and something inside him gave way—emotions dammed for too long.

"Yeah, definitely. They've supported me through some of the lowest moments in my life," he agreed, leaning toward her for the first time. "And the phoenix is to symbolize starting over. But not just in my career, in my life, too. I didn't think I'd make it back on a team again, let alone play for England. It wasn't just the injury, it was fear."

And he tapped his chest.

"Inside, I didn't believe in myself. But then I met an amazing sports psychologist who helped me get back on track."

"You're referring to Anna Scott," said the journalist, her eyes glinting with the excitement of a potential exclusive.

The Team England publicist was shaking her head, making a slashing movement with her hand, warning him not to talk about Anna. He saw her, no question, but the devil in him decided to ignore her insistent advice and give the interviewer what she wanted. And it might be the only way he could get Anna to hear him.

For a moment, pain flared behind his eyes.

"Yes, I'm talking about Anna Scott. She pulled me out of a very dark place, helped me start playing again, and playing well—winning. Without her, I'd never have made it."

The interviewer leaned toward him, her tone warm, confidential, *just two old friends having a chat*, but her body quivered with excitement.

He knew it. He knew all about reading body language, knew what she wanted. And maybe, just maybe it was the last roll of the dice.

"And you started a relationship with Ms. Scott?"

The audience were silent, a collective holding of breath. Wondering if he'd take another step toward the cliff edge.

"I think you know that already, Jasmine," he said, arching one eyebrow at her. "The newspapers and gossip sites wouldn't leave her alone. She was torn apart by the Press. And I couldn't do *anything* to help her. Journalists crucified her."

The interviewer squirmed uncomfortably, then squared her shoulders.

"Were you in a relationship with her from the beginning?"

His eyes darkened, whether with anger or passion, no one but Nick could tell.

"All relationships have a beginning, but to answer your question, no. Despite the allegations, that's not how it was."

"How was it exactly?"

How was it? Perfect. Perfectly wrong.

"She healed me, we became … friends—good friends—and then … she left."

He spoke as if at confessional, quietly, humbly, almost as if he'd forgotten the interviewer was there.

She stared at him, a shocked but avid expression on her face, and she leaned even closer, her red nails wrapped around the clipboard, her script abandoned.

"And then what?"

Nick blinked slowly, his eyes coming back into focus as he buried his feelings deeper.

"And then I got picked for the England team."

Not the answer she wanted.

The interviewer twitched a shoulder in irritation.

"What happened to Dr. Scott? What happened to Anna?"

"Nothing happened."

Her forehead creased with frustration.

"But … but that can't be the end of the story!"

He leaned back and gave her a small smile.

"'Fraid so. That's it. That's the end."

"I don't believe that!"

Nick didn't want to believe it either.

CHAPTER TWENTY-SEVEN

Anna stepped onto the gangplank that led from the jumbo jet to the arrivals hall at Heathrow airport.

It bounced slightly as she walked, making her feel off balance. And wasn't that the truth. She hadn't spoken to Nick since the day of her father's funeral.

She didn't know if she was doing the right thing, but as her mother had pointed out, there was only one way to know for sure.

So, she'd bought an open-ended return ticket to London. She didn't know how long she'd be staying.

Waiting in line at Immigration, she glanced across at a newspaper stand on the other side of the row of booths.

Nick's Heart to Heart: Rugby Player Shows Soft Sides

She knew it must be about *him*, but she wondered what the headline referred to. The Immigration Officer did a double-take when he saw the name on her passport, checked her paperwork and studied her face intently, but he didn't hold her up or cause any delay.

Anna rushed over to buy the newspaper. As she read the story of his TV interview, her eyes filled with tears. No one had ever been so candid about the way they felt about her. It was humbling and a little scary. But hopeful. She felt hope for the first time in so long.

The journey to Nick's house took 45 minutes and Anna watched the dawn break, a thin, watery sun beginning to rise. But as the taxi drove along Nick's road, she still had no idea what she'd say.

She struggled out with her suitcase and handed a shockingly large number of bills to the cab driver. Then, taking a deep breath, she knocked on the door.

After half a minute, she heard some muffled cursing and the door was yanked open by a bad-tempered 6' 5" Samoan with a hangover.

"What?"

"Hi, Fetuao. How are you?"

He blinked, then a huge smile spread across his face.

"Anna Scott! *Malō!* You're here! Nick is gonna split his shorts!"

"Um, great?"

He grinned widely and pulled her into a hug.

"The boy's been pining for you." He drew back, his face serious. "It was a bad thing they did to you. We're all behind you—and our boy."

"Thank you. That means a lot to me."

"Sure. Come on in. Did you see any paps out there?"

Anna looked horrified.

"No! But I wasn't really looking."

Fetuao shrugged and shook his head.

"Been coming and going ever since..."

He shrugged again, picked up her enormous suitcase with one hand and led her inside.

"You been here before?"

"No."

"Huh. Well, Nick's upstairs, second on the left. He had a late night."

Fetuao stowed her suitcase by the door and abandoned her at the bottom of the stairs while he shuffled into the kitchen. From the back, he looked even more rumpled, and Anna smiled. He was one of the good guys.

The house was quiet, although it was nearly nine o'clock. She heard Fetuao turn on the radio, singing along to something. Down the corridor, she could hear snoring.

Steeling herself, she knocked softly on the second door on the left.

Then she heard Nick's sleepy, grumpy voice.

"Fuck off, Fetu."

Smiling to herself, she pushed the door open—and nearly got hit by a flying pillow.

"What part of fuck off didn't you understand?!"

"Um, it's Anna."

She risked opening the door a couple of inches again and saw the duvet slip off Nick's shoulder as he sat up in bed. Stunned, she stared at the new tattoo that covered the other half of his chest, a phoenix spreading its wings.

"Anna?" He stared at her and she took a tentative step inside. "Shit, Anna!"

"Hi, Nick," she said shyly, unable to meet his gaze.

The room was messy with clothes scattered over every flat surface, but the walls were bare. A photograph of him with his parents and sister was displayed on his dresser, but that was the only personal thing in the room.

Then she spied his guitar, half-hidden with a t-shirt hanging from the neck. He'd never brought it to her apartment; she'd like to hear him play that one day.

He cleared his throat and her gaze snapped back to his intense eyes.

"Will you play for me?"

"What, now?"

"Please. I've always wanted to hear you play."

Nick rubbed the stubble on his cheeks, a faint pink staining the skin.

"Okay. Um, what do you want to hear?"

"Anything. Anything you want to play me."

Nick picked up the guitar tentatively and began to sing softly.

Shivers ran through Anna, and when she heard the lyrics, her breath caught and tears started in her eyes.

His voice stayed low and intimate, and when he finished, it was several seconds before he met her gaze.

"The woman in the song has sad, grey eyes?"

He shrugged sheepishly.

"It's one of my dad's favourites. He played it all the time when we were kids. Yeah, *Girl with Grey Eyes*."

"Who's it by?"

"A Scottish band, 'Big Country'."

"It's beautiful. Thank you for playing it for me."

He glanced up to meet Anna's eyes, silvery-grey in the dawn light.

"I watched the match against Ireland. I heard what you said. Was it a message for me? Did you mean it?"

An uncertain smile lifted his lips.

"I didn't know how else to tell you. I was desperate. I didn't care if I came over like a dickhead. I just ... I needed you to know how I felt. I needed you to *hear* me."

Anna nodded her head slowly.

"It was the most wonderful thing anyone has ever done for me. Ever. And I love you so damn much."

His mouth dropped open and then he lunged across the room, grabbing her and pulling her against his body in a hug, unembarrassed by his magnificent, naked body.

Anna's skin flushed as they clung together, her hands gliding over his smooth, golden skin. There was just so much of him, so warm, so male.

"I can't believe you're really here," he murmured into her hair, his soft lips brushing against the skin of her neck, his beard tickling her. "Are you staying? This time, are you staying?"

She pulled back so she could see his eyes, those glorious hazel-green eyes, the longing in his expression.

"If you want me. Yes, I'm back. I don't know what I'll do or where I'll go..."

"Doesn't matter," he said quickly. "Just ... don't leave me again."

She laughed as tears sprang to her eyes.

"You really mean it? I've brought you nothing but trouble!"

He shook his head vehemently, his eyes flaring.

"You're the best thing that's ever happened to me."

"Better than beating Ireland in your first international?" she teased.

"Yep, almost as good as that," he grinned, sitting back on the bed and pulling her with him.

He stopped abruptly.

"Are you allowed to be here? You're not going to get into trouble, are you?"

Anna touched a finger to his lips.

"The police decided that there's no case to answer. I'm a free woman."

Nick kissed the tip of her finger then rested his forehead against hers.

"Thank God," he said. "Thank God."

Then he kissed her: deeply, reverently, joyfully. And as she rested her hand on his bare chest, she could feel his pulse pounding wildly beneath the silky skin. Her fingers drifted across the breadth of his chest, following the intricate lines of ink.

"This is new, the tattoo."

"It's a phoenix."

"I see that. It's beautiful."

Half of Nick thought he was still dreaming. He'd woken up hearing her voice and he'd seen her and held her and the world started spinning his way again, but it didn't seem real. It didn't seem possible that after all this time she'd come back.

When she hadn't got in touch after the Ireland match, the little spark of hope he'd had was extinguished. But now...

He kissed her again, savouring every second, every brush of her tongue against his, every time their teeth clashed in a messy, unplanned, unpredictable kiss. And that fucking tongue stud—it was so hot. He remembered vividly the way she'd dragged it across his simmering flesh, driving him to distraction.

He was in a hurry to claim her, but wanted to make it last, too. His brain warred with his body, but it was Anna who slowed him down.

"We have forever, but if we didn't, what would you do?"

"I'd kiss you in the daylight."

Anna laughed in surprise.

"What?"

"All the time we were together, we had to hide. I don't want to hide anymore. I want everyone to know."

Anna's smile slipped.

"With all the pictures out there, I'm pretty certain people know," she said sadly.

Nick grabbed her wrists and brought her hands to his lips.

"No! They just know the rubbish the papers printed. It was a soap opera to them, nothing real. But it's my life and your life, and I want it to be *our* life. So I want to kiss you in daylight. I want to walk with you in a park. I want to take you out for dinner and not care who sees us. Fuck the lot of them! It's no one else's business. I'm not ashamed of us, are you?"

Anna smiled softly.

"For a man of few words, you sure do know how to say all the right things."

She pulled away from him and walked to the window, pulling back the curtains and letting the cool, grey, London sun paint the walls with a faint glow.

Then she turned to face him.

"I don't care who's watching. Kiss me!"

Laughing, defiant, tumbling onto the sheets, they kissed and held each other, bare skin sliding together as Anna's flesh turned rosy and a flush coloured Nick's tanned cheeks.

He undressed her slowly, worshipping her body, exploring the flesh he'd been without too long, relishing every moan and sigh, the silk of her skin under his rough fingers.

Then he paused, his fingers tangling in the delicate necklace, the gold chain with a rugby ball pendant.

"You're still wearing it?"

"Yes. I've never taken it off."

His arms trembled as the muscles bunched when he braced himself over her, and his eyes closed when he pressed inside her. Anna sighed and moaned, arching her back to meet him, wrapping her long legs around him, her nails scoring thin red lines down his back and buttocks.

He groaned as he felt his balls tighten and it was too soon, but Anna wasn't holding back either. She bit his ear and licked his throat, then swore as he pressed her into the mattress with his hips, kissed her breasts as they bounced with his thrusts, his head buried in her neck.

God, she'd missed this, his urgency, this intimacy, this reckless abandon of self to become *them*, to become more than *she* and *him*. A union, a joining, a coming together in heat and lust and need. And love. With him there was always love.

Anna gasped, flying and falling as Nick drove inside her harder and deeper, finishing with a shudder, a profanity, and a long moan of pleasure as he finally let himself go.

Breathless and gasping, they lay in a sweaty tangle, pale sunlight dancing across flushed and heated skin.

Nick held her hand and kissed the knuckles gently.

"I'm better with you here. You make it all worthwhile."

Anna slept, falling into a wonderful, dream-filled sleep, relief and exhaustion pulling her under.

As Anna slept, Nick watched her, his eyes absorbing every curve, every angle, every breath in her body.

It still felt dreamlike that she was here, that she'd come back. The only way he knew it was real was because happiness soared in his heart. He felt whole, he felt complete. But it felt fragile, as if it could break again at any moment, as if what they had could still be taken away from them.

Nick thought about what they'd already been through: his injury, his court case, her arrest, her father's death, losing the job she loved. Anna had lost so much already and he'd regained everything, even her.

But what if it all went away again? It could, easily. If he got injured, something that put him out of the game for good, would they go on as a couple? Could they?

How could they make a living? What would they do? Where would they live?

But as he watched the gentle rise and fall of her chest, his fears fell away.

They'd find their path. The world had taught them some harsh lessons, but they'd survived.

Nick smiled grimly to himself, his expression defiant.

She'd made him stronger, now he would be strong for her.

"Have you got a dress in your suitcase?"

Anna raised her eyebrows at Nick's odd question.

"I have a few, but I don't think they're your size."

Before she knew what was happening, she was on her back with Nick pinning her to the bed and tickling the hell out of her.

She resisted as long as she could but had to give in.

"Uncle!" she yelled, red faced, tears running down her cheeks.

"Uncle who?" asked Nick, pausing in his tickling.

"It means I give in!" Anna gasped.

Nick flopped down beside her.

"Oh, right. That's okay then."

When she'd gotten her breath back, she turned on her side to look at him.

"Why were you asking about a dress?"

Nick scratched his beard as his forehead wrinkled.

"I've got this fundraiser thing to go to tonight. I want you to come with me."

Anna was cautious. She wanted to say yes, but maybe it was too soon. What was the protocol for announcing to the world that they were together when they'd spent so long forced to stay apart?

She pursed her lips. One way to find out, and now seemed as good a time as any.

"Who's it for?"

"A children's charity," he answered, then met her eyes. "It's something the Phoenixes do every year. Jason says it should be fun."

"Will Sim Andrews be there?"

Nick nodded.

"Maybe it's not a good idea that I go."

"I think it's a great idea," Nick argued, rolling onto his side and propping his head on his hand.

Anna took a deep breath.

"Okay, but we don't blindside him again. We should tell him first."

"Fine by me."

~

Nick looked handsome in his tux, but Anna didn't feel quite as pulled together as she'd liked to have been, bearing in mind she'd only had a few hours' notice and this was their first public appearance together. But after the initial flurry of interest as they'd arrived on the red carpet, it had been reassuringly low key.

Her simple silk sheath dress needed to be ironed quickly but it draped elegantly as she walked. Unfortunately, there wasn't much she could do about the bags under her eyes, despite an industrial application of concealer.

Nick had phoned Sim Andrews to break the news. It had been a short but positive conversation. Since the police weren't charging Anna, Sim's views towards her had thawed somewhat, and the Phoenixes' Head Coach made it a point to come over and kiss her on the cheek. He told her how proud he was that two of his team were playing for England, and that Fetuao was also playing for his national side. Nothing important was said, but the fact that he was speaking to her at all gave her a warm glow. And when he offered his condolences for the loss of her father, it was heartfelt.

After an hour, Nick had been called away for the charity's Press photographs and Anna found herself by the buffet table.

"Boring, isn't it?" smiled the woman standing next to her.

"Trying to decide whether or not to chance the shrimp?"

The woman laughed.

"Ah, that's definitely not boring, that's risky. Who knows how long it's been sitting here under the hot lights. My advice: avoid!"

Anna smiled. "Thank you for the tip!"

The woman held out her hand.

"I'm Isabel Buxton. I'm a senior producer on 'Loose Women'."

The way she said it, Anna suspected that she ought to know what that was.

Isabel raised her eyebrows expectantly.

"I'm sorry, I'm not familiar with that. I haven't been in the UK very long," she hedged.

Isabel chuckled but didn't seem offended.

"I'll let you off then. It's a TV panel show, by women, for women, about women. We have four female presenters, and we discuss everything from current affairs and daily politics, women's issues, viewers' concerns, as well as some celebrity gossip. We're on during the week at lunch time and we've been going since 1999. We're just coming up to 2,500 shows," she said proudly.

Anna was on her guard.

"I know, I know," Isabel sighed, correctly reading her expression. "You've been the subject of a media witch hunt and you probably don't want anything to do with journalists."

Anna gripped her glass of warm champagne more tightly.

"No 'probably' about it."

Isabel nodded.

"Fair enough. But I'm assuming that coming here with Nick tonight was a statement of sorts?"

It hadn't been planned, but it definitely seemed to be working out that way. She didn't say anything out loud. Now she knew who Isabel worked for, she was even more cautious.

"But wouldn't you like a chance to put *your* side of the story? It would be on live TV, so no editors. You could tell *your* story *your* way."

Isabel held out a rectangle of cardboard.

"This is my business card. We're doing a show on social media manipulation in a few weeks. I think you'd make a great guest."

She pressed the card into Anna's hand.

"You've been a victim of the media—wouldn't you like the chance to steer that ship for a change? At least think about it ... and stay away from the shrimp."

"How did you know I'd be here tonight?"

"I didn't," Isabel said with a wink. "I'm just a shameless opportunist. But it's one way not to be a victim anymore."

Anna had to admire Isabel's chutzpah as she watched her walk away. Then she felt Nick's warm hands slide around her waist as he nuzzled her neck, the soft skin beneath her earlobe. It seemed to be one of his favourite places.

"Who was that?"

"Friend or foe ... I'm not sure. She's a TV producer. She wants me to go on a show named 'Loose Women' and talk about my side of the story, as she calls it."

"My mum watches that," Nick said.

"Really?"

"Yeah, she said there's some good stuff on there."

Anna was thoughtful.

"What are you going to tell your parents ... about us?"

Nick frowned.

"What do you mean?"

"Well, won't they be worried now that I'm back?"

Nick grinned at her.

"Nah. Mum told me that once I'd stopped arseing about, you'd come home. Dad does what Mum tells him. They like you Anna. They'll be happy for us. Don't worry about it."

"Well ... okay. And Trisha?"

He gazed at her seriously.

"She told me to do the interview that was on last night. She said I was trying to be too clever by quoting your mantra and I should do something more obvious."

"No, I was already on my way, but I really want to watch that interview."

"Make sure you tell her that for me," he grinned. "She's a know-all pain in my arse. She'll hate it that she was wrong."

"You want me to tell her that, too?"

"Bloody hell! Not if you want me to live. But since you brought it up, what did you tell your mum when you came back?"

Anna smiled and squeezed Nick's waist.

"It was more her telling me. She told me to hurry back to my 'young man' and stop wasting time."

"I like the sound of your mum."

"Yes, she'd really like you, too. I'm sorry that I didn't introduce you at Dad's funeral..."

"It was a tough time."

"It was. But I never thanked you for coming. It meant a lot to me."

Gently, he held her fingers in his hand and looked down.

"You said you wished you'd never met me. It sounded like you meant it."

Anna glanced away, her lips trembling.

"It was a shitty thing to say and you didn't deserve that. I'm really sorry. I blamed myself for Dad's death, the strain I'd put him under. It was a cruel thing to say to you. I honestly didn't mean it."

Nick's eyes widened in understanding.

"You think the stress about us ... you think that ... that did it?"

She hesitated.

"Maybe, yes; maybe, no. No, not really. It didn't help. But he'd been on pills for high blood pressure for years, but he wouldn't do anything about improving his diet. Mom was always nagging him, but he wouldn't listen. Galloping Gary Scott—no one could stop him when he wanted something." She sighed. "I wish you could have met him."

"Me, too."

There was a pause as the all too frequent tears formed in Anna's eyes and Nick squeezed her hand again.

"Mom says she'll come visit soon."

"Yeah? That would be brilliant. Maybe she could come for one of my matches." He gave her a side-long glance. "I've been picked to play for England against South Africa next month."

Anna's expression brightened immediately.

"Oh my God! That's amazing!"

He kissed her softly.

"Nah. It's more amazing that you came home."

CHAPTER TWENTY-EIGHT

IT WAS A BAD IDEA. TERRIBLE IDEA. WHAT ON EARTH WAS SHE THINKING?

Anna gripped her hands together to stop them shaking. Brendan nudged her in the ribs.

"You're acting like a crack addict waiting for a fix. And stop sweating! You're ruining your makeup!"

Anna had thought about Isabel's offer for several days and in the end decided to do it. She'd go on 'Loose Women' and give her side of the story. It had been Isabel's comment about not being a victim that had gotten to her. Maybe it was time to take charge. She couldn't bring herself to approach any of the newspapers who'd had a hand in vilifying her, so this TV chat show seemed the best way to go.

Either that, or she was talking herself into an epic fail.

Nick had been reluctant for Anna to put herself back in the spotlight, but understood that she needed to do *something*. After they'd talked it through, he'd finally agreed that it was something she needed to do and he'd given his grudging approval. Not that she needed it, but it was nice to have it.

Nick was at an away-game and hadn't been able to come with her to the TV studio, so he'd suggested that Brendan would be a good person to take for support.

Anna was rethinking that as he fussed around her, tugging her neckline lower as Anna tugged it up again.

At least she'd felt somewhat reassured when Isabel welcomed her warmly and introduced her to the lead anchor, a friendly woman in her late fifties named Ruth, who seemed down to earth and straight forward. The other presenters had been pleasant, too, and Anna had the unusual sense of being with women who were supportive, rather than attacking her. It felt good.

The studio audience had been warmed up, the titles played, and Ruth went into her opening spiel.

"We're talking today about social media. We've all got Facebook accounts, Twitter accounts, Instagram, Snapchat, Whatsapp—we all know how quickly information can get out there. But what happens when you're the focus of all that attention? And what if it's largely negative? What if it hurts you? What then? Today, our guest is a woman who knows all too well what negative media intrusion can do. She was accused of lying under oath about being in a relationship with rugby ace Nick Renshaw, an allegation of perjury that never reached court due to lack of evidence. Please welcome Dr. Anna Scott."

Anna walked on with a nervous smile and sat in the middle of the panel of four women, facing towards the audience as they applauded politely.

RUTH: Hello, Anna. Thank you for coming.

ANNA: Thank you for inviting me.

RUTH: Perhaps you could give us an account of what happened to you, Anna?

ANNA: I was crucified by the Press for something I didn't do. I was arrested and spent the night in a cell. I was never told the name of my accuser. The police found no evidence that I lied; no evidence of any wrong-doing because there was nothing to find. But I lost my job, my home, everything.

RUTH: [*PAUSE*]

LINDA: But you were in a relationship with Nick Renshaw. You still are?

ANNA: Yes, we're together now. We weren't at the time in question. I came to the UK in the summer of 2014. I'm a qualified medical doctor and chose to specialise in sports psychology. My late father was friends with Steve Jewell, the then head coach at Manchester Minotaurs rugby team. Steve had two new players, one coming back from long-term injury, and he wanted me to work with them.

COLLEEN: And the injured player was Nick Renshaw?

ANNA: Yes. I worked with him for several months, along with a number of other rugby players, soccer players and local athletes. Then I had the chance to move to London to work with teams down here. I decided to open a second clinic. While I was doing that, Nick had some problems of his own.

NADIA: He beat up his fiancée when he caught her cheating on him.

ANNA: He admitted to causing damage to her car and to his former friend's home where he saw them together, intimately involved, should I say. She was injured accidentally, even the judge said so at the time. But Nick pleaded guilty and was fined and did community service.

LINDA: You spoke up for him at the court case.

ANNA: His lawyer asked me if I'd appear as a character witness. I agreed.

RUTH: And you weren't in a relationship with Nick at this time.

ANNA: No.

RUTH: When did this professional relationship become something more?

ANNA: In stages. He wrote to thank me for my support at his court case. I emailed back. It became an online friendship. But then my work took me to London, as I said, and we didn't stay in touch. I met him again when he came to play for the Finchley Phoenixes.

NADIA: And you weren't allowed to, what's the phrase, fraternize with the players?

ANNA: No.

NADIA: But you did.

ANNA: Yes.

RUTH: Why risk it?

NADIA: Have you seen him? He's gorgeous! Well hot!

[*LAUGHTER*]

ANNA: We were both single, we liked each other. I think maybe we were both a little lonely, too, as we'd both recently relocated to London. My original contract was for six weeks, but it got extended. So we had to keep hiding. We hadn't planned on falling in love.

RUTH: How did the Club find out?

ANNA: We went to Nick's family for Christmas. I had a wonderful day with lovely, wonderful warm people, and then in the evening we went for a walk after dinner. Unfortunately, we bumped into his ex-fiancée. They'd broken up when she cheated on him with his best friend while he was recovering from surgery. They'd been broken up for months before Nick and I became a couple. But she saw us, and put two and two together and got five. I'll always remember what she said: "You won't get away with this."

COLLEEN: And she told the newspapers.

ANNA: [*PAUSE*] I don't know. Someone did. It was trial by social media. I had to delete my Facebook and Twitter accounts because the abuse was so bad. And then I was arrested for perjury. I had my phone, iPad and laptop seized, and I was taken away in a police van. The police had been wrongly informed that I'd been in a relationship with Nick at the time of his court case and that I'd lied about it. My conditions of bail meant that I wasn't allowed to see him. For three months. While all this was going on my father died. It was the lowest point of my life. Within a few weeks, I'd lost my job, my reputation, the man I loved, and my own dear father.

RUTH: [*PAUSE*] I can only imagine how traumatic that must have been.

ANNA: Thank you. It was ... difficult. And then while I was at home in New York with my mother, my lawyer emailed to say that the police had found no evidence that a crime had been committed: there was no case to answer. But I'd already lost everything, so I didn't care.

COLLEEN: Those personal images of you with Nick—that must have been hard.

ANNA: The police told me that hackers get into 'phones of interest'. Apparently, at that point, I became a victim of a crime, which is kind of ironic. They did try to follow it up, I believe. It was looked into by the police's hi-tech crime unit, Cy-Comms, but, well, once the images are out there, it's a struggle to take them down.

COLLEEN: And no one was ever prosecuted for that?

ANNA: No.

NADIA: And there was that ex-boyfriend of yours, too. The one you had an affair with ... the married man.

ANNA: Ah, yes, the married man. Well, I was young and he was my supervisor for my PhD thesis. I fell for the oldest line in the book, that he was going to leave his wife for me. But ... I did know that he was married, so I have to take some of the blame, I know that...

NADIA: What happened?

ANNA: When the university authorities found out, they discussed expelling me, but I was so close to finishing my PhD that they let me work from home. He was given a slap on the wrist and sent on a sabbatical. He was back teaching within a year. What no one ever mentions was that it wasn't the first time he'd had an affair with a student.

NADIA: So you're saying he was just a dirty old man?

ANNA: I'm saying that I wasn't the first naïve woman who'd believed his lies. When the truth came out, he couldn't drop me fast enough. I felt so stupid, so humiliated. I couldn't cope, couldn't function ... that's why everything that happened this time makes it so ... so...

NADIA: Crap?

[LAUGHTER]

ANNA: Yes! Definitely that! Nick was single, I was single— neither of us cheated. I know that his club had a no-fraternization clause in our contracts. We should have come clean at the beginning. Nick wanted to, but I was scared I'd lose the contract, scared I'd lose my job. Pretty ironic, huh?

RUTH: When did you get back with Nick?

ANNA: [*SMILES*] I saw what he said after the England versus Ireland match. I was watching it in New York on my mom's laptop.

COLLEEN: About that, what did he mean?

ANNA: He was telling me not to give up. Not to be defeated. It was very personal. He knew it would mean something special to me ... and it did.

RUTH: And then he gave that very emotional interview.

NADIA: That was so romantic! And to do it in public like that! Wow! What did you think?

ANNA: I didn't know about it until I was in London. I'd already planned to come back. When I got off the plane at Heathrow, I saw a newspaper headline. It was...

COLLEEN: You must have felt very emotional.

ANNA: Oh, definitely.

LINDA: What do you feel about the people who accused you?

ANNA: I don't feel anything.

NADIA: After what they did to you? How they ruined your life?

ANNA: The death of my father ... it puts things into perspective. Nick and I are together again, that's more important than holding onto any bitterness.

COLLEEN: I'd be madder than a snake! Don't you want to make them pay? Not even a little bit?

ANNA: No, they're not worth my time. I'm going to look to the future now.

RUTH: And what does that look like?

ANNA: [*LAUGHS*] I have no idea. I'm not allowed to be a sports psychologist anymore—I had my licence revoked. Maybe I'll write self-help books about how not to screw up your career!

RUTH: Thank you for talking us today, Anna. It's been a pleasure.

ANNA: Thank you for having me.

As soon as she'd started the interview, she felt calm. It was almost like talking to a group of girlfriends. Yes, she'd conveniently omitted to mention her fireside inferno with Nick, but that was private and no one would ever know. But now that she was off-camera, her hands shook as she unclipped the microphone from her shirt, and she couldn't remember a word that she'd said.

Brendan swept her into a hug.

"You were magnificent, Annie!"

Her phone vibrated in her pocket.

Knocked it out of the park. Love you, babe. X

Two days later, Anna got an email from one of the tabloid newspapers who'd printed the lies about her. They wanted to offer her a job as a regular columnist, writing on self-help and personal advice. She laughed when she read the email.

She stopped laughing when she saw how much they offered to pay her.

"What do you think, Nick?"

"I don't know. Do you want to be an agony aunt?"

"It's advice columnist! Maybe, yeah. I like that I'd be able to help people."

"Even if it's working for one of those newspapers?"

His lip curled as he spoke.

"I'm not naïve, Nick. I know how these people work. But newspapers? They're just the vessel—as good or as bad as the people working for them. Maybe I can even it up a little." She sighed. "It's not like I have anything better to do. And they'll pay for me to hire an assistant for a few hours a week—I could ask Brendan. I miss that crazy guy."

Nick pulled her into his arms and kissed her thoroughly.

"Anything you want to do is okay with me, babe."

"Anything?" she asked silkily.

"Yeah. Especially when you've got that look in your eye."

She shrieked as he slung her over his shoulder in a fireman's lift and headed for the stairs.

"*Mio Dio!*" said Giovanni as he walked in through the front door. "What is it I should say? Get a room!"

"That's what we're doing, mate," Nick called over his shoulder.

"I think we'll have to get our own place, sooner rather than later," Anna said breathlessly as Nick carried her up the flight of stairs.

"Jealous bastards," laughed Nick.

He had several things on his to-do list: getting their own place was just one of them. But for now, it could wait.

CHAPTER TWENTY-NINE

SEVEN MONTHS LATER...

Saturday 29th October 2016
  Rugby World Cup Final, Twickenham: England V Samoa
  Nick had been awake for two hours, his brain churning. Sleep was far, far away. Unfortunately, so was Anna.

Although it was probably just as well. If she'd been lying next to him, he'd have wanted to do more than wake her up.

He cringed and tried to push the thought out of his head. It just wasn't appropriate given the person who was currently sleeping a few feet away from him.

Jason snorted loudly and Nick rolled his eyes. He'd shared a room with his teammate enough times to know that the guy was a snorter—one of those people who didn't really snore, but every now and again, let out a rip-roaring snort like a constipated warthog. It was irritating and very hard to ignore. Other people on the England team wouldn't room with him anymore, so Nick was stuck.

He didn't mind. Much.

Deciding he couldn't stay in bed any longer, he rolled free from the sheets and did a few stretches, recognising the familiar jangle of nerves. Generally, he was a pretty laidback bloke, even on game days, but this was a World Cup match, and it was the Final. The last time England had won was more than a decade ago. Expectations were riding high for a repeat after all those years.

He closed his eyes and allowed himself a moment to think about what that meant, what it had taken to get to this point, this moment: the sacrifices, the effort, the years, the many disappointments, the injuries, the successes. And Anna. Without Anna, he wasn't sure he'd be here at all.

She must have been thinking of him as well, because his phone vibrated with an incoming text.

> **My darling Nick,**
> **I know you'll be great today. Whatever happens, I'm so proud of you.**
> **And I'll never stop loving you.**
> **Think it.**
> **See it.**
> **Believe it.**
> **Do it.**
> **Your personal sports psychologist and inamorata ©.**
> **Ax**

He smiled. That was so typical of her, using twenty words when just three would do. He grinned and snapped a picture of himself giving a thumbs up next to a sleeping Jason.

Her reply was brief and made him laugh.

> **Are you trying to make me jealous?**
> **It's working! Still love ya! Ax**

He smiled to himself, thinking of her at home in the little house they'd recently bought together. Given the chance, she'd have taken up the whole bed last night, sleeping like a starfish. Maybe she was making coffee now or maybe putting out some nuts for the birds in their tiny backyard. He was proud that even with London prices, they'd been able to afford some outdoor space: a patio and small square of grass with a spindly aspen tree that they'd planted together.

Or maybe she was reading the news on her laptop and deciding what to put in her column on Monday.

Maybe she was thinking about starting the self-help book that she'd been talking about writing.

No, she was probably making pancakes for breakfast and talking to her mother who'd flown across for the Final.

Jason grunted and rolled over.

"W's goin' on?"

"Nothing, yer mad sort. Quick game of rugby then off to the pub."

"'kay."

Jason rolled away and went back to sleep. *Incredible.*

Nick shook his head. The guy was something else.

He picked up the hotel's phone and called room service for porridge, fruit and coffee, deciding he'd have poached eggs with the team later on. Then he downed some vitamins with a glass of water and headed for the bathroom.

He'd just stepped out of the shower when there was a knock at the door. He wrapped a towel around his waist and pulled it open.

An older man in a waiter's uniform was pushing a breakfast cart, loaded with fresh fruit, a carafe of coffee, two cups, and two bowls of porridge kept warm under insulated lids. Also, somewhat incongruously, there was a vase with a red rose in it.

"Good morning, sir. It's a beautiful day, no sign of any rain."

"Great, thank you."

The waiter pushed the trolley inside, situating it by the window and pretending not to see the naked form of Jason who was only just stumbling to the bathroom.

"Eh, sorry about that," said Nick, rubbing his freshly shaven face.

"Nothing to apologise for, sir. If I could just ask you to sign this."

"Yes, of course."

Nick signed for the food and fumbled in his wallet for some change for a tip.

"No, I really couldn't accept anything, sir," the waiter said with a genteel wave of his hand. "It's my pleasure. And may I add, every one of the kitchen staff wishes you their best of British for today," and he gestured toward the red rose in its vase, the same as the logo stitched onto Nick's Team England kit. "We'll all be watching you on the telly later. And, ahem, I've got five quid on you to score the winning try."

"That's really nice of you. Thank you very much."

The man pushed a small notebook in front of him.

"If I could just get your autograph, sir. For my daughter."

"Sure, no problem. What's your daughter's name."

"Ah, well, if you could just sign it, that would be lovely. I wouldn't want to impose."

"I don't mind," Nick smiled. "What name shall I put?"

The man's cheeks reddened.

"Barry."

Nick's eyebrows shot up, but he did as he was asked, signing his name with a flourish, then adding the date.

To Barry, best regards on Cup Final day.
Nick Renshaw, 29.10.16

The man held the little notebook as if Nick had just given him the recipe for turning lead into gold.

"Thank you," he said reverently, tucking the little book in his waistcoat pocket then bowing himself out of the room.

Nick smiled to himself. It felt good to give pleasure to a fan, although Barry was a funny name for a girl.

Oddly enough, the strange encounter had settled his nerves, and he decided that the red rose was coming home with him later. Anna would like that.

He ate his porridge with some dried fruit and nuts on top, then two bananas.

Jason slumped at the table a few minutes later and inhaled his food eagerly. Neither of them felt like talking, already turning inwards and preparing themselves mentally.

Then they both dressed in their Team England suits, crisp white shirts and team ties, with polished black dress shoes. They were representing their country, and tracksuits wouldn't cut it today.

Finally, they packed up their bags and headed for the team bus.

It had been decorated overnight, and hung festooned with red and white balloons and the famous St. George's flag draped across the engine block.

Photographers milled around at the front of the hotel, along with several hundred fans who cheered them as if they'd already won.

Nick signed a few more autographs then climbed into the bus, sitting next to Paul, one of the other Backs.

"Big day," he said.

Nick grinned. "The biggest."

He thought back to his old club up in Rotherham, where a capacity crowd was fewer than 2,000 people. It was so different now, and he felt the weight of responsibility to those fans, the ones who came out and cheered in all weathers.

Today they were blessed with sunshine, surprisingly warm for October, one of those perfect afternoons of an Indian Summer. The sky was a solid blue with only the palest clouds high, high above.

The drive to Twickenham should have taken just a few minutes, but all along the route, St. George flags decorated the streets of redbrick Victorian houses, and good luck banners hung from windows and lampposts everywhere. For a few weeks of the World Cup year, everyone was a rugby fan.

The streets were lined with men, women and children dressed in white and, red and waving flags, cheering as the bus drove past slowly.

All of the players grinned and waved back, feeling their spirits rise with the fans on this special day.

As they drew closer, the towering walls of the stadium came into view, the massive oval shape dominating the landscape.

Even though they'd all seen it before, the players craned their necks to catch the first glimpse of where, God willing, they'd make history.

It was the largest dedicated Rugby Union stadium in the world and had stood there for over a hundred years. Before that, the ten acre site had been used to grow cabbages, and even to this day, the stadium was affectionately known as the Cabbage Patch.

Nick's chest swelled with pride as he thought of all the famous players who'd been there before him, wondering if they'd felt the same sense of destiny.

At the players' entrance, there were more photographers, and Nick stood with the rest of his teammates in front of the team bus, smiling for the cameras. More autographs and more well-wishers, then the players disappeared inside.

Now, it was down to the serious business of the day.

They changed out of their Paul Smith suits and into training kit, ready for their work-out, getting their muscles warmed up. The physiotherapists were already there, waiting in their uniforms to rub, pummel, strap, and ease muscles and joints.

Following that was second breakfast of poached eggs, more fruit, protein shakes and vitamins.

There were fifteen players and eight subs, along with all the staff working to get the team into tip top shape before they stepped onto the field.

As the clock ticked down toward kick-off, the atmosphere began to thicken, tension in the air, in the very walls around them. Nick tuned out, disappearing into himself, shutting out everything around him as he plugged in his headphones, listening to his music. He breathed deeply and slowly, using Anna's relaxation techniques. Just thinking about her eased a knot of anxiety inside him. No matter what, she'd be there for him—he knew that without a doubt. It was a good feeling. The best.

~

Up in the commentary box, the BBC sports commentators were also warming up.

Jimmy Smith: Welcome to the BBC's coverage of the Rugby World Cup Final 2016. We're here with former internationals Jonny Wilkinson who scored the winning drop goal in the 2003 Rugby World Cup, and Stuart Reardon who has been capped for England ten times, and Great Britain five times. Jonny, what are you hoping for from this Cup Final?

Jonny: We're all very excited for this game today. Samoa brings to the table athletic, strong, physical, very physical players who always play exciting rugby. It's going to be a great game today. Wouldn't you say, Stu?

Stuart: Yes, it's a bright, sunny day with a firm ground, there'll be lots of play today. Because of the weather conditions, it'll be a fast-flowing game, wide passes, hopefully high-scoring, definitely. It'll be a Backs game today. Samoa are a great team. Very big, physically aggressive side, like Jonny said. England will have to be strong in the middle, and use the skill out-wide with the extremely fast and skilful Backs England have got—I fancy their chances today! It'll be an exciting game!

Jonny: Whoever controls the ball most and wins field position, will win the game. England have got too much for Samoa.

Jimmy: Nick Renshaw, wearing the number 17 shirt, will be up against his great buddy Fetuao Tui who he plays with at Finchley. Tui is in the number 12 shirt. How do you think that will go, Stu?

Stuart: It'll be very competitive, there'll be a great battle between those two today. There'll be a bit of banter for sure. Even though they're great mates at the club, that all goes out the window when you're playing for your national side, and I'm sure it'll be a massive physical and athletic competitive game. It'll be good to see who comes out on top.

Jonny: It's quite tough playing against a good friend, but they won't be thinking about that today. It's a big responsibility playing for your country. You keep it clean but play as tough as you can.

Stuart: If they're against each other in the field, they'll both want to win the ball ... and it's bragging rights when you get back to your club level team. Whatever happens, they'll have a laugh and a joke and a drink after.

Jimmy: So how do you rate England's chances today, Stu?

Stuart: England are looking really well today, they're in fantastic form. They've been playing some exciting football throughout this tournament building up to this game, so today is going to be no different. Everyone's been really pleased by how Nick's done in this series. He was a surprise pick—a lot of eyebrows were raised at Nick's selection in this team, but he's proved that he deserves this shot and he's playing really well. He's come through a lot of issues and a lot of media intrusion, so it'll be good to see how he deals with it all and how he plays today.

Nick stared up at the number 17 shirt hanging above him in the England colours, the name RENSHAW proudly stencilled across the back. He'd *worked* for that shirt, he'd *earned* that shirt, and now he was going to do it proud.

For every person who said he wouldn't make it, he'd prove them wrong.

For every person who'd encouraged him and believed in him, he'd prove them right.

He was ready.

He pulled the tight-fitting silky material of the 17 shirt over his body, slipped the shorts over his lucky Speedos, then laced his boots tightly.

The players grouped together, arms around each other's shoulders, as Coach looked at them all seriously.

"Big day, lads. But you've trained hard, you're fit, and I know you've got this. Stick to the game plan. We've watched hours of video, we know where their weaknesses are, so we're going to tie them in the middle and look to spread to their right—the left side defence is weak. Keep the mistakes to a minimum. They're a tough team, but we're tougher. They're a hard team, but we're harder. You're going to go out there and play your hearts out, and I know you will. Make me proud, make England proud, but most of all, make yourselves proud!"

"Raaah!"

They were led out by the England mascot and two young boys who played for their schools. They'd both won competitions to be there on this special day and were equal parts proud and incredibly shy.

Four foot nothing and skinny as twigs, they led out the England team of tall, heavily-muscled men, clad in the white uniforms with the red rose of England stitched over their hearts.

Walking next to them were the huge, darkly tanned Samoan players, solemn and serious, grinning and excited.

Fetuao winked at Nick.

"Hello, shorty."

At 6' 5", Fetuao towered over most of the England players.

Nick grinned back.

"Big buggers fall harder. See you at the try line!"

The tunnel was dimly lit and it echoed with the thunder of thousands of feet above them.

Nick felt like a gladiator going into battle—which wasn't far from the truth.

The pounding echoed in his blood and he felt the pulsing adrenaline flame through him. He rolled his shoulders, forcing himself to breathe deeply.

Anna was nearby, and he whispered her name, like a prayer.

He knew that the designated seats for the families were behind the tunnel and he hoped he'd be able to get a quick glimpse of Anna in that sea of faces. She was sitting with Trish and his parents, as well as her mother who'd flown in two days earlier. But just knowing they were nearby was enough.

He sucked in a breath and walked out in front of 82,000 people, a mix of emotions pummelling him: fear, excitement and honour, butterflies in his stomach. The roar of the crowd hit him like a blast of super-heated air, and the hairs on the back of his neck stood up at the wall of sound. It was so loud, the music and fans chanting, with fireworks blasting off as the teams stepped onto the field. It was breath-taking, surreal, beyond anything he'd ever experienced.

The bright swathe of green stretched in front of him, a perfect set of stripes pointing toward the H-shaped goal posts.

There wasn't a single empty seat, and the noise rose upwards on and on, a wave of cheers, the enthusiastic, excited roar of the crowd.

The England fans were singing, their voices rising in a crescendo. Nick closed his eyes as the emotion hit him in the centre of his chest.

Thousands of people were here to watch the game. To watch him play. It was the moment that he'd dreamed about his whole life, worked for and prayed for, but here he was living it.

Thoughts cascaded through his mind about what it took to get here, what his job would be on the field, what he needed to do, the game plan.

And he felt a deep well of gratitude for being selected by Coach, a man who'd kept faith in him and given him this chance; grateful for all the help he'd had along the way. And now he was proud and determined to show what he could do.

It was hard to believe that not so long ago he'd been injured, dropped by his club, cheated on by his fiancée, jobless, friendless and hopeless. At the beginning of the season, he wasn't even in the starting team. And now he was here, at the home of British rugby, because he never gave up.

He felt a quiet pride, thinking of the many years it had taken to reach this point, to build his body, his fitness, his skills and his unbreakable spirit.

To be here, representing his country on the biggest stage of his career. He knew that Anna and his family were watching and proud of him, they knew his struggles through different jobs, the hours he'd put in.

He wanted to succeed for them as much as for himself. To prove that he was and would always be, undefeated.

He was ready.

The teams lined up for the official photographs and flashbulbs popped in front of their eyes. They were bathed in light, the sun beaming down on bronzed skin and perfectly hewn bodies, their tight uniforms clinging to them.

Nick glanced up, awed by the scale of the scene, taking a moment to enjoy who he was, where he was, and what he was about to do.

Then it was time for the national anthems to be sung.

An amplified voice rang out around the stadium.

"Please be upstanding for the Samoan National Anthem."

There was a soft hush and then the sweet, tranquil sounds of the South Sea Islands music rose in the air. The team stood straighter, their eyes glassy with emotion as they filled their lungs and sang. Around the arena, a few red flags with a patch of blue with white stars waved boldly and the words echoed quietly:

Vaai i na fetu o loo ua agiagia ai / Look at those stars that are appealing.

Then it was the turn of the England team. Nick lifted his chin and sang with everything in him, the words meaning more than ever before. And up in the Royal Box, he knew that members of the Royal Family were watching. Not Her Majesty, but Princes William and Harry, for sure.

God Save Our Gracious Queen
Long Live our Noble Queen
God Save the Queen.

It was staggering, hearing nearly a hundred-thousand voices belting out the words. Nick felt his heart racing, pride and humility mixed inside him.

As the final notes died away, a huge roar erupted from the crowd.

Now, they were just minutes from the kick-off.

As the noise dipped again, the Samoan side lined up, faces grim as they performed their *haka*, the traditional war cry.

They flexed their muscles and roared at the England team, stamping the ground as they stuck out their tongues, eyes narrowed and threatening.

Nick didn't know what the words meant, but he recognised the aggression on their faces, the challenge thrown down. The England players formed a long line, linking their arms, staring back at the Samoans who shouted across the field.

The challenge was delivered and accepted, and then the teams jogged to their starting positions. Two of the players ran to the 22 yard line, knelt, said a quick prayer and crossed themselves.

Nick no longer noticed the fans—instead, his intense focus was on the other players and the rugbys ball. He was in the zone.

The referee blew the whistle and the two sides surged together.

Nick was fast, sprinting forward and grabbing the ball from the Hooker and racing down the field, a blur as he sidestepped two players.

On the other side of the stadium Anna cringed as all 17 stone of Fetuao tackled Nick, sending him crashing to the ground. She swore she heard the sound of him hitting the dirt, even though she knew that couldn't be possible.

She'd seen many, many rugby matches by now, but worried that she'd be watching this one through her fingers. Nick's mother gripped her arm and buried her face.

"I can't watch! I can't watch! Tell me when it's over!"

"Mum! It's only a minute into the first half!" Trisha scolded, her cheeks pink from the excitement.

Nick picked himself up, checking that all his limbs were attached. Yep, no damage done. Fetuao winked at him and called him a pussy Pommie.

The game was fast, passes flashing across the field, and Nick was in his element. This was his game. This was how he played rugby. God, he loved it! Every dirty, brutal, painful second of it!

His muscles surged, thighs pumping furiously as he raced toward the goal, catching a glimpse of Fetuao as the huge Samoan tried to trample him into the ground for a second time. Suddenly, he felt an iron grip around his waist and his legs were swept from under him, just yards from the try line.

Nick tried to hide the ball under his body as three more players piled on top of him, flattening him across the field, but it was wrenched free and the pressure suddenly disappeared.

He climbed to his feet, frustration painted on his face, and he ran his hands over his short hair.

"Come on!" he yelled. "Get in!"

Whether he was talking to himself or his teammates, no one knew. Anna clamped her hand over her mouth and tried not to cry out.

Up in the commentary box, emotions were running high.

Jonny: That's a great attacking position for Samoa now. Latu gets the ball, spins it out to Nanai. Missed pass out to Fanene and he tries ... he beats the first tackle. He's held up five yards from the line.

Stuart: The white jerseys are all over there! Out to Foster who's on the right wing although he's the left wing. What's he doing?

Jonny: He's held up a yard from the line, now the ball comes back. Paul Dawson from the right touchline, out to Renshaw swinging across. Jonson in midfield drives. England will get a penalty.

Jimmy: The ref blows the whistle. Good play by the English Backs but what happened to the Forwards? The Samoans were all over them!

Jonny: The Samoans are taking an upper hand, that's for sure. Lomu touches down but there was a body check there.

Stuart: Nice pass out to Renshaw. He's running for the line! Go, Nick! Go ... ow, he got hammered there, completely milled. I wouldn't want to be feeling that tomorrow.

Anna had closed her eyes a fraction of a second before Nick was tackled. Next to her, Nick's mum cried out. The women clung together until Trish told them grumpily that they could look now.

Nick staggered to his feet, shook his head, then jogged back into position.

At half time, the teams left the field, bruised, bloodied in some cases, and with England trailing 12 points.

Nick gulped down water and fruit juice, then chewed some sweets for a sugar hit. He knew that they hadn't played as well as they could. He knew it, his teammates knew it, and Eddie Jones knew it.

"Come on, boys, we know where we've gone wrong," Eddie barked, his voice half choked with passion. "We're behind on the scoreboard and need everyone here to step up to the plate, show me what you can do. Go out there and play better than your opposite number. Stick to the game plan—let's do what we know we can do. It's a massive occasion, everyone's watching. We need to do what we've practised; everyone in here now! Look at the guy at the side of you. Look at the guy in front of you. We're here to win this. We've worked hard to win this. Wse deserve to win this!"

He turned to Nick.

"We need you to pick up your game. Be sharp, act first, where's your urgency gone? We need points, and it's down to you and the Backs to get them. Show me what you can do. Go out there and prove it! This is your time."

Nick felt the words in his core. Yes! This was *his* time—here and now.

Eddie was on a roll, his passion inspiring the team.

"Gav, I need you to control our field position better. We control that and we control the game. Make them work harder for every yard. Vince, are you even on the field? You've got five minutes to show me why I put you out there, or I'll pull you off pitch and give someone else a chance! It's up to you!

"Paul! Show me why I picked you—show me what I know you can do! And the rest of you—I picked you, I backed you, I selected you! You're the best and you can do this! We've trained hard! We've put all the hours in! Now is your time to shine! We need 100 percent. When we leave that field, we need to know that we've given everything to win this game. Play like we've practised, play for each other, play for the badge, play for your country!

"We're only trailing by a few points! That's nothing to what we can do! We know how many points we can score. Stick to the game plan, let the ball play! Go out there and enjoy it! It's a special occasion! Have pride in your shirt! Show everyone watching on TV what this team is about! Show what you can do! Raaaaah!"

The captain stepped forward, signalling them all to huddle, desperate to gain some momentum from his tired team.

"We can still win this! But you've got to want it! You've got to need it! It's about all of you, not one person. This is our journey and we can see the prize at the end. Stick to the plan, make those conversions. Mostly, *get in there!*"

"Get in!" the men roared back.

They ran back onto the field, renewed and determined.

Nick glanced toward the tunnel entrance and saw Anna jumping up and down, an England flag in one hand and a Stars and Stripes in the other. Probably the only Stars and Stripes in the whole stadium.

Energy flooded through him and his eyes narrowed as he focussed on the game.

He grabbed the ball and accelerated down the field, moving with the speed and precision of a panther as he dodged the huge Samoan players. It was stunning, watching him weave through the wall of defenders, passing the ball, plucking it from the air as it was thrown back to him, charging hard, running for the line! He'd scored a try!

Slowly, England began to recover the ground they'd lost, pushing forward with their attack, getting the ball and keeping the ball, playing harder, playing faster, being tougher.

The fans were screaming themselves hoarse and drums were being pounded around the stadium. No one was sitting, not even in the Royal Box. Princes William and Harry were on their feet and even the Duchess of Cambridge was yelling her encouragement, her eyes bright and excited.

Nick was soaked with sweat, his England shirt clinging to his body as the match reached the closing minutes. England were still trailing Samoa by four points. It was going to the wire, it could go either way, and everyone knew it.

The cheers and shouts grew louder until no one standing in the Twickenham stadium could hear themselves above the tidal wave of sound. Nick felt like he was underwater, hearing only the waves crashing overhead.

He had to dig deep inside himself. He had to find the reserves of energy, to find out if he had what it took to be a winner.

He thought of all the people who'd believed in him, the people who loved him. And he thought of Anna.

He glanced around, taking in the tired faces of his teammates, knowing that they were on their last legs, they didn't have much left to give, wondering if there was anything in the reserve tank. But the huge Samoans weren't looking much better, the strain showing everywhere.

In the stands, the crowd were jumping up and down, urging the team on, yelling their hearts out, desperation in the shrill noise, the excitement of the World Cup Final. They believed in the team. They believed they could still win.

Nick's head came up and even though there were just seconds left to play, he felt that belief sweep through him.

The ball went wide and Nick sprinted into position as Owen passed to Jason, and then to Andy.

And he saw his opportunity.

Ignoring a desperate Eddie Jones, ignoring the game plan, he raced down the wing, catching the ball at full speed and tucking it under his arm, a man on a mission. His eyes narrowed, all his energy focussed on that distant white stripe. His legs pumped furiously and his heart thundered as the world shrunk around him.

Fetuao thundered down behind him with Lani, the two of them coming in for a pincer movement, refusing to let the game go without a fight.

Eddie Jones had his head in his hands, almost unable to watch, knowing that his reputation and career were on the line with the young team he'd chosen, with the choices that he'd made.

He opened his eyes as Nick rocketed past, beating Lomu. Paul Dawson came up behind him, and now it was two England players and two Samoans racing for the line, Lani and Fetu storming up the field.

The referee glanced at his watch and the crowd's roars grew even louder with just seconds left to play.

Eng-er-land! Eng-er-LAND!

Seeing Fetu and Lani converging on him, Nick passed to Paul, who side-stepped the massive Samoan and threw the ball back to Nick.

He snatched it from the air, adrenaline shooting through him as he put his head down, running hard down the left wing, racing for the line!

The ball was tucked tightly under his left arm, his right arm thrust out to fight off any tackle.

The crowd were screaming, Fetu was right behind him, the referee was lifting his whistle, could he do it, could he do it?

Nick launched himself into the air, the ball tucked beneath his arm as the line appeared in front of him. He felt Fetu's hand against his back, trying to grab his shirt, but it was too late.

The ground raced up to meet him, a bone-jarring, teeth-rattling jolt as he crashed and skidded across the green turf, crossing the line as the referee blew the final whistle and the crowd went wild.

Stuart: Oh yes, across the line! Nick Renshaw has scored for England! Get in there! The ref's blown the whistle! England win the World Cup! See you later, Samoa!

Jonny: The stadium's erupted! The fans can't believe it!

Jimmy: What an exciting game today and what a thrilling finish! Nick's had a turbulent build up to this series but he's come through with flying colours, clinched the winning try. What a finish! What a game! What a day! England win the Rugby World Cup 2016! No one who saw this match will ever forget it! England win!

Nick lay on the ground, his hands over his eyes, feeling the waves of emotion as 82,000 people cheered and yelled, jumping up and down, tears on their faces.

Suddenly, all his teammates were there, joy and euphoria in their voices as they crowded around him, pulling him to his feet, pounding his back and hugging him so tightly he could barely breathe. This meant everything to him, to them, to their country. Everything.

Fetu came up to Nick and the big man had tears in his eyes. There were no words as the two friends embraced.

Nick stood and finally looked around him, taking in the extraordinary scenes as the crowd celebrated, strangers hugging strangers. He allowed himself to feel it all.

His moment.

His day.

His life.

His eyes searched for Anna's in the crowd, and his heart filled with a fierce joy. Today he'd made her proud and made his country proud.

And most of all, he'd made himself proud.

Today, he'd won.

Today, he was undefeated.

EPILOGUE

FOUR-AND-A-HALF YEARS LATER...

"Well, it's been quite an astonishing few years for you, hasn't it?"

Nick smiled brightly at the interviewer.

"By the way, congratulations on your MBE at Buckingham Palace—that's a great honour. Nick Renshaw MBE! I believe that the Queen is a fan."

Nick coughed with embarrassment.

"I don't know about that, but it was an amazing day. I felt really proud. Yeah, it was a real honour."

Nick relaxed back in his seat, one arm stretched along the top of the sofa. His crow-black hair glinted under the studio lights and his eyes danced with happiness.

"Not quite what you might have expected back in 2014 when you'd been dropped by your club at the time."

"You could definitely say that, Jasmine."

"How did it feel, playing in your testimonial match last week?"

"Wow, I'm not even sure how to answer that. Um, pretty amazing and humbling. I wasn't expecting anything like that."

He rubbed his beard thoughtfully, the salt-and-pepper colour adding a distinguished air to his appearance.

"Did you know that it was the largest number of fans at a rugby testimonial ever?"

Nick's eyes widened and a slight flush brightened his cheeks.

"No, um, no. That's news to me. Wow!"

"I think it's a measure of just how much the fans love you. Isn't that right, ladies and gentleman?"

The studio audience cheered and clapped, howling their appreciation.

Nick grinned widely and waved at the people who were there for him.

Jasmine smiled then gave a theatrical sigh.

"So, I have to ask ... is this the end of Nick Renshaw's rugby career? No plans to coach? Can you really just walk away from something that's been your whole life?"

He gave a quiet chuckle.

"I'm retiring from rugby, not moving to Mars, Jasmine."

"But you're not going to coach?"

He shook his head, his dark hair flopping over his forehead.

"Not immediately, no. But never say never." He gave a small smile. "I've been playing rugby for 24 years of my life, professionally for 16. I think it's time to do something different now. I know that I'll miss the banter with my friends and rugby mates. I'll miss the pranks, team bonding, chatting with all the lads, taking the mickey out of each other."

He paused.

"I've made some really good friendships through rugby, and the laughs I've had along the way are priceless, all good memories. Even the injuries I've sustained and come back from. It's shaped me into the man I am today. I'm a strong, grateful, resilient person who is always chasing progress. I know who I am, my tough past shaped me into a better man. I don't regret any of it. I'm grateful for it all. But, you know, my life is about more than just rugby. I've met an amazing woman that I want to share my life with."

Nick glanced across, catching Anna's gaze and seeing the love shining in her eyes.

The interviewer smiled coyly and leaned towards him.

"Do I hear wedding bells, Nick?"

He winked at her but didn't answer. That was private, but it was also true that Anna was wearing a beautiful ring with three flawless diamonds. Each one represented a different stage in their relationship: the past, the present and the future.

After everything that had happened, he'd never thought he could trust another woman, but he trusted Anna with his life, with his soul and with his heart.

It was also true that they'd delayed plans for a wedding twice already, once when Anna's mother was sick, and once again when they'd both been working crazy hours and Nick was travelling all the time. But now Nick was retired, yes, they had plans.

"I think you'll be disappointing a lot of your female fans if that's true."

Sighing loudly, the reporter smiled at him and batted her eyelashes playfully.

"Nick, you've been one of the most successful England Captains *ever*, leading your team to a second World Cup earlier this year which has never been equalled before. You're the fifth most capped player *ever*. Your retirement from professional rugby really is the end of an era. Is there anything you'd like to say to your fans?"

He nodded, his face serious.

"Yeah, there is."

And he cleared his throat, staring right into the camera.

"Thank you doesn't seem like enough words. You've been there for me through thick and thin. You've been there for me when I was down and felt defeated. You were there as I clawed my way back up, with your messages, thoughts and prayers; all the times people told me to fear nothing, to never give in. Maybe you think saying those words is a small thing, but it's not, because it gave me hope when that was something in very short supply. You believed in me at a time when I didn't believe in myself. And when I was honoured to play for England, I played those games for all of you with my whole heart. So, to all my fans and supporters, thank you. I couldn't have done it without you."

Applause broke out in the studio and even the cameramen and sound engineers were cheering. Up in the producers' booth, people were smiling and clapping.

As one, the studio audience rose to their feet, applauding a man who'd been down as far as it was possible for a human being to sink, standing in front of them, a true man, a leader of men.

Nick swallowed back the tide of emotions and glanced to the side of the studio where Anna stood.

She was wiping tears from her cheeks when he caught her eye. She smiled a watery smile and mouthed three little words: *I love you!*

And he knew, in that moment, he knew. He'd been a broken man, defeated when he met the love of his life. But now, the future was beautiful and it held no fear.

With his hand over his heart, he said the words she'd taught him so long ago:
When your world crashes down...
When they all say you're out...
When your body is broken...
I will rise...
I will return...
And I will be undefeated.

THE END

Swipe the page to read more about Nick and Anna in *Model Boyfriend*...

EXTRACT FROM MODEL BOYFRIEND

The training sessions had been going well all week. The lads for Nick's testimonial were enjoying being back with old teammates and rivals, back where they'd felt most alive. Some of them were still playing professionally, but the rest were already enjoying their retirement, if that was the right word. Fit, active men in their thirties—all retired. But the competitive spirit never left them, even when they left the game professionally.

Perhaps being a rugby player is a rite of passage where the sport becomes your identity, your skin, embedded in your heart and deep in your blood—so it never leaves you.

Nick felt it—that his whole identity was wrapped up in the sport that he'd loved for so long.

He shook his head to clear the rolling, twisting thoughts.

Enough! I'm getting sentimental in my old age, he thought with a sigh.

He glanced around the locker room with a feeling of pride and gratitude as friends, colleagues and former teammates changed into their shorts, shirts and boots, and ... what the hell?

He did a double-take when he saw another face from his past: Kenny Johnson.

With a jet of fury that took his breath away, Nick was sent spinning back to the day when Kenny had destroyed their friendship and killed his trust; the day he'd seen Kenny screwing his ex-fiancée. The Best Man and the Bride-to-Be.

For a split second, the sense of betrayal was fresh and raw.

As Nick stared at his former friend, Kenny walked toward him, his expression unsure, as if Nick might lunge and beat the shit out of him—an act that had landed Nick in court five years ago, with a criminal record to match.

Kenny had broken the guy-code.

Nick stared at the other man's broken nose and worn, battered face, surprised to see remorse in Kenny's eyes. Nick thought about what it must have cost Kenny in pride, to come here today, into the lion's den.

The two men locked eyes, a thousand unsaid words roaring through the air, but then Nick blew out a long breath. Ultimately, Kenny had done Nick a favour by showing him that Molly was a liar and a cheat. It also meant that Nick had gone on to have a relationship with Anna, well, there was no comparison. He loved Anna with his whole being; Molly was nothing but a dark stain on his memory.

He hadn't seen either of them in years.

One of the other players saw Kenny and called out.

"Ken, you mad sort! What are you doing here?"

Kenny forced a grin.

"Hey up, lads, you're looking good out there. Some of you have still got it and some of you never had it, eh?"

"Piss off, Ken, you big pudding!" snorted Tufty, who was probably twenty pounds heavier since he'd retired. "I'll show you what I've got!"

"In your dreams, ya sausage!" Kenny turned away, his smile fading as he met Nick's frown. "You got time for a quick chat?"

Nick could see the hopeful expression on his face, the regret. He remembered that they'd been friends, mates, before Kenny had betrayed him. He decided that he wanted to hear what the man had to say.

So did everyone else in the locker room if the covert looks and sly glances were anything to go by. They all knew what had happened between Nick and Kenny.

Nick nodded.

"Sure, let's go for a walk." Then he turned to the other players. "Lads, top session! I'll catch up with you in the clubhouse. First pint on me."

Nick walked out of the room in silence followed by Kenny, and they headed to the Stands, staring out at the vast stadium, the rows of empty seats.

The silence grew uncomfortable as Nick waited for Kenny to speak.

"I never got to play here," said Kenny, hesitant, awed, and Nick could hear the wistfulness in his voice. "Not like you. You've had an amazing career—you were always the one, old golden balls," and he laughed sadly. "But that's not why I'm here." He sighed. "It's been a long time..."

Nick nodded, but didn't speak.

Kenny grimaced and stumbled on, his words coming slowly and awkwardly.

"I know I'm not your favourite person. I wouldn't blame you if you hated me. If it had been the other way around, well, I wouldn't have pissed in your ear if you'd been on fire."

Nick turned away.

"I'd never have done that to a friend," Nick said quietly but firmly. "Friendship means something to me, not just words."

Kenny dropped his eyes to the ground, shoving his hands in his pockets and shuffling his feet.

"I know. Believe me, I know," and he raised his eyes to meet Nick's stony stare. "But I just wanted to say I'm sorry for what happened. I should have known better, I should have been better. I'm not perfect, who is? But we all make mistakes—and that was the worst one of my whole life—I lost my best friend." He hunched his shoulders. "Anyway, so what I'm saying, the past is the past. And I can't change it, but I want to make things right, as much as I can. I'm so fucking sorry for what I did. I've regretted it every day since." He squared his shoulders. "I'm here because I want to play—I want to show my respect for your career by playing in your testimonial." He paused. "If you'll have me?"

Nick hesitated, seeing two roads ahead of him. He could carry on hating Kenny for what he did five years ago, or he could accept his apology and move on. It could never be the way it had been, but maybe it was time to let it go.

"Yeah," said Nick slowly. "It's been a long time, Ken. "We've known each other a lot of years. I'm not the type to hold a grudge, but what you did and what happened to me as a consequence of your actions—and my actions—can't be undone. We can't go back to how we were, the trust is gone."

Kenny lowered his head, shame colouring his roughened features.

Nick took a deep breath.

"I can't play alongside you again, we'll never be teammates, but I appreciate you stepping up and wanting to take part. I'm sure Coach will be happy to have you in the opposing side. I'll let him know you're available. I accept your apology."

Kenny swallowed as Nick held out his hand.

"Thanks, mate. That's ... well, thank you."

"I'm in a good place now," said Nick quietly as they shook hands. "I think things happen for a reason."

～

At the end of the following week, Brian Noble, the coach who'd volunteered to train the teams for the testimonial, gathered them all together. Including Kenny.

"That's the last session down. Well done, lads. It's been a pleasure working with you this fortnight. I'm impressed ... and surprised how some of you got through the last few days of training."

He pointed at the group of older players who'd been retired a while, and they laughed, chucking towels at his head.

"Twickenham is a sell-out for our Nick, so if there's ever a place for ex-teammates to settle any beef between each other, it's on that field, in front of a sell-out crowd."

Kenny joined in the laughter, but Nick caught his faint grimace.

It had been a challenging week for him, and a few of Nick's teammates had given him a hard time, but he'd toughed it out.

"See you all on Saturday!"

~

Nick arrived at the stadium over an hour before the other players. Anna had offered to come with him, but she also understood when he told her that he needed to do this for himself.

As he walked along those empty corridors, his footsteps echoed, surrounded with all the incredible memories—the crowds, the cheers, the electric atmosphere, the emotions, the sense of pride and achievement, winning the World Cup twice, the pinnacle of his career. And now, it was the last time that he'd play here. It didn't seem real.

The locker room smelled of pine-scented disinfectant. The team's shirts were already hanging in place. Nick walked around the room, touching them with a sense of awe, a tug of sadness. After today, he was on the outside. If he ever came back to visit, he'd be the one watching all the action, but no longer part of it. He was benched for the rest of his life.

When he reached the iconic number 17 shirt, his shirt, he sat down with heavy thoughts, memories filling his mind.

He forced himself to think about today's game. He was genuinely excited to play.

In theory, the game would be more relaxed than competition games, but he knew that as soon as the first bone-crushing tackle went in, as athletes, every one of them would want to win.

He picked up his kitbag and pulled out his lucky Speedos. They looked a bit threadbare these days because he'd worn them in every game since Anna had given them to him. He'd be wearing them today.

As he unfolded the Speedos, a note fluttered to the floor. He picked it up, brushing the crumpled paper flat, then reading the looping, handwritten words.

My darling Nick,

Enjoy today, my love. You deserve this. You've worked so hard to get here, on and off the field. Be yourself. Be amazing.

I love you,

A x

PS Don't get injured!

He smiled at the postscript. No, he definitely wasn't going to get injured today.

It was a small moment of peace, a few seconds of calm in what would be a crazy day.

The locker room began to fill up, first with the physios and then all the other players.

Over the next few hours before the game, Nick hardly had a moment to think. He had Press interviews, friends and former teammates to say hello to and reminisce for a few minutes, the joys and sorrows of shared experiences, a shared life.

The England manager Eddie Jones was there, along with Nick's friend from the Phoenixes, Jason Oduba, who should have been playing but had picked up a groin strain. Young Ben Richards was there, shy and quiet, a new signing for the Phoenixes. It seemed right to Nick to have a rookie playing—a way of passing the torch, perhaps.

He also had a meet and greet with the Chief Executive of West Bowing RFU, the amateur club he'd played in as a kid. He was donating £100,000 of the gate money to them.

The man pumped his hand vigorously, emotion shining in his kind old eyes.

"Thank you so much! This means a lot to us, that you've remembered us. All the youngsters we'll be able to help with this money—you don't know what it means!"

Nick nodded, embarrassed, because he did know what £100,000 meant to a small amateur club.

He was happy to donate the money but truthfully it was no skin off his nose. It was either donate it or let the taxman take it.

A player was allowed to keep a certain sum from the ticket sales at his retirement testimonial game, but above that, it was taxable. Nick preferred that the money went to his old club. But the rest of the gate money was his—and it had to last the rest of his life.

It seemed like half the world wanted to shake his hand that day: old teammates, a few celebrities, friends, rivals, and of course, Kenny.

The guy was still a dickhead, but Nick had forgiven him, and that felt good.

He smirked at Nick, then sauntered over to shake hands, grinning as he took out his two front teeth, the result of an injury from a long-ago game.

"Give my regards to Anna."

Nick raised an eyebrow as he shook Kenny's hand.

"You can give them yourself later, but I can't guarantee she won't punch you in the face. Mate."

Kenny laughed and went to get changed.

The noise level in the locker room gradually escalated as the excitement and anticipation built. When no one was looking, Nick popped a tramadol into his mouth and swallowed it down with water, massaging his aching shoulder. So many injuries, so many surgeries—he should be glad this was over.

Finally, the coach told everyone to be quiet.

"Well, lads, you all know why you're here. I'll hand you over to your Captain for the last time, Nick Renshaw."

A ribald cheer went up, and Nick grinned at the sea of faces, eyeing him expectantly.

"Thanks for playing today, lads. I really appreciate your support. I know you're not getting paid for this, but I am."

Everyone laughed.

"I know it's a friendly, but let's be honest, there's no such thing as a friendly rugby game." There were nods and smiles all around. Nick gave an evil grin. "And the first person to smash Kenny gets a thousand pounds."

The look on Kenny's face was priceless—well, worth a grand, at least.

"All joking aside, enjoy the game and let's put on a real show for the fans. Rah! By the way, nobody is allowed to tackle me!"

With a final laugh and slaps on the back, they left the locker room.

Nick walked out onto the field, hand in hand with two ten-year-old mascots, kids from his old amateur club. The look of awe on their young faces was another reminder of everything he was saying goodbye to.

The noise on the field was louder than a train rushing towards him, louder than a tsunami thundering down. From the darkness of the tunnel, he watched the cheerleaders dancing to *Let's Get Ready to Rumble* and smiled. *God, I'll miss this.*

Then as the teams strode onto the field, the music changed to Bowie's *Heroes*, the Phoenixes' theme tune, Nick's team for the last four years. A massive roar from the crowd, a wall of noise, drowned out the music, and they started to chant—82,000 fans on their feet: "Ren-*shaw!* Ren-*shaw!* Ren-*shaw!*"

Emotion hit Nick in the centre of his chest.

They're here for me...

It didn't seem real. He waved to the crowd, and the roar became deafening.

It was overwhelming, completely staggering. Nick had played for sell-out games, for national games, for World Cups, but he'd never experienced this, *and I never will again.* The mix of emotions was hard to explain, even harder to deal with.

It was intense, his heart racing, and the pride of that moment would stay with him his whole life.

He glanced toward where Anna was sitting with his family, catching a glimpse of her waving crazily, jumping up and down, her mouth opening and closing as she sang along with the crowd.

Unable to take it in, his emotions overloaded, Nick jogged into position, anticipation racing through his blood. The referee blew the whistle, and he did what he was born to do.

~

Two hours later, Nick was dripping with sweat, his lungs heaving, staring up at the fans who were on their feet, clapping and cheering, all chanting his name one final time: Ren-*shaw!* Ren-*shaw!* Ren-*shaw!*

The compere waved him to the side and held the microphone between them, his voice echoing around the massive stadium.

"Great game today, Nick! What a way to finish! I bet you couldn't have written it any better, selling out Twickenham! How does it feel to finish your career here?"

Nick closed his eyes briefly, his emotions intense, confused, in turmoil. He forced himself to focus, to do what was expected of him.

"Thank you, Jim. Thanks for your kind words." He forced a smile. "First of all, I'd like to thank everyone who turned out today, the fans, the coaches, the players—it's been good to see some old faces out here, and some new ones. A massive thank you to all my Board, all the organisers who've made this happen. I'm not quite sure how I feel: this place, this ground. Coming here as a young boy, then coming here as an adult and winning two World Cups..."

The crowd erupted, and Nick had to wait until the cheers died down so he could continue.

"It's hard to believe I won't be back. I've had an amazing career and been very fortunate. It takes more than one person to win a game and I've had a great team supporting me, and not just the other players. I'd like to thank my manager, my family, my coach, Eddie Jones—there are too many to mention, but you know who you are. Thank you! Nick Renshaw signing off—peace out, Twickenham!"

Nick waved at the fans and the crowd shouted his name again, for the final time.

As Nick left the field, the other players were standing in front of the tunnel, clapping and thumping him on the back as he walked between them. The ones who'd been through this already knew how he felt; the younger players just enjoyed the post-game euphoria.

Nick wished he could have just five minutes of silence to get his head together, but that wouldn't happen.

He glanced up at the family and friends box and saw Anna with his sister and parents, all waving wildly. Even from this distance, he could see that Anna was crying as she blew him kisses.

He waved back tiredly, took one last look at the stadium that had been his second home, then headed for the locker rooms.

Time for a series of hot showers and ice baths, one after the other, to speed up the healing process of microtrauma in his muscles.

He didn't need a physio today since he hadn't been injured, thank God. Anna wouldn't have been impressed if he'd limped off the field.

Instead of changing into casual clothes, he wore a suit, white shirt and dark tie. His unwashed number 17 shirt was stuffed into his kitbag. He'd decide what to do with it later. Some players kept their kit; some auctioned it off for charity.

Then, with the rest of his teammates, he headed to the bar, but was stopped fifty times along the way by people who wanted to shake his hand or pat him on the back. He was smiling when he entered the bar.

The first person he saw was his ex-fiancée. A woman he despised.

"What the fuck?"

Molly McKinney smiled at him, her icy blue eyes as cold as her personality.

The name brought many memories with it, most of them bad. Nick's scheming, cheating ex-fiancée had effectively ended Anna's career as a sports psychologist by selling information about Anna's illicit relationship with Nick to the Press.

When Anna had worked for the Finchley Phoenixes at the same time as Nick, the club had no-fraternization clauses in their contracts. She was fired as soon as the relationship became public.

Anna had also spent a night in a police cell because of Molly's lies—an accusation of perjury in court. It was later proved false, but by then the damage had been done.

Molly strutted toward him, her breasts even bigger than last time he saw them, almost falling out of the electric blue dress she wore.

"Hey, Nicky! Great game! You was awesome!"

She swooped in to kiss him, but Nick stepped back, stunned, his lip curling with distaste. She was the last person he'd expected to see.

"Are you here for Kenny?" he asked.

It wasn't an unreasonable question, but Molly's face turned red and her eyes narrowed.

"Are you having a laugh? That loser! I came for you, Nicky. Old times sake and all that ... we was good together."

Luckily, the cavalry in the shape of Anna and Brendan arrived before Molly could annoy Nick even further.

"Love what you've done with your new tits," snarked Brendan. "Don't let the door hit you on your Kim Kardashian on the way out."

"What's she doing here?" Anna whispered.

Nick shook his head, bewildered.

"I have no idea," Nick said truthfully.

"I'd be happy to have her scrawny arse chucked out," Brendan offered eagerly.

For a second, Nick was tempted, but then he shook his head.

"Nah, she'd probably love making a scene. Just ignore her—she knows she's not welcome."

He glanced over to see Molly being tugged into a corner by Kenny, who seemed even less pleased to see her, if that was possible. They started a heated conversation as she yanked her arm free and poked him in the chest.

"Rather him than me," he muttered.

Someone thrust a glass of champagne into his hand and Nick forgot about Molly. The drinks kept arriving at his table, and the couple of glasses of wine that he'd planned to have were long in the past as people kept buying him more drinks: shots, beers, more wine, another bottle of champagne.

He thanked everyone who bought him a drink, but passed them all to the other players and they disappeared fast enough.

He barely tasted the delicious three-course meal, and later he couldn't remember anything that was said to him.

But then the toasts started, and with all eyes on him, Nick drank first one glass, then another and another, long since passing his two-drink limit, until they all began to blur. He should stop, he knew he should, but he no longer cared.

It had been a long time since he'd drunk this much, and Anna watched him with worried eyes. She couldn't blame anyone for wanting to buy Nick a drink to celebrate with him, and there were very few people who knew that he'd had a serious drinking problem earlier in his career.

She didn't say anything, but she may, however, have kicked him in the shins. Nick just grinned, his smile loose and his eyes glazed.

The compere rounded up the speeches, thanking everyone, then ran through the highlights of Nick's career and presented him with car keys for a brand new Range Rover Sport, a gift from his sponsors.

In return, Nick said a few words and was able to hand over a cheque for £100k to his old amateur club.

"Adios, amigos!" he slurred. "Goodbye career. Hello retirement."

Anna took charge of the keys to the new car, then slid her arm around his waist.

"Well done, babe. I'm proud of you. Now put that drink down and get your sexy ass in the taxi. Oh boy, you'll be in a world of hurt tomorrow."

Her words rang with truth.

Download *MODEL BOYFRIEND* now...

REVIEWS

We really hope that you enjoyed Nick and Anna's story.

Reviews are love! Honestly, they are! But it also helps other people to make an informed decision before buying this book.

So we'd really appreciate if you took a few seconds to do just that.

Thank you!

Jane & Stu

For more news about Jane's books, (and a **free** short story each month by Jane) www.janeharveyberrick.com

And random news about Stu! www.stuart-reardon.co.uk (it's a jungle out there!)

OUR WRITING PARTNERSHIP...

...started like this

Jane & Stu get ready to skydive, Colorado 2018

"Stu, I have this idea for a book we could write together—a rugby romance! We'll base it on your experiences of being a professional rugby player and, um, you know, romance!"

"Sounds great, Jane. But I'm not a writer."

"Well, you can tell stories, so you can write."

"Um..."

"What's the biggest crowd you ever played in front of?"

"Old Trafford, 80,000 people."

"Blimey!"

"Yeah, it was amazing."

"Okay, well, write about that. Tell me what it felt like to walk out in front of that many people. What could you hear? What could you see? What was going through your mind?"

"I'll give it a go."

[Waits for message box to pop up, drums fingers, a day later ... oh good, he's done it. Reads text.]

"Oh wow!"

[Hair stands up on the back of Jane's neck as she's swept away by Stuart's words.]

"Oh my God! That was sooooo good!"

"You think so?"

"YES!!!!"

"Okay."

"No, not 'okay'! It was fantastic! Honestly, the hair stood up on the back of my neck! Can you write some more like that?"

"Sure."

And from that, our book was born.

MORE ABOUT JANE & STUART

STUART

Stuart is a retired England International Rugby League player who's career spanned 16 years as a professional playing for several top League clubs. He has had several major injuries that nearly ended his career just as in *Undefeated*, the amazing collaboration with Jane.

Currently he is a filmmaker, YouTuber, videographer, photographer, author, model, and fitness addict.

He lives in Cheshire with his beautiful fiancée Emma and their young son, Phoenix Rai.

And if you're wondering why the story is set in the world of Rugby Union rather than Rugby League, well, it's simply that Union is a much better known game, especially outside the UK.

Sorry to all the League fans out there!

JHB

I enjoy watching surfers at my local beach as I walk with my little dog, and weaving stories of romance in the modern world, with all its trials and tribulations.

It's been the best fun working with Stu on this story. More than fun, fascinating and enlightening, too. A writing partnership turned into a true friendship; Stu and Em have been there for me during the most difficult time of my life.

And I really love to hear from readers, so please do drop me a line.

www.janeharveyberrick.com

ACKNOWLEDGMENTS

Stu

I only got into the whole book world through becoming friends with Lynda Throsby years ago. Lynda got me into it as a cover model; Lynda and her husband Peter helped me set up my online fitness program, helped me really grow what I'm doing, and become organized. Without all of the above, I wouldn't have met you and there wouldn't be a book called *Undefeated*! So thank you Lynda :) you are a star.

Jane

Wanting to write, being a writer, it's a lifelong lesson, and one that we're still learning. But there are a number of people who have helped guide and sculpt *this* book. So we'll start with these women, all amazing in their own rights, all different, all supportive.

From us

To Tonya Allen, beta reader and travel buddy

To the Reardonites and Jane's readers for their love and loyalty

To Sheena Lumsden for behind the scenes support

To all the bloggers who give up their time for their passion of reading and reviewing books—thank you for your support

To our readers—you rock!

ROMANCE WITH STUART REARDON

My lovely co-author with these titles

Two book series - contemporary romance
*Undefeated
*Model Boyfriend

Three book series - romcom
*Gym Or Chocolate?
*The World According to Vince
*The Baby Game

Standalone
Survivor Love Island *(romcom)*
*Touch My Soul *(novella)*

MORE BOOKS BY JHB

Series Titles

*The Education Series
An epic love story spanning the years, through war zones and more...
*The Education of Sebastian (Education series #1)
*The Education of Caroline (Education series #2)
*The Education of Sebastian & Caroline (combined edition, books 1 & 2)
Semper Fi: The Education of Caroline (Education series #3)

*The Traveling Series
All the fun of the fair ... and two worlds collide
*The Traveling Man (Traveling series #1)
*The Traveling Woman (Traveling series #2)
*Roustabout (Traveling series #3)
*Carnival (Traveling series #4)
*Gypsy (Traveling series #5)

The Justin Trainer Series
The bodyguard and the billionaire
Guarding the Billionaire (Justin Trainer series #1)
Saving the Billionaire (Justin Trainer series #2)

* The EOD Series
Blood, bombs and heartbreak
*Tick Tock (EOD series #1)
* Bombshell (EOD series #2)

MORE BOOKS BY JHB

The Rhythm Series
Blood, sweat, tears and dance
*Slave to the Rhythm (Rhythm series #1)
*Luka (Rhythm series #2)

Standalone Titles
Contemporary Romance
The Lilac Cadillac
Battle Scars
One Careful Owner
*Lifers
At Your Beck & Call
The New Samurai
Exposure

New Adult
*Dangerous to Know & Love
Dazzled
Summer of Seventeen

Paranormal
*The Dark Detective: Venator (Book #1)
*The Dark Detective: Paukúnnum (Book #2)

Novellas
Playing in the Rain
*Behind the Walls

Anthologies of Short Stories
*The Year Book Volume 1
*The Year Book Volume 2
*The Year Book Volume 3

Audio Books
One Careful Owner
(*narrated by Seth Clayton*)

On the Stage
Later, After: Playscript
Trailer

With Alana Albertson
Father Figure

MORE BOOKS BY JHB

* These titles are published in languages other than English.
Please check Jane's website for details—and receive **a free short story every month** when you sign up for her newsletter :)

QR code for Jane's website

JANE WRITING AS BERRICK FORD

Police Thrillers, UK

Dead Water
Dead Man's Dive
Dead Reckoning
Dead Shore

www.berrickford.com